DAYTIME SHOOTING STAR

Story & Art by
Mika Yamamori

CONTENTS

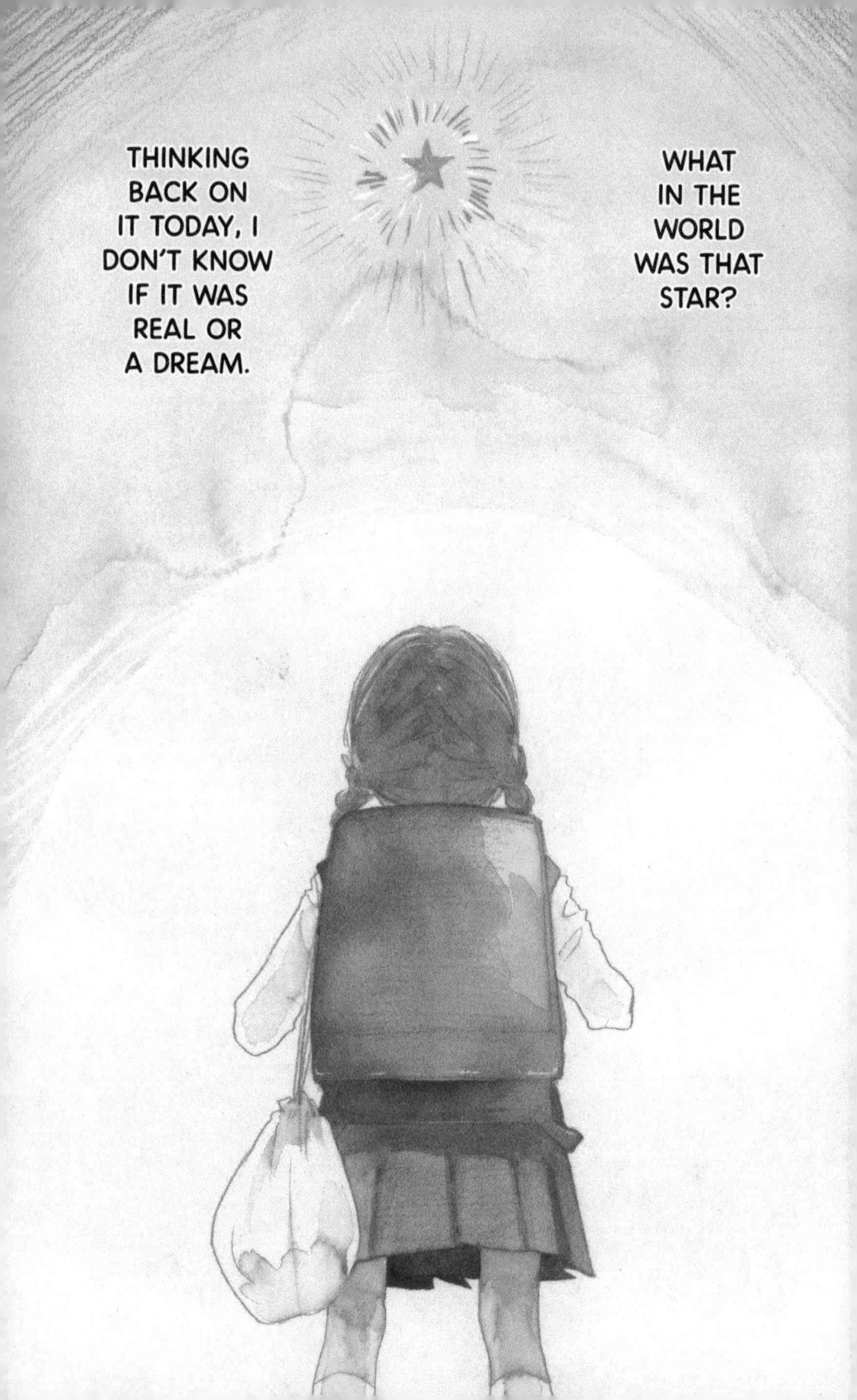
WHAT IN THE WORLD WAS THAT STAR?
THINKING BACK ON IT TODAY, I DON'T KNOW IF IT WAS REAL OR A DREAM.

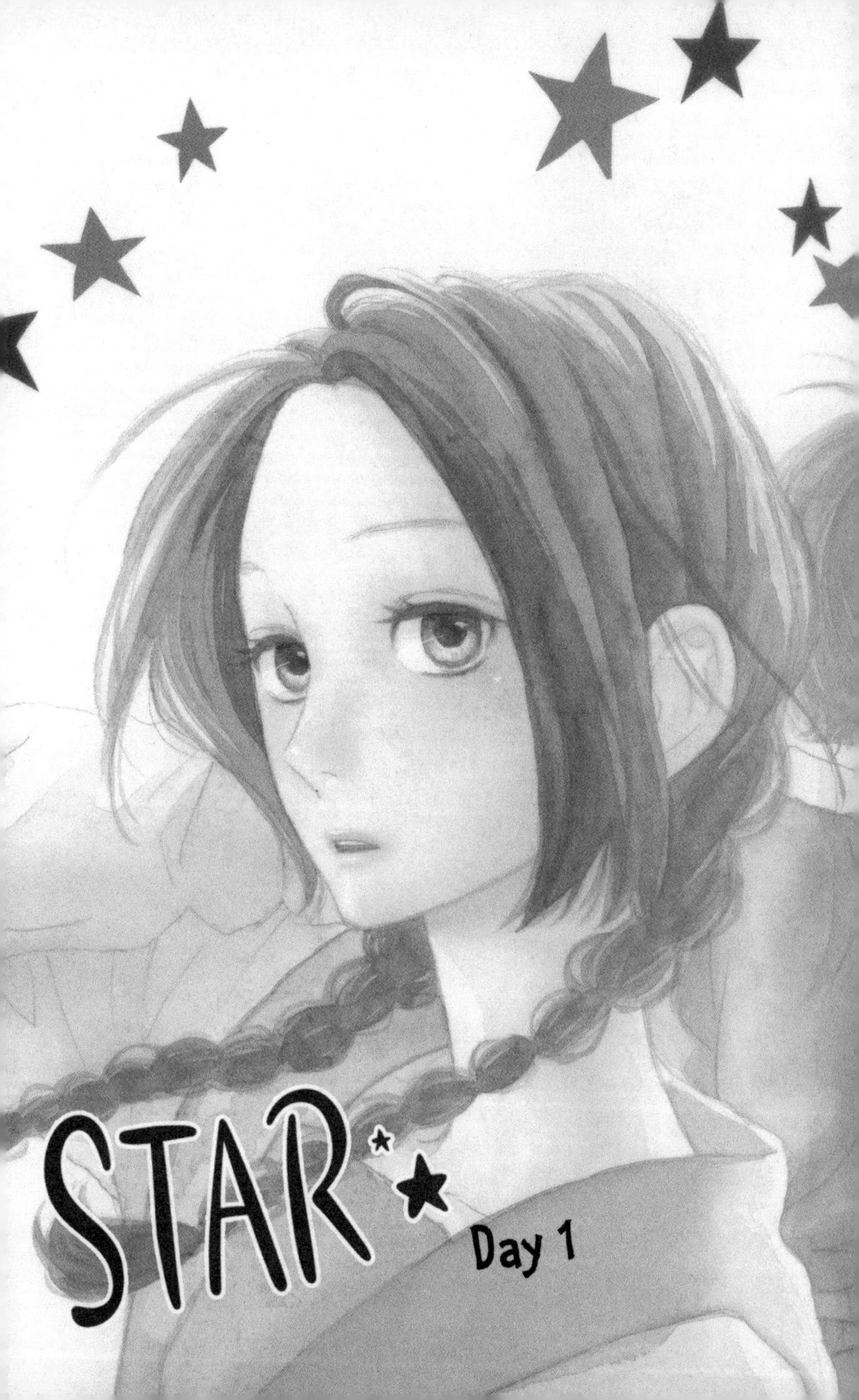
STAR
Day 1

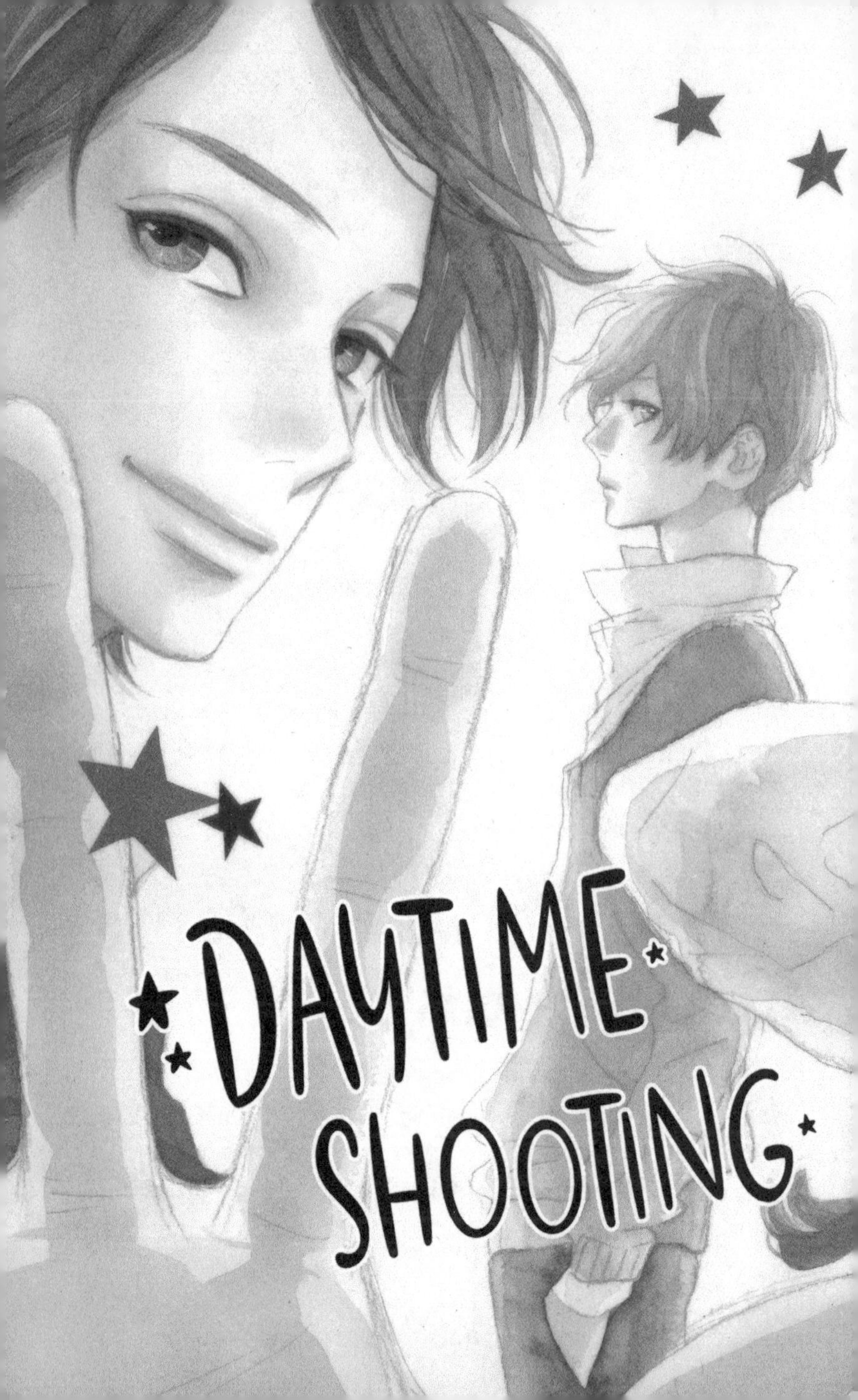
DAYTIME SHOOTING

And so...

Greetings to those of you reading my work for the first time, and to those who have read my previous series.
Oh, hello. I'm Mika Yamamori.
STRAINED BACK
My "howdy" pose

This is the start of my second series. Hurray! KLAP KLAP KLAP It's been two and a half months since *Sugars* ended. So much has happened. This is my first biweekly series, so perhaps I should call this my first series. Just hear me out.

I thought twice a month would be easy!!

It's crazy! It's one deadline after another! Is this right? I'd really like to know how the other *Margaret* mangaka live their lives. Also, working on a series is kind of subdued and difficult. I'm still not used to it. I wish I could land a brainbuster on myself as I struggled on *Sugars*.

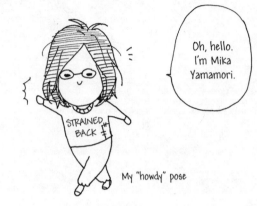

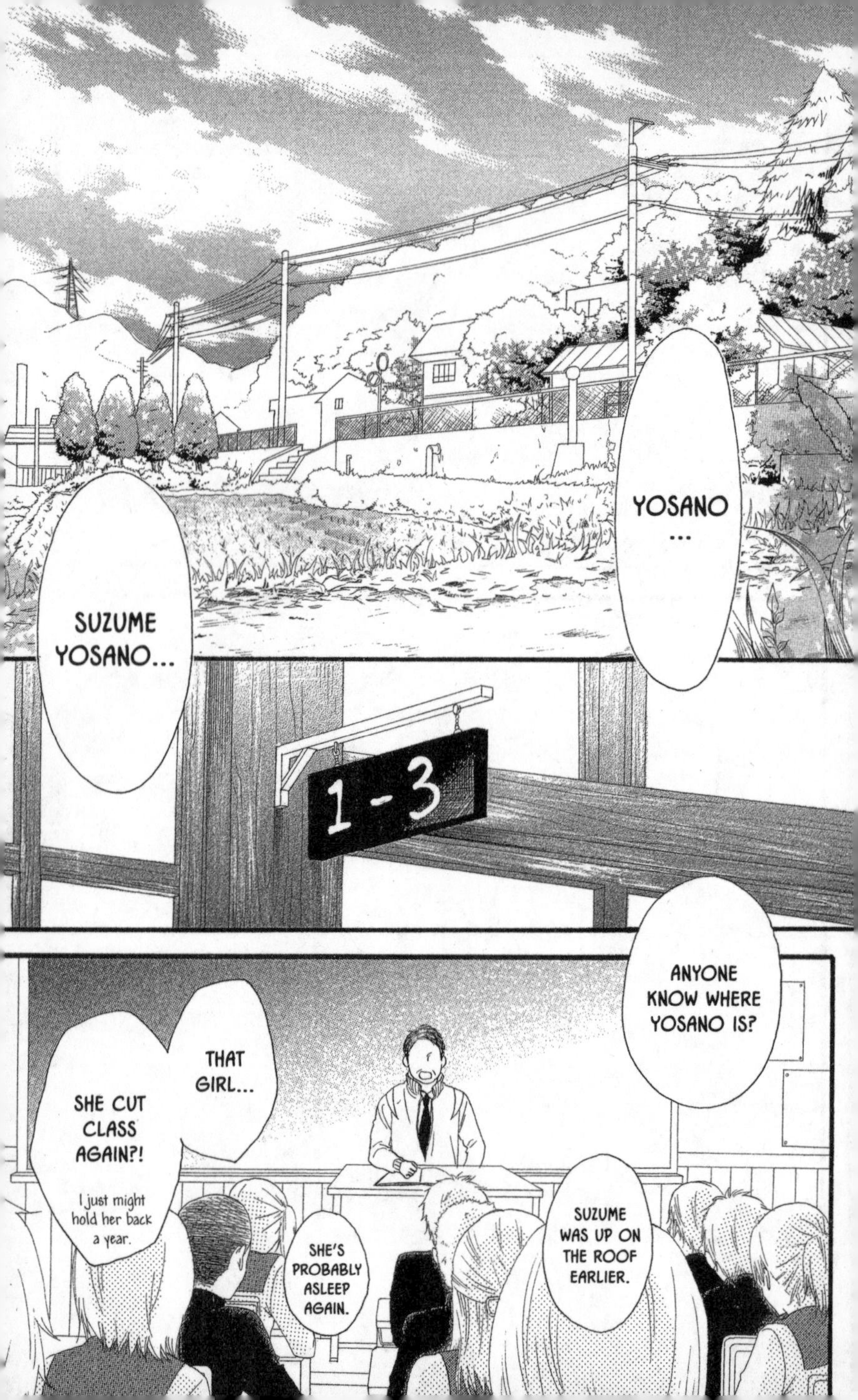
YOSANO ...
SUZUME YOSANO...
1-3
ANYONE KNOW WHERE YOSANO IS?
THAT GIRL...
SHE CUT CLASS AGAIN?!
I just might hold her back a year.
SUZUME WAS UP ON THE ROOF EARLIER.
SHE'S PROBABLY ASLEEP AGAIN.

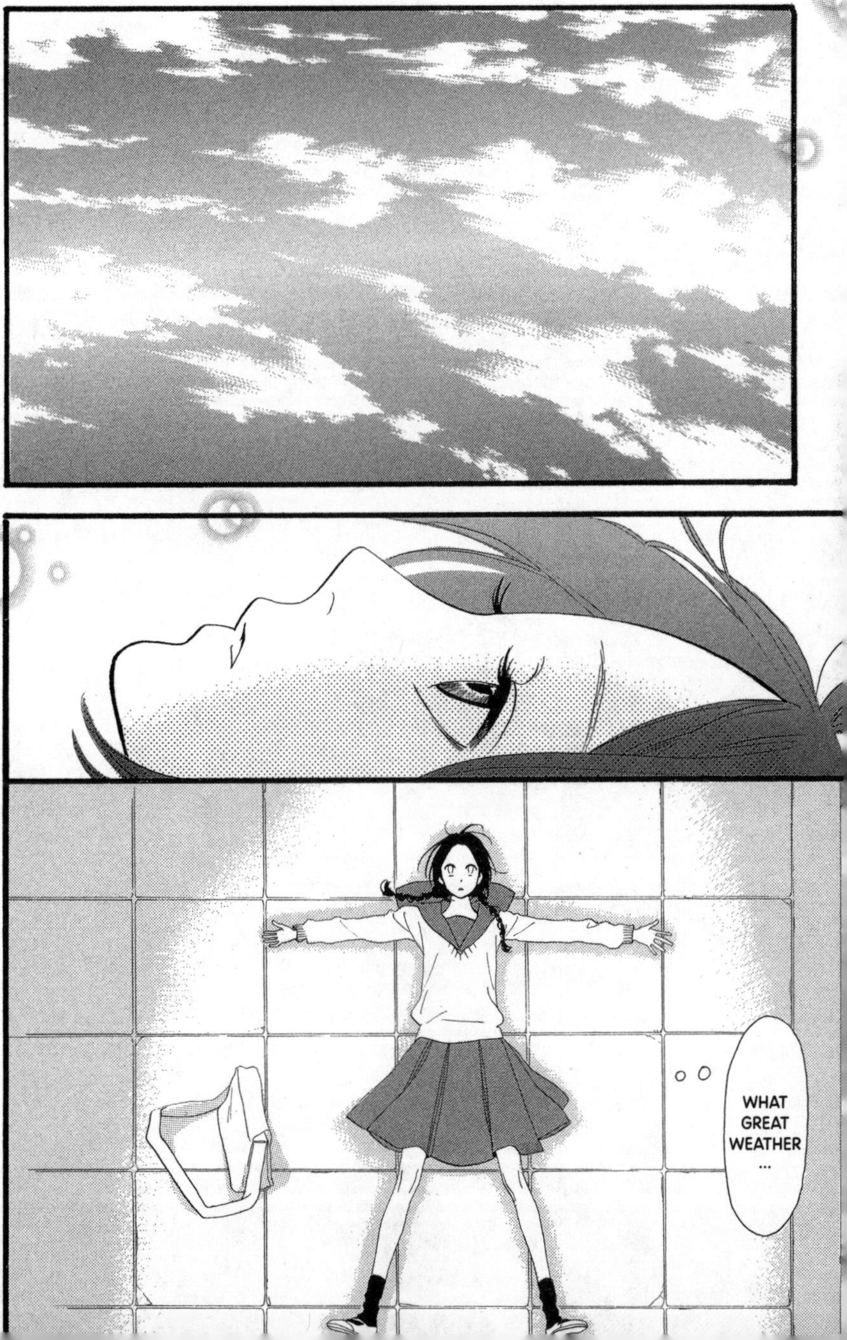
WHAT GREAT WEATHER ...

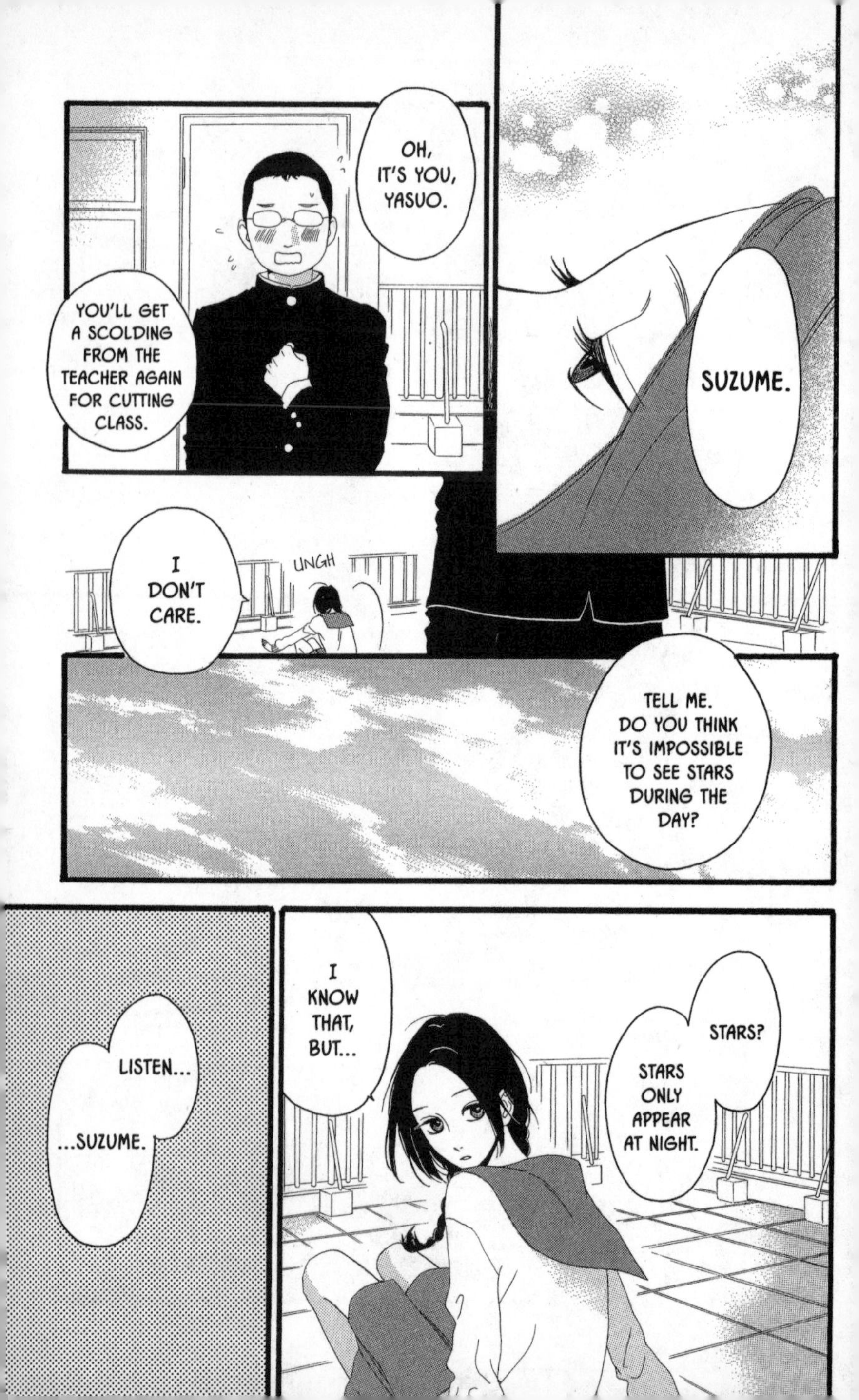
SUZUME.
OH, IT'S YOU, YASUO.
YOU'LL GET A SCOLDING FROM THE TEACHER AGAIN FOR CUTTING CLASS.
UNGH
I DON'T CARE.
TELL ME. DO YOU THINK IT'S IMPOSSIBLE TO SEE STARS DURING THE DAY?
STARS?
STARS ONLY APPEAR AT NIGHT.
I KNOW THAT, BUT...
LISTEN...
...SUZUME.

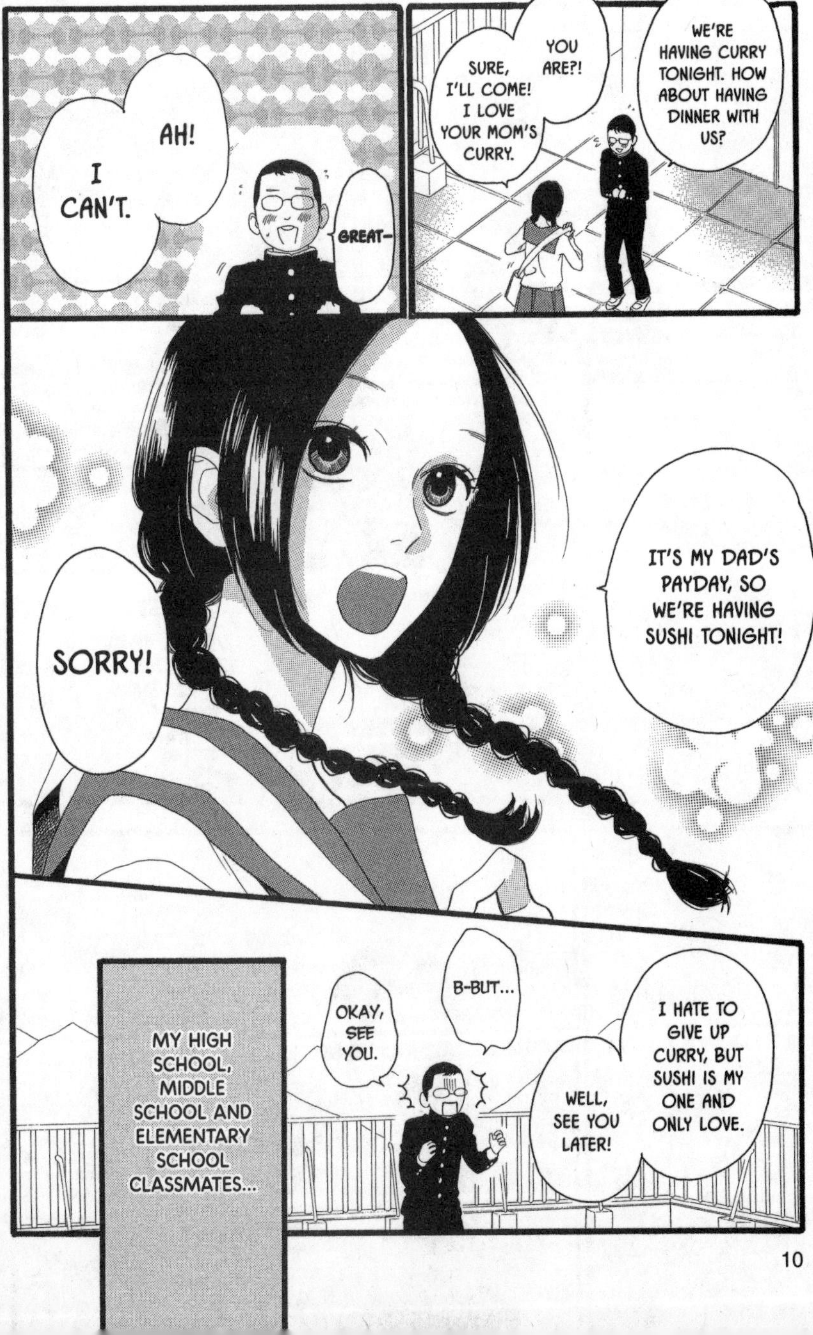
WE'RE HAVING CURRY TONIGHT. HOW ABOUT HAVING DINNER WITH US?
YOU ARE?!
SURE, I'LL COME! I LOVE YOUR MOM'S CURRY.
GREAT—
AH! I CAN'T.
IT'S MY DAD'S PAYDAY, SO WE'RE HAVING SUSHI TONIGHT!
SORRY!
I HATE TO GIVE UP CURRY, BUT SUSHI IS MY ONE AND ONLY LOVE.
WELL, SEE YOU LATER!
B-BUT...
OKAY, SEE YOU.
MY HIGH SCHOOL, MIDDLE SCHOOL AND ELEMENTARY SCHOOL CLASSMATES...

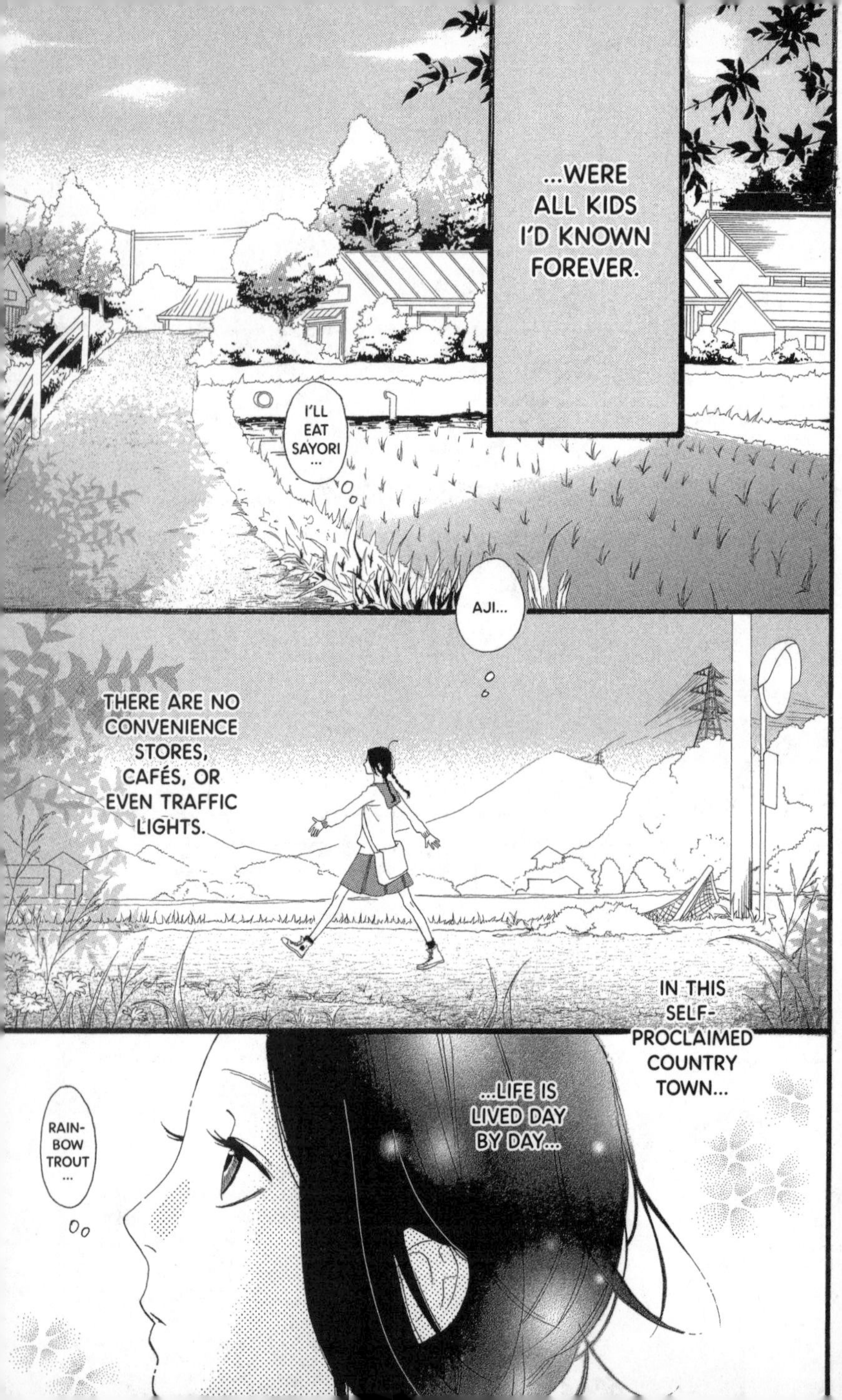
...WERE ALL KIDS I'D KNOWN FOREVER.
I'LL EAT SAYORI...
AJI...
THERE ARE NO CONVENIENCE STORES, CAFÉS, OR EVEN TRAFFIC LIGHTS.
IN THIS SELF-PROCLAIMED COUNTRY TOWN...
...LIFE IS LIVED DAY BY DAY...
RAINBOW TROUT...

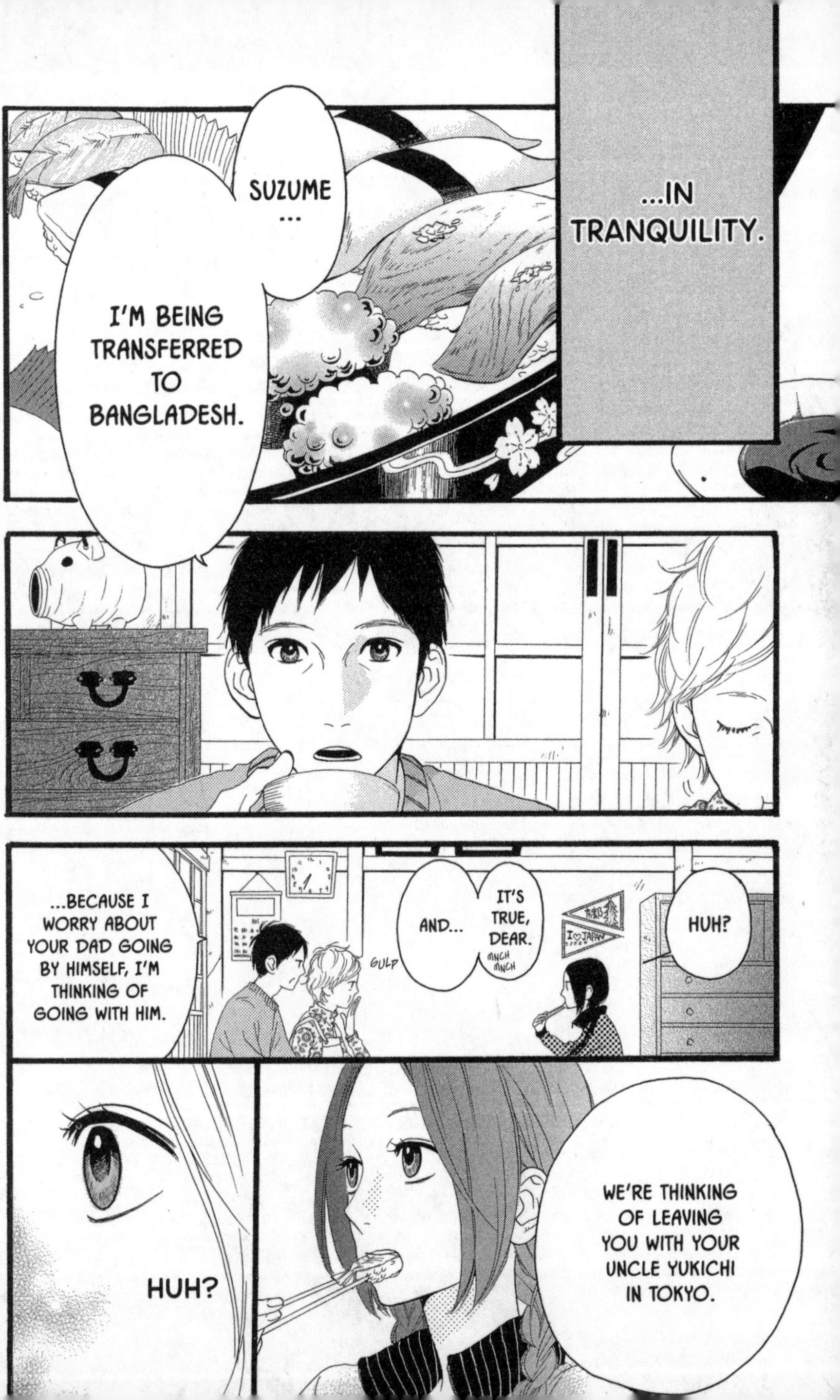
...IN TRANQUILITY.
SUZUME ...
I'M BEING TRANSFERRED TO BANGLADESH.
HUH?
IT'S TRUE, DEAR.
MNCH MNCH
AND...
GULP
...BECAUSE I WORRY ABOUT YOUR DAD GOING BY HIMSELF, I'M THINKING OF GOING WITH HIM.
WE'RE THINKING OF LEAVING YOU WITH YOUR UNCLE YUKICHI IN TOKYO.
HUH?

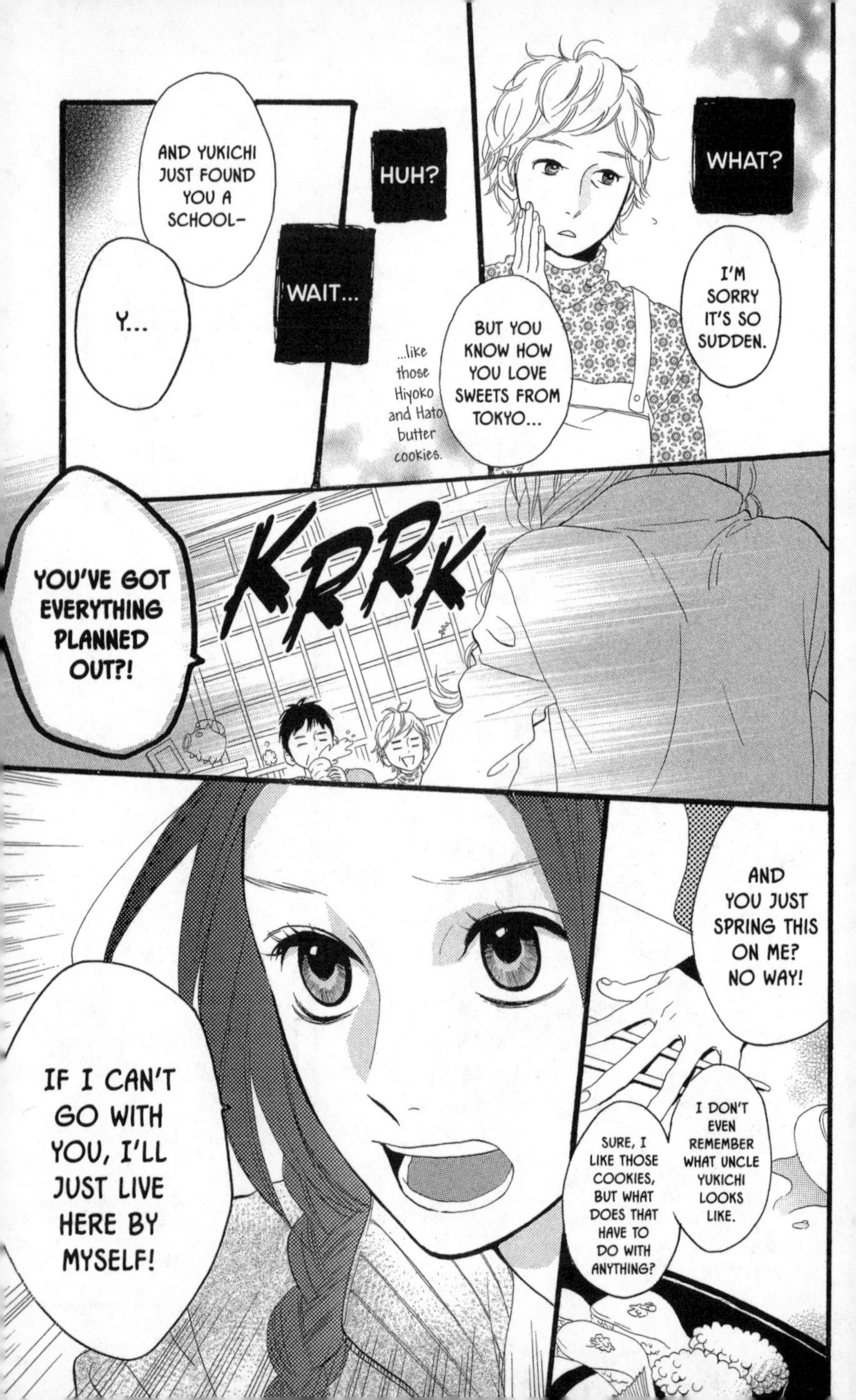
WHAT?
I'M SORRY IT'S SO SUDDEN.
BUT YOU KNOW HOW YOU LOVE SWEETS FROM TOKYO...
...like those Hiyoko and Hato butter cookies.
AND YUKICHI JUST FOUND YOU A SCHOOL–
HUH?
WAIT...
Y...
KRRK
YOU'VE GOT EVERYTHING PLANNED OUT?!
AND YOU JUST SPRING THIS ON ME? NO WAY!
I DON'T EVEN REMEMBER WHAT UNCLE YUKICHI LOOKS LIKE.
SURE, I LIKE THOSE COOKIES, BUT WHAT DOES THAT HAVE TO DO WITH ANYTHING?
IF I CAN'T GO WITH YOU, I'LL JUST LIVE HERE BY MYSELF!

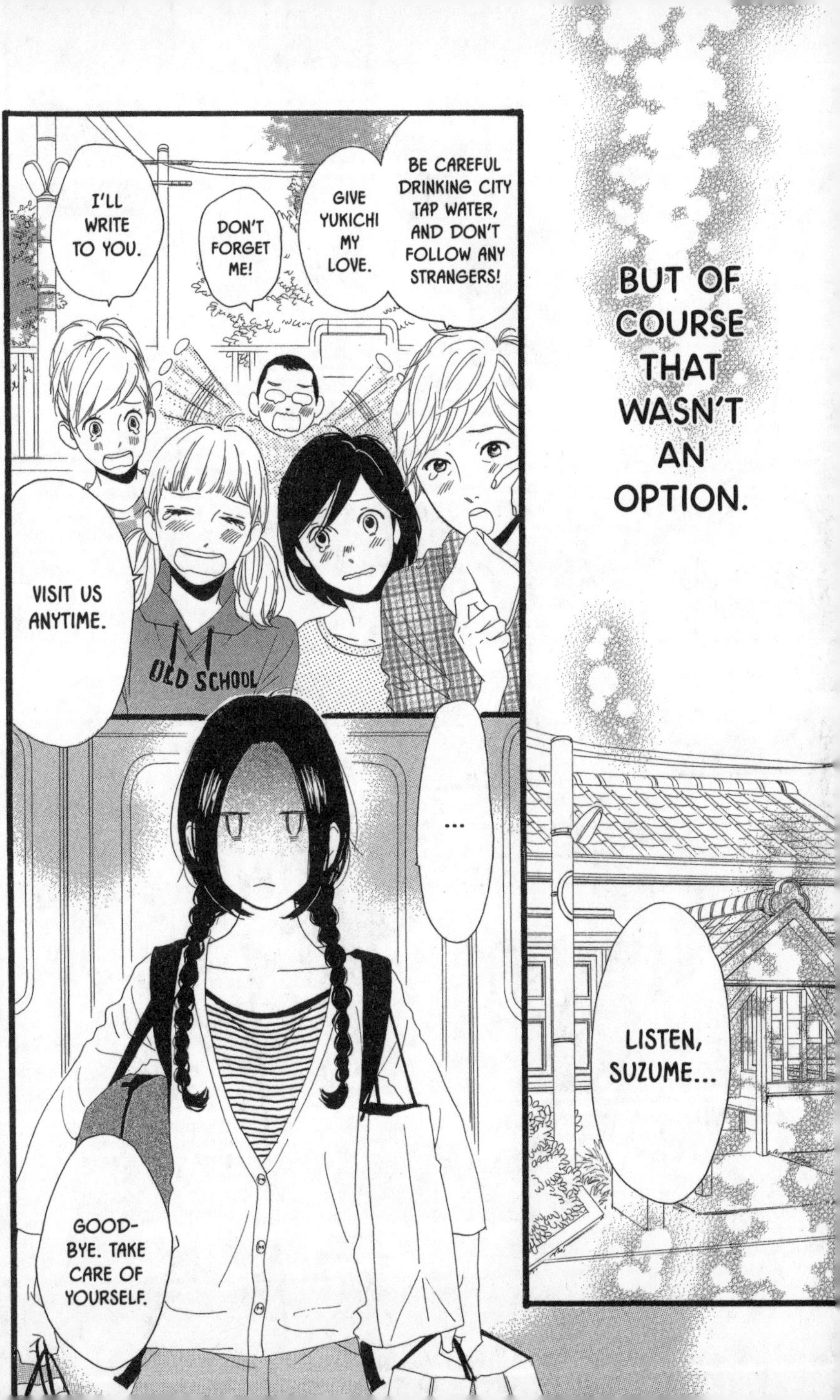
BUT OF COURSE THAT WASN'T AN OPTION.
LISTEN, SUZUME...
BE CAREFUL DRINKING CITY TAP WATER, AND DON'T FOLLOW ANY STRANGERS!
GIVE YUKICHI MY LOVE.
DON'T FORGET ME!
I'LL WRITE TO YOU.
...
VISIT US ANYTIME.
OLD SCHOOL
GOOD-BYE. TAKE CARE OF YOURSELF.

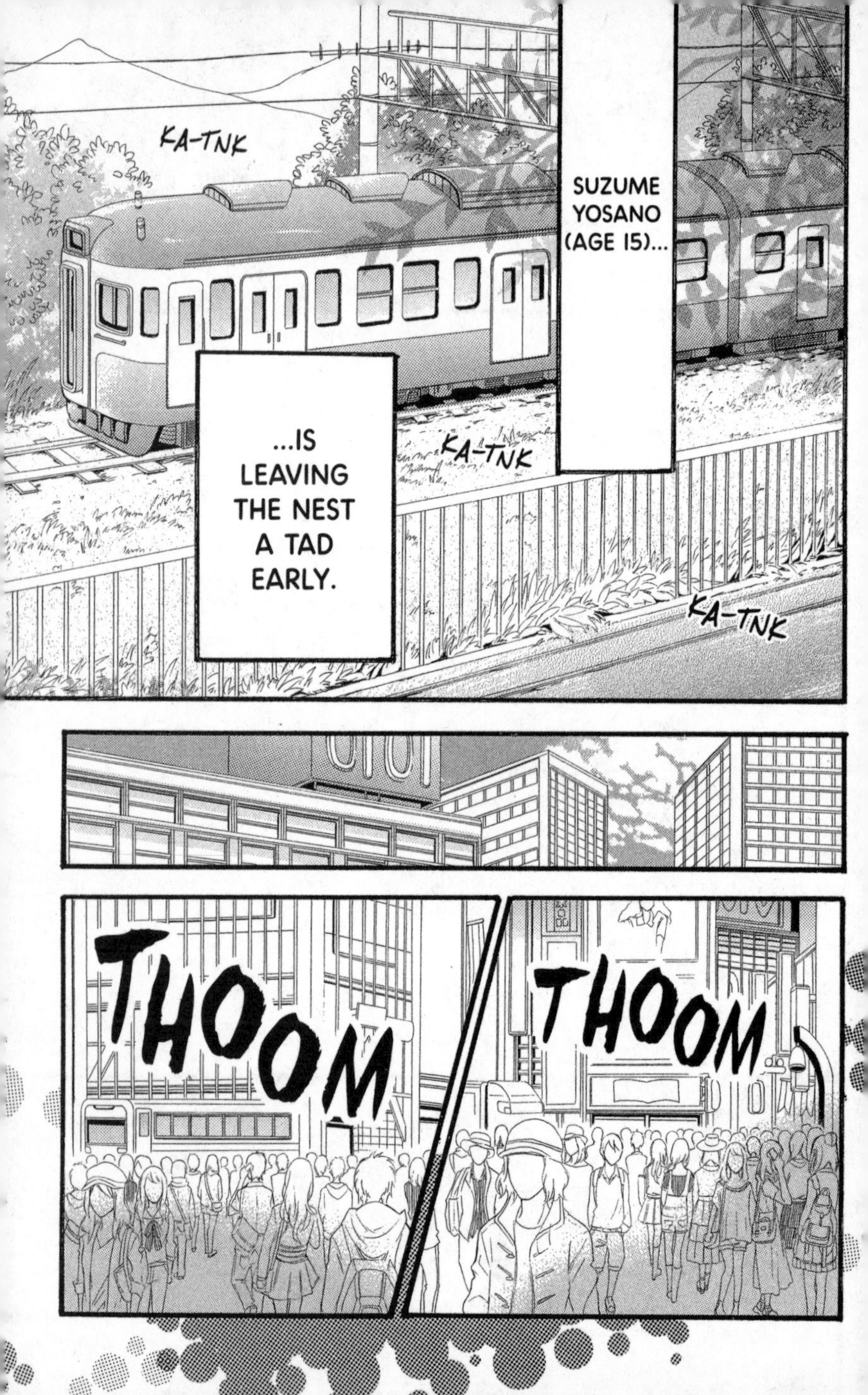
SUZUME YOSANO (AGE 15)...
...IS LEAVING THE NEST A TAD EARLY.
KA-TNK
KA-TNK
KA-TNK
THOOM
THOOM

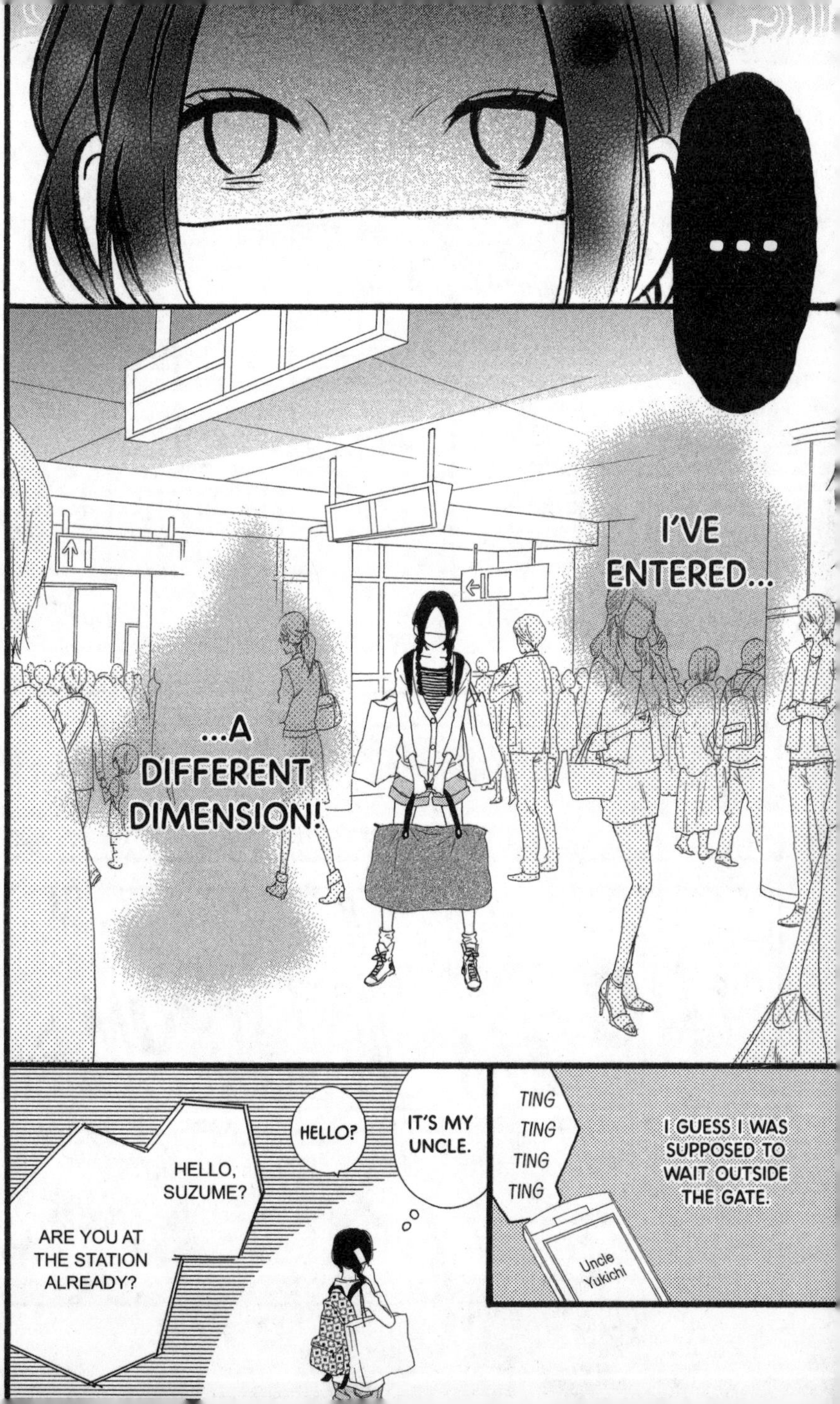
...
I'VE ENTERED...
...A DIFFERENT DIMENSION!
I GUESS I WAS SUPPOSED TO WAIT OUTSIDE THE GATE.
TING TING TING TING
Uncle Yukichi
IT'S MY UNCLE.
HELLO?
HELLO, SUZUME?
ARE YOU AT THE STATION ALREADY?

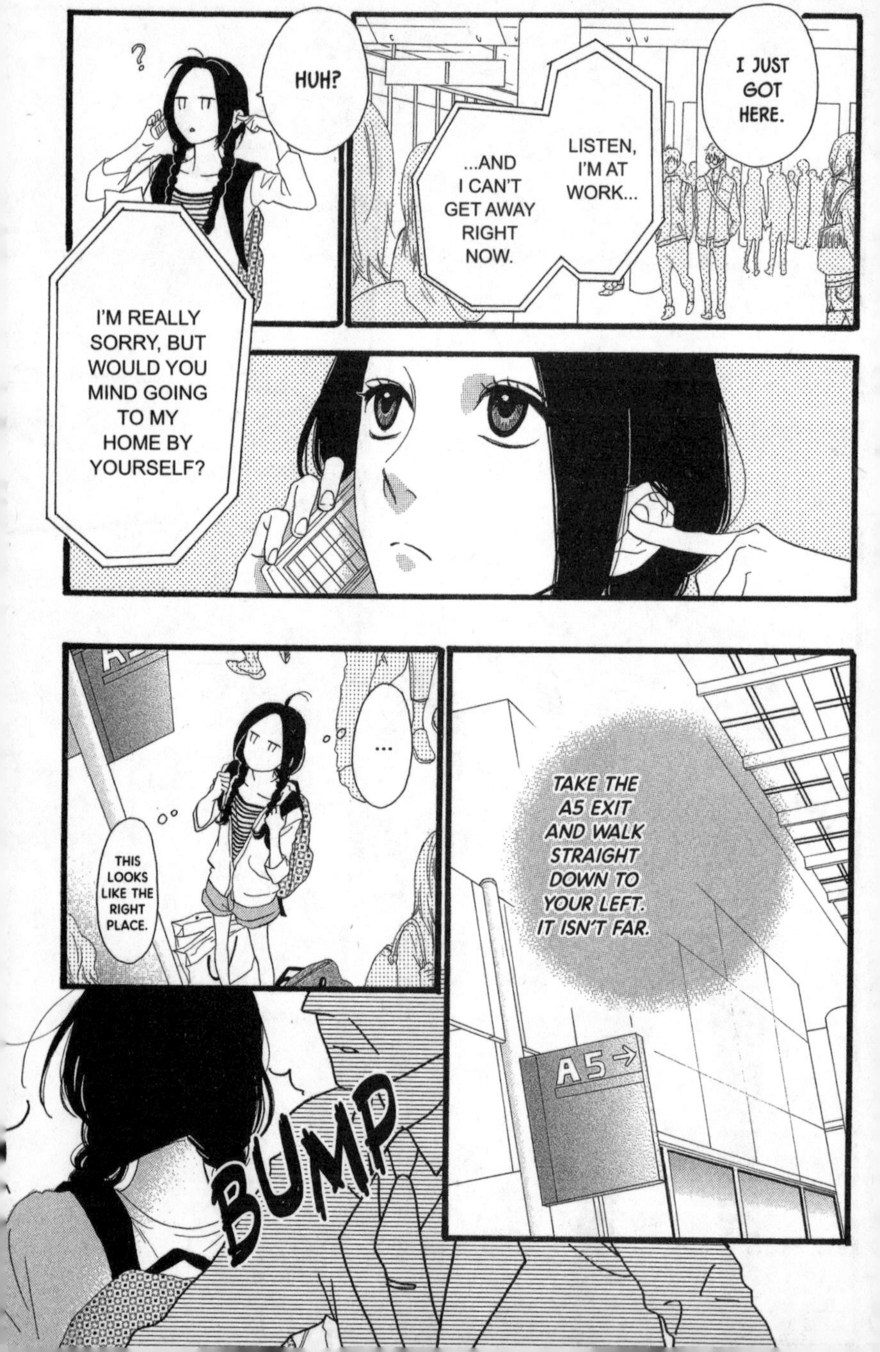
I JUST GOT HERE.
LISTEN, I'M AT WORK...
...AND I CAN'T GET AWAY RIGHT NOW.
?
HUH?
I'M REALLY SORRY, BUT WOULD YOU MIND GOING TO MY HOME BY YOURSELF?
TAKE THE A5 EXIT AND WALK STRAIGHT DOWN TO YOUR LEFT. IT ISN'T FAR.
A5 →
...
THIS LOOKS LIKE THE RIGHT PLACE.
BUMP

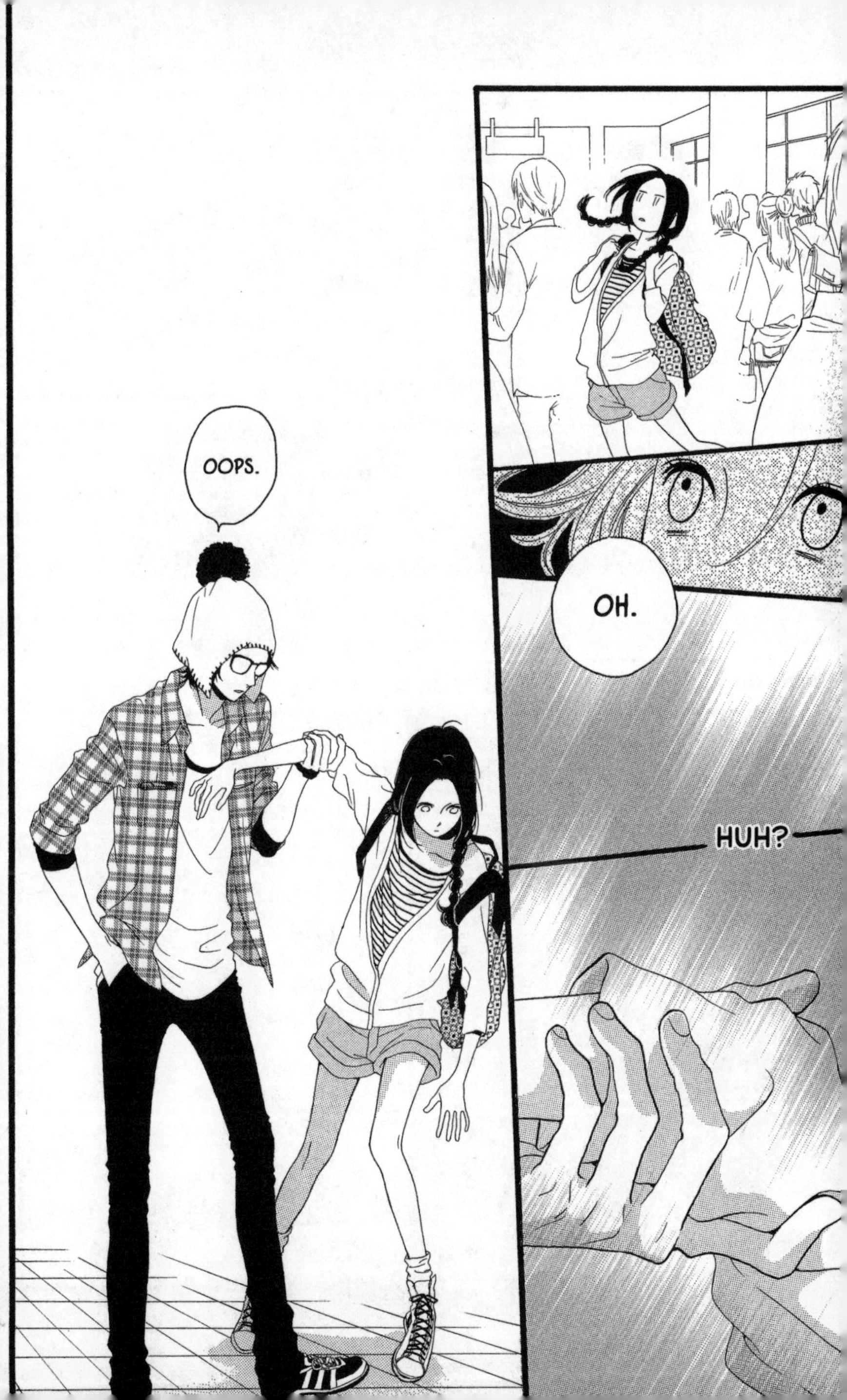
OH.
HUH?
OOPS.

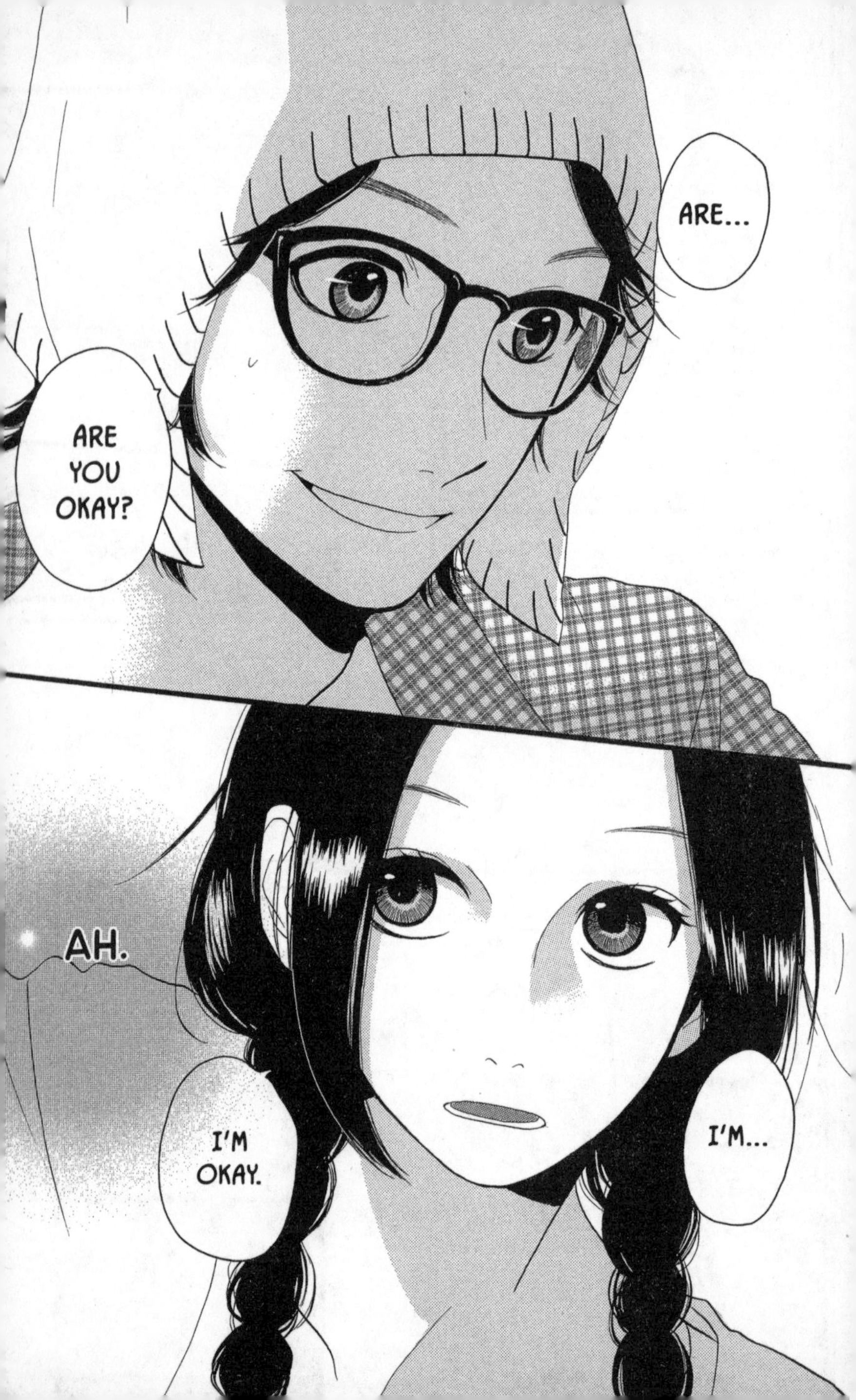
ARE...
ARE YOU OKAY?
AH.
I'M...
I'M OKAY.

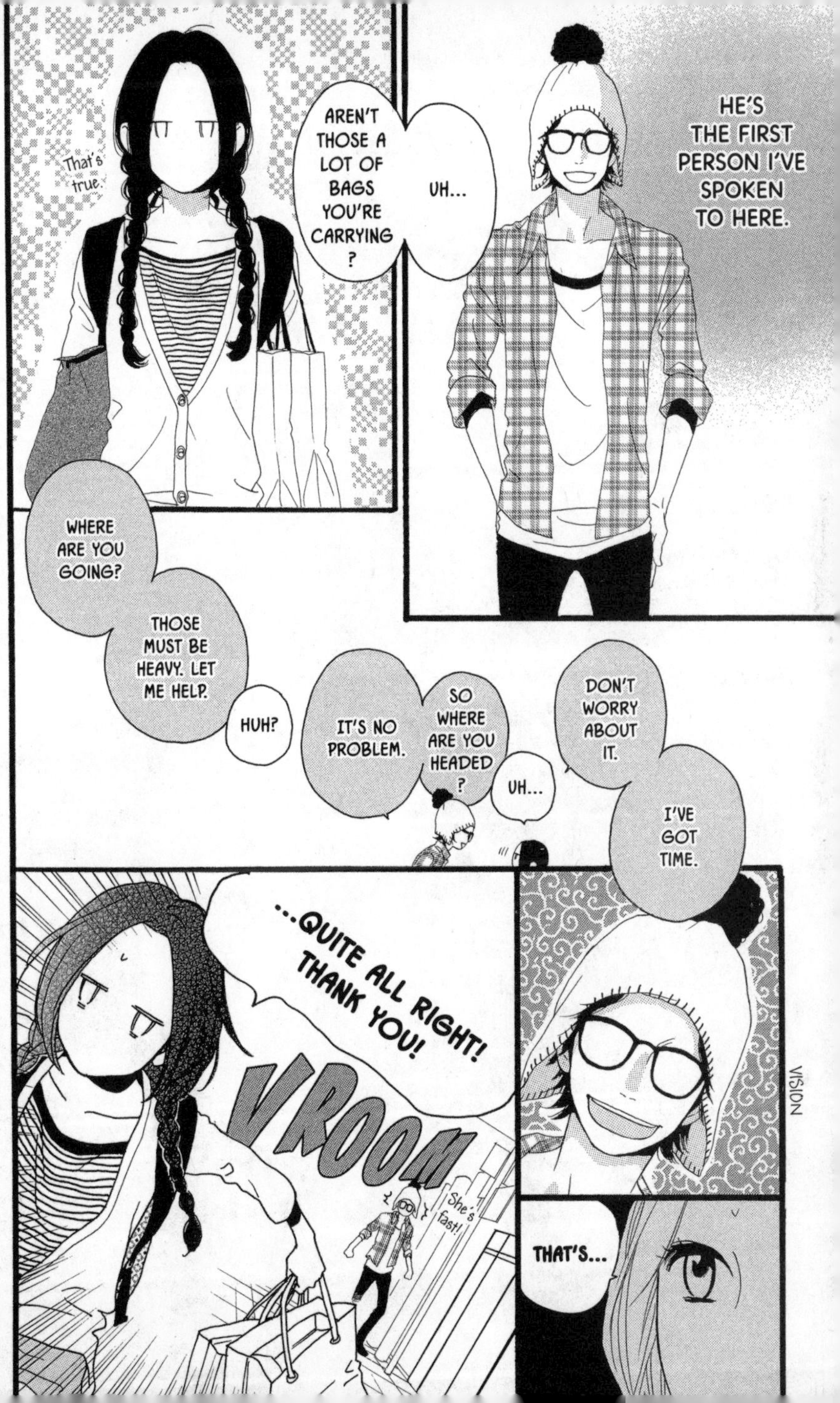
HE'S THE FIRST PERSON I'VE SPOKEN TO HERE.
AREN'T THOSE A LOT OF BAGS YOU'RE CARRYING?
UH...
That's true.
WHERE ARE YOU GOING?
THOSE MUST BE HEAVY. LET ME HELP.
HUH?
IT'S NO PROBLEM.
SO WHERE ARE YOU HEADED?
UH...
DON'T WORRY ABOUT IT.
I'VE GOT TIME.
THAT'S...
...QUITE ALL RIGHT! THANK YOU!
VROOM
She's fast!
VISION

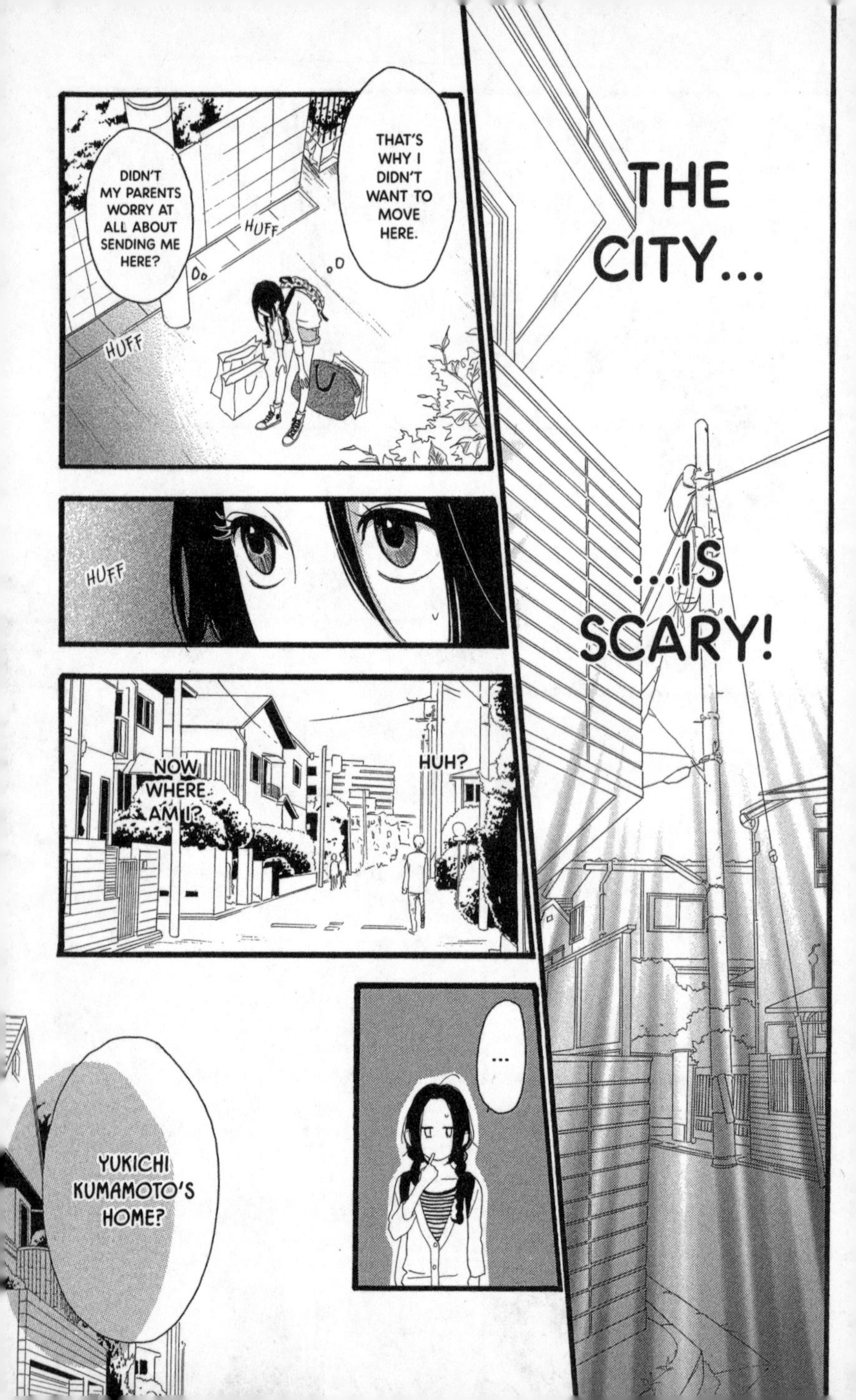
THE CITY...
...IS SCARY!
THAT'S WHY I DIDN'T WANT TO MOVE HERE.
HUFF
DIDN'T MY PARENTS WORRY AT ALL ABOUT SENDING ME HERE?
HUFF
HUFF
HUH?
NOW WHERE AM I?
...
YUKICHI KUMAMOTO'S HOME?

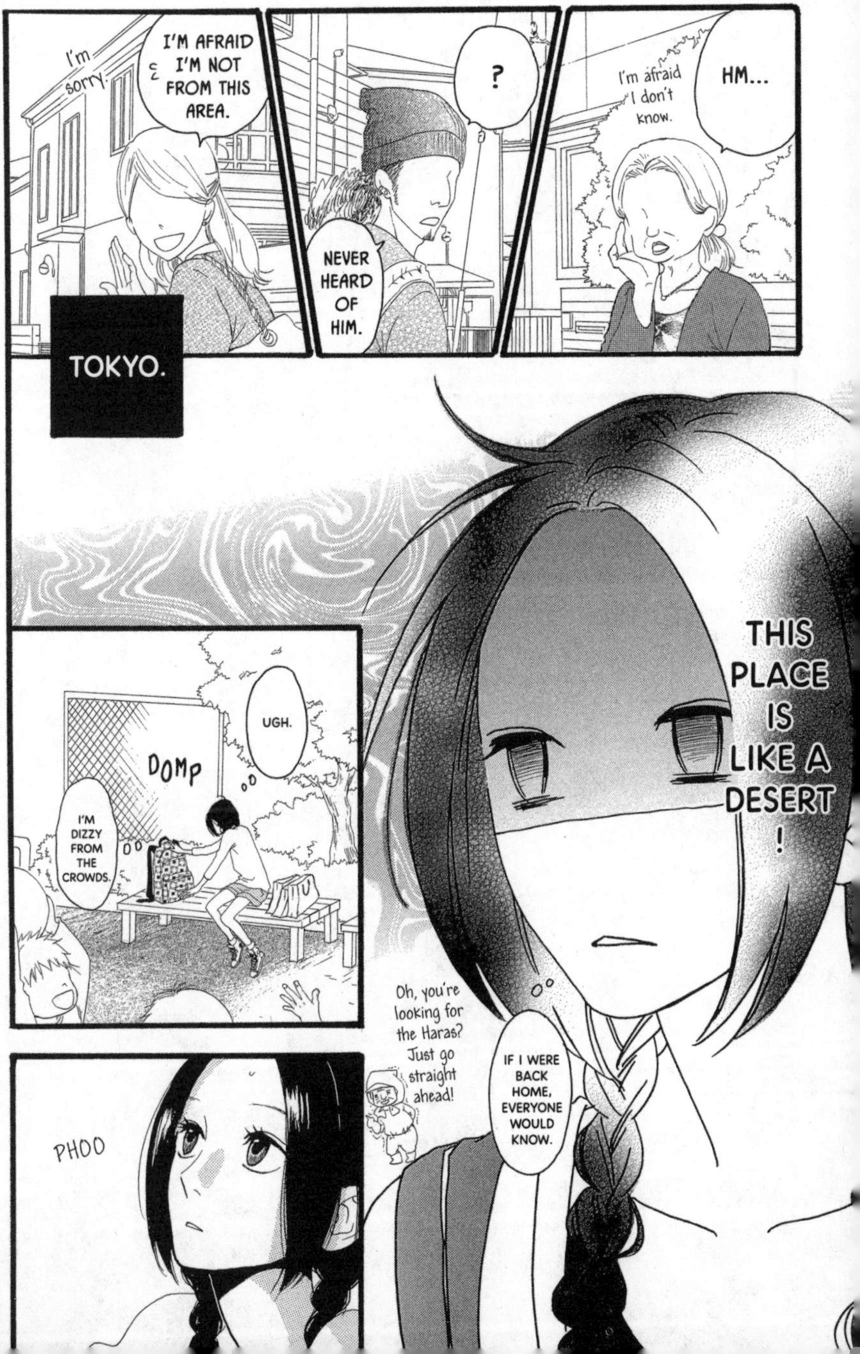

HM...
I'm afraid I don't know.
?
NEVER HEARD OF HIM.
I'M AFRAID I'M NOT FROM THIS AREA.
I'm sorry.
TOKYO.
THIS PLACE IS LIKE A DESERT!
IF I WERE BACK HOME, EVERYONE WOULD KNOW.
Oh, you're looking for the Haras? Just go straight ahead!
UGH.
DOMP
I'M DIZZY FROM THE CROWDS.
PHOO

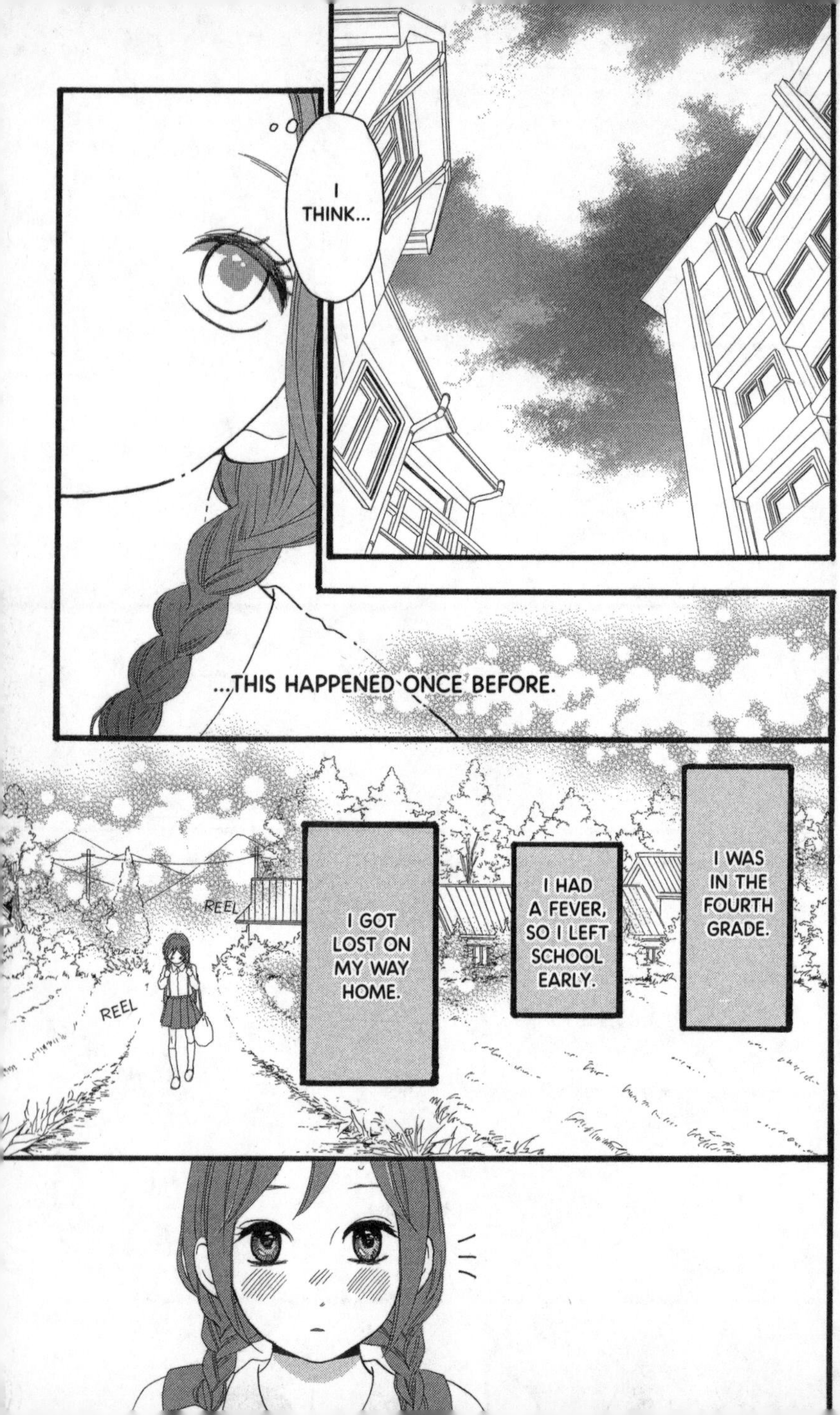
I THINK...
...THIS HAPPENED ONCE BEFORE.
I WAS IN THE FOURTH GRADE.
I HAD A FEVER, SO I LEFT SCHOOL EARLY.
I GOT LOST ON MY WAY HOME.
REEL
REEL

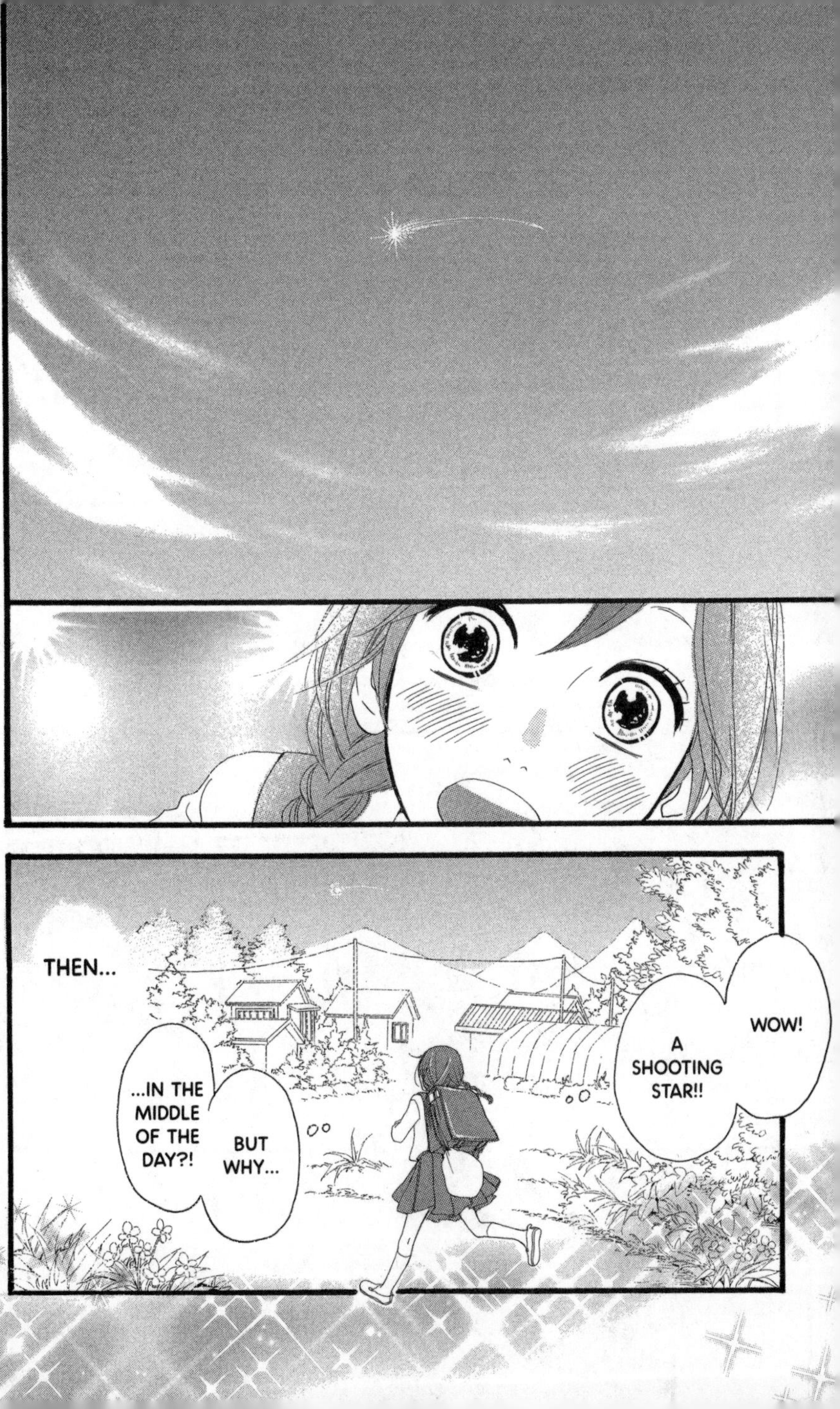
WOW!
A SHOOTING STAR!!
BUT WHY...
...IN THE MIDDLE OF THE DAY?!
THEN...

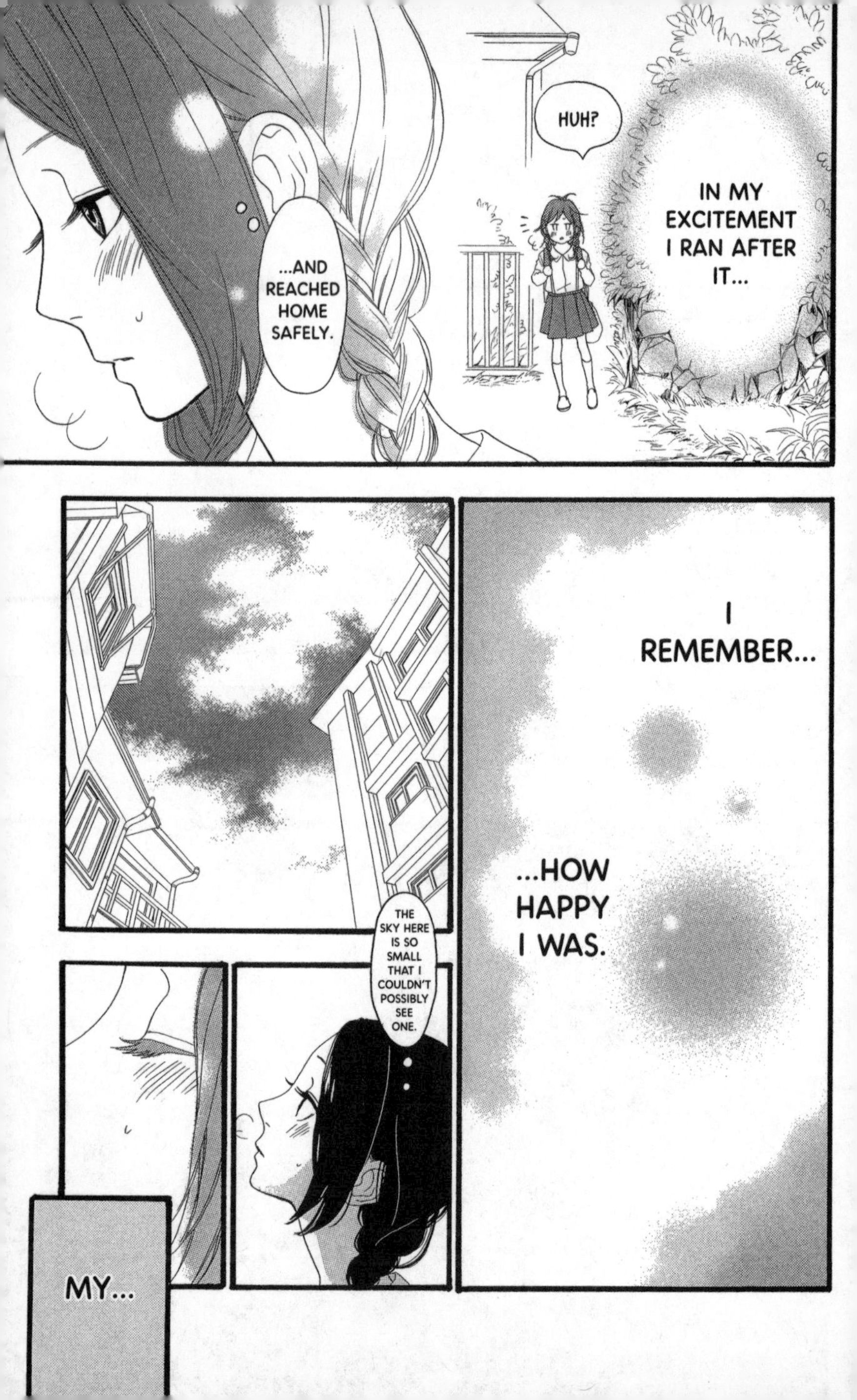
IN MY EXCITEMENT I RAN AFTER IT...
HUH?
...AND REACHED HOME SAFELY.
I REMEMBER...
...HOW HAPPY I WAS.
THE SKY HERE IS SO SMALL THAT I COULDN'T POSSIBLY SEE ONE.
MY...

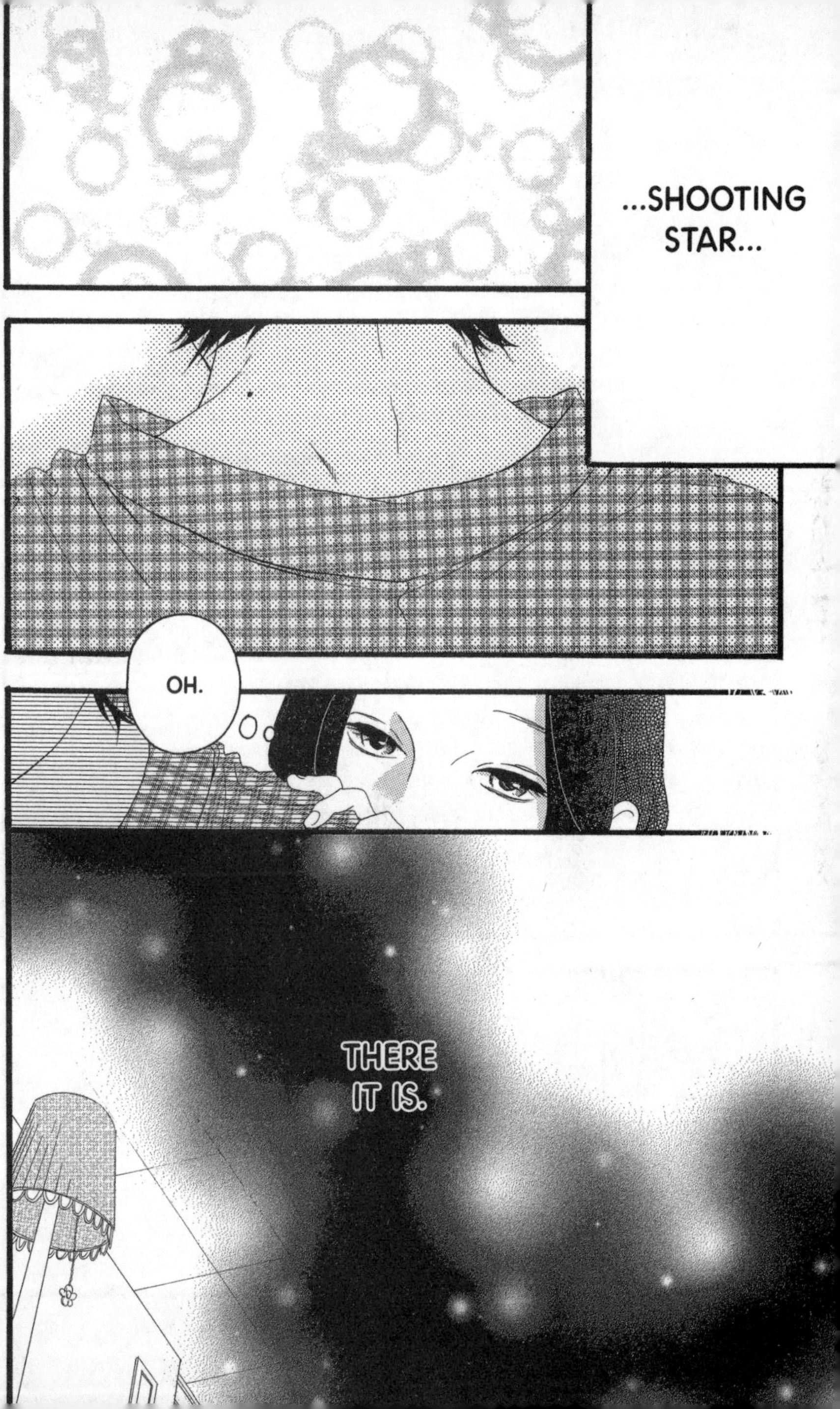
...SHOOTING STAR...
OH.
THERE IT IS.

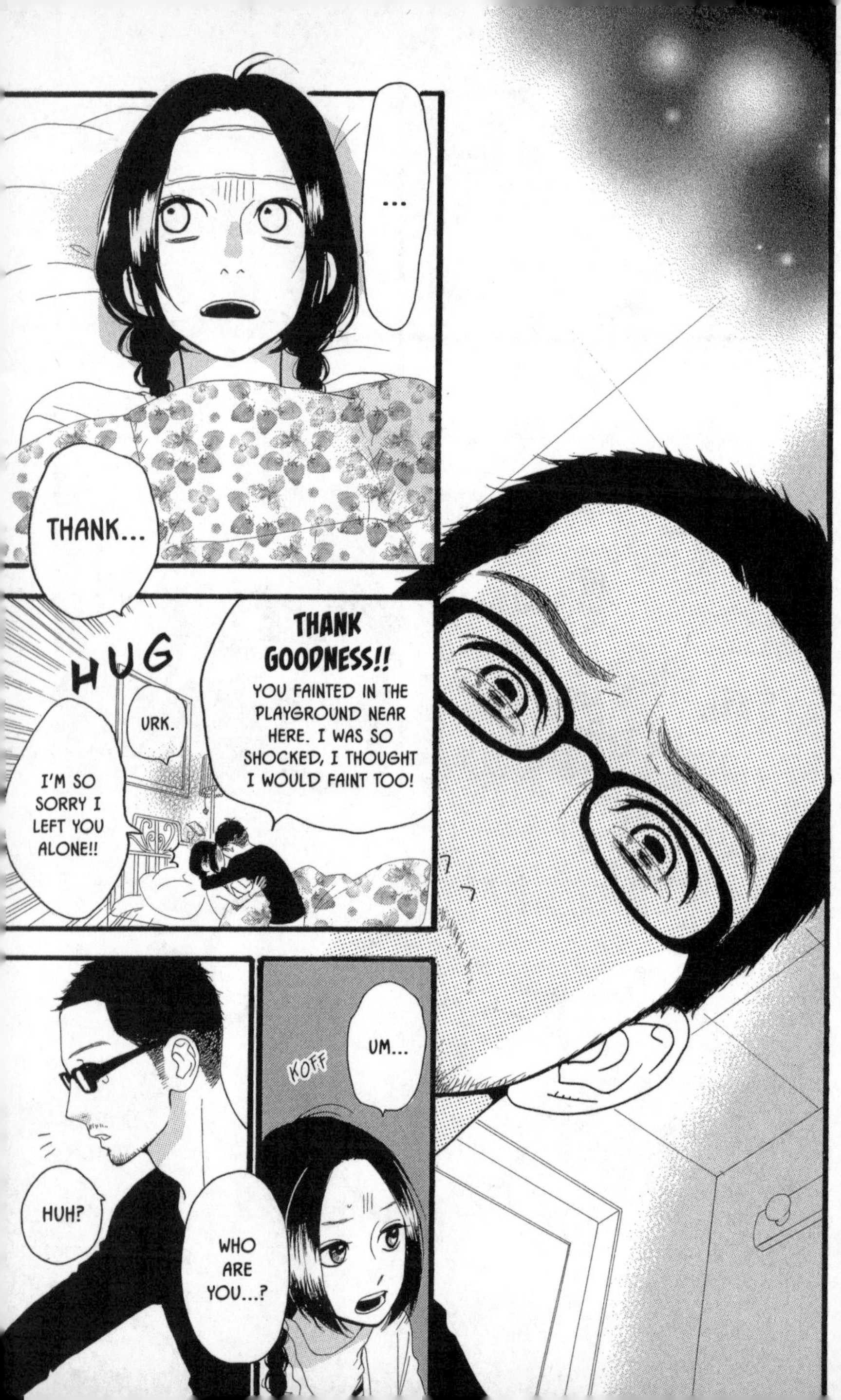
...
THANK...
THANK GOODNESS!! YOU FAINTED IN THE PLAYGROUND NEAR HERE. I WAS SO SHOCKED, I THOUGHT I WOULD FAINT TOO!
HUG
URK.
I'M SO SORRY I LEFT YOU ALONE!!
UM...
KOFF
WHO ARE YOU...?
HUH?

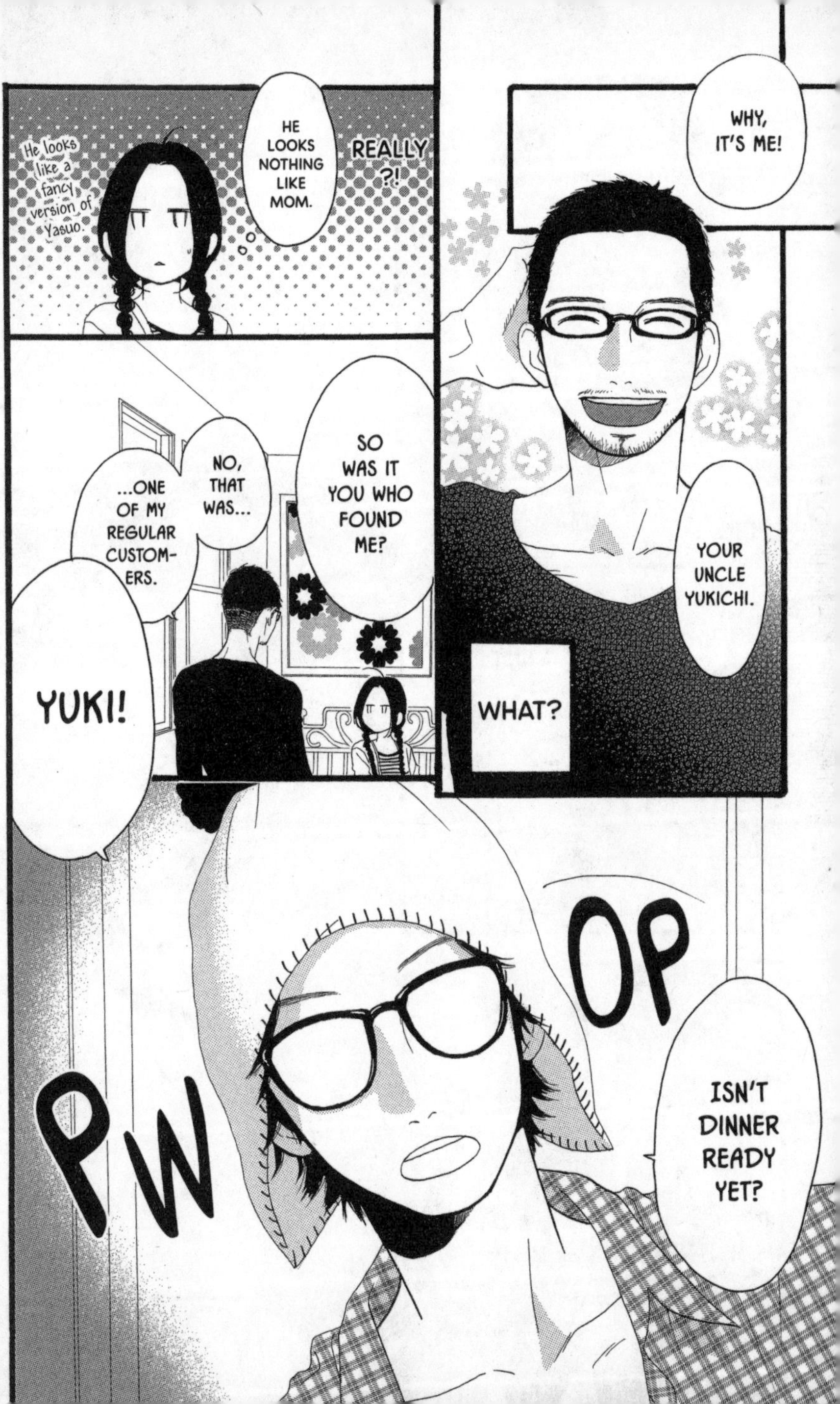
WHY, IT'S ME!
YOUR UNCLE YUKICHI.
WHAT?
REALLY ?!
HE LOOKS NOTHING LIKE MOM.
He looks like a fancy version of Yasuo.
SO WAS IT YOU WHO FOUND ME?
NO, THAT WAS...
...ONE OF MY REGULAR CUSTOM-ERS.
YUKI!
PWOP
ISN'T DINNER READY YET?

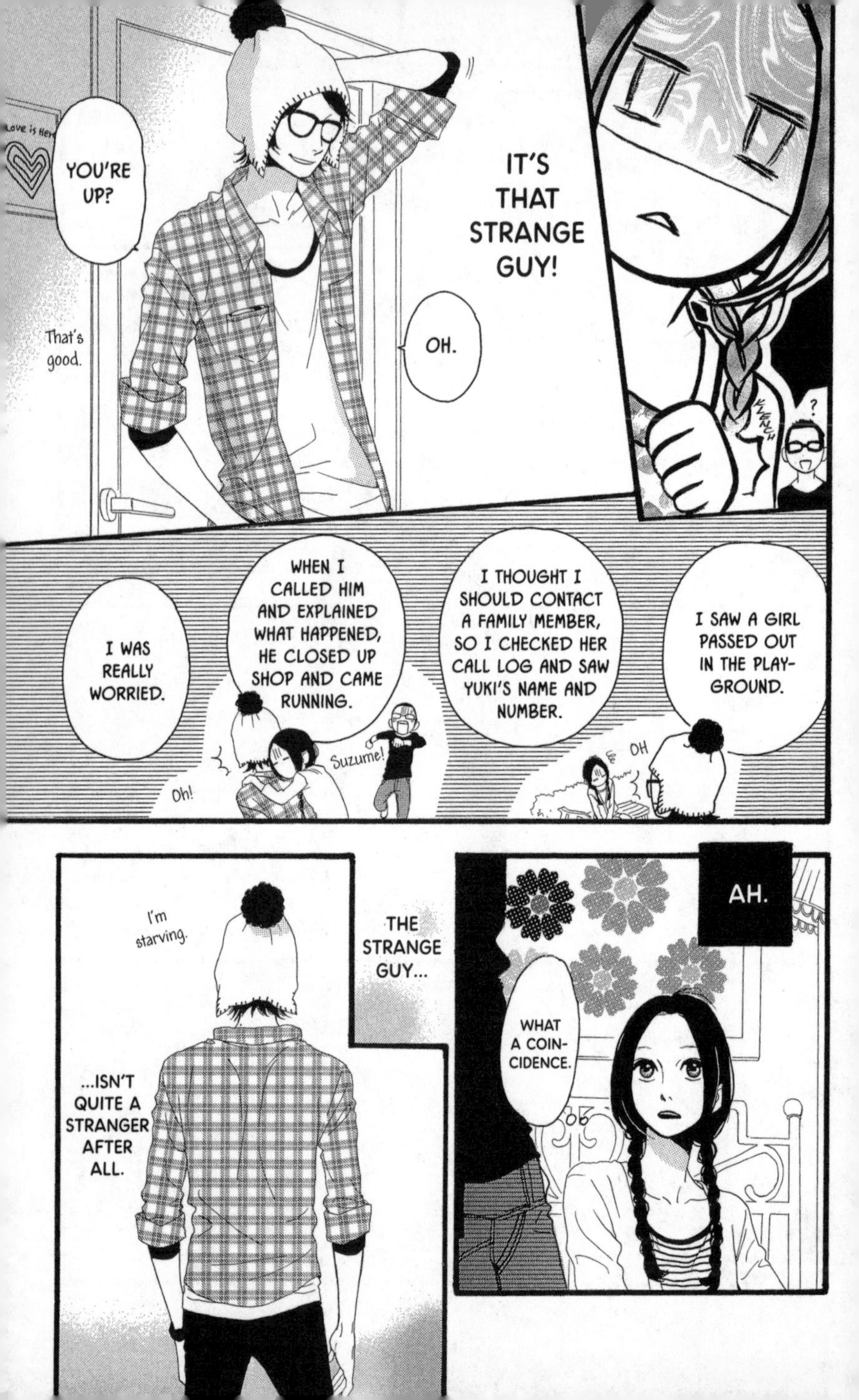

KLENCH
?
IT'S THAT STRANGE GUY!
OH.
YOU'RE UP?
That's good.
Love is Here
I SAW A GIRL PASSED OUT IN THE PLAYGROUND.
OH
I THOUGHT I SHOULD CONTACT A FAMILY MEMBER, SO I CHECKED HER CALL LOG AND SAW YUKI'S NAME AND NUMBER.
Suzume!
WHEN I CALLED HIM AND EXPLAINED WHAT HAPPENED, HE CLOSED UP SHOP AND CAME RUNNING.
I WAS REALLY WORRIED.
Oh!
AH.
WHAT A COINCIDENCE.
THE STRANGE GUY...
I'm starving.
...ISN'T QUITE A STRANGER AFTER ALL.

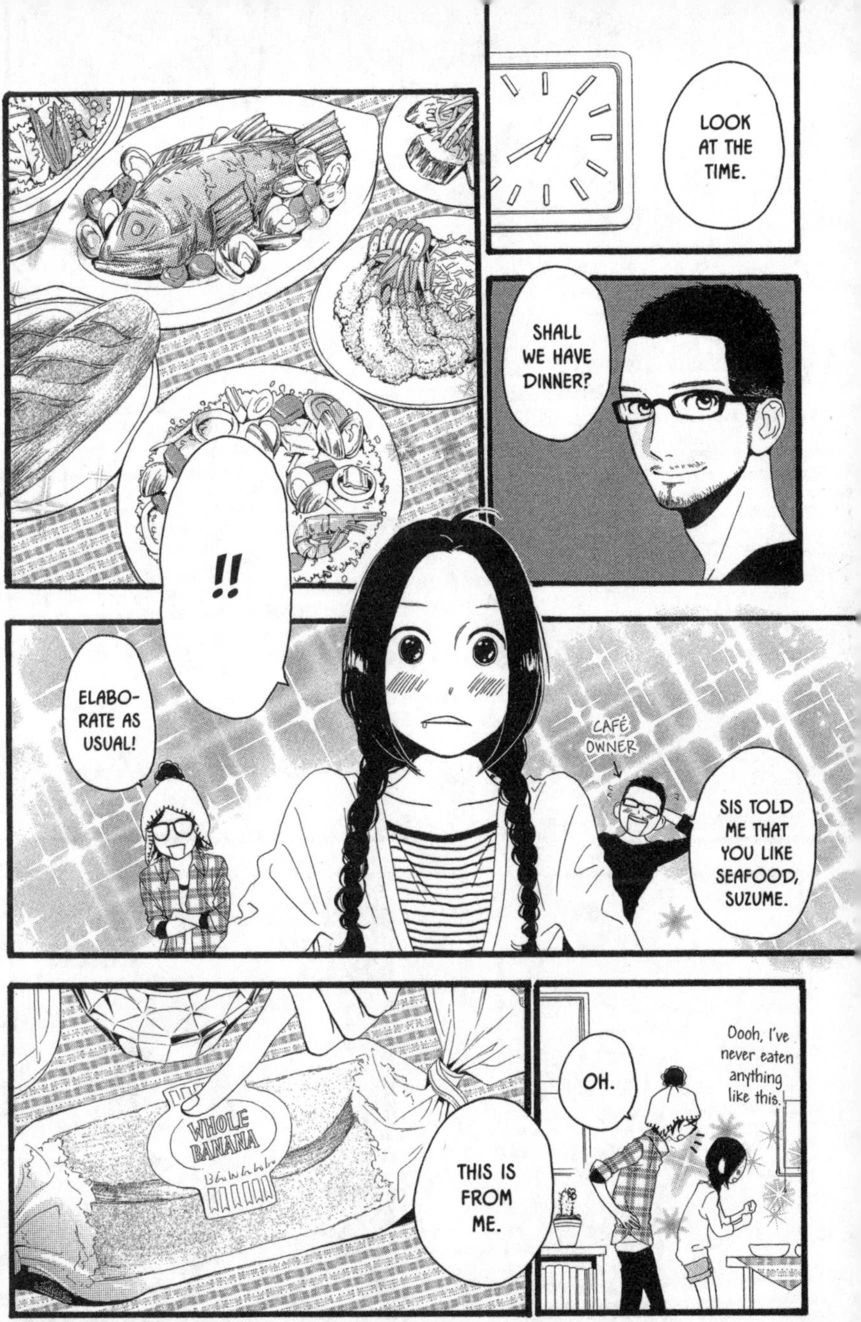
LOOK AT THE TIME.
SHALL WE HAVE DINNER?
!!
SIS TOLD ME THAT YOU LIKE SEAFOOD, SUZUME.
CAFÉ OWNER
ELABO-RATE AS USUAL!
Oooh, I've never eaten anything like this.
OH.
THIS IS FROM ME.
WHOLE BANANA

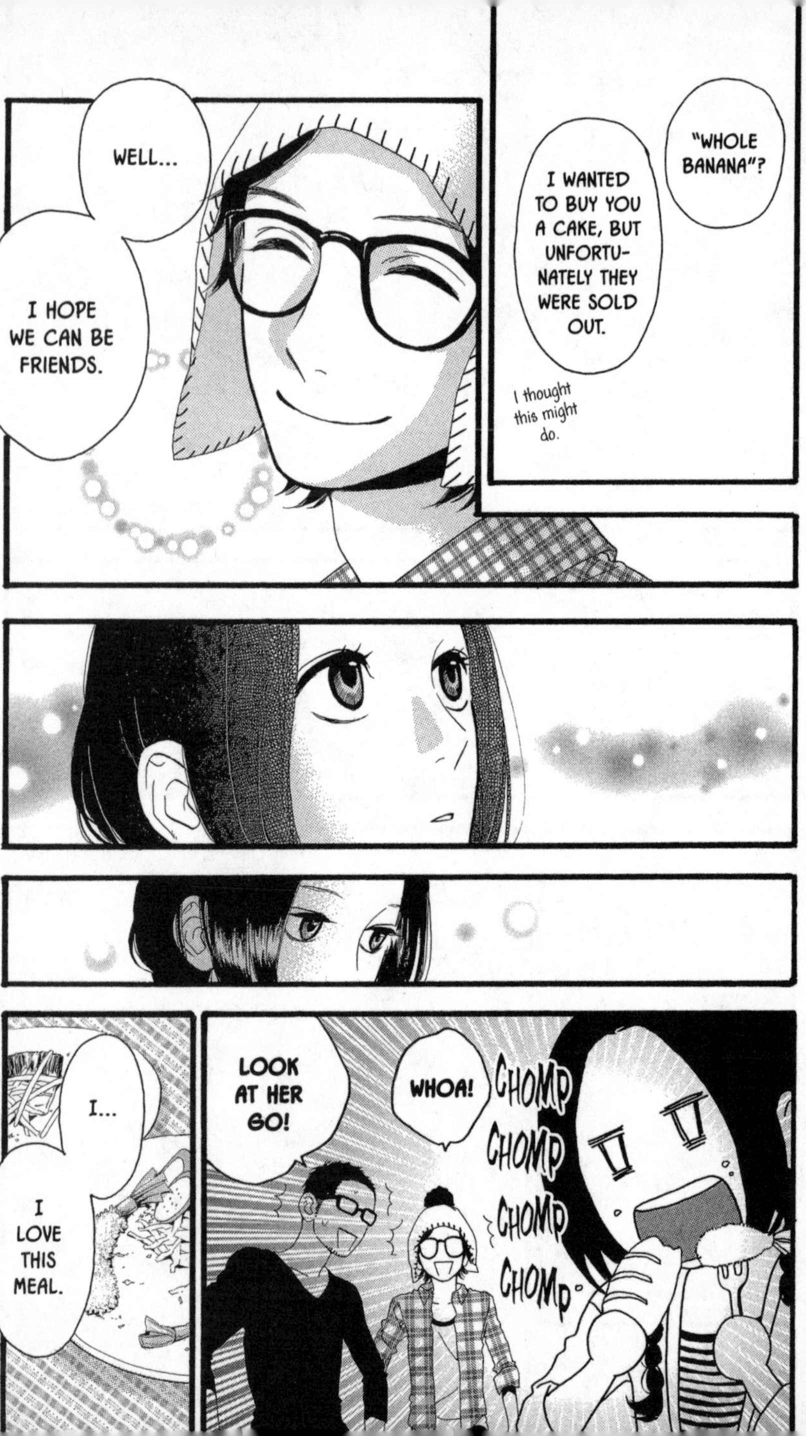
"WHOLE BANANA"?
I WANTED TO BUY YOU A CAKE, BUT UNFORTU- NATELY THEY WERE SOLD OUT.
I thought this might do.
WELL...
I HOPE WE CAN BE FRIENDS.
CHOMP CHOMP CHOMP CHOMP
WHOA!
LOOK AT HER GO!
I...
I LOVE THIS MEAL.

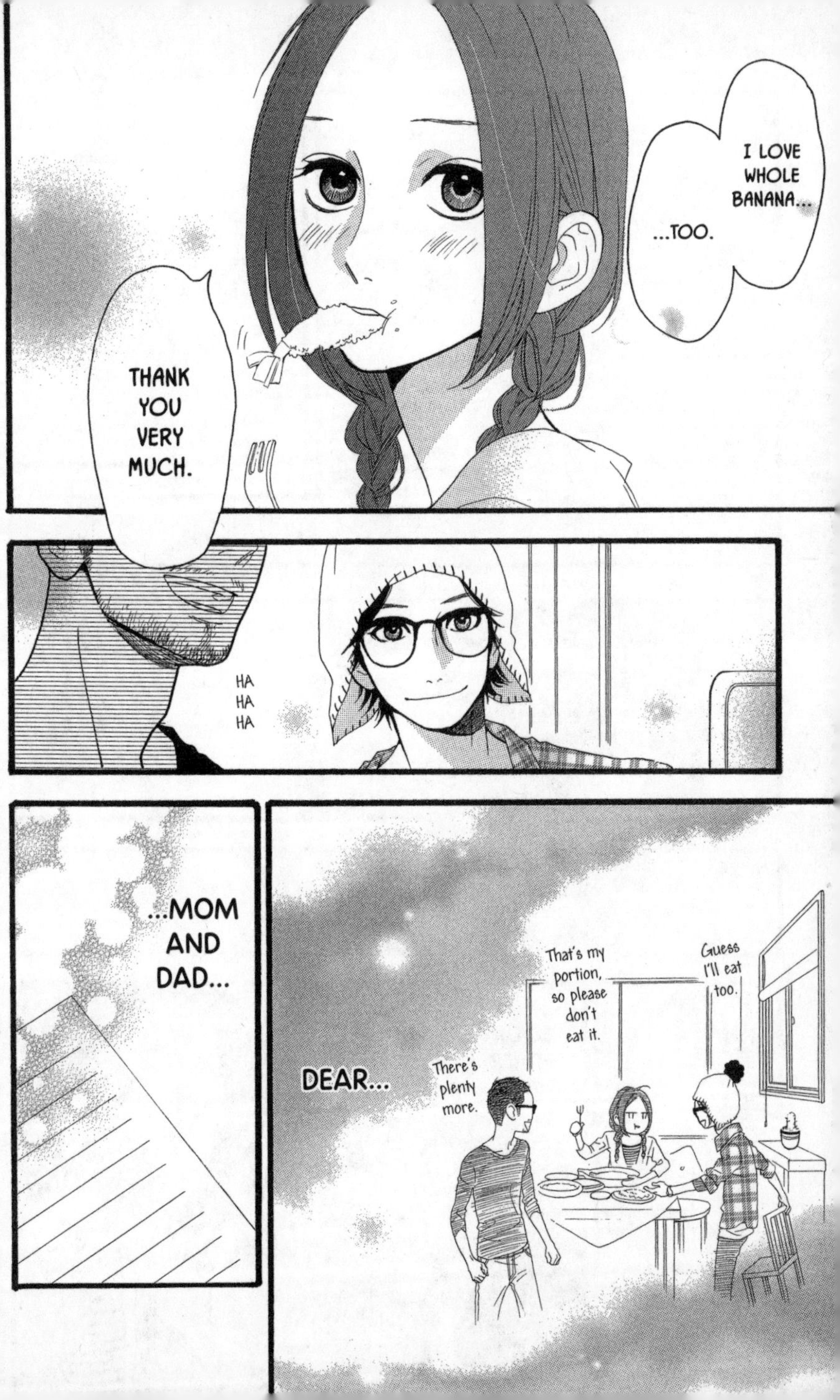
I LOVE WHOLE BANANA... ...TOO.
THANK YOU VERY MUCH.
HA HA HA
Guess I'll eat too.
That's my portion, so please don't eat it.
There's plenty more.
DEAR...
...MOM AND DAD...

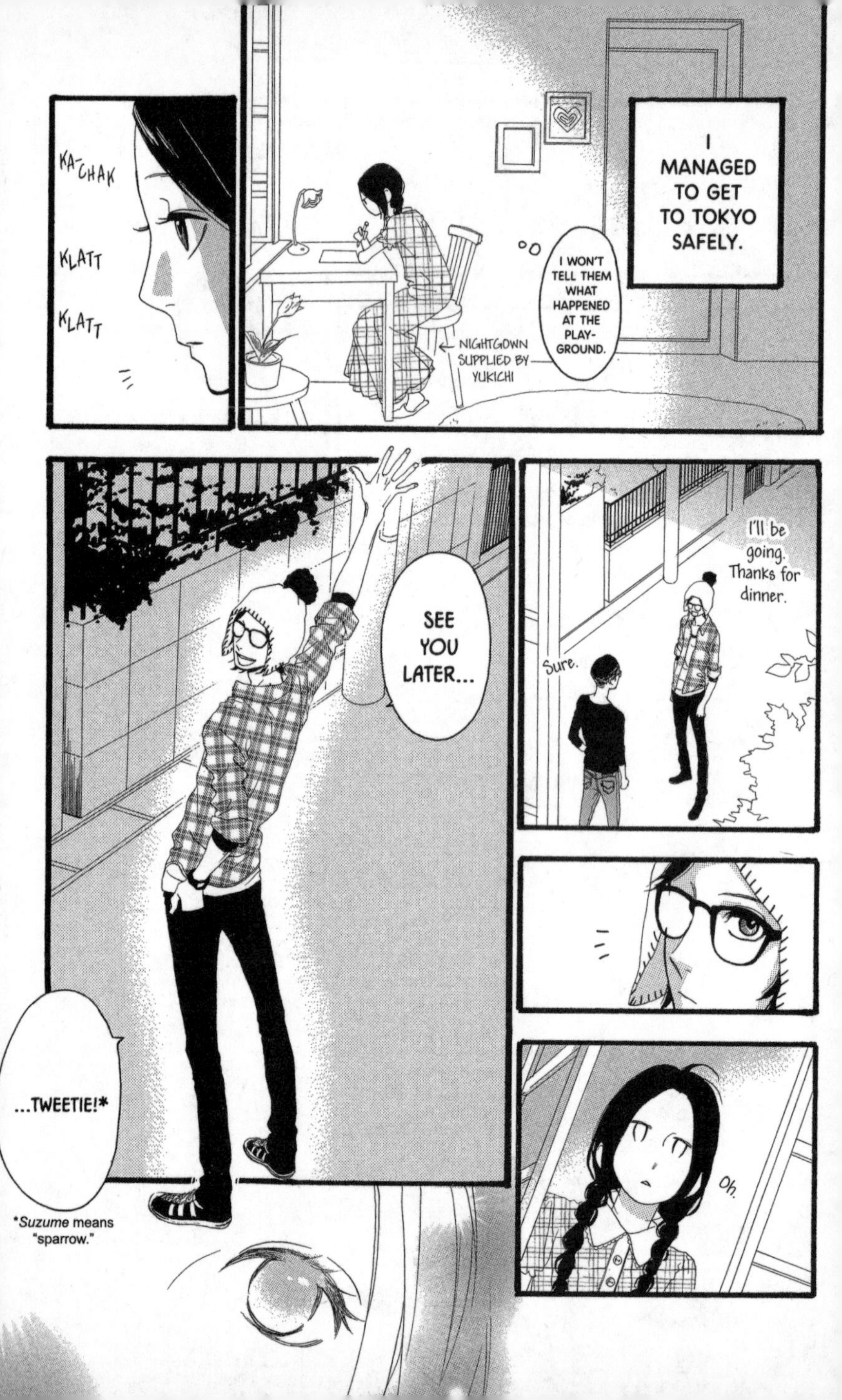
I MANAGED TO GET TO TOKYO SAFELY.
I WON'T TELL THEM WHAT HAPPENED AT THE PLAY-GROUND.
NIGHTGOWN SUPPLIED BY YUKICHI
KA-CHAK
KLATT
KLATT
I'll be going. Thanks for dinner.
Sure.
Oh.
SEE YOU LATER...
...TWEETIE!*

*_Suzume_ means "sparrow."

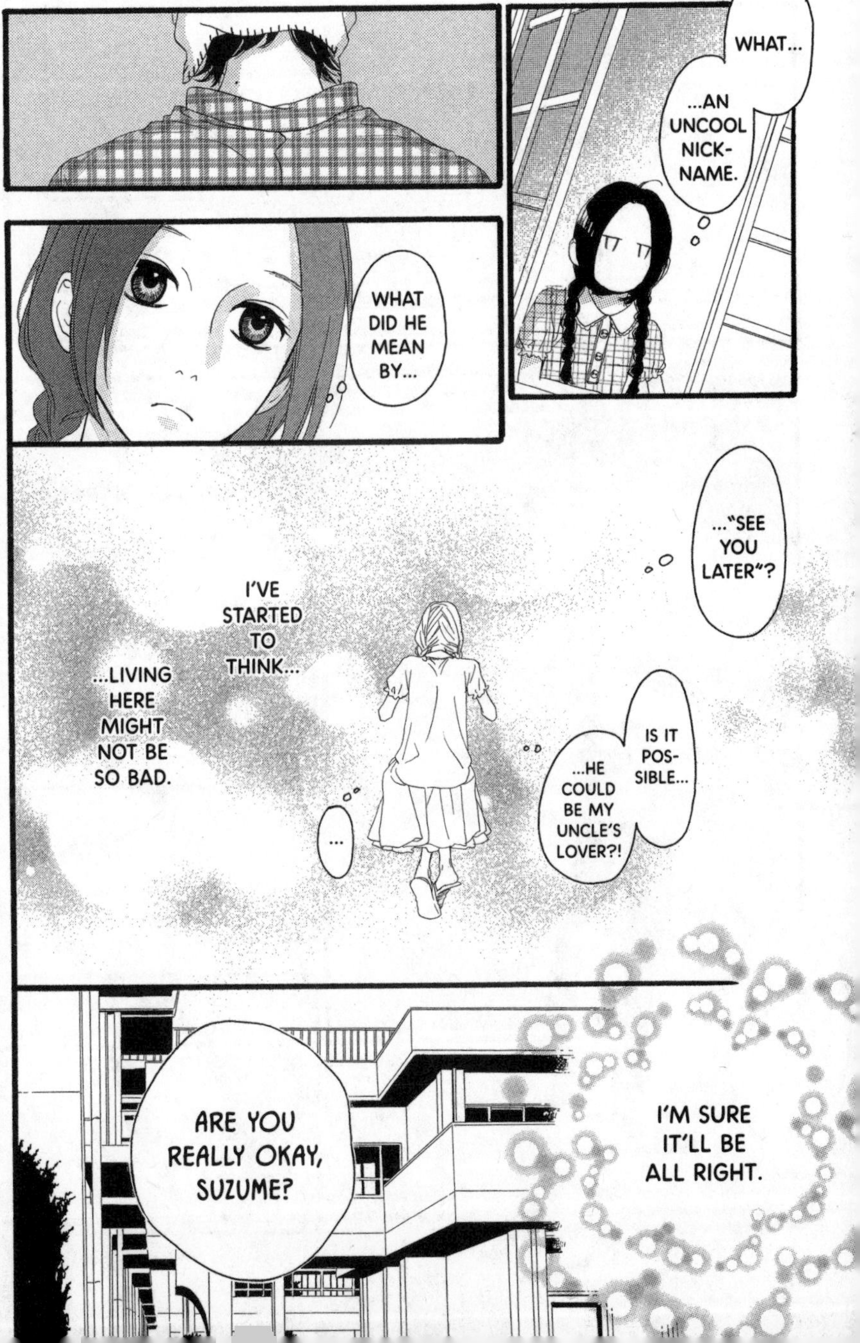
WHAT...
...AN UNCOOL NICK-NAME.
WHAT DID HE MEAN BY...
..."SEE YOU LATER"?
IS IT POSSIBLE...
...HE COULD BE MY UNCLE'S LOVER?!
...
I'VE STARTED TO THINK...
...LIVING HERE MIGHT NOT BE SO BAD.
I'M SURE IT'LL BE ALL RIGHT.
ARE YOU REALLY OKAY, SUZUME?

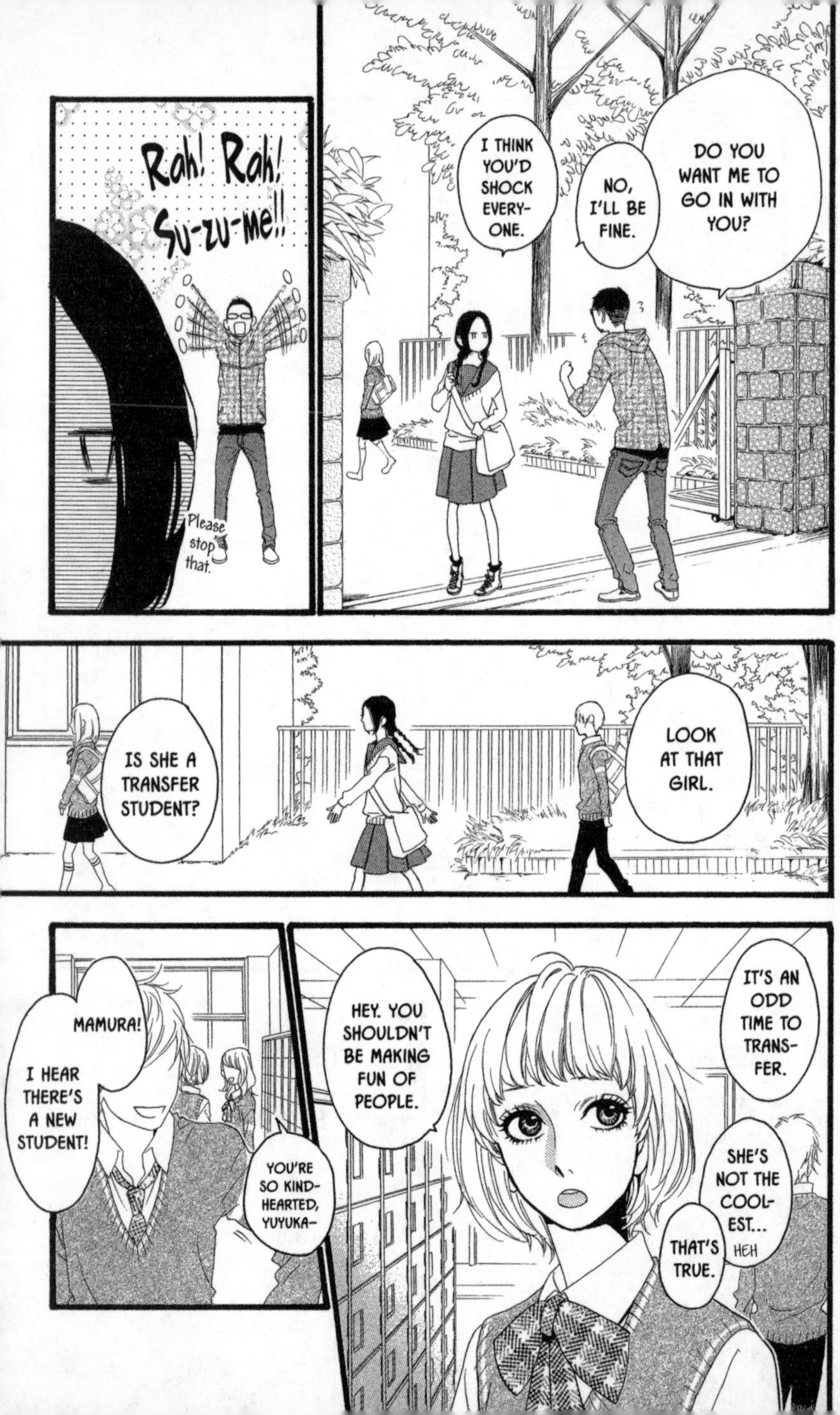
DO YOU WANT ME TO GO IN WITH YOU?
NO, I'LL BE FINE.
I THINK YOU'D SHOCK EVERYONE.
Rah! Rah! Su-zu-me!!
Please stop that.
LOOK AT THAT GIRL.
IS SHE A TRANSFER STUDENT?
IT'S AN ODD TIME TO TRANSFER.
SHE'S NOT THE COOLEST...
HEH
THAT'S TRUE.
HEY. YOU SHOULDN'T BE MAKING FUN OF PEOPLE.
YOU'RE SO KIND-HEARTED, YUYUKA-
MAMURA!
I HEAR THERE'S A NEW STUDENT!

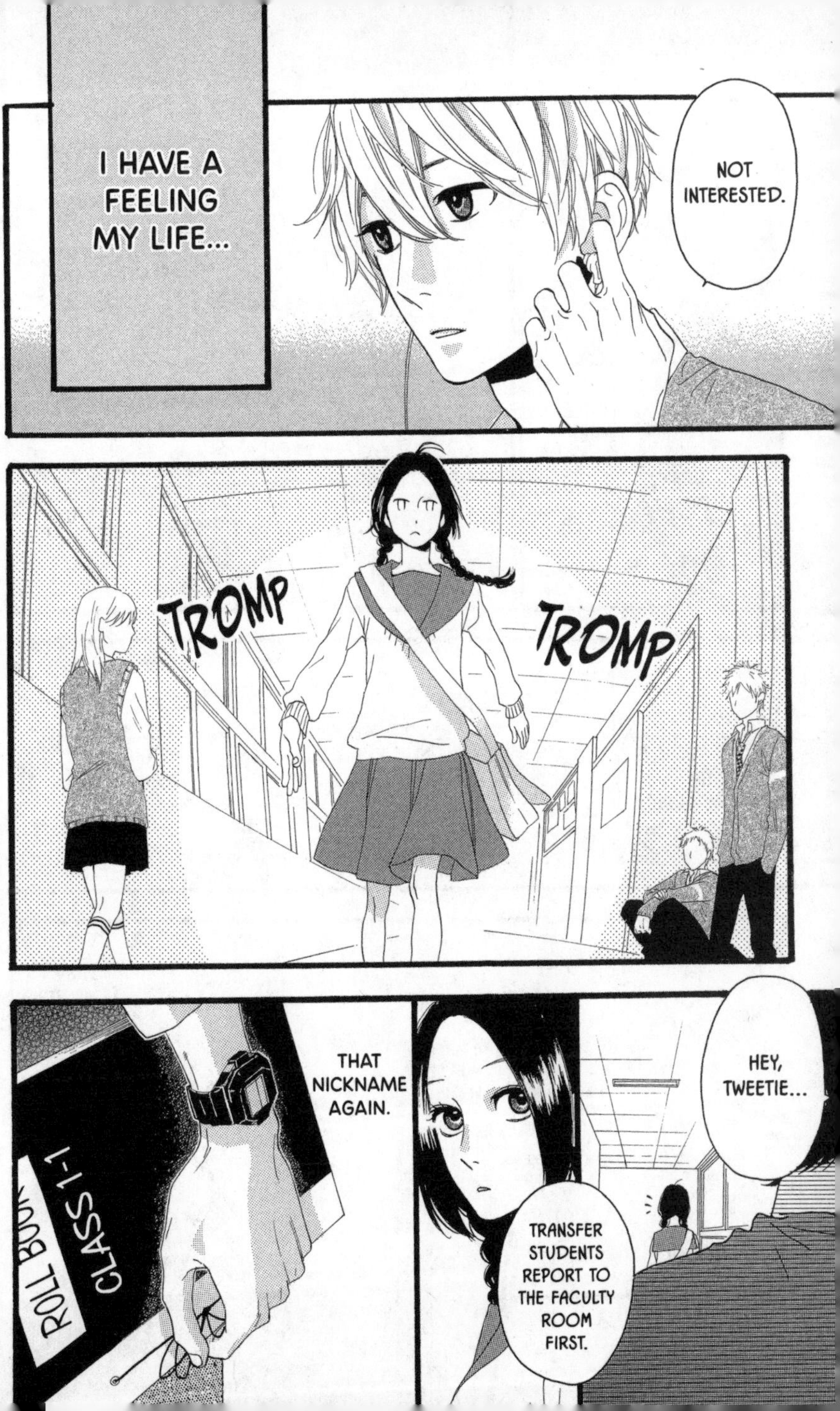
NOT INTERESTED.
I HAVE A FEELING MY LIFE...
TROMP
TROMP
HEY, TWEETIE...
TRANSFER STUDENTS REPORT TO THE FACULTY ROOM FIRST.
THAT NICKNAME AGAIN.
ROLL BOO
CLASS 1-1

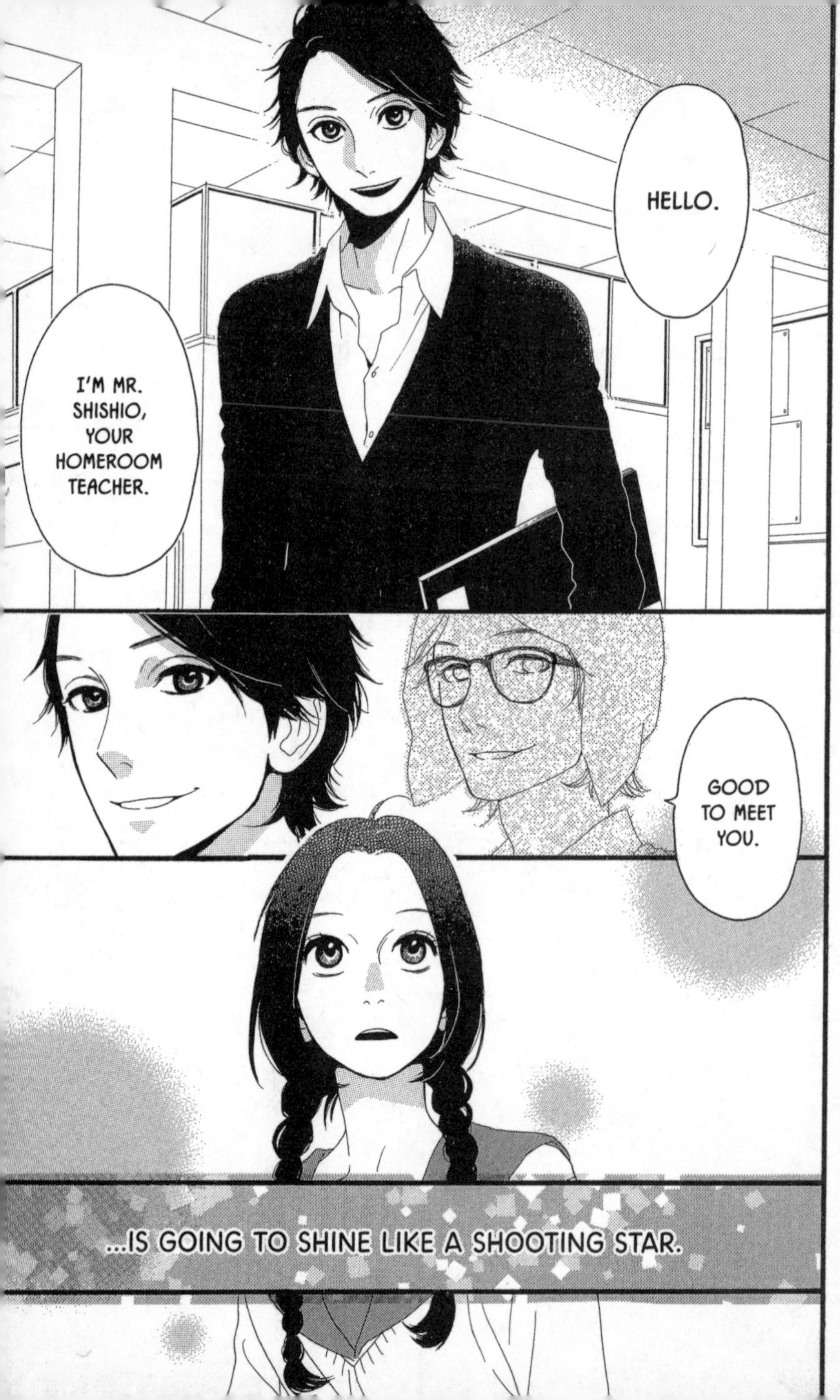
HELLO.
I'M MR. SHISHIO, YOUR HOMEROOM TEACHER.
GOOD TO MEET YOU.
...IS GOING TO SHINE LIKE A SHOOTING STAR.

And so...

I don't have much to write in these spaces anymore...so I'm having my assistants draw some of the characters from *Sugars* and *Daytime Shooting Star.* ♪ Heh! I've always wanted to try this. ♫

One assistant, Sanae Kameyama (nickname Kame-chan), didn't know which series to pick, so she drew me two pictures. Thank you, Kame-chan! Please enjoy her work.

I'd better decide what to write or draw on these pages in the future. (Personally I enjoy reading this section in other manga, so I really want to fill this space.)

Should I call for submissions? Oh, you don't think I should? All right, then....

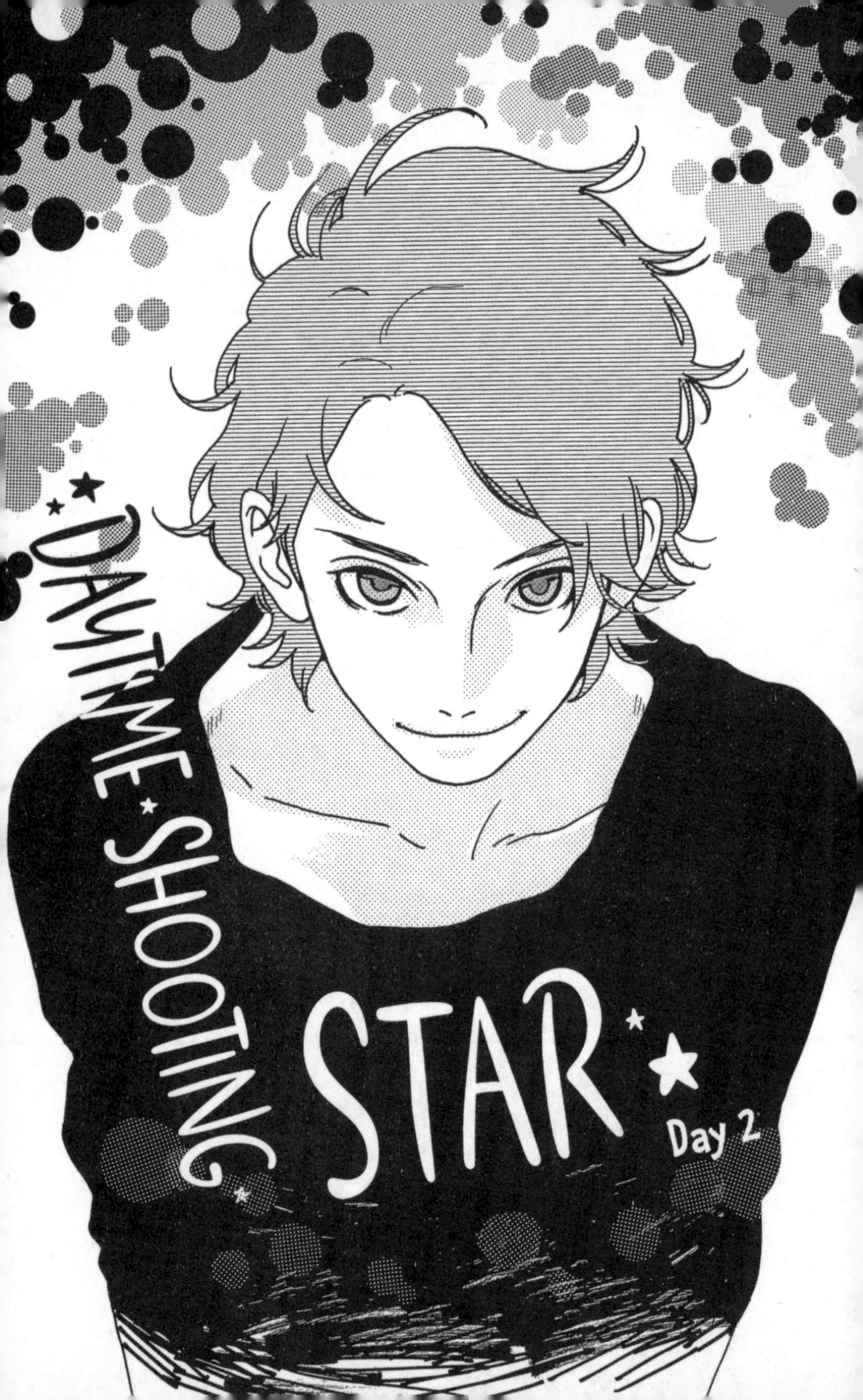
DAYTIME SHOOTING STAR
Day 2

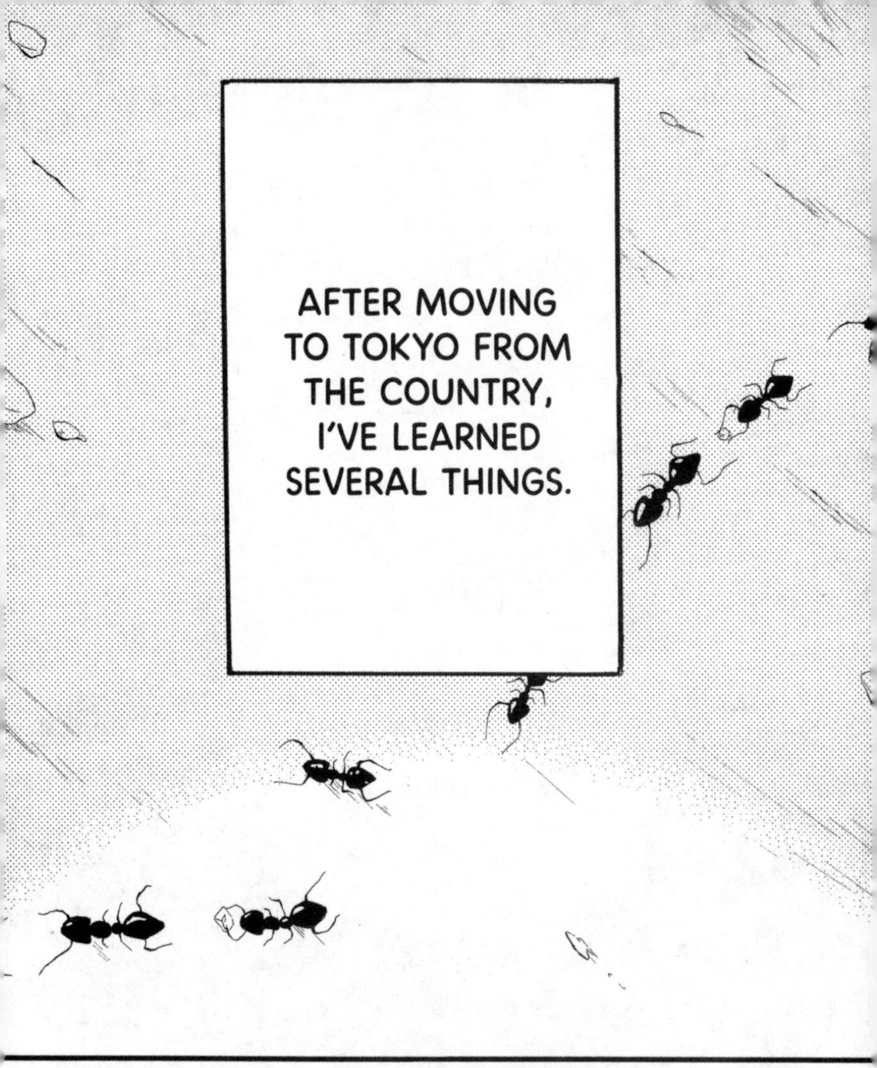
AFTER MOVING TO TOKYO FROM THE COUNTRY, I'VE LEARNED SEVERAL THINGS.

Suzume's Monologue

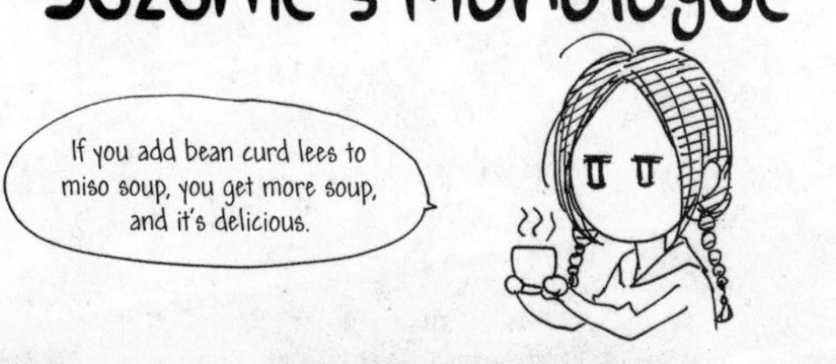
If you add bean curd lees to miso soup, you get more soup, and it's delicious.

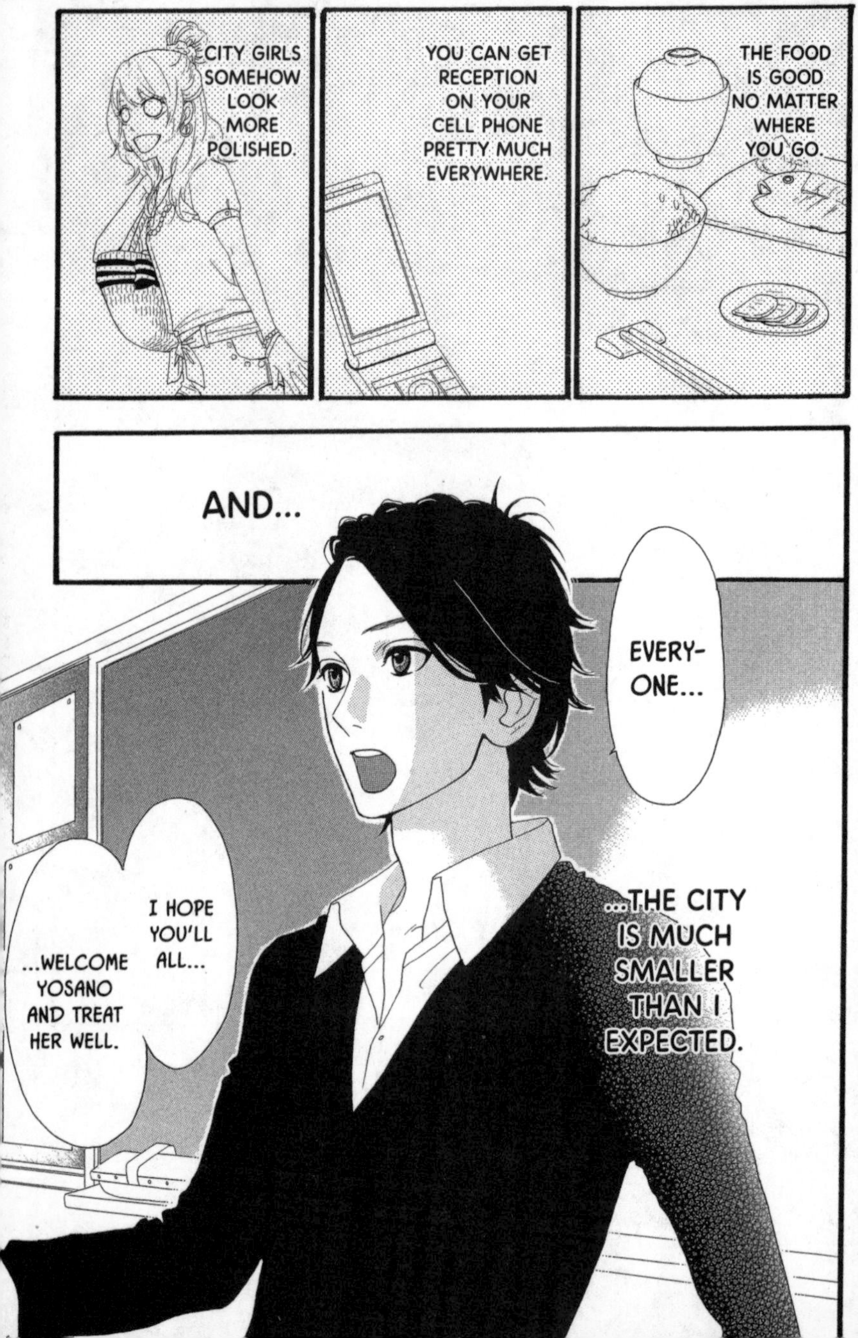
THE FOOD IS GOOD NO MATTER WHERE YOU GO.
YOU CAN GET RECEPTION ON YOUR CELL PHONE PRETTY MUCH EVERYWHERE.
CITY GIRLS SOMEHOW LOOK MORE POLISHED.
AND...
EVERY-ONE...
...THE CITY IS MUCH SMALLER THAN I EXPECTED.
I HOPE YOU'LL ALL...
...WELCOME YOSANO AND TREAT HER WELL.

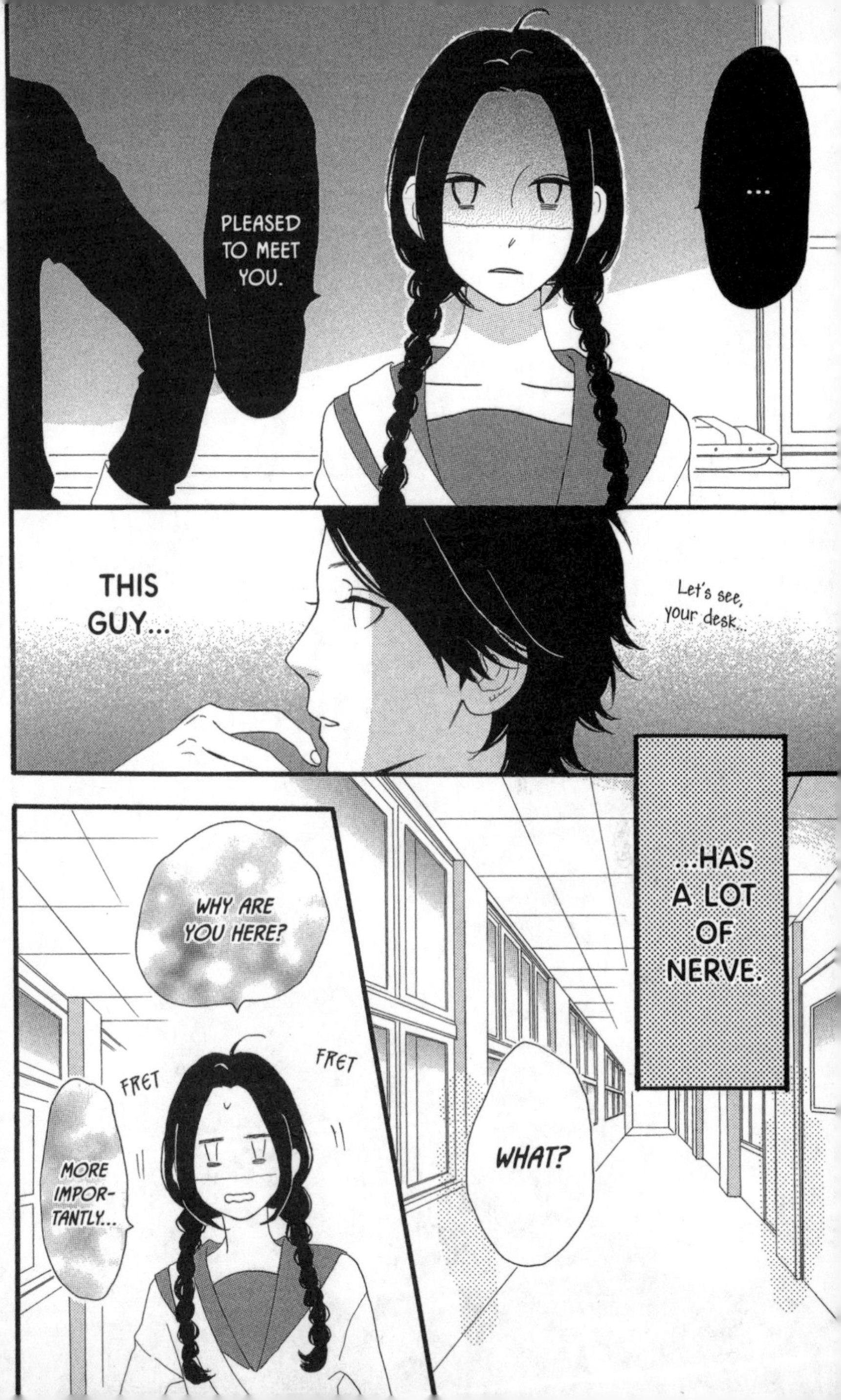
...
PLEASED TO MEET YOU.
Let's see, your desk...
THIS GUY...
...HAS A LOT OF NERVE.
WHAT?
WHY ARE YOU HERE?
FRET
FRET
MORE IMPORTANTLY...

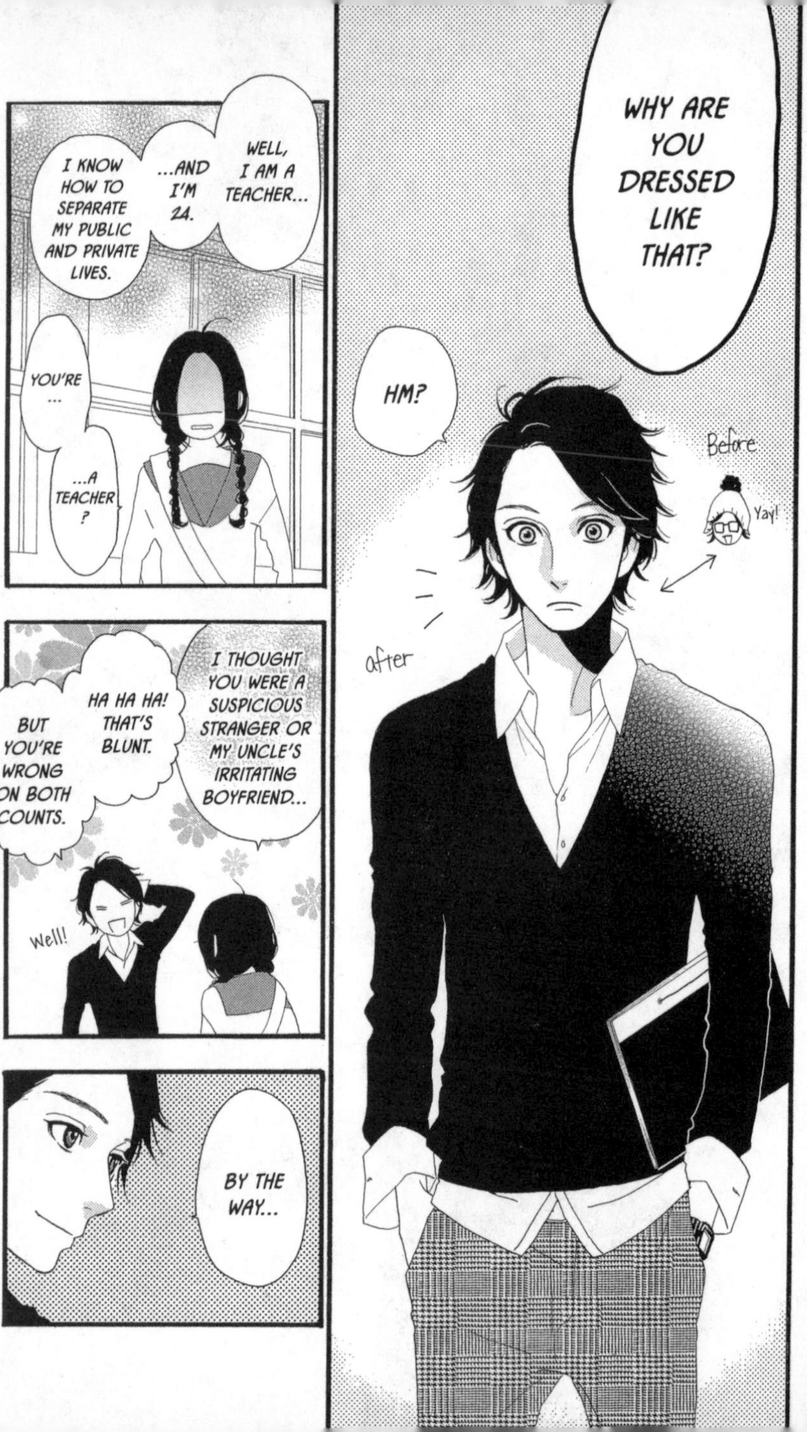
WELL, I AM A TEACHER...
...AND I'M 24.
I KNOW HOW TO SEPARATE MY PUBLIC AND PRIVATE LIVES.
YOU'RE ...
...A TEACHER?
I THOUGHT YOU WERE A SUSPICIOUS STRANGER OR MY UNCLE'S IRRITATING BOYFRIEND...
HA HA HA! THAT'S BLUNT.
BUT YOU'RE WRONG ON BOTH COUNTS.
Well!
BY THE WAY...
WHY ARE YOU DRESSED LIKE THAT?
HM?
Before
Yay!
after

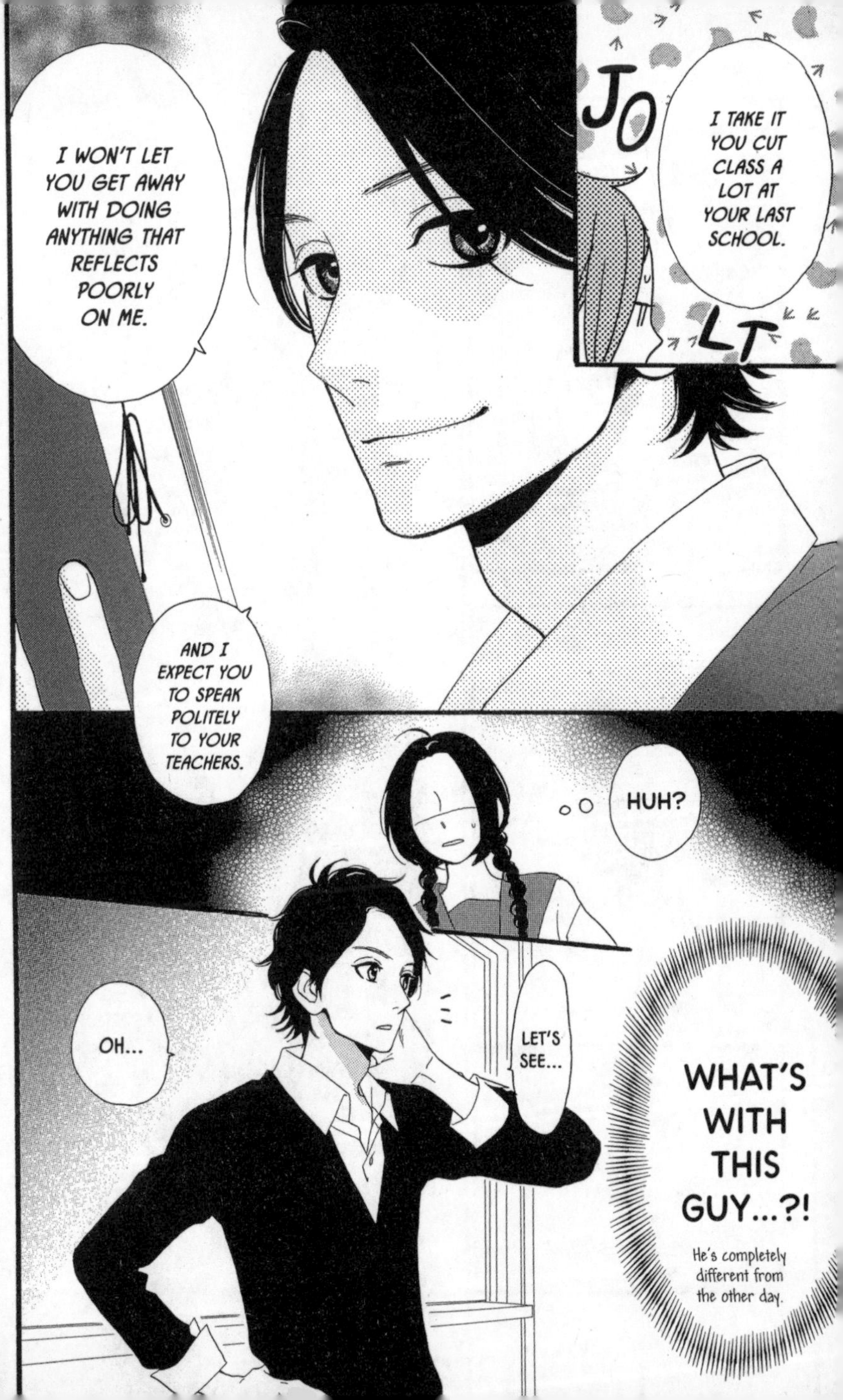
JOLT
I TAKE IT YOU CUT CLASS A LOT AT YOUR LAST SCHOOL.
I WON'T LET YOU GET AWAY WITH DOING ANYTHING THAT REFLECTS POORLY ON ME.
AND I EXPECT YOU TO SPEAK POLITELY TO YOUR TEACHERS.
HUH?
WHAT'S WITH THIS GUY...?!
He's completely different from the other day.
LET'S SEE...
OH...

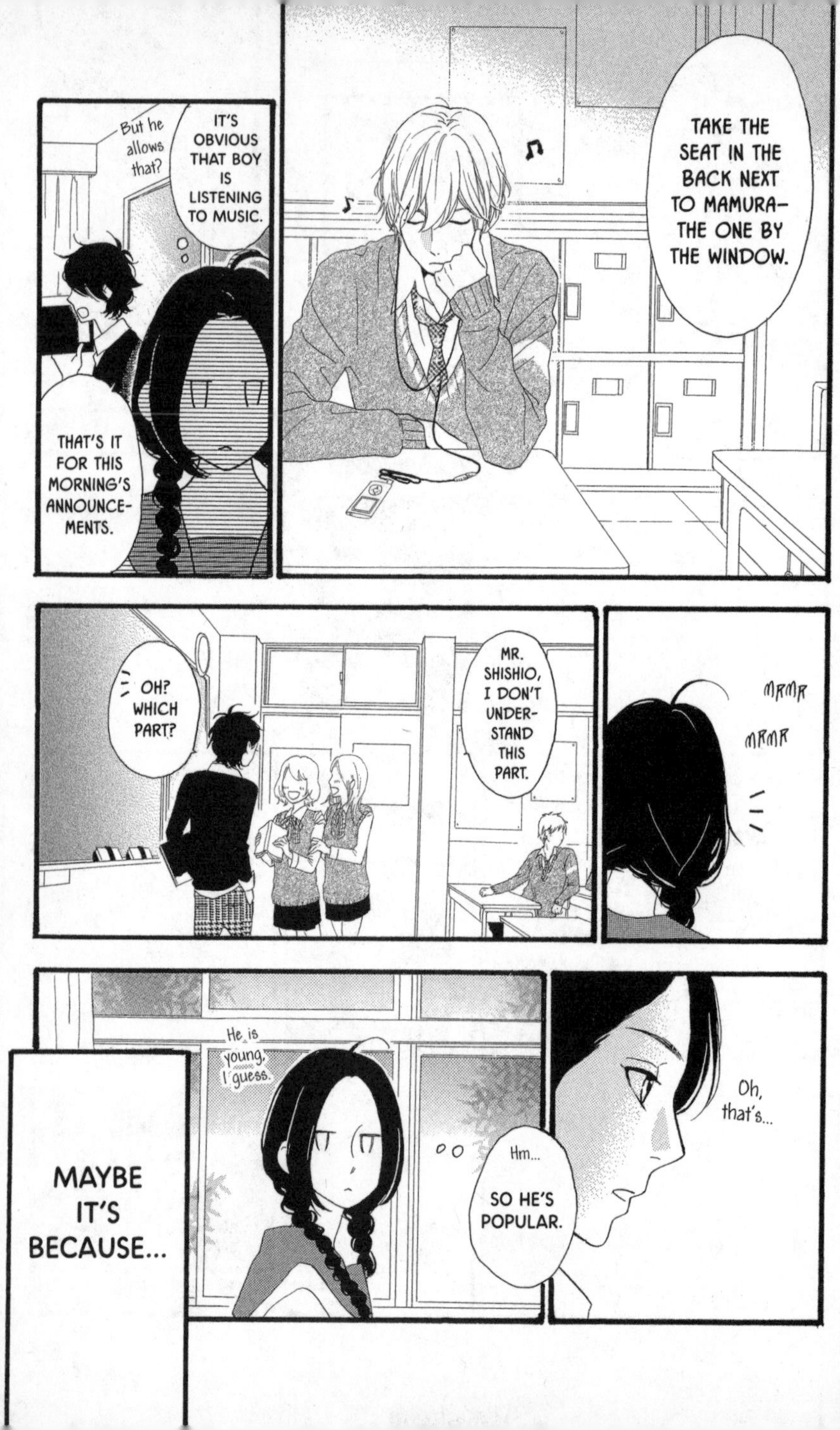
TAKE THE SEAT IN THE BACK NEXT TO MAMURA— THE ONE BY THE WINDOW.
IT'S OBVIOUS THAT BOY IS LISTENING TO MUSIC.
But he allows that?
THAT'S IT FOR THIS MORNING'S ANNOUNCEMENTS.
MRMR
MRMR
MR. SHISHIO, I DON'T UNDERSTAND THIS PART.
OH? WHICH PART?
Oh, that's...
Hm...
SO HE'S POPULAR.
He is young, I guess.
MAYBE IT'S BECAUSE...

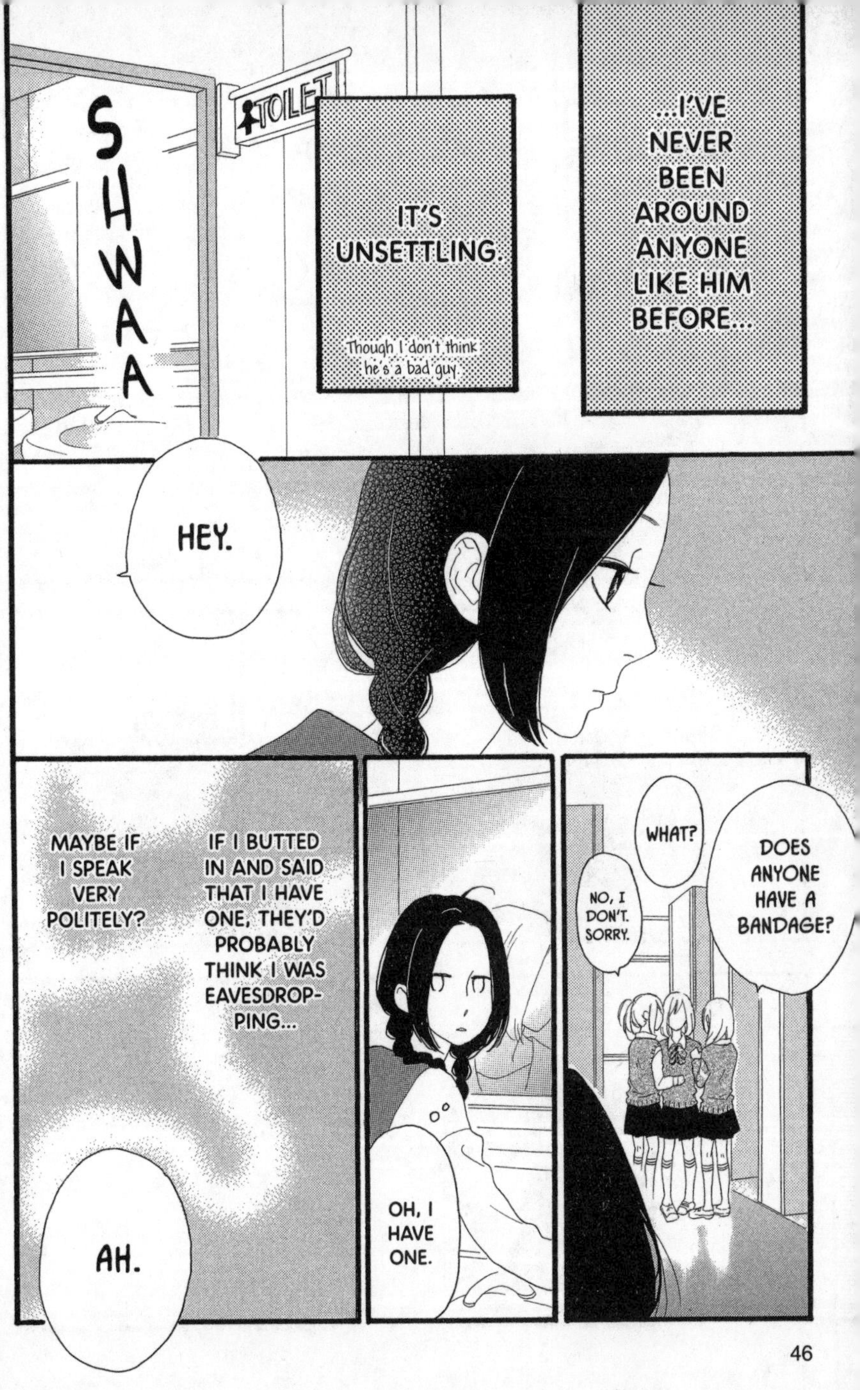
...I'VE NEVER BEEN AROUND ANYONE LIKE HIM BEFORE...
IT'S UNSETTLING.
Though I don't think he's a bad guy.
TOILET
SHWAA
HEY.
DOES ANYONE HAVE A BANDAGE?
WHAT?
NO, I DON'T. SORRY.
OH, I HAVE ONE.
IF I BUTTED IN AND SAID THAT I HAVE ONE, THEY'D PROBABLY THINK I WAS EAVESDROP-PING...
MAYBE IF I SPEAK VERY POLITELY?
AH.

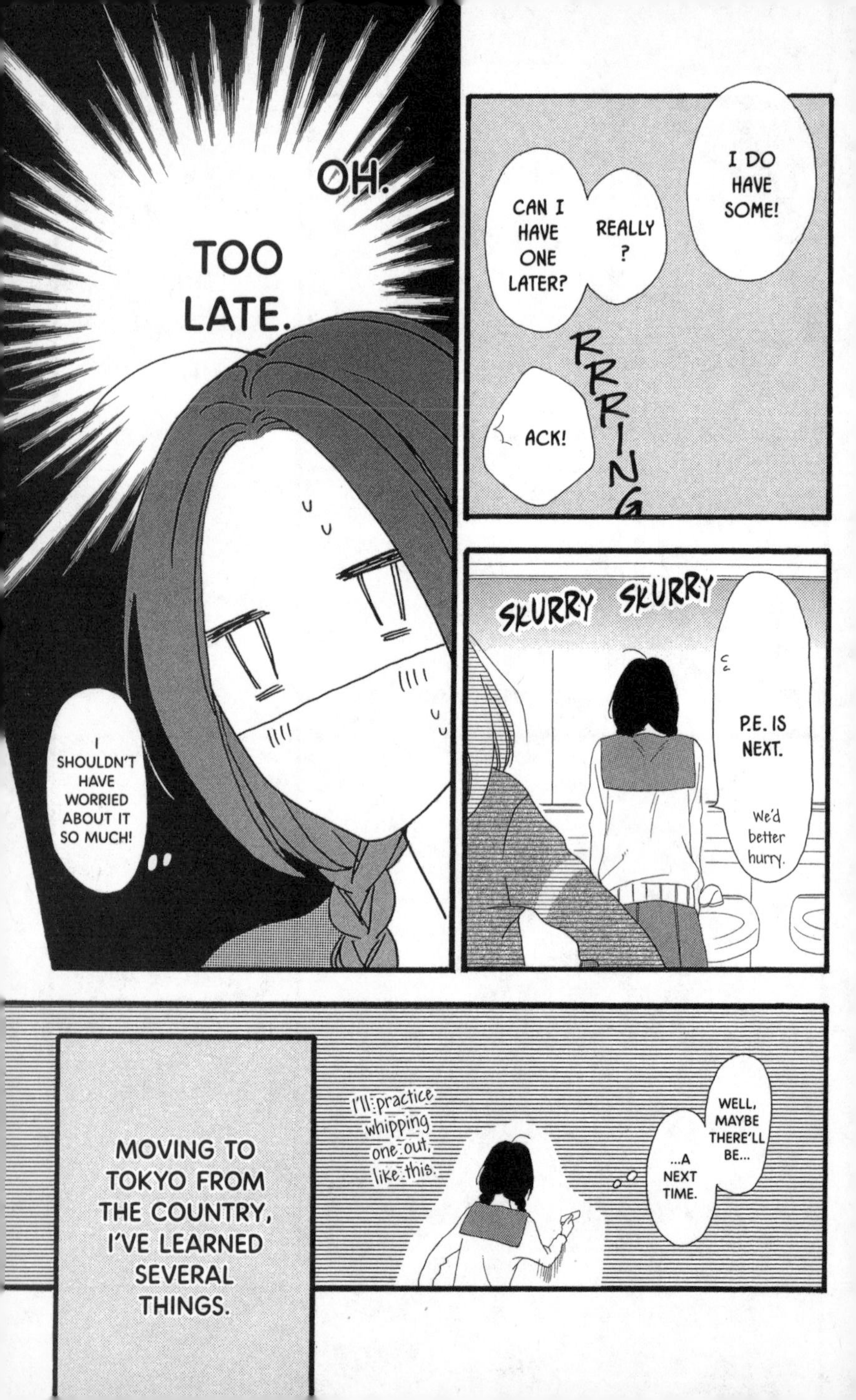
I DO HAVE SOME!
REALLY?
CAN I HAVE ONE LATER?
RRRING
ACK!
SKURRY SKURRY
P.E. IS NEXT.
We'd better hurry.
OH.
TOO LATE.
I SHOULDN'T HAVE WORRIED ABOUT IT SO MUCH!
WELL, MAYBE THERE'LL BE...
...A NEXT TIME.
I'll practice whipping one out, like this.
MOVING TO TOKYO FROM THE COUNTRY, I'VE LEARNED SEVERAL THINGS.

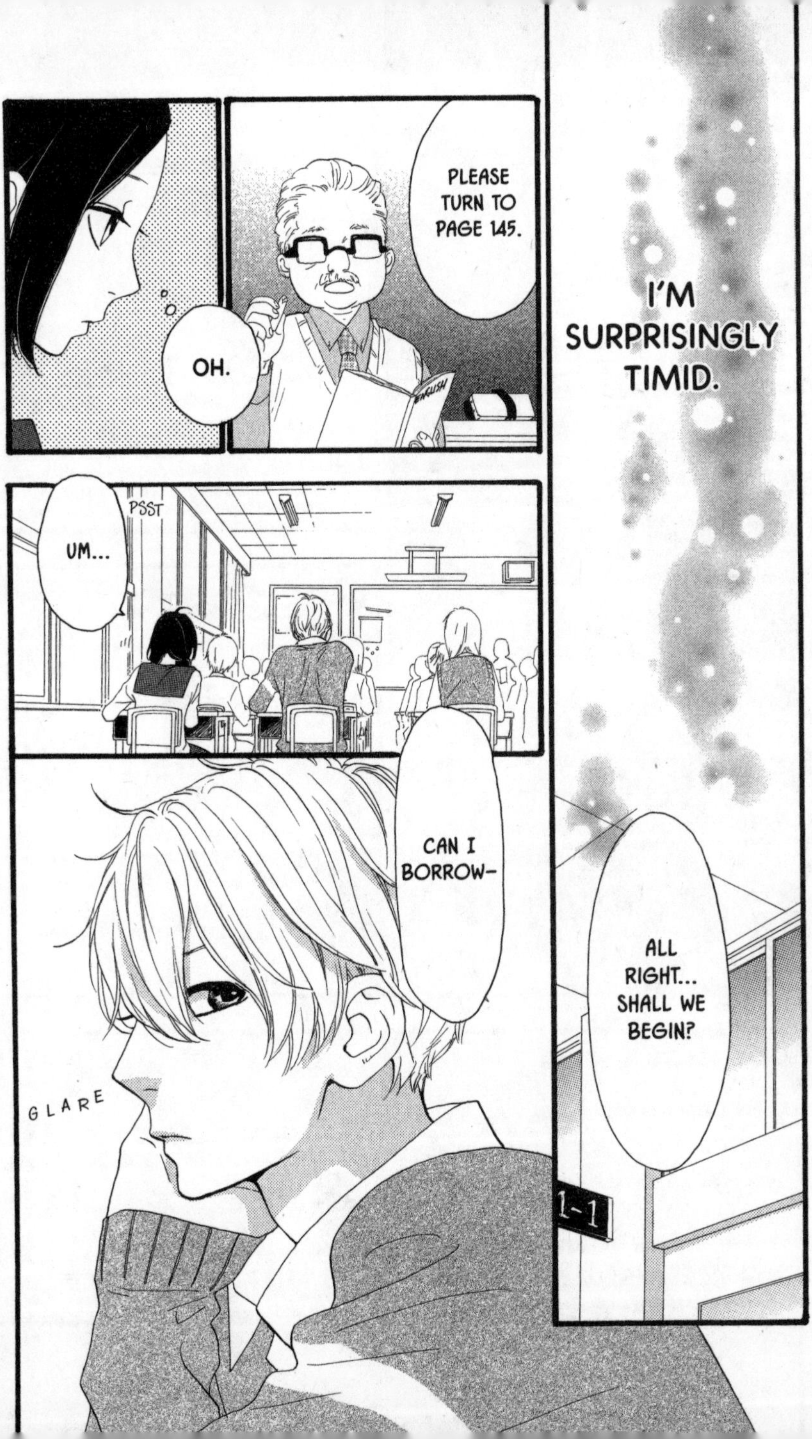
I'M SURPRISINGLY TIMID.
1-1
ALL RIGHT... SHALL WE BEGIN?
PLEASE TURN TO PAGE 145.
ENGLISH
OH.
PSST
UM...
CAN I BORROW-
GLARE

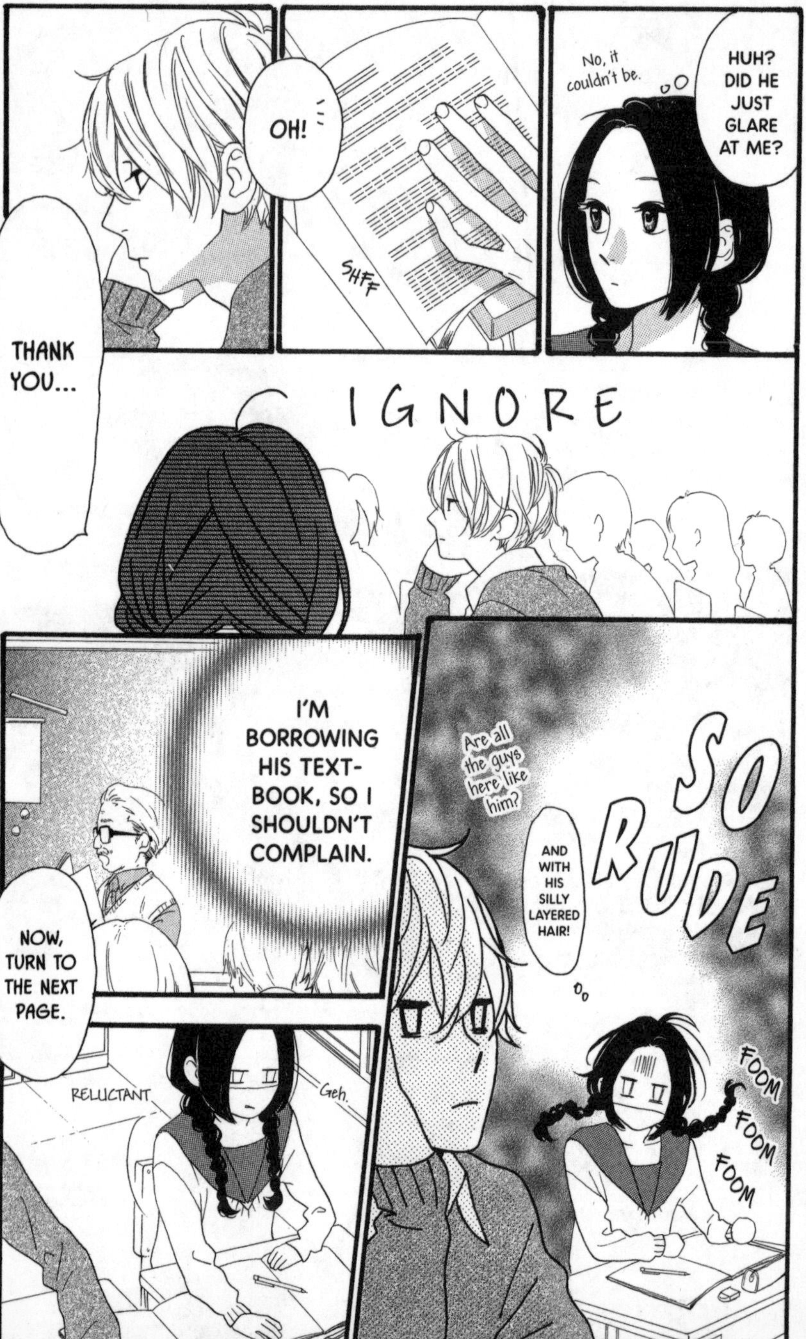

HUH? DID HE JUST GLARE AT ME?
No, it couldn't be.
OH!
SHFF
THANK YOU...
IGNORE
SO RUDE
Are all the guys here like him?
AND WITH HIS SILLY LAYERED HAIR!
FOOM FOOM FOOM
I'M BORROWING HIS TEXT-BOOK, SO I SHOULDN'T COMPLAIN.
NOW, TURN TO THE NEXT PAGE.
Geh.
RELUCTANT

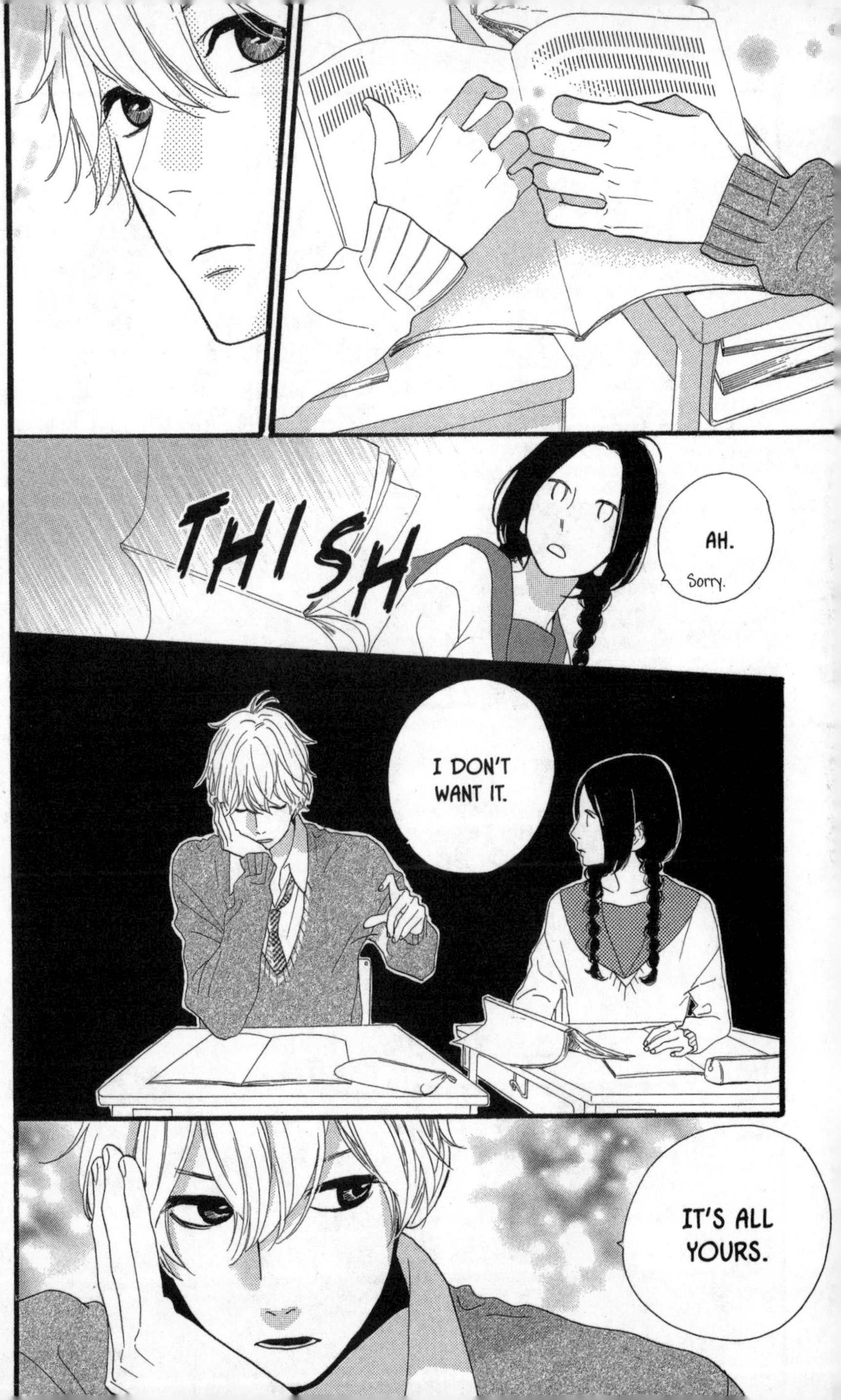
THISH
AH.
Sorry.
I DON'T WANT IT.
IT'S ALL YOURS.

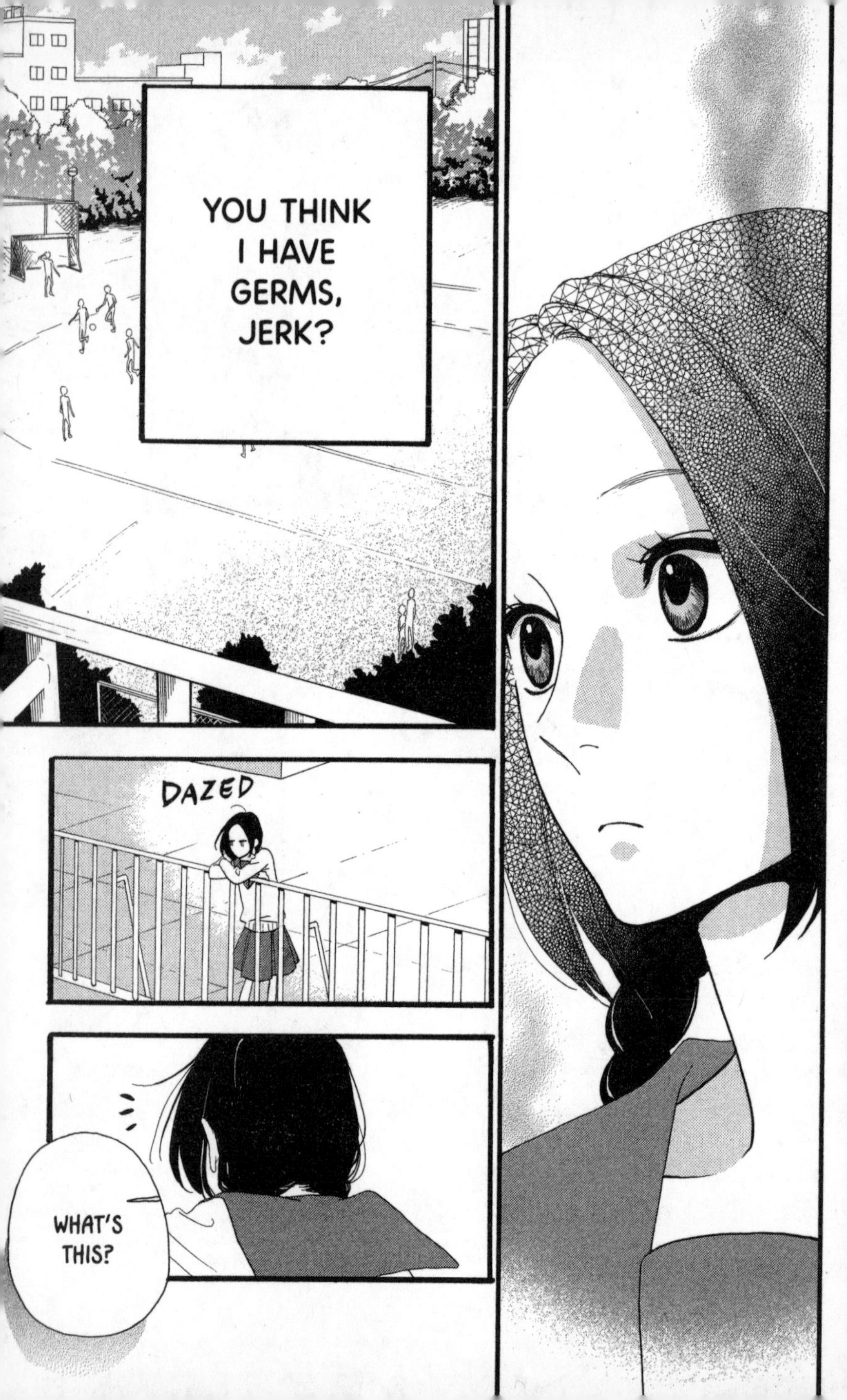
YOU THINK I HAVE GERMS, JERK?
DAZED
WHAT'S THIS?

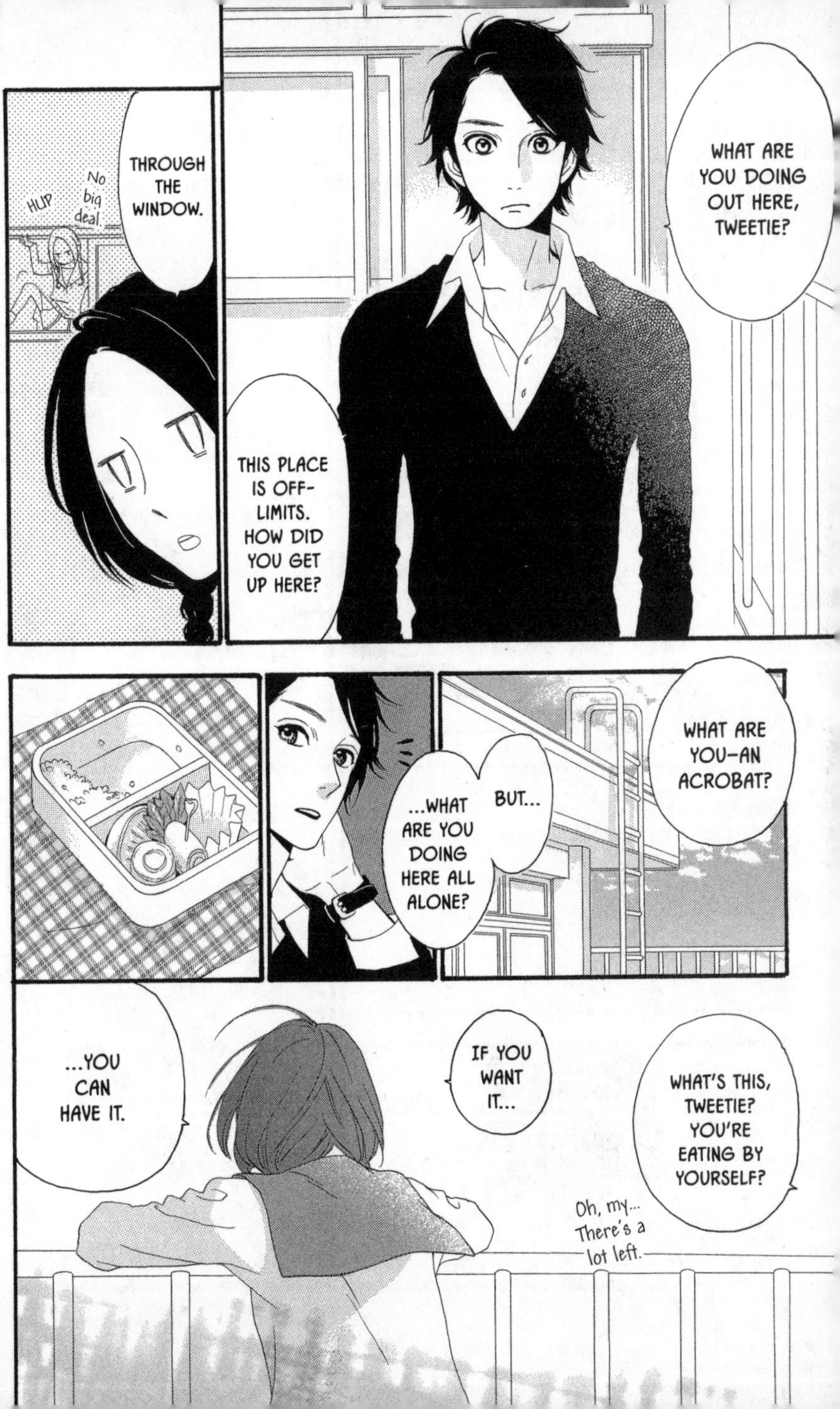
WHAT ARE YOU DOING OUT HERE, TWEETIE?
THIS PLACE IS OFF-LIMITS. HOW DID YOU GET UP HERE?
THROUGH THE WINDOW.
No big deal.
HUP
WHAT ARE YOU—AN ACROBAT?
BUT...
...WHAT ARE YOU DOING HERE ALL ALONE?
WHAT'S THIS, TWEETIE? YOU'RE EATING BY YOURSELF?
Oh, my... There's a lot left.
IF YOU WANT IT...
...YOU CAN HAVE IT.

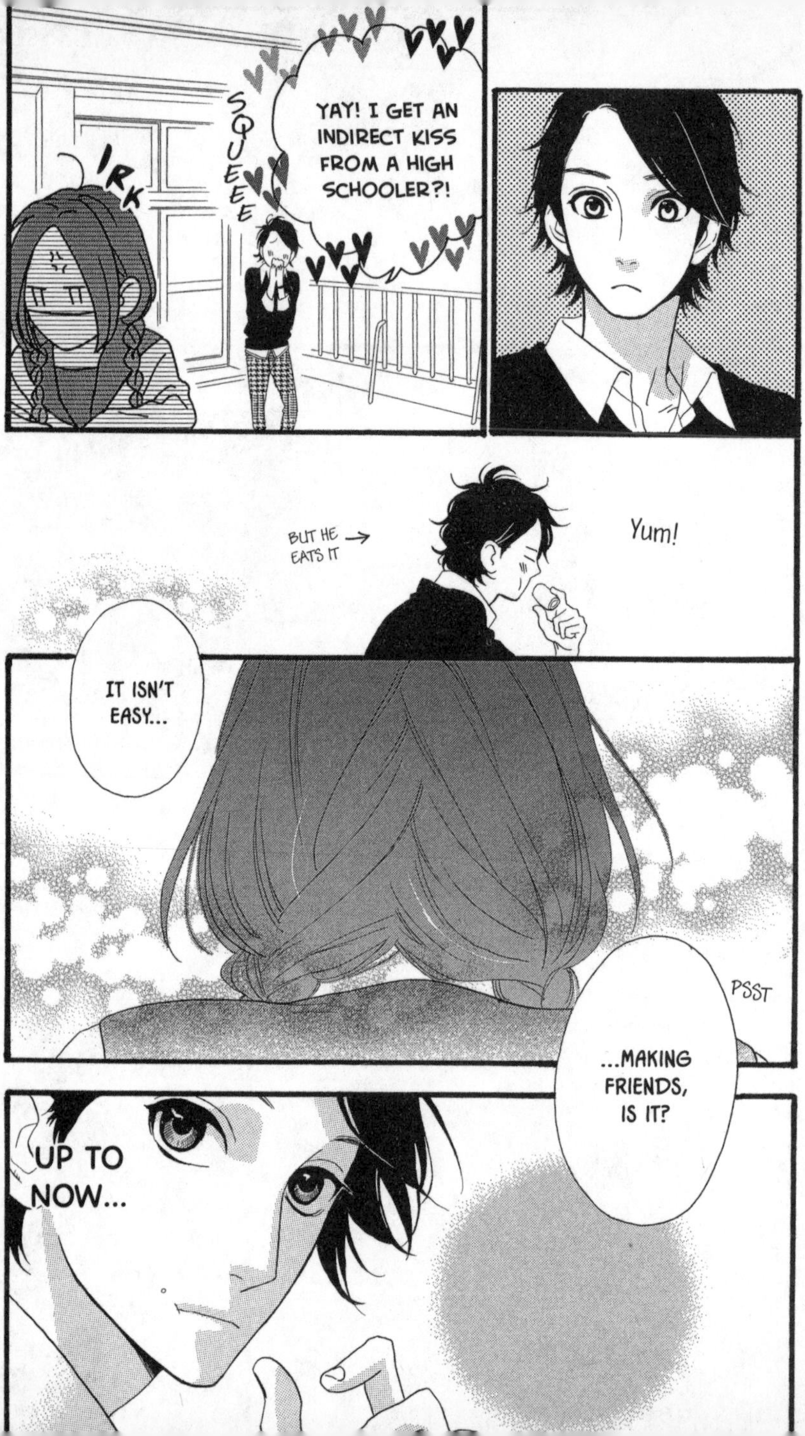
YAY! I GET AN INDIRECT KISS FROM A HIGH SCHOOLER?!
SQUEEEE
IRK
Yum!
BUT HE EATS IT
IT ISN'T EASY...
PSST
...MAKING FRIENDS, IS IT?
UP TO NOW...

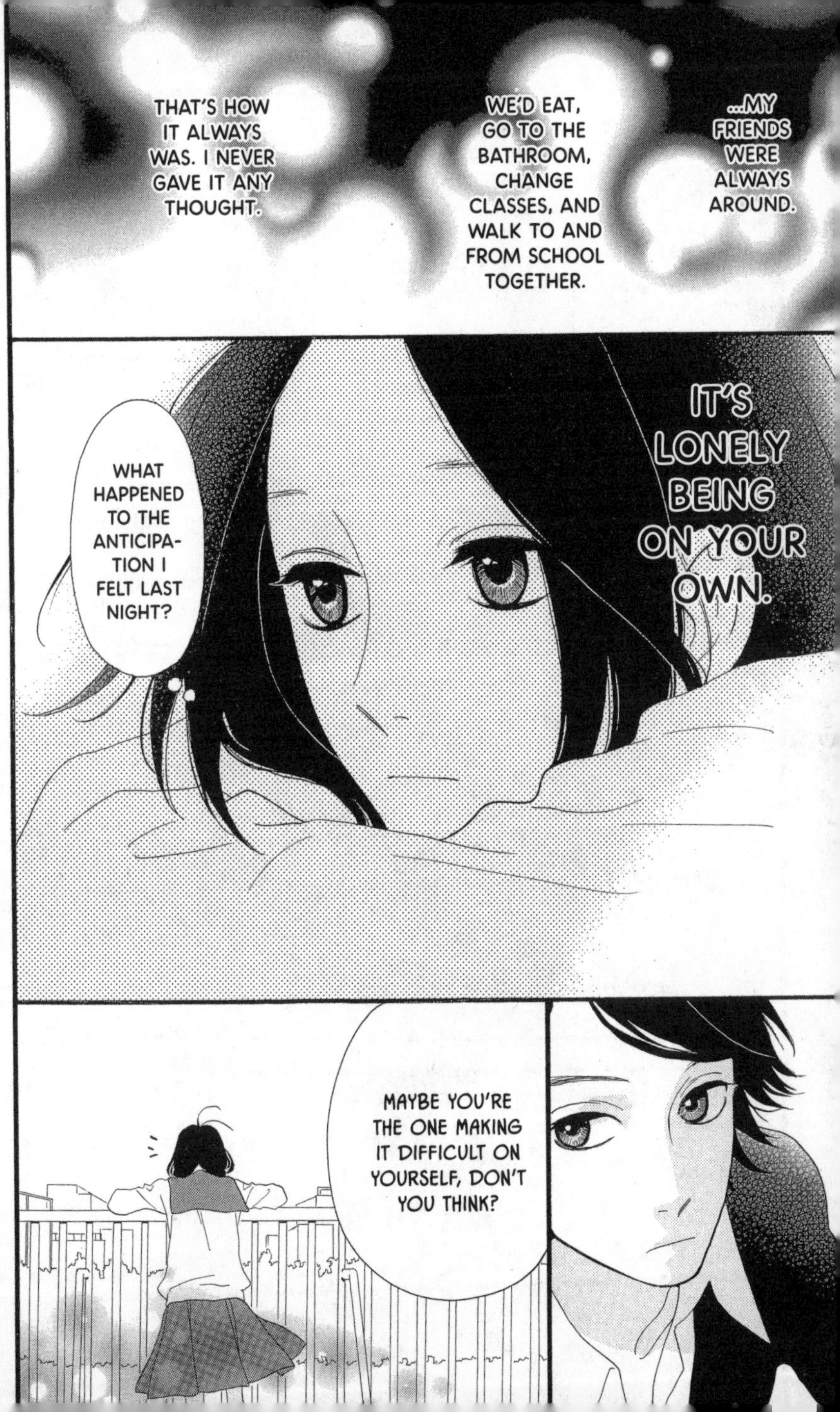
...MY FRIENDS WERE ALWAYS AROUND.
WE'D EAT, GO TO THE BATHROOM, CHANGE CLASSES, AND WALK TO AND FROM SCHOOL TOGETHER.
THAT'S HOW IT ALWAYS WAS. I NEVER GAVE IT ANY THOUGHT.
IT'S LONELY BEING ON YOUR OWN.
WHAT HAPPENED TO THE ANTICIPA-TION I FELT LAST NIGHT?
MAYBE YOU'RE THE ONE MAKING IT DIFFICULT ON YOURSELF, DON'T YOU THINK?

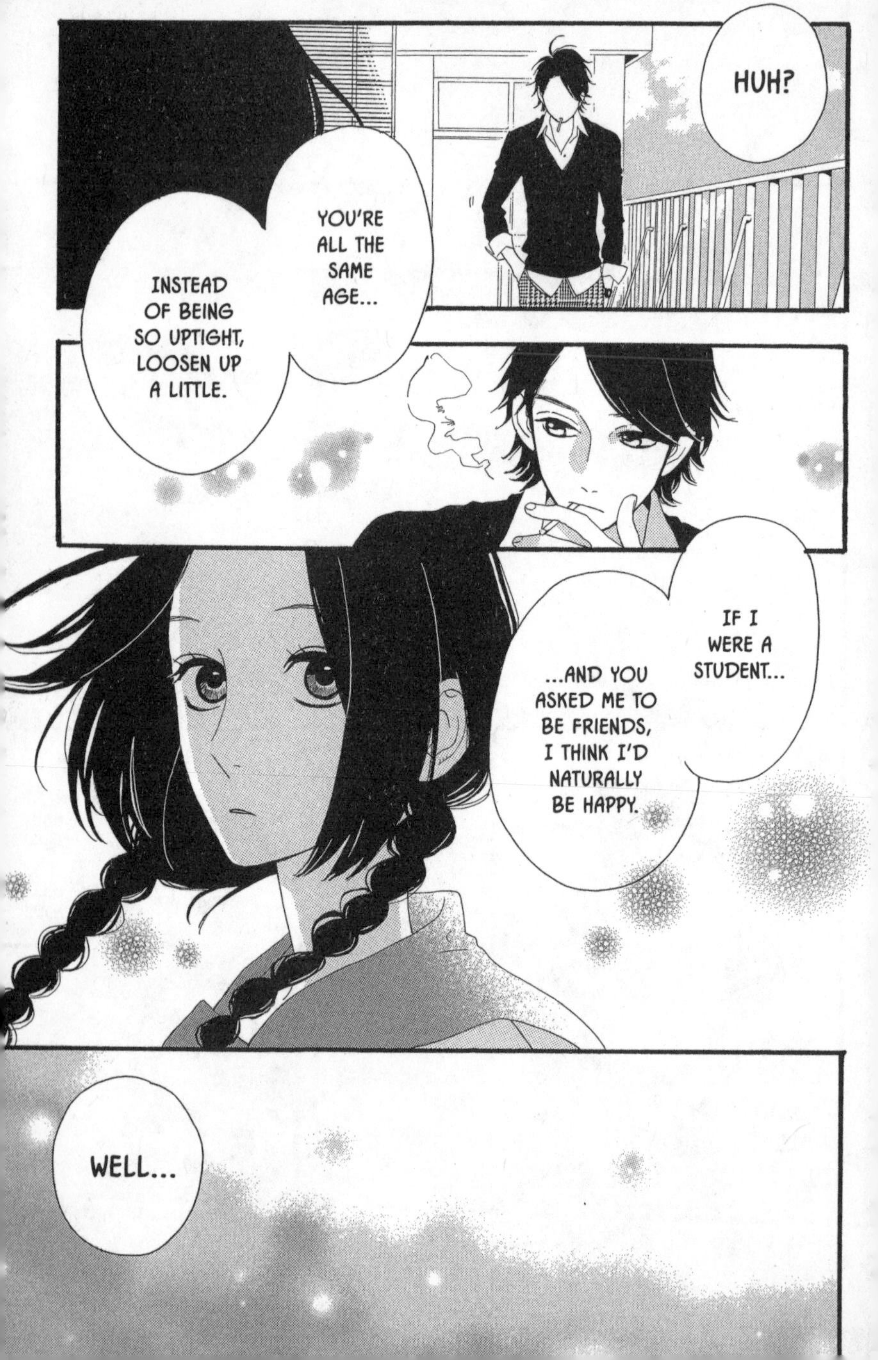
HUH?
YOU'RE ALL THE SAME AGE...
INSTEAD OF BEING SO UPTIGHT, LOOSEN UP A LITTLE.
IF I WERE A STUDENT...
...AND YOU ASKED ME TO BE FRIENDS, I THINK I'D NATURALLY BE HAPPY.
WELL...

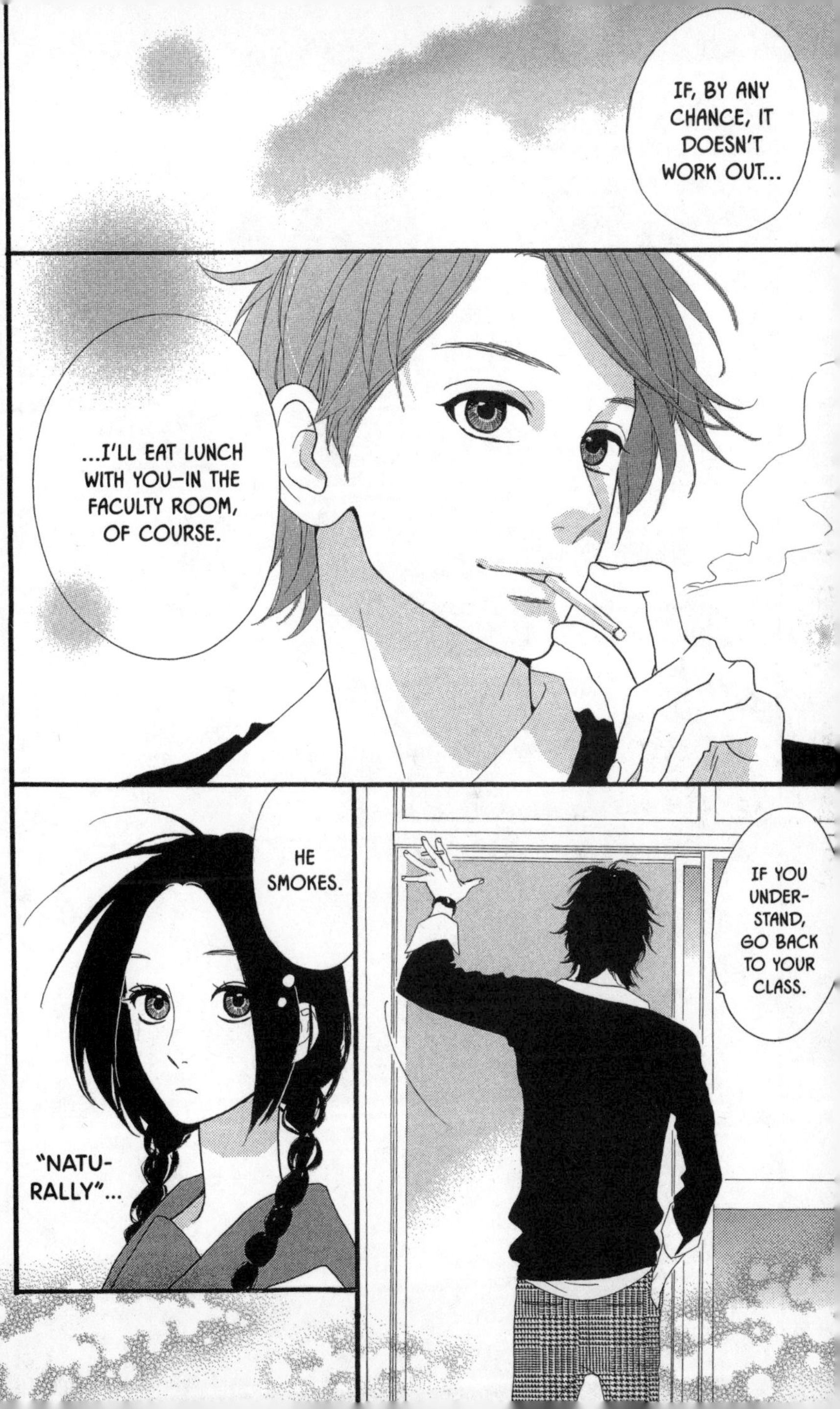
IF, BY ANY CHANCE, IT DOESN'T WORK OUT...
...I'LL EAT LUNCH WITH YOU—IN THE FACULTY ROOM, OF COURSE.
IF YOU UNDER-STAND, GO BACK TO YOUR CLASS.
HE SMOKES.
"NATU-RALLY"...

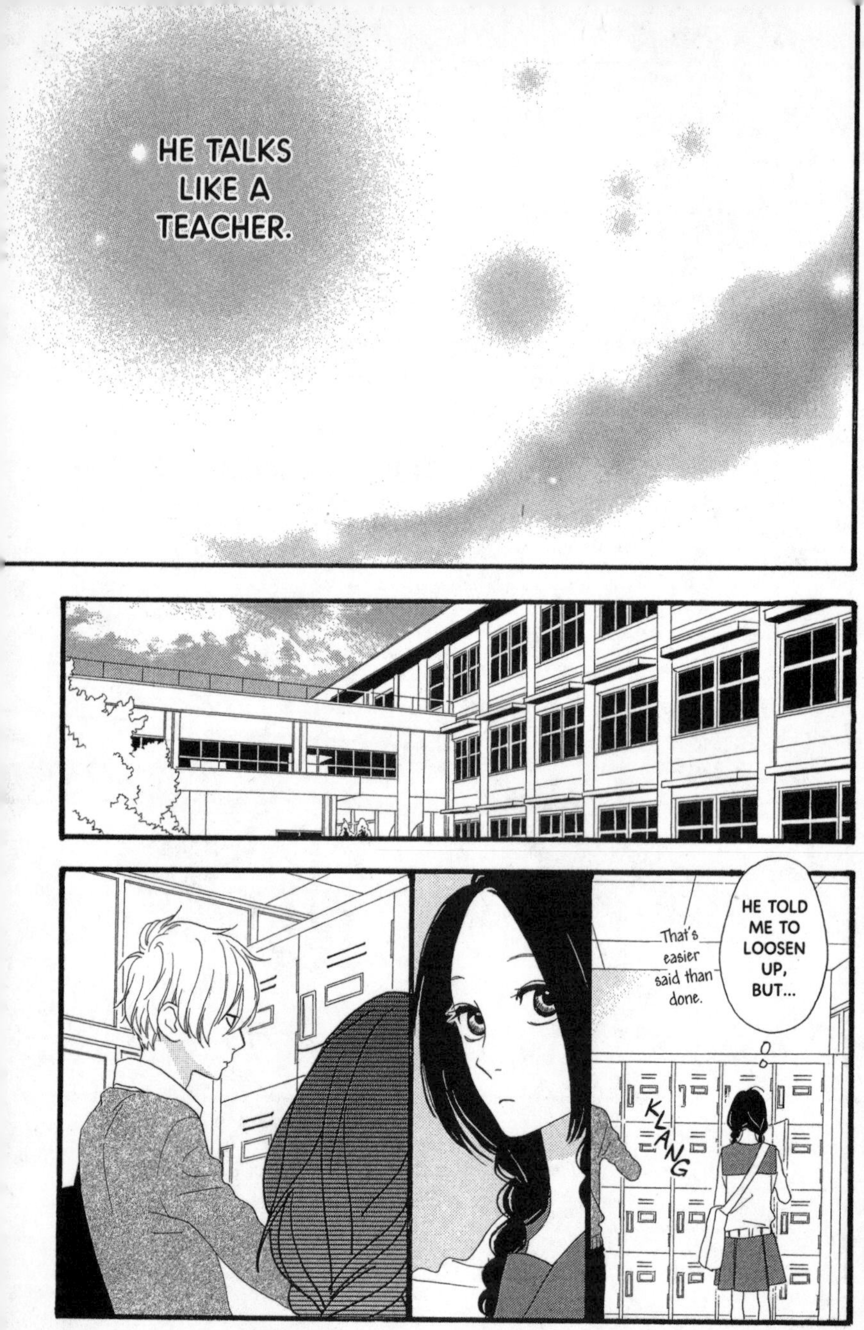
HE TALKS LIKE A TEACHER.
HE TOLD ME TO LOOSEN UP, BUT...
That's easier said than done.
KLANG

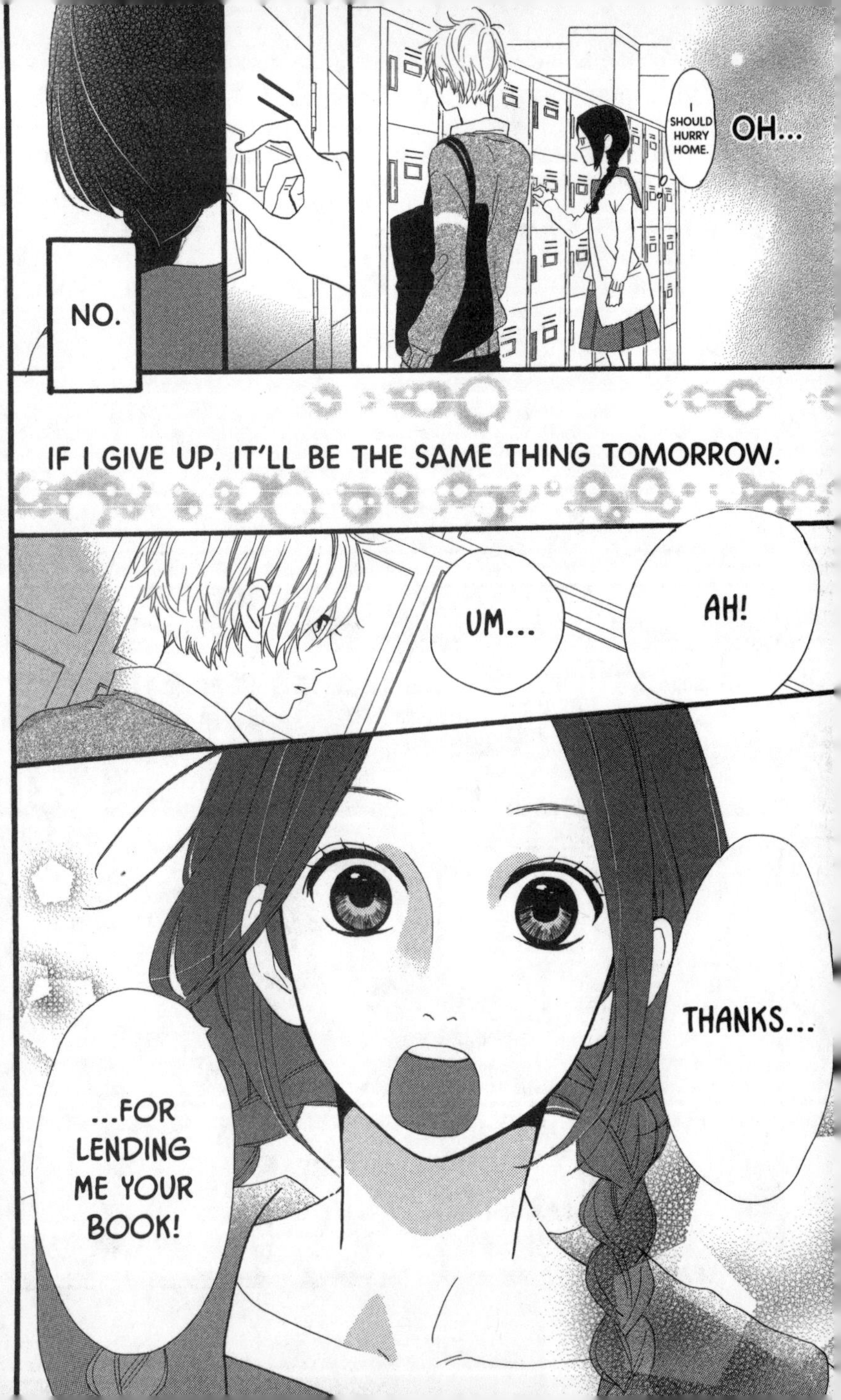
OH...
I SHOULD HURRY HOME.
NO.
IF I GIVE UP, IT'LL BE THE SAME THING TOMORROW.
AH!
UM...
THANKS...
...FOR LENDING ME YOUR BOOK!

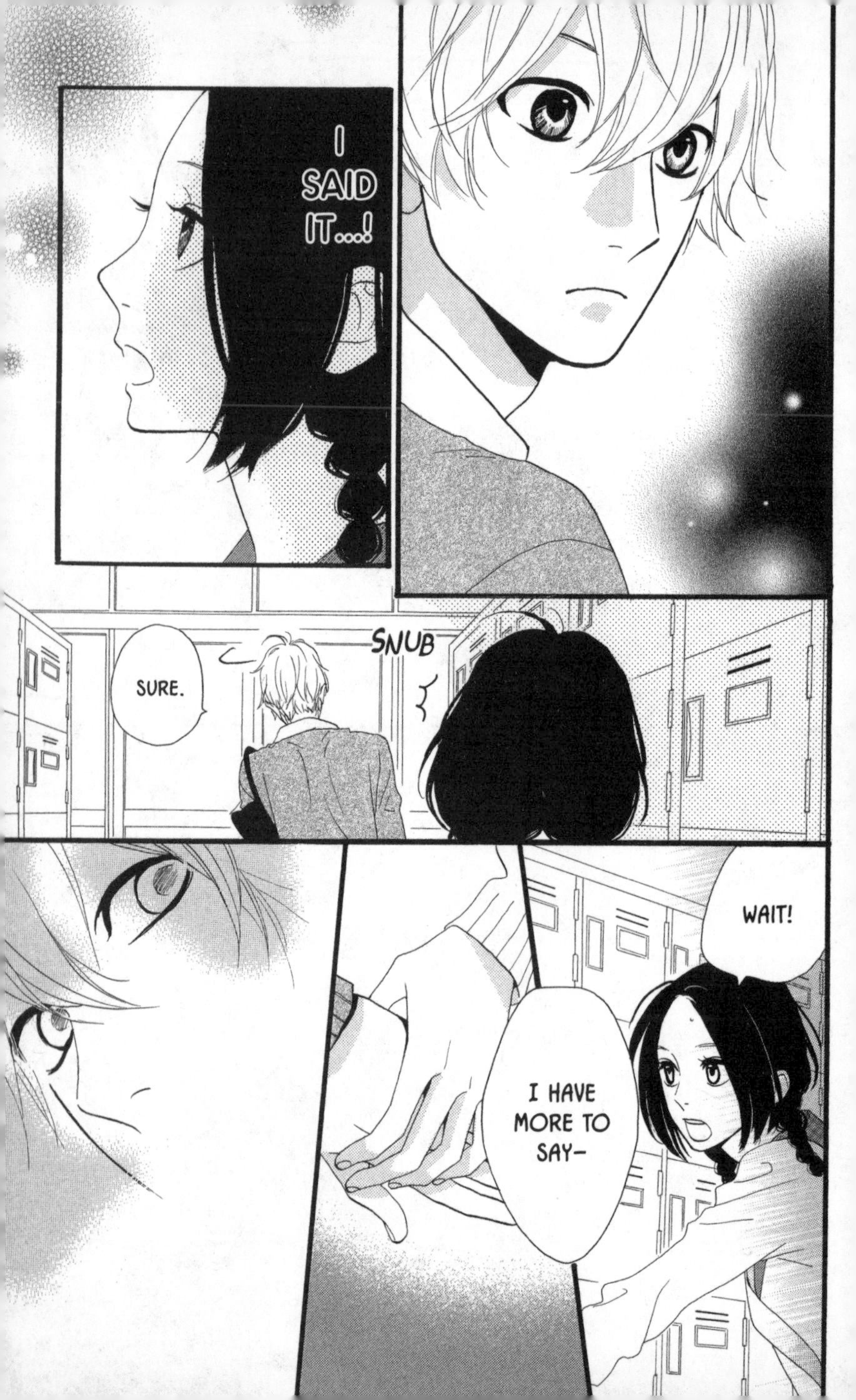
I SAID IT...!
SNUB
SURE.
WAIT!
I HAVE MORE TO SAY–

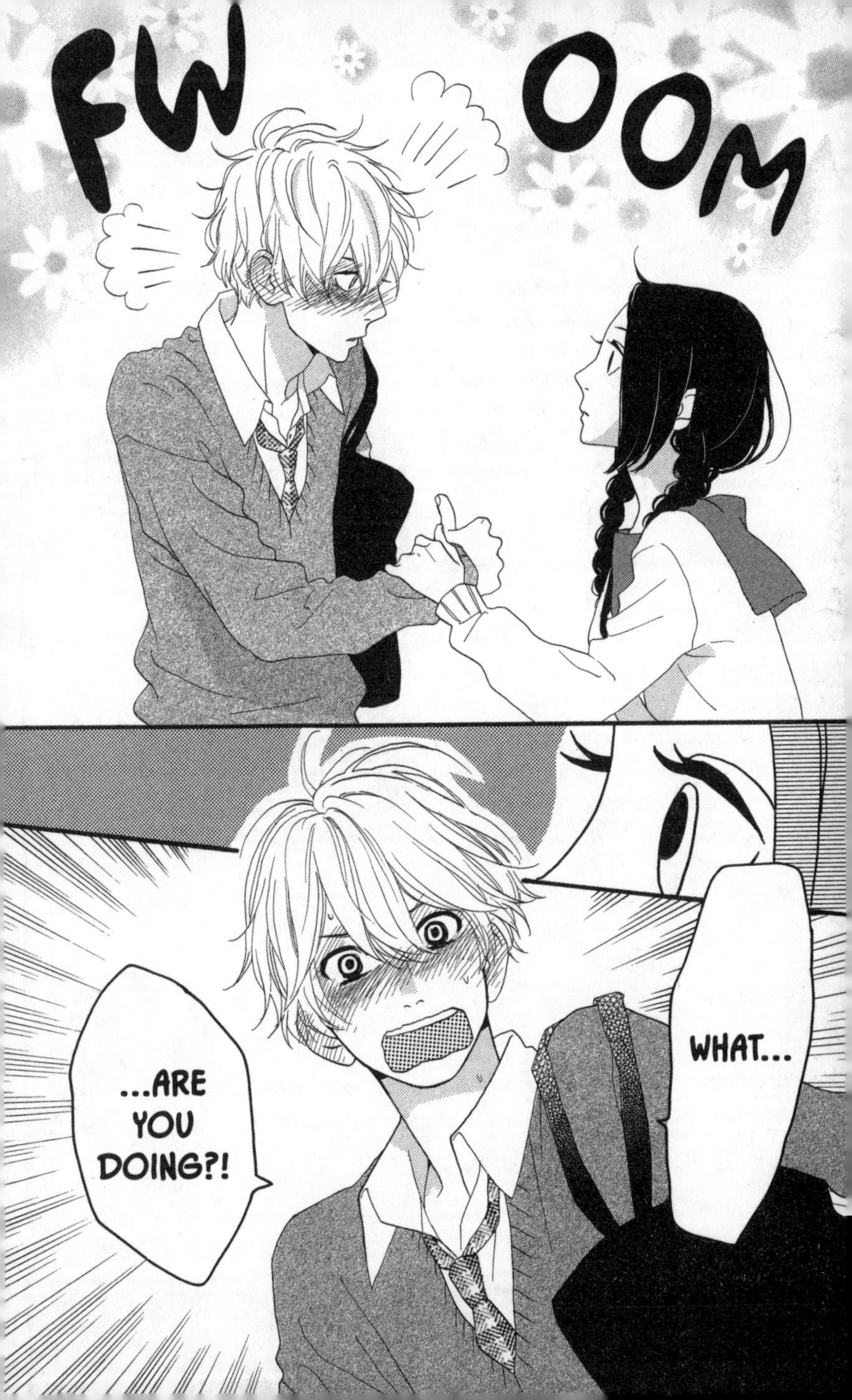
FWOOM
WHAT...
...ARE YOU DOING?!

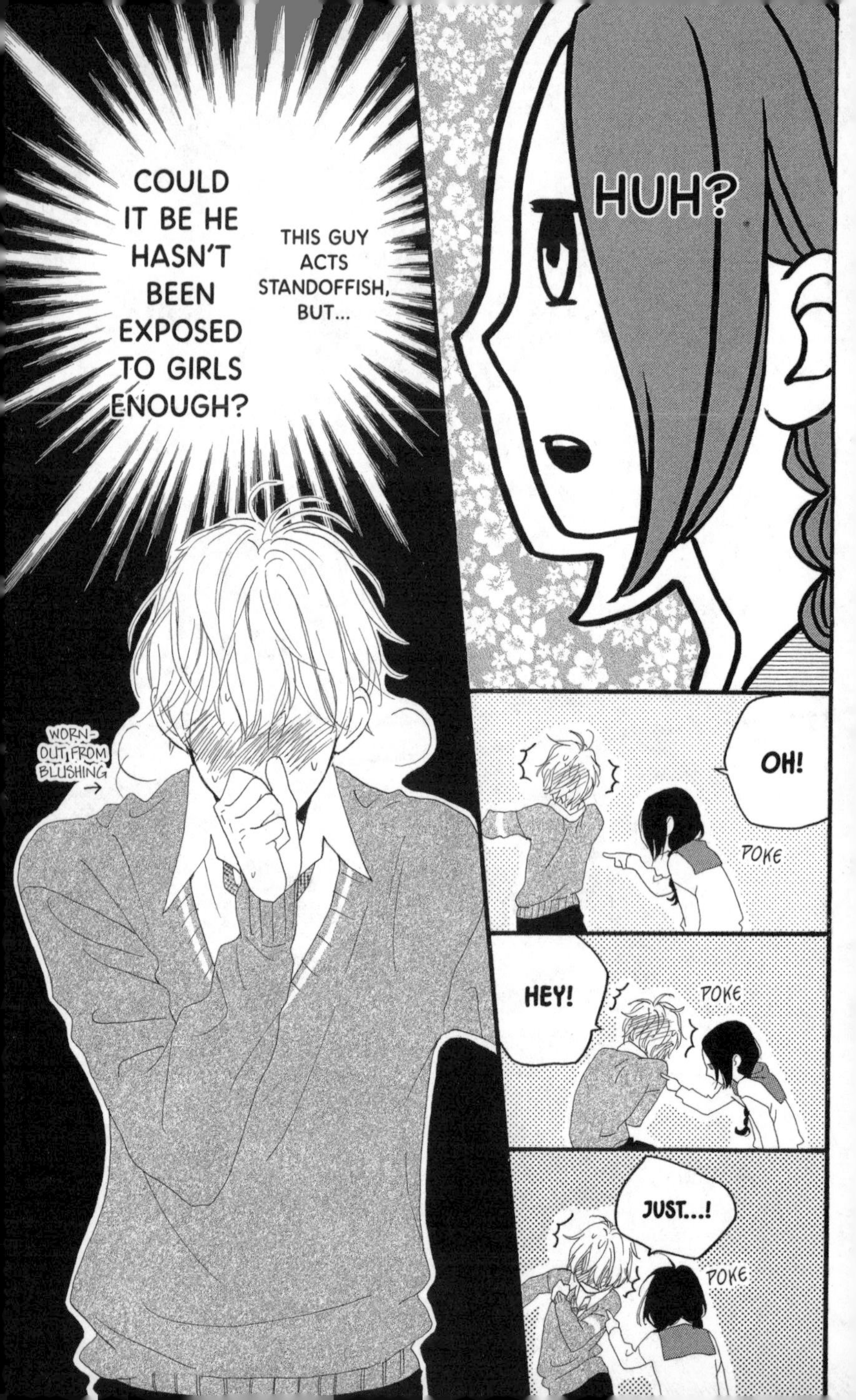
HUH?
OH!
POKE
HEY!
POKE
JUST...!
POKE
THIS GUY ACTS STANDOFFISH, BUT...
COULD IT BE HE HASN'T BEEN EXPOSED TO GIRLS ENOUGH?
WORN-OUT FROM BLUSHING

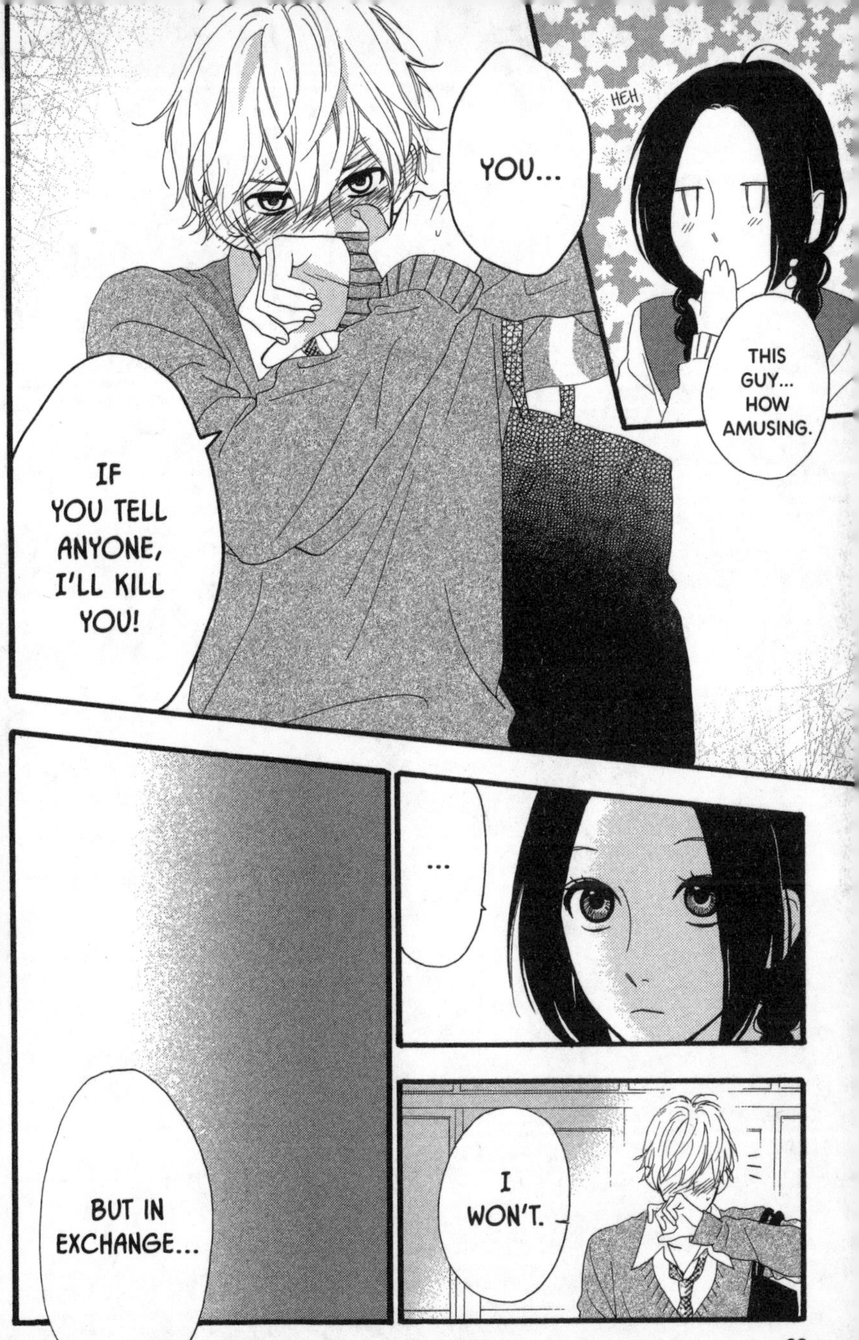
HEH
THIS GUY... HOW AMUSING.
YOU...
IF YOU TELL ANYONE, I'LL KILL YOU!
...
I WON'T.
BUT IN EXCHANGE...

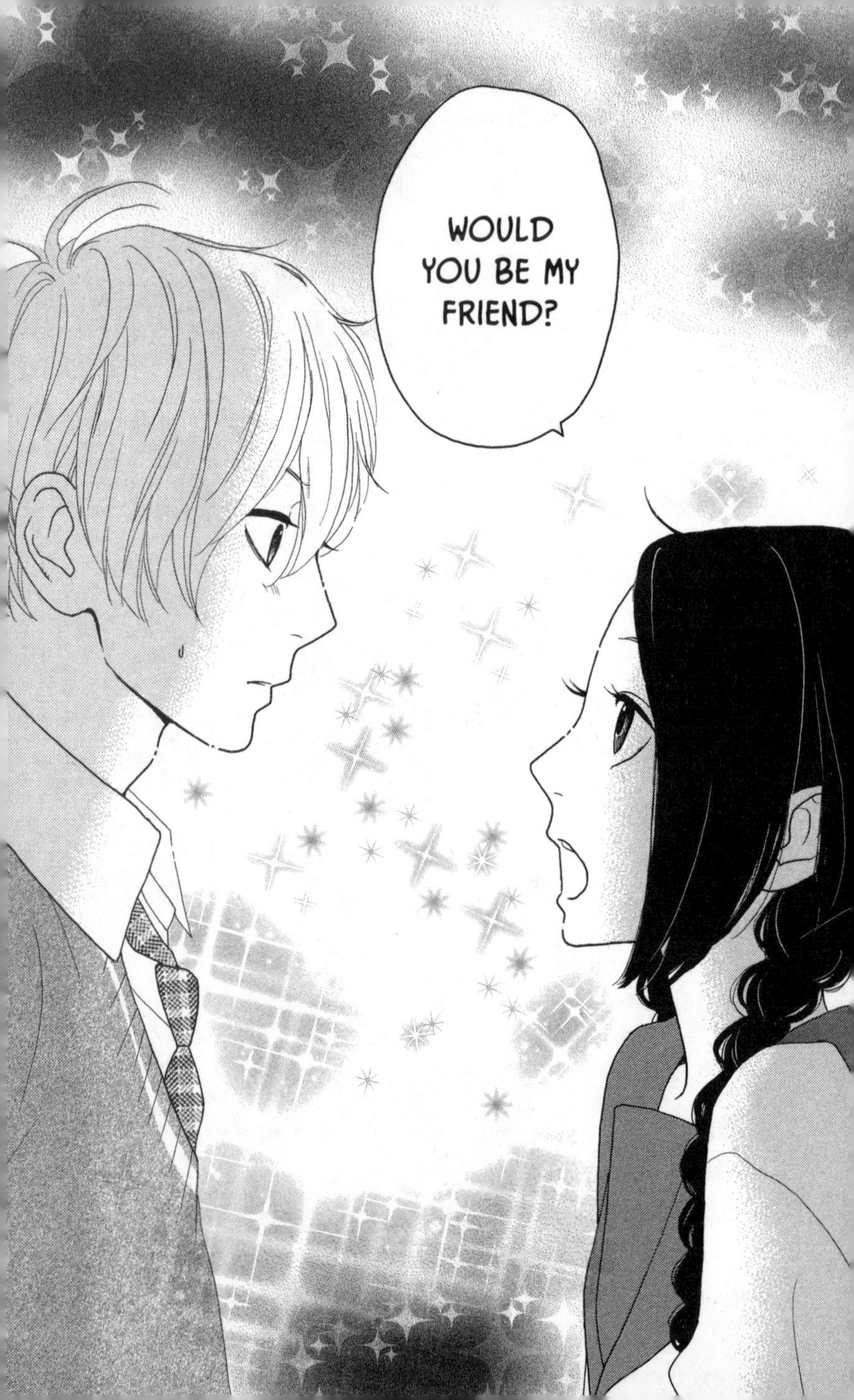
WOULD YOU BE MY FRIEND?

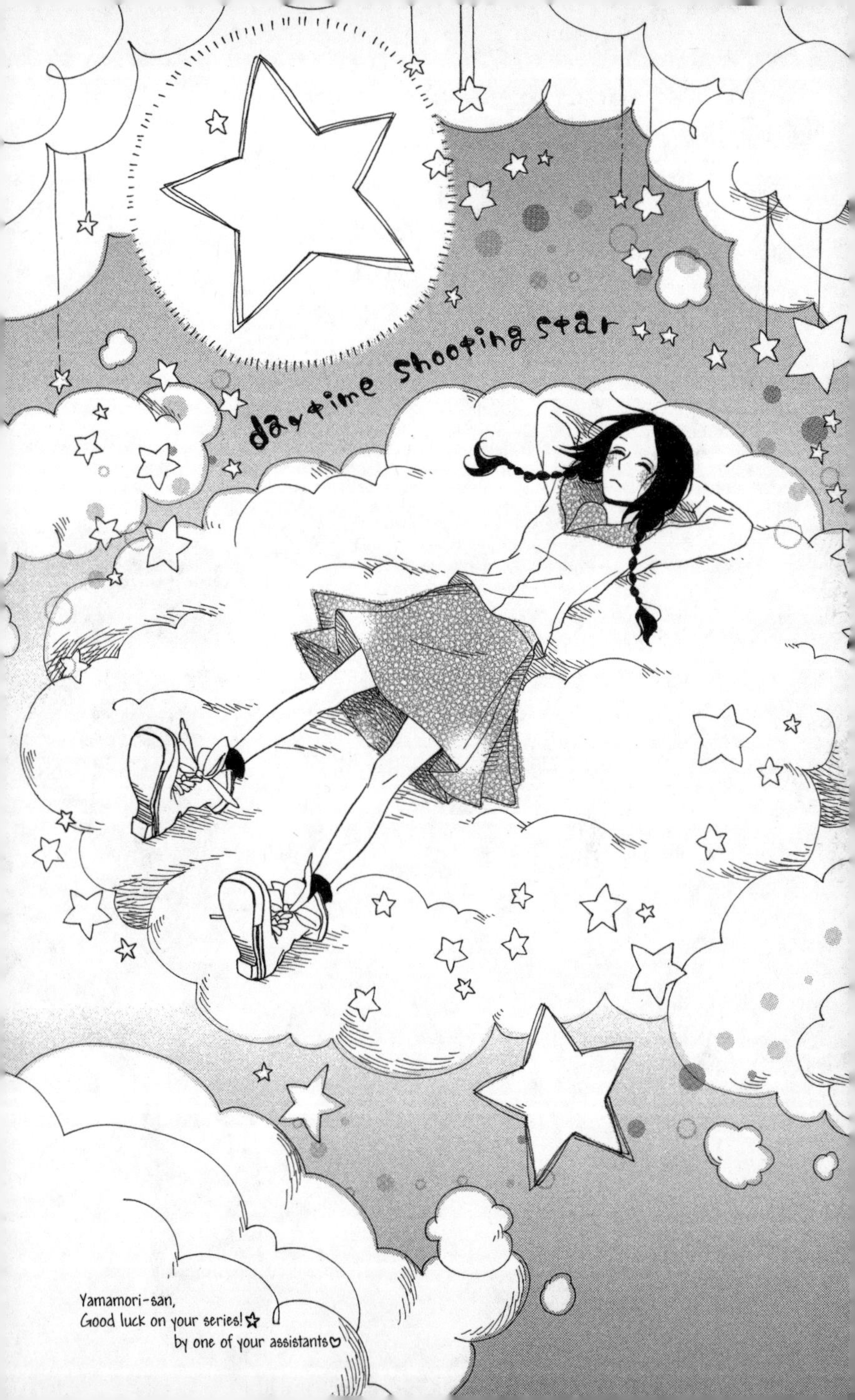
daytime shooting star
Yamamori-san,
Good luck on your series!
by one of your assistants

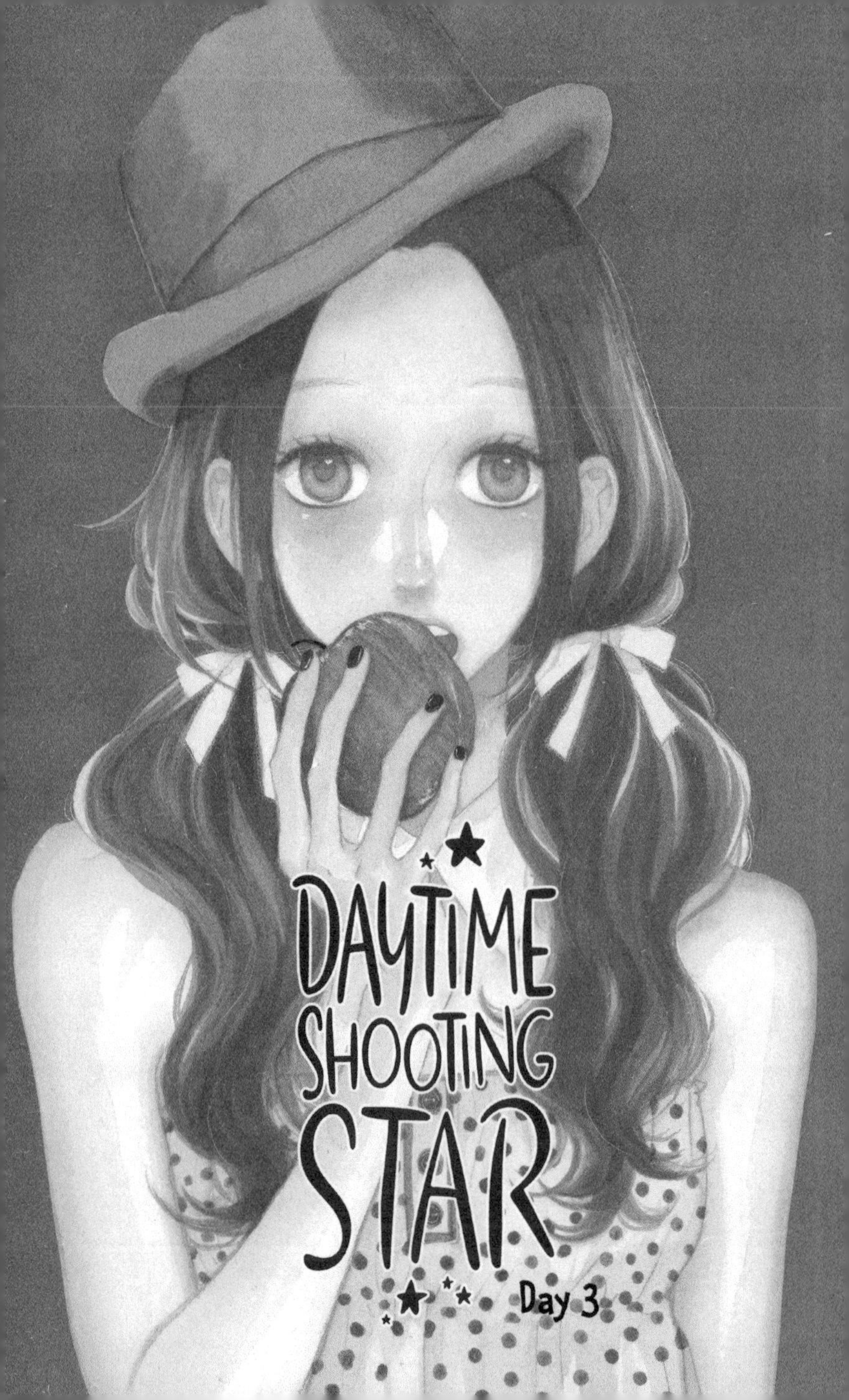
DAYTIME SHOOTING STAR
Day 3

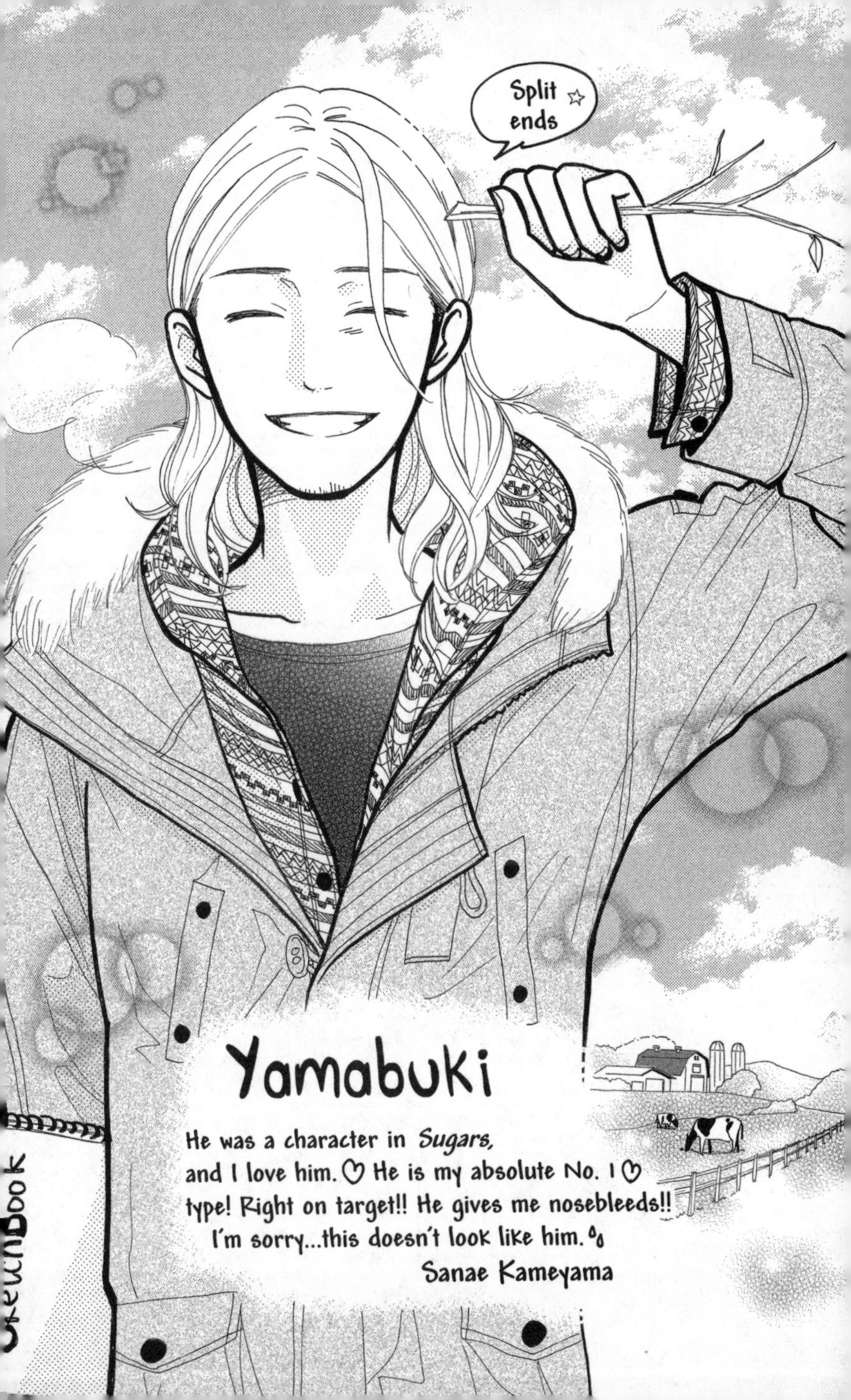
Split ends ☆
Yamabuki
He was a character in *Sugars,* and I love him. ♡ He is my absolute No. 1 ♡ type! Right on target!! He gives me nosebleeds!! I'm sorry...this doesn't look like him.
Sanae Kameyama

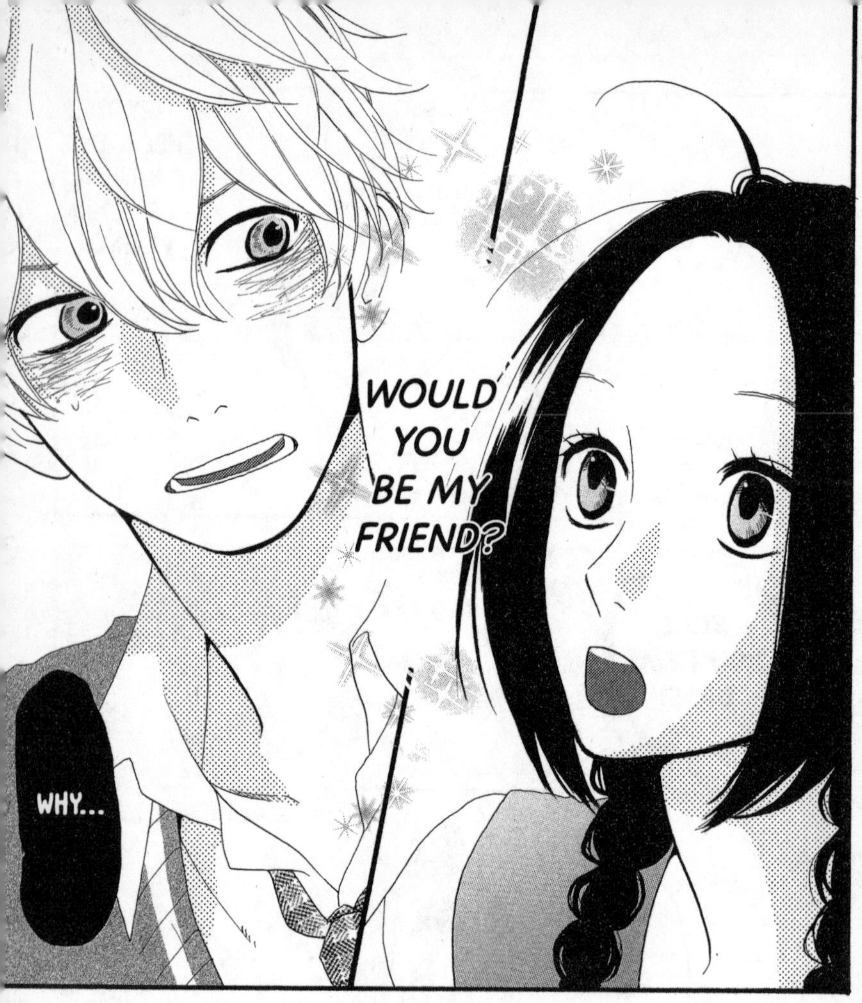
WOULD YOU BE MY FRIEND?
WHY...

Suzume Yosano

Born Dec. 1
Height: 5'4"
Weight: 110 lbs

Blood Type: A
① Likes: fish, white rice
② Talents/Hobbies: sports, sleeping
③ Recent Troubles: My uncle forces me to study.

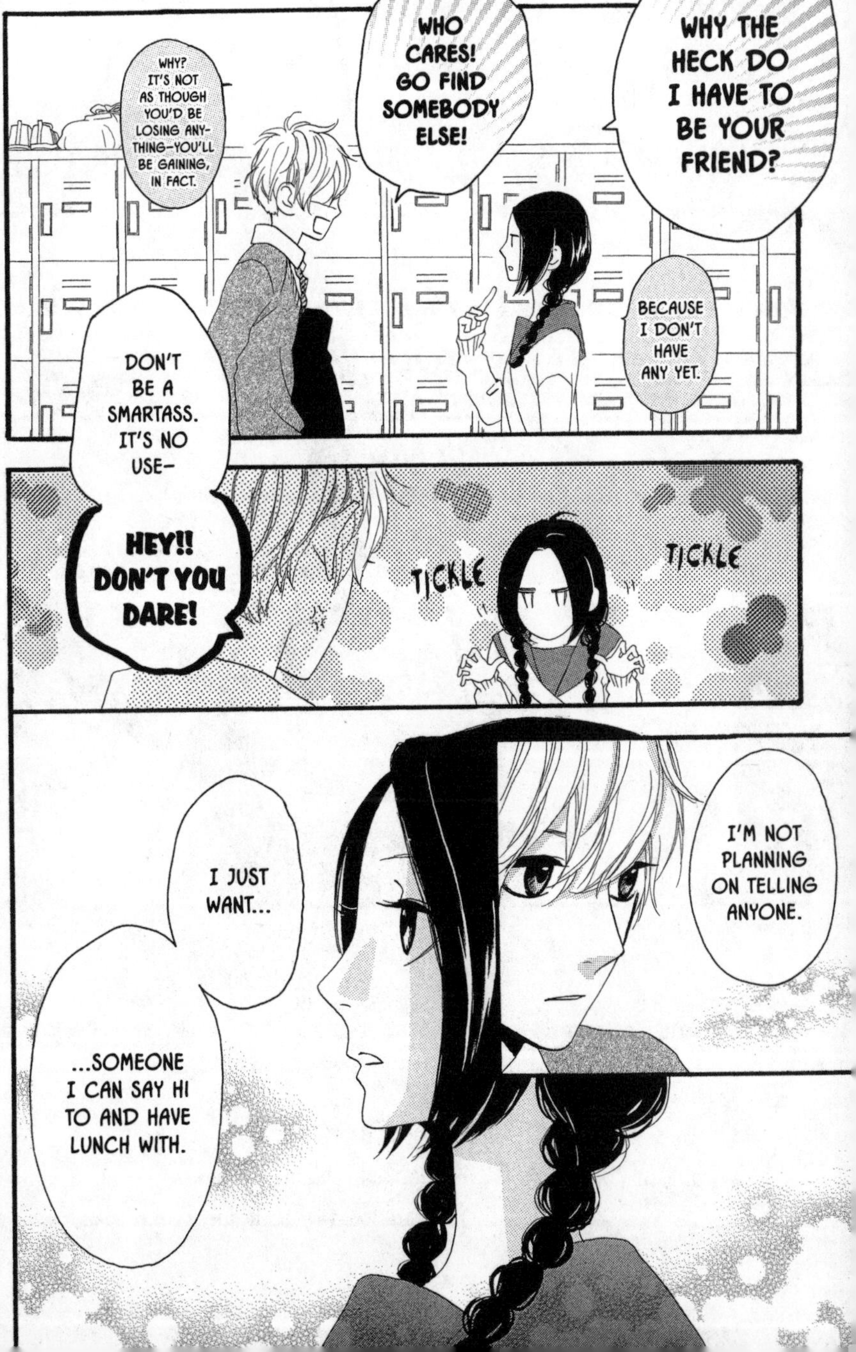
WHY THE HECK DO I HAVE TO BE YOUR FRIEND?
BECAUSE I DON'T HAVE ANY YET.
WHO CARES! GO FIND SOMEBODY ELSE!
WHY? IT'S NOT AS THOUGH YOU'D BE LOSING ANY-THING—YOU'LL BE GAINING, IN FACT.
DON'T BE A SMARTASS. IT'S NO USE—
TICKLE
TICKLE
HEY!! DON'T YOU DARE!
I'M NOT PLANNING ON TELLING ANYONE.
I JUST WANT...
...SOMEONE I CAN SAY HI TO AND HAVE LUNCH WITH.

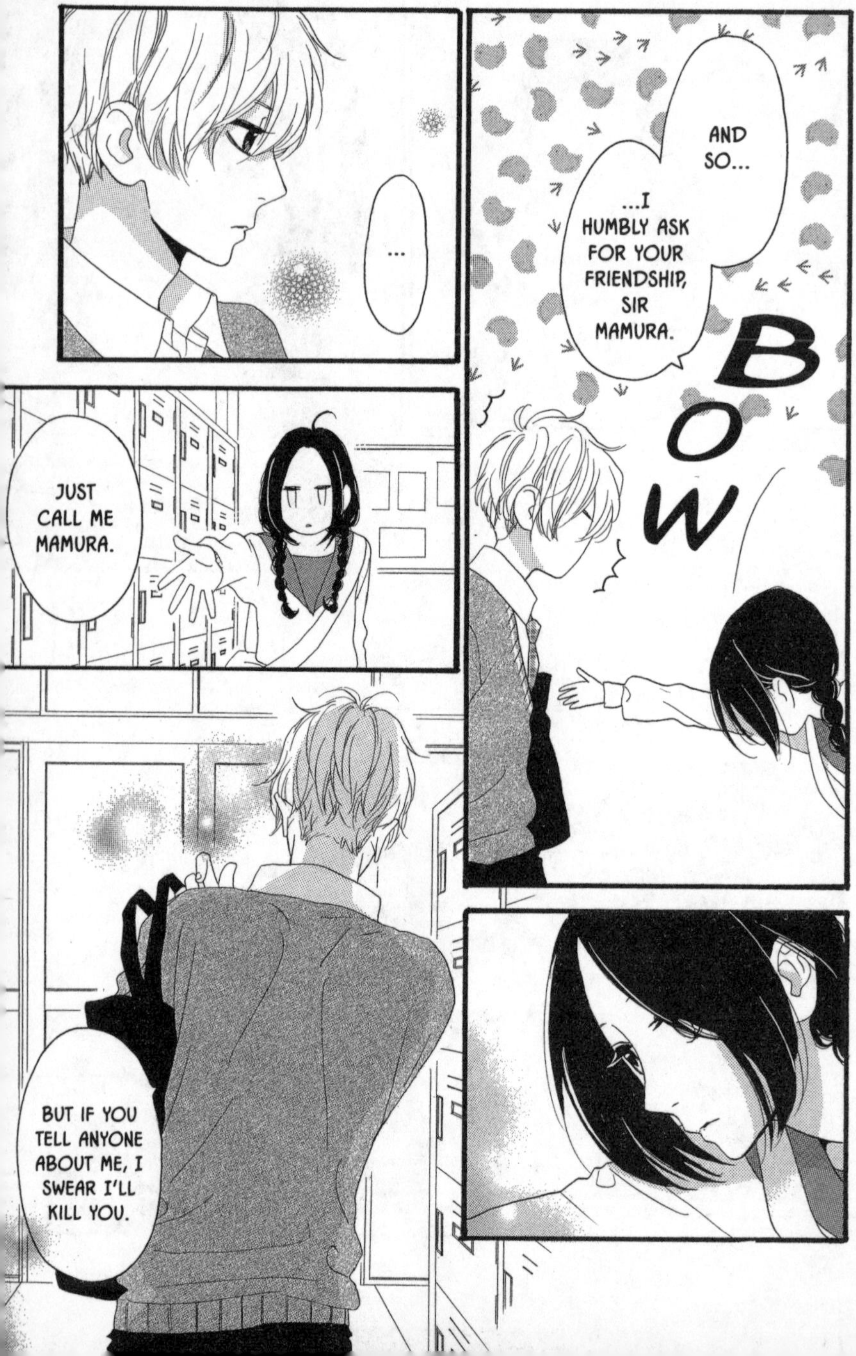
AND SO...
...I HUMBLY ASK FOR YOUR FRIENDSHIP, SIR MAMURA.
BOW
...
JUST CALL ME MAMURA.
BUT IF YOU TELL ANYONE ABOUT ME, I SWEAR I'LL KILL YOU.

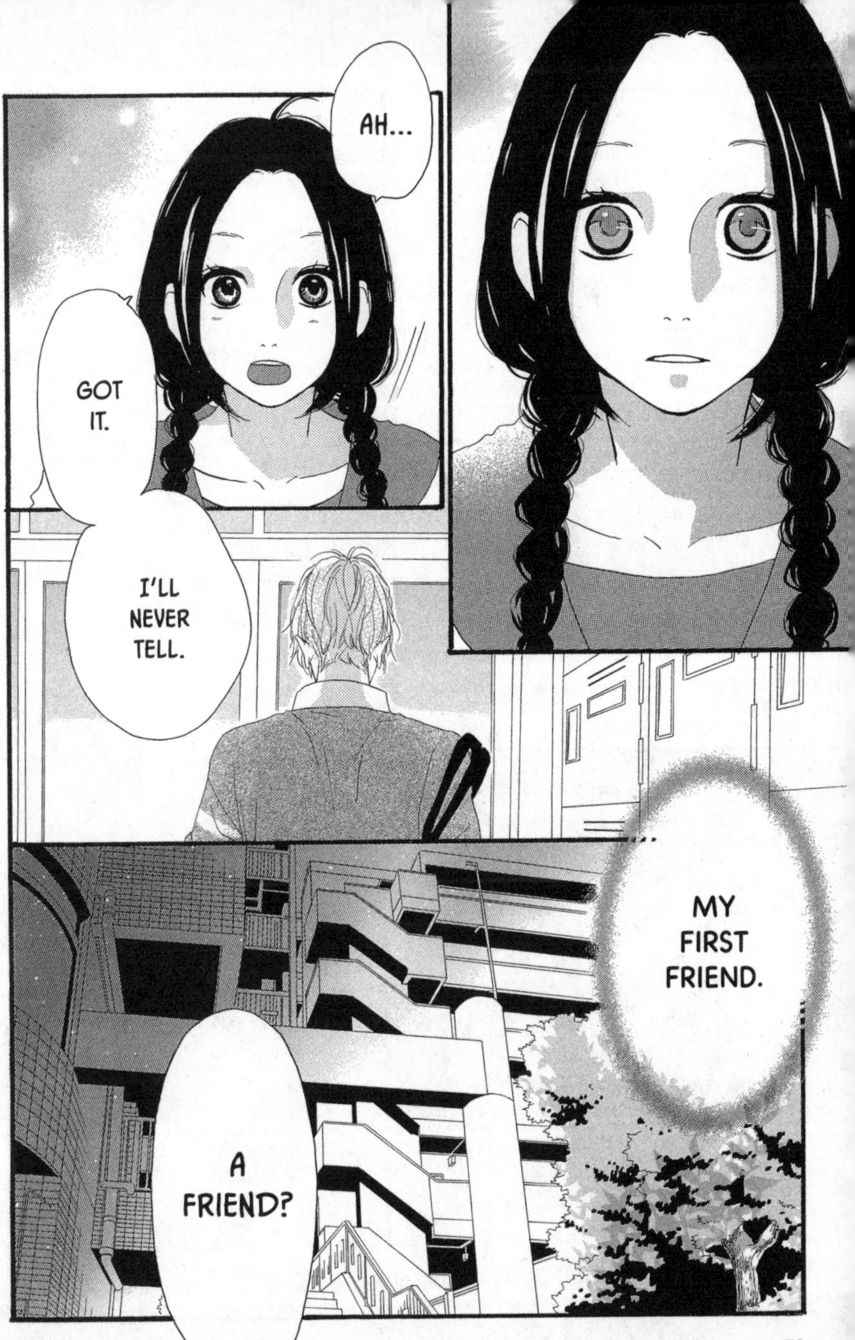
AH...
GOT IT.
I'LL NEVER TELL.
MY FIRST FRIEND.
A FRIEND?

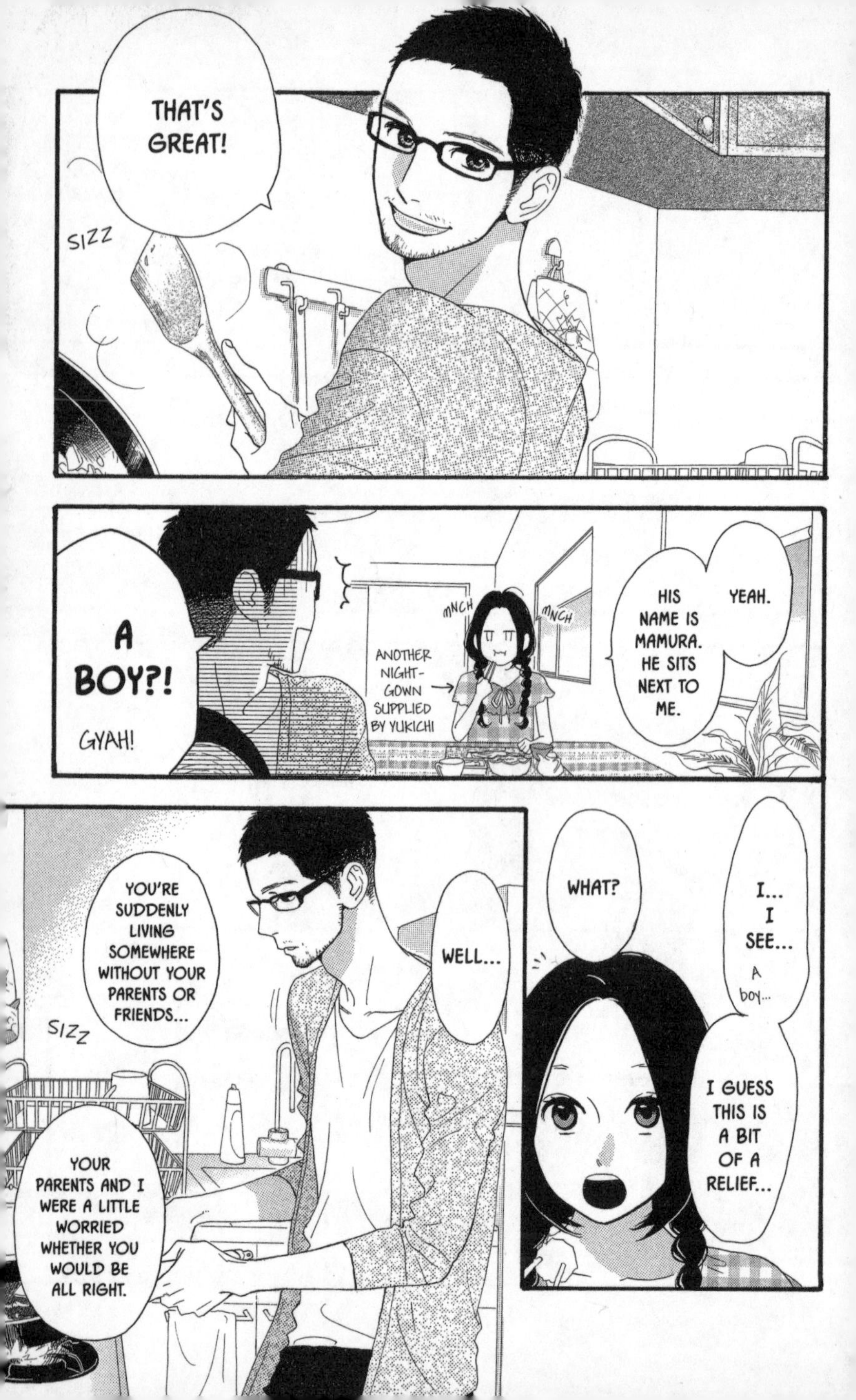
THAT'S GREAT!
SIZZ
YEAH.
HIS NAME IS MAMURA. HE SITS NEXT TO ME.
MNCH
MNCH
ANOTHER NIGHT-GOWN SUPPLIED BY YUKICHI
A BOY?!
GYAH!
I... I SEE...
A boy...
I GUESS THIS IS A BIT OF A RELIEF...
WHAT?
WELL...
YOU'RE SUDDENLY LIVING SOMEWHERE WITHOUT YOUR PARENTS OR FRIENDS...
SIZZ
YOUR PARENTS AND I WERE A LITTLE WORRIED WHETHER YOU WOULD BE ALL RIGHT.

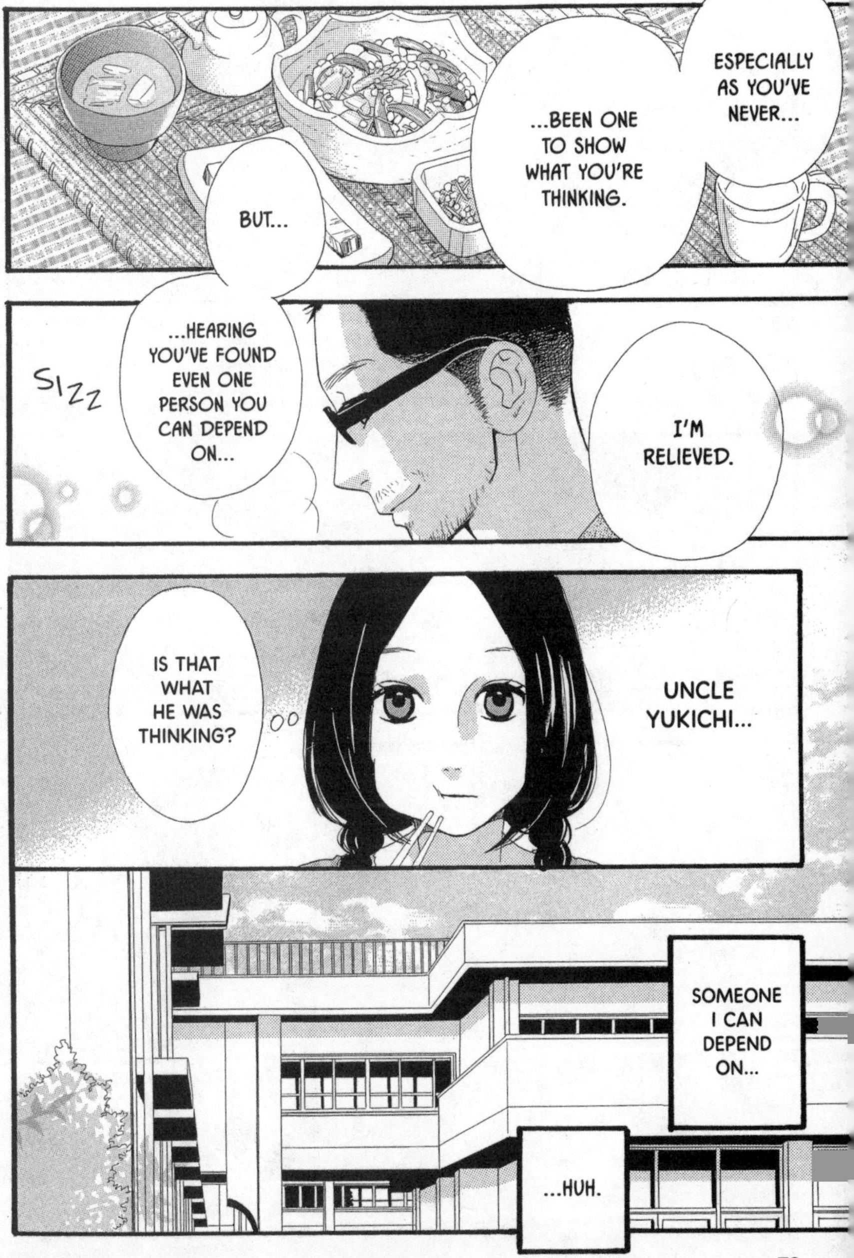
ESPECIALLY AS YOU'VE NEVER...
...BEEN ONE TO SHOW WHAT YOU'RE THINKING.
BUT...
...HEARING YOU'VE FOUND EVEN ONE PERSON YOU CAN DEPEND ON...
I'M RELIEVED.
SIZZ
UNCLE YUKICHI...
IS THAT WHAT HE WAS THINKING?
SOMEONE I CAN DEPEND ON...
...HUH.

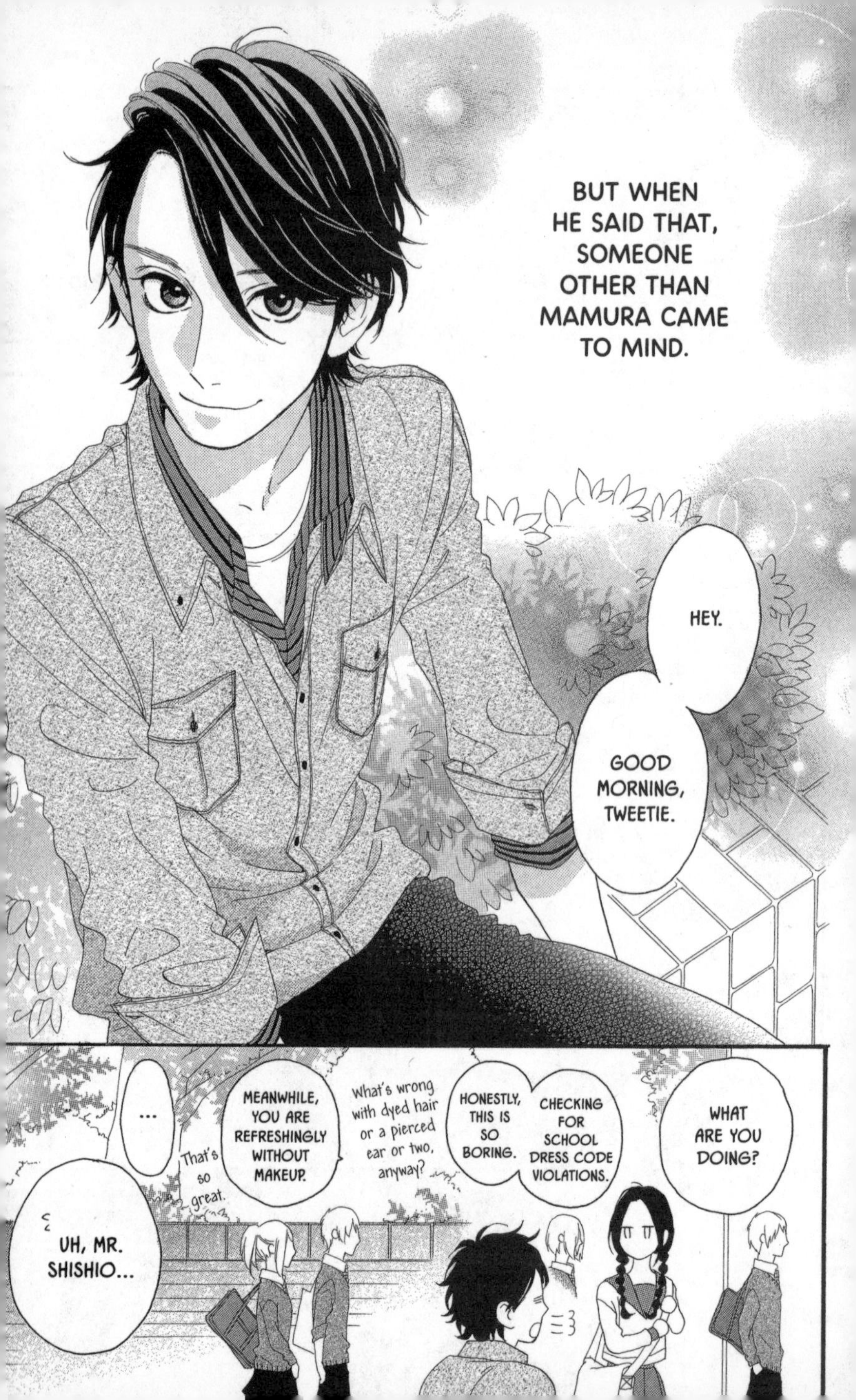
BUT WHEN HE SAID THAT, SOMEONE OTHER THAN MAMURA CAME TO MIND.
HEY.
GOOD MORNING, TWEETIE.
WHAT ARE YOU DOING?
CHECKING FOR SCHOOL DRESS CODE VIOLATIONS.
HONESTLY, THIS IS SO BORING.
What's wrong with dyed hair or a pierced ear or two, anyway?
MEANWHILE, YOU ARE REFRESHINGLY WITHOUT MAKEUP.
That's so great.
...
UH, MR. SHISHIO...

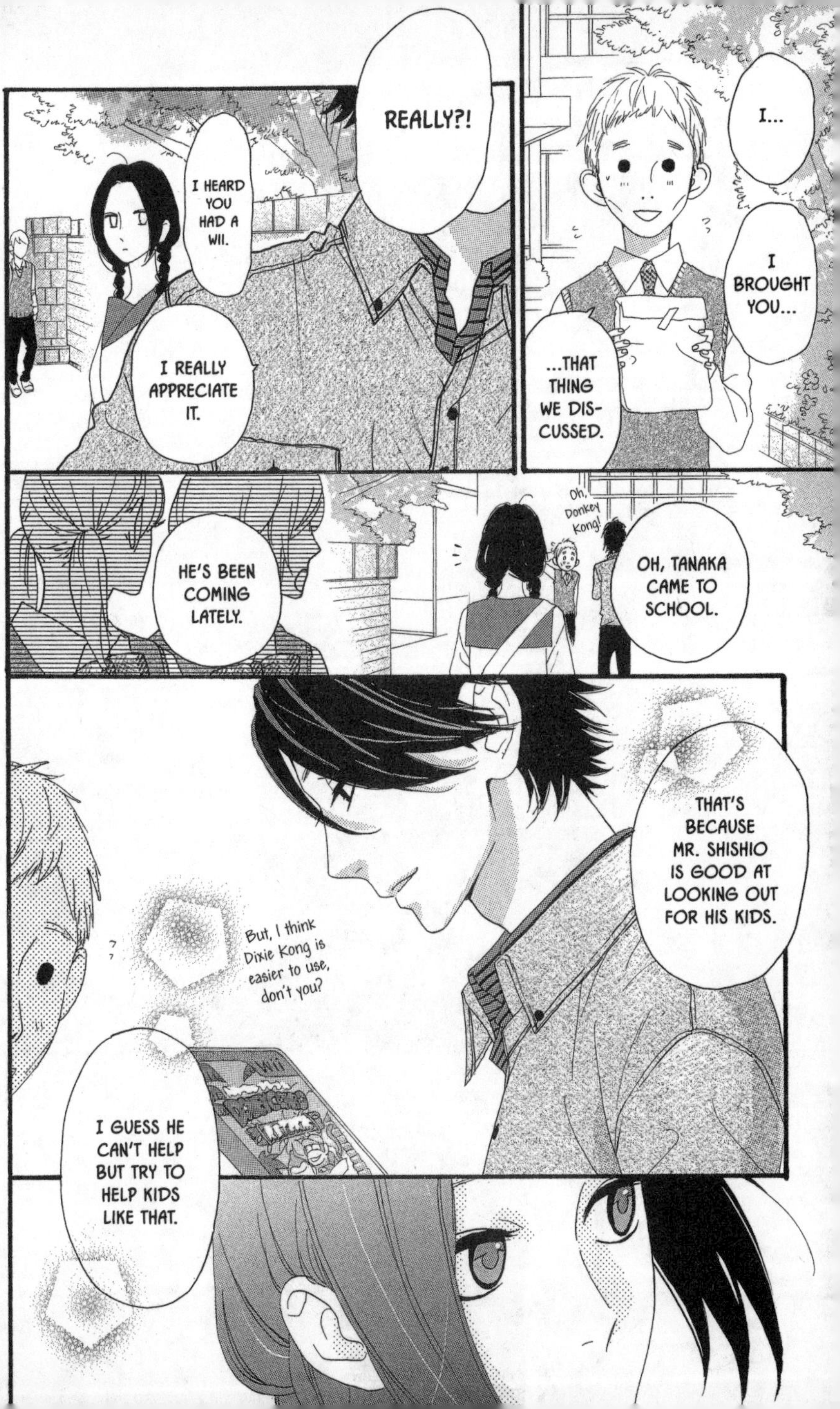
I...
I BROUGHT YOU...
...THAT THING WE DISCUSSED.
REALLY?!
I HEARD YOU HAD A WII.
I REALLY APPRECIATE IT.
OH, TANAKA CAME TO SCHOOL.
Oh, Donkey Kong!
HE'S BEEN COMING LATELY.
THAT'S BECAUSE MR. SHISHIO IS GOOD AT LOOKING OUT FOR HIS KIDS.
But, I think Dixie Kong is easier to use, don't you?
I GUESS HE CAN'T HELP BUT TRY TO HELP KIDS LIKE THAT.

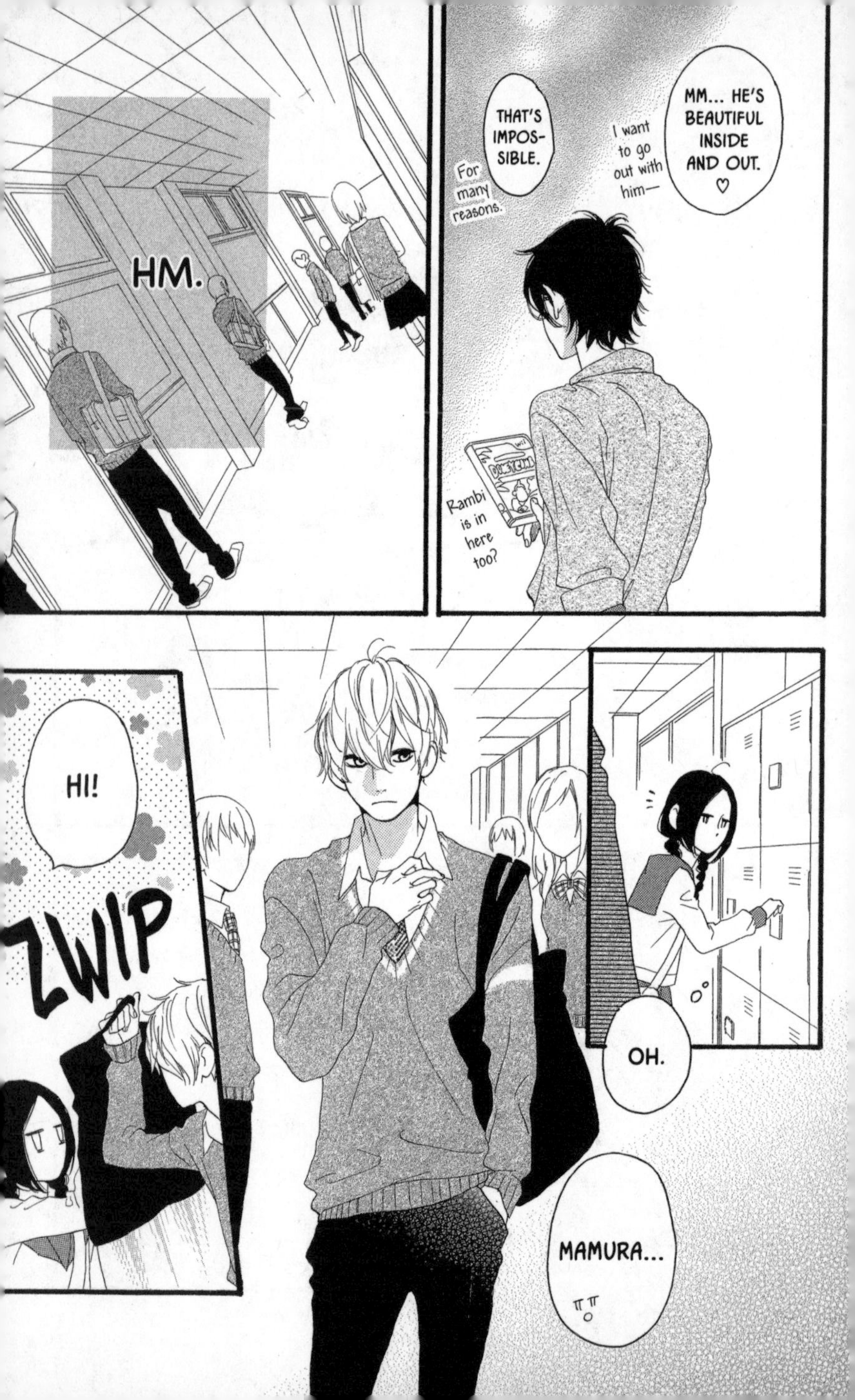
MM... HE'S BEAUTIFUL INSIDE AND OUT. ♡
I want to go out with him—
THAT'S IMPOSSIBLE.
For many reasons.
Rambi is in here too?
HM.
OH.
MAMURA...
HI!
ZWIP

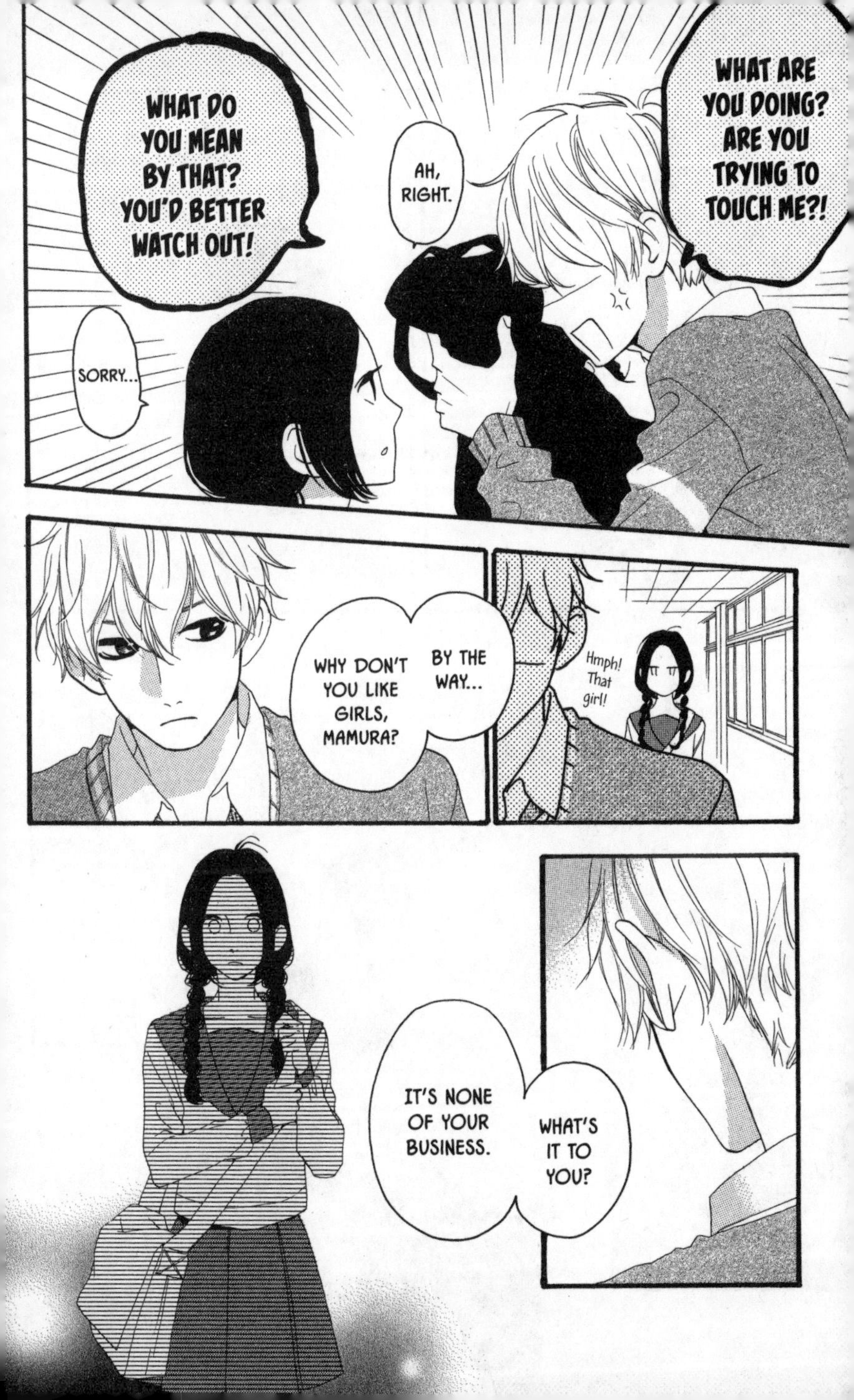
WHAT ARE YOU DOING? ARE YOU TRYING TO TOUCH ME?!
AH, RIGHT.
WHAT DO YOU MEAN BY THAT? YOU'D BETTER WATCH OUT!
SORRY...
Hmph! That girl!
BY THE WAY...
WHY DON'T YOU LIKE GIRLS, MAMURA?
WHAT'S IT TO YOU?
IT'S NONE OF YOUR BUSINESS.

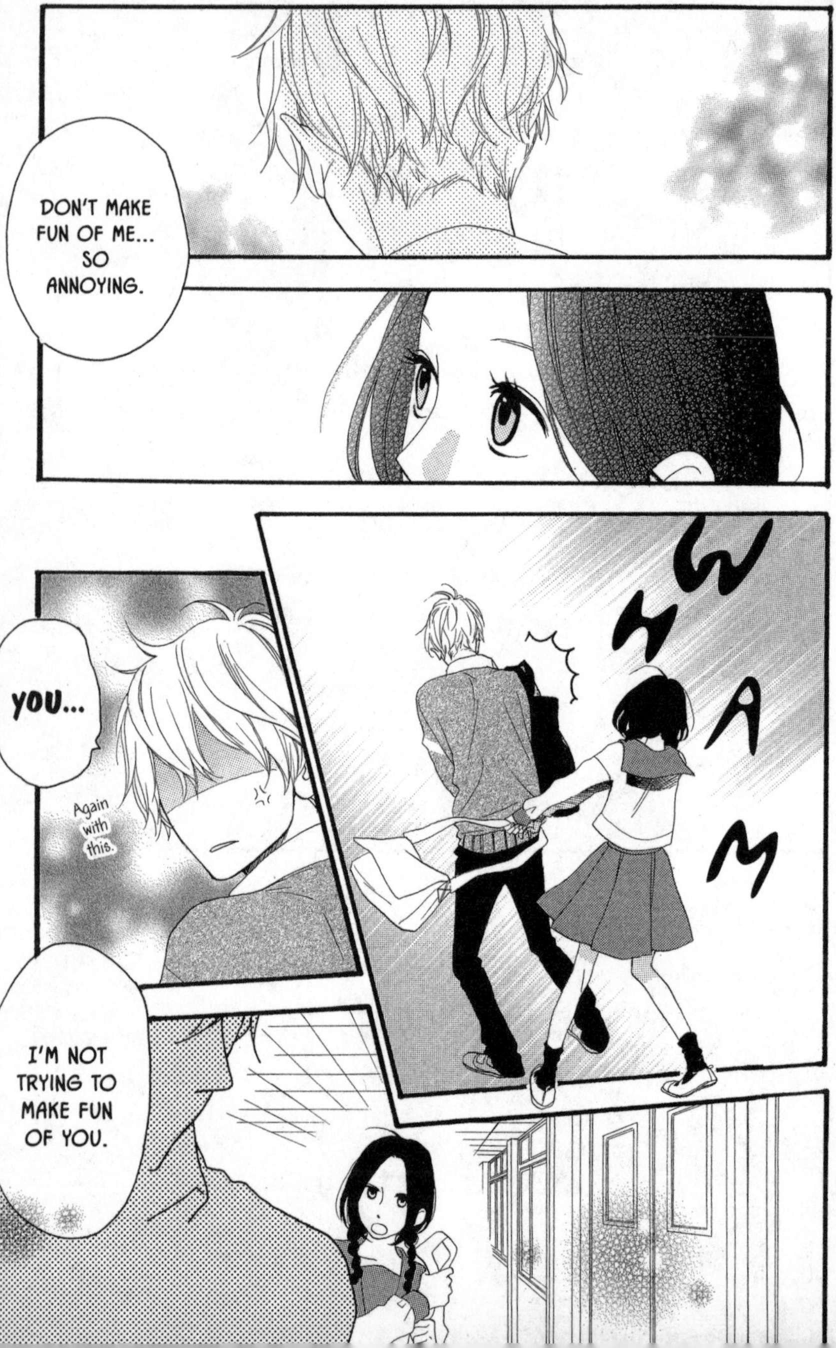
DON'T MAKE FUN OF ME... SO ANNOYING.
WHAM
YOU...
Again with this.
I'M NOT TRYING TO MAKE FUN OF YOU.

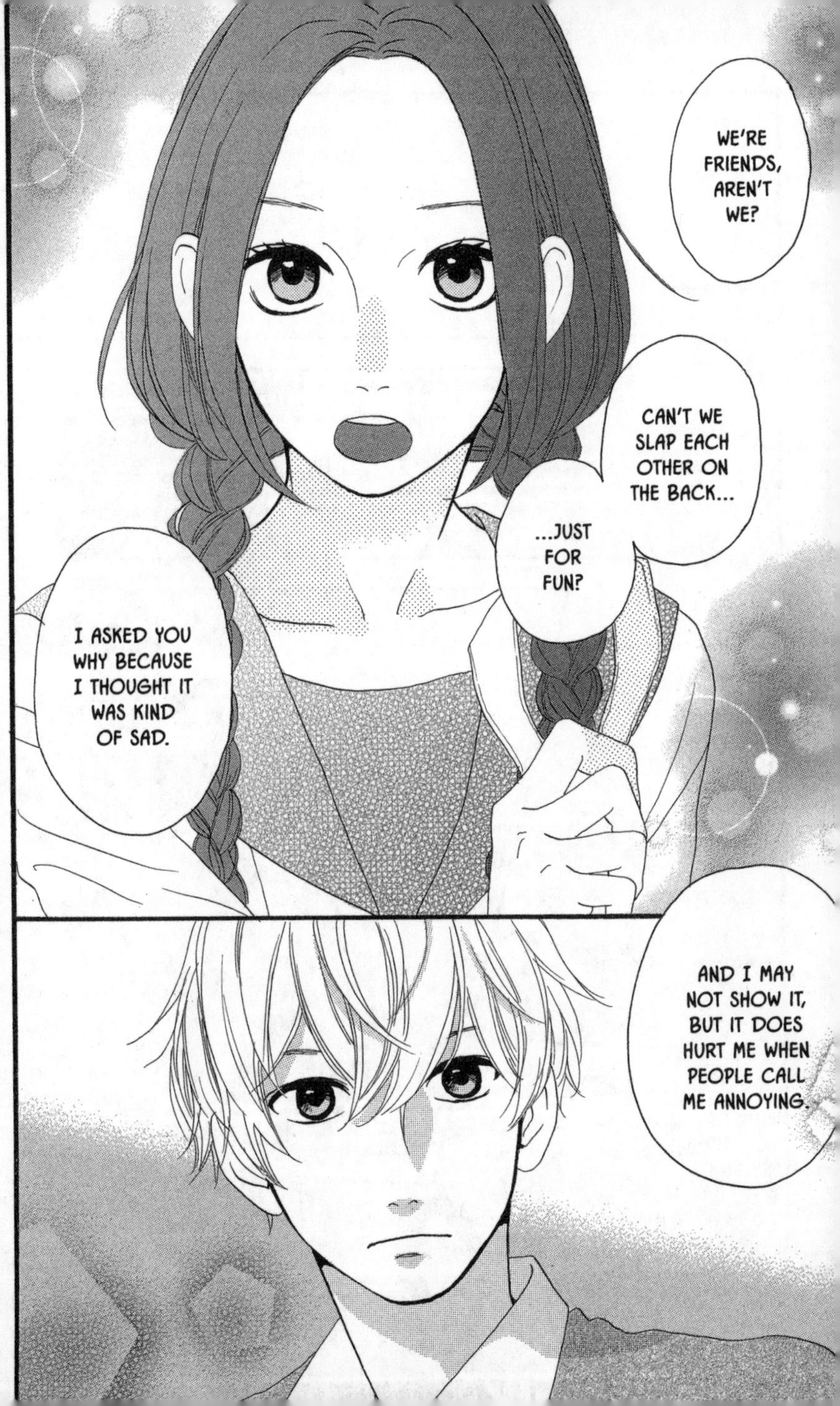
WE'RE FRIENDS, AREN'T WE?
CAN'T WE SLAP EACH OTHER ON THE BACK...
...JUST FOR FUN?
I ASKED YOU WHY BECAUSE I THOUGHT IT WAS KIND OF SAD.
AND I MAY NOT SHOW IT, BUT IT DOES HURT ME WHEN PEOPLE CALL ME ANNOYING.

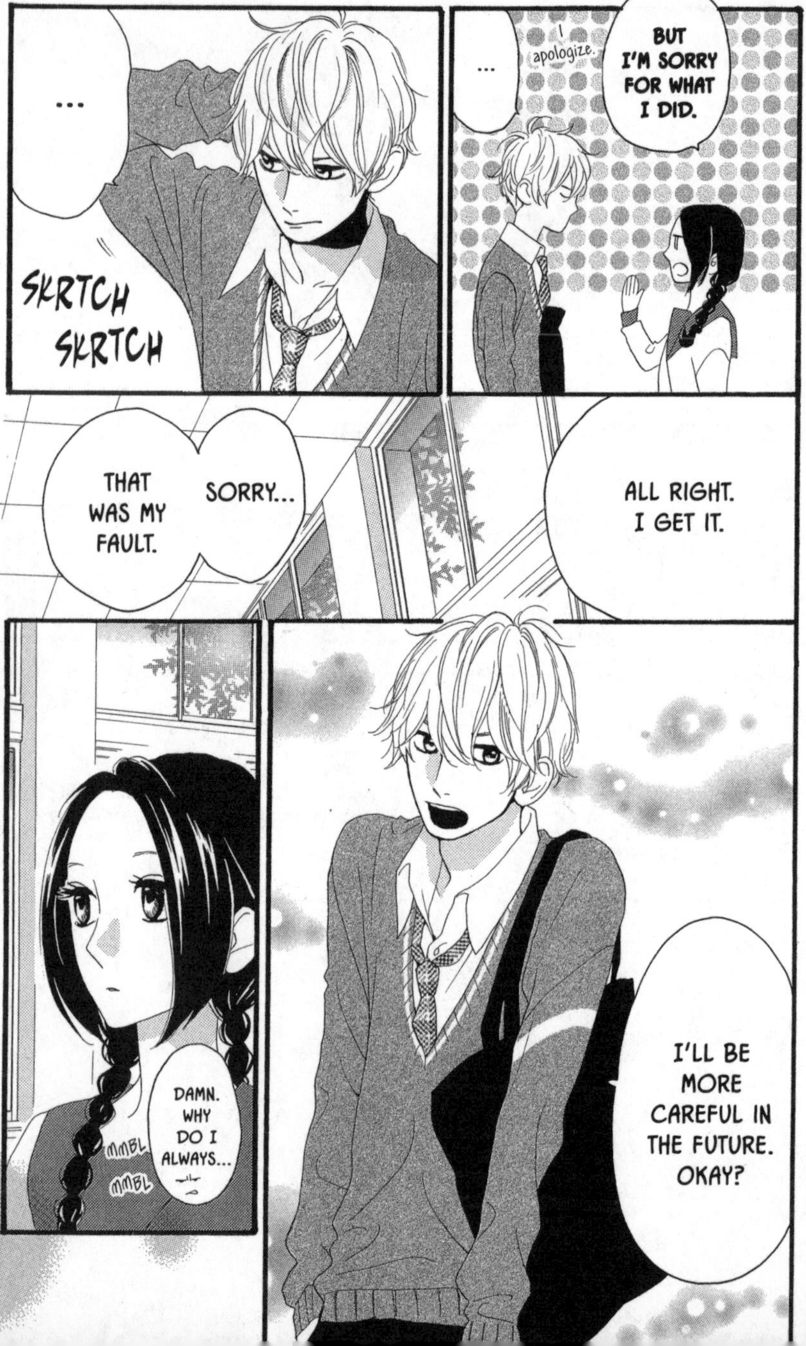
BUT I'M SORRY FOR WHAT I DID.
I apologize.
...
...
SKRTCH SKRTCH
ALL RIGHT. I GET IT.
SORRY...
THAT WAS MY FAULT.
I'LL BE MORE CAREFUL IN THE FUTURE. OKAY?
DAMN. WHY DO I ALWAYS...
MMBL MMBL

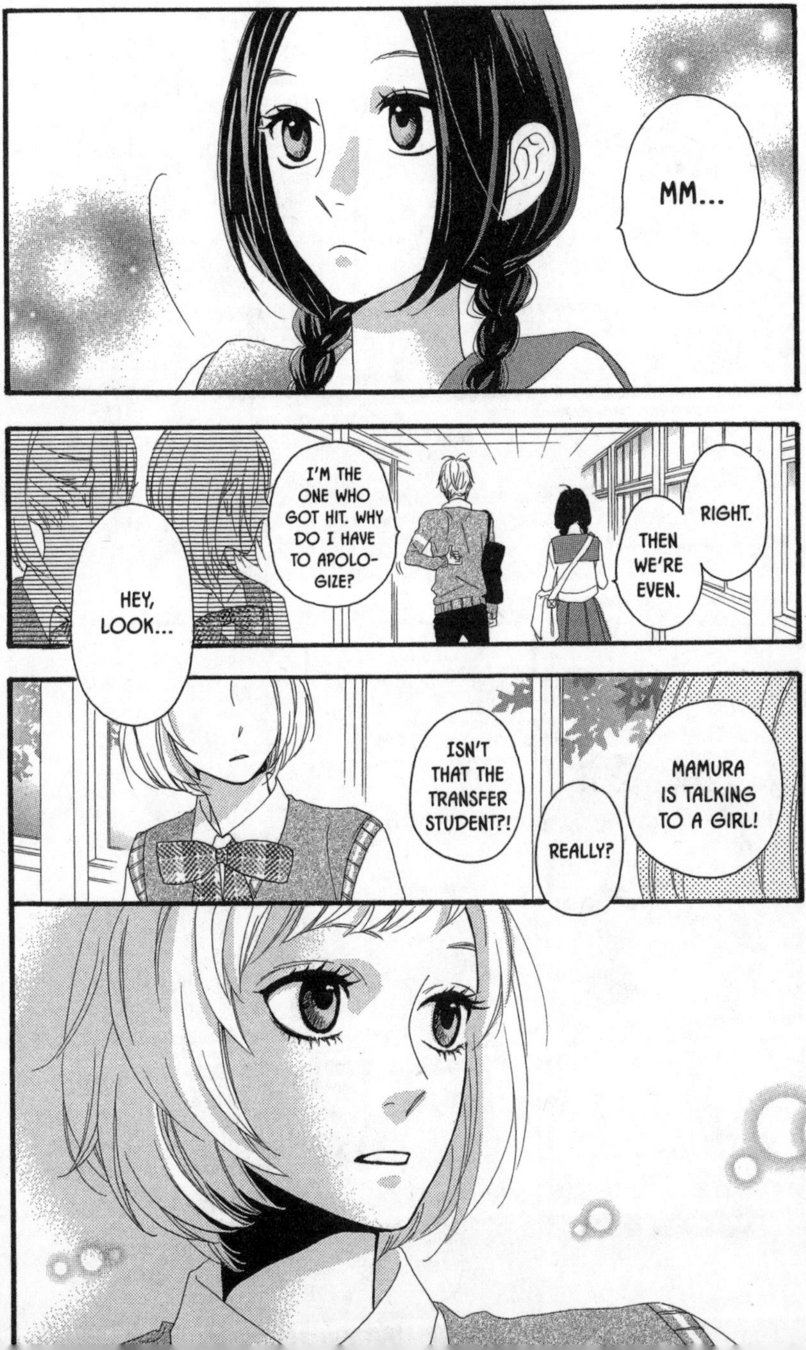
MM...
RIGHT.
THEN WE'RE EVEN.
I'M THE ONE WHO GOT HIT. WHY DO I HAVE TO APOLOGIZE?
HEY, LOOK...
MAMURA IS TALKING TO A GIRL!
REALLY?
ISN'T THAT THE TRANSFER STUDENT?!

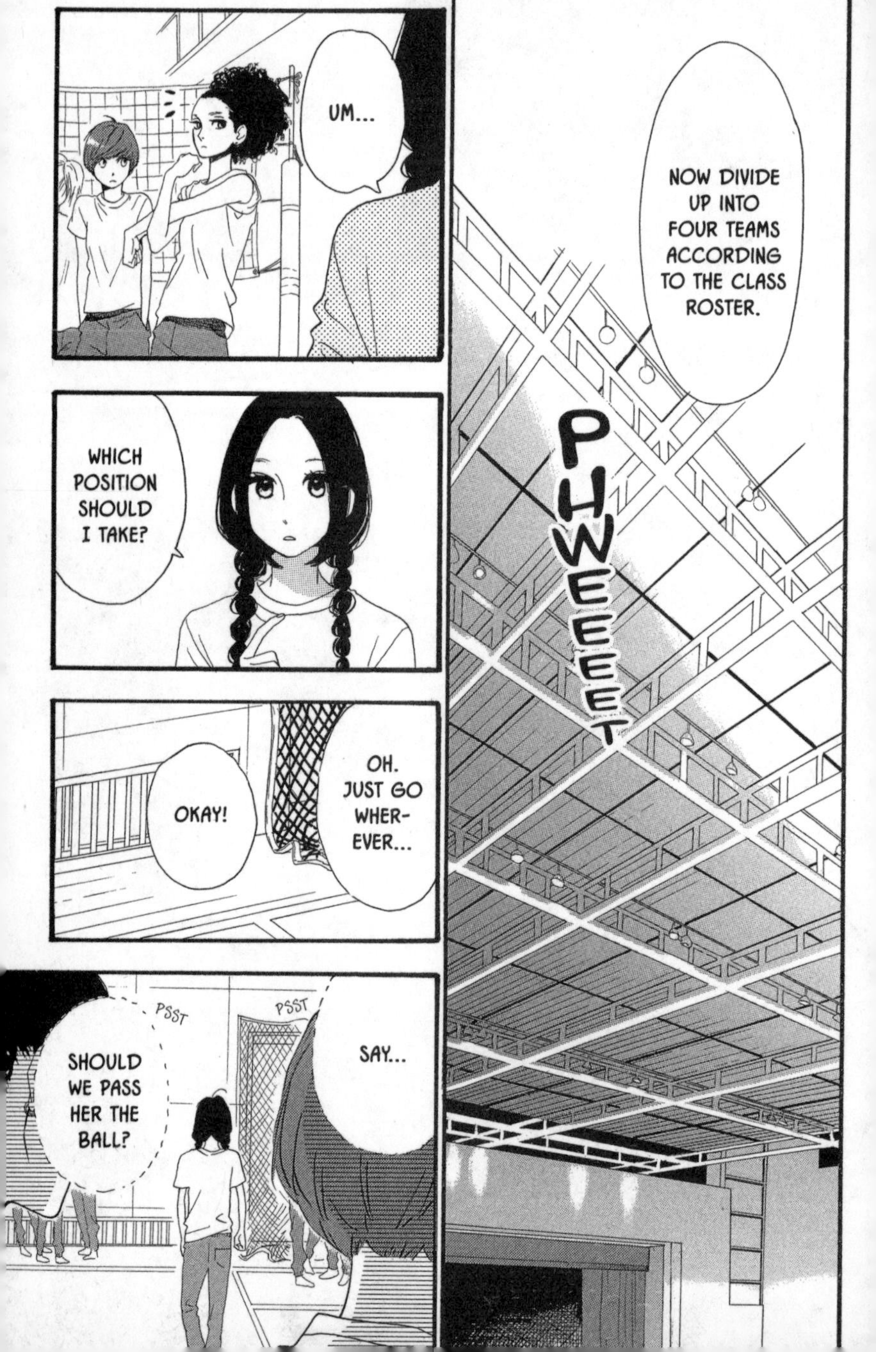
NOW DIVIDE UP INTO FOUR TEAMS ACCORDING TO THE CLASS ROSTER.
PHWEEEET
UM...
WHICH POSITION SHOULD I TAKE?
OH. JUST GO WHER-EVER...
OKAY!
PSST
SAY...
PSST
SHOULD WE PASS HER THE BALL?

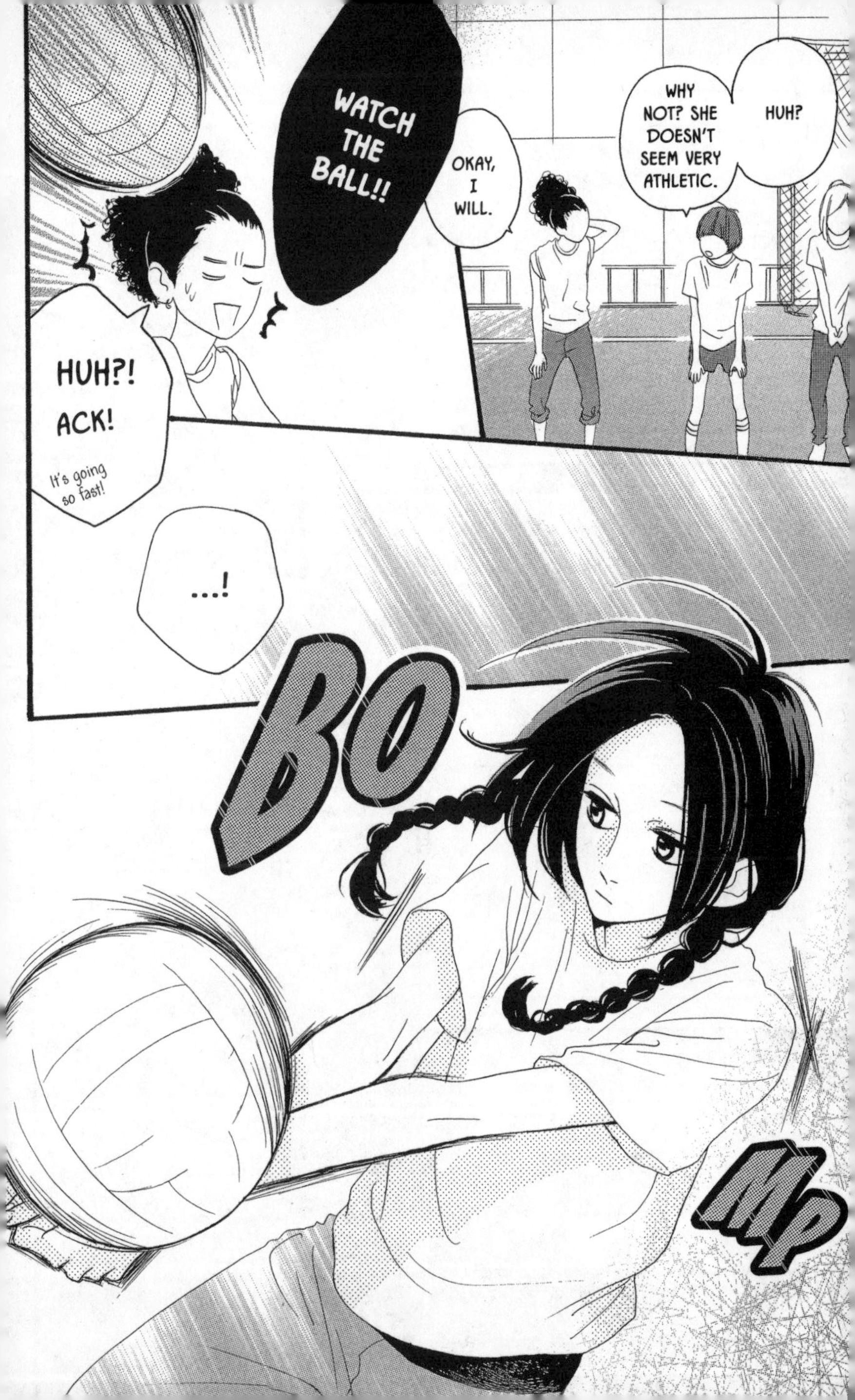
HUH?
WHY NOT? SHE DOESN'T SEEM VERY ATHLETIC.
OKAY, I WILL.
WATCH THE BALL!!
HUH?! ACK!
It's going so fast!
...!
BOMP

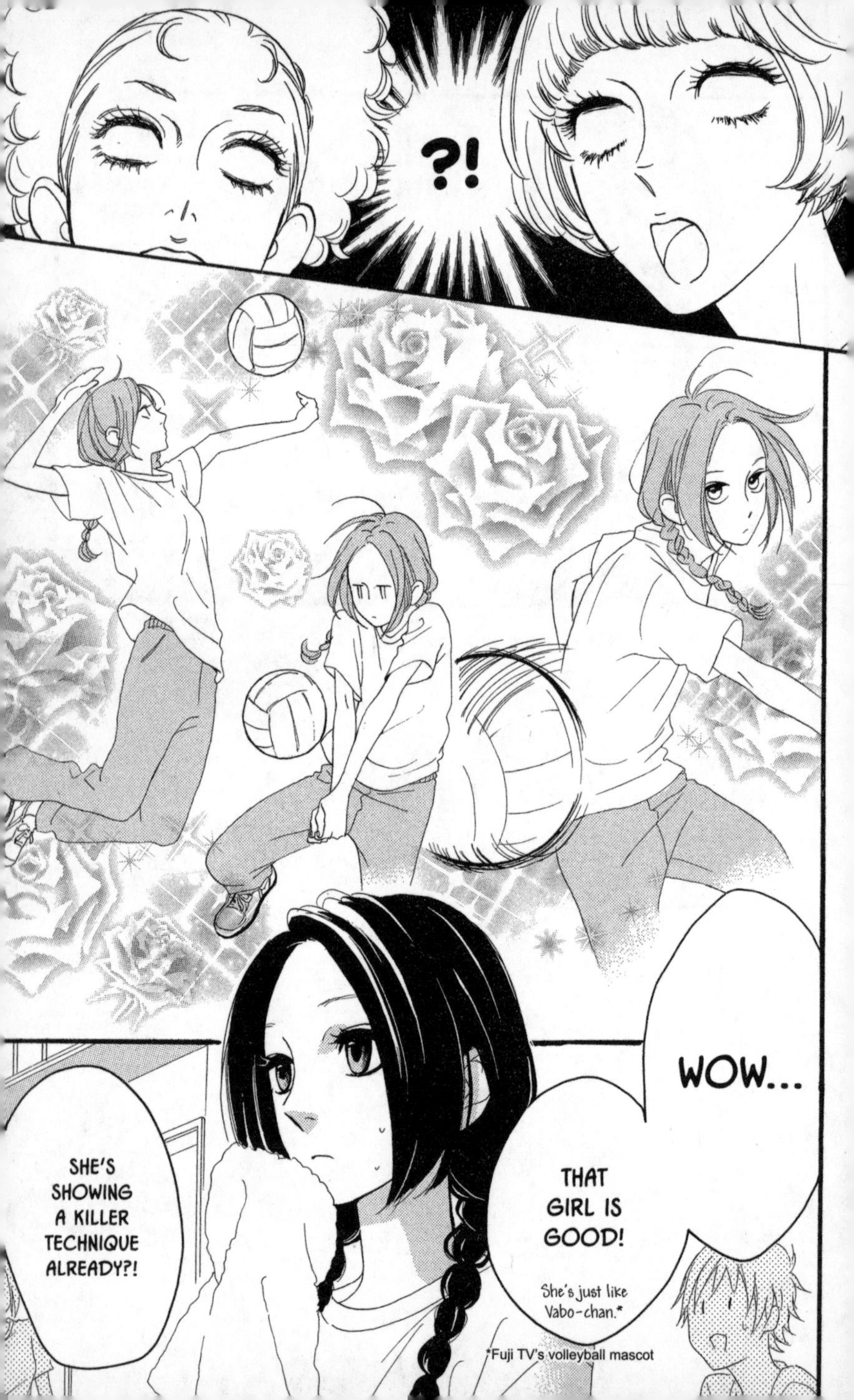
?!
WOW...
THAT GIRL IS GOOD!
She's just like Vabo-chan.*
SHE'S SHOWING A KILLER TECHNIQUE ALREADY?!
*Fuji TV's volleyball mascot

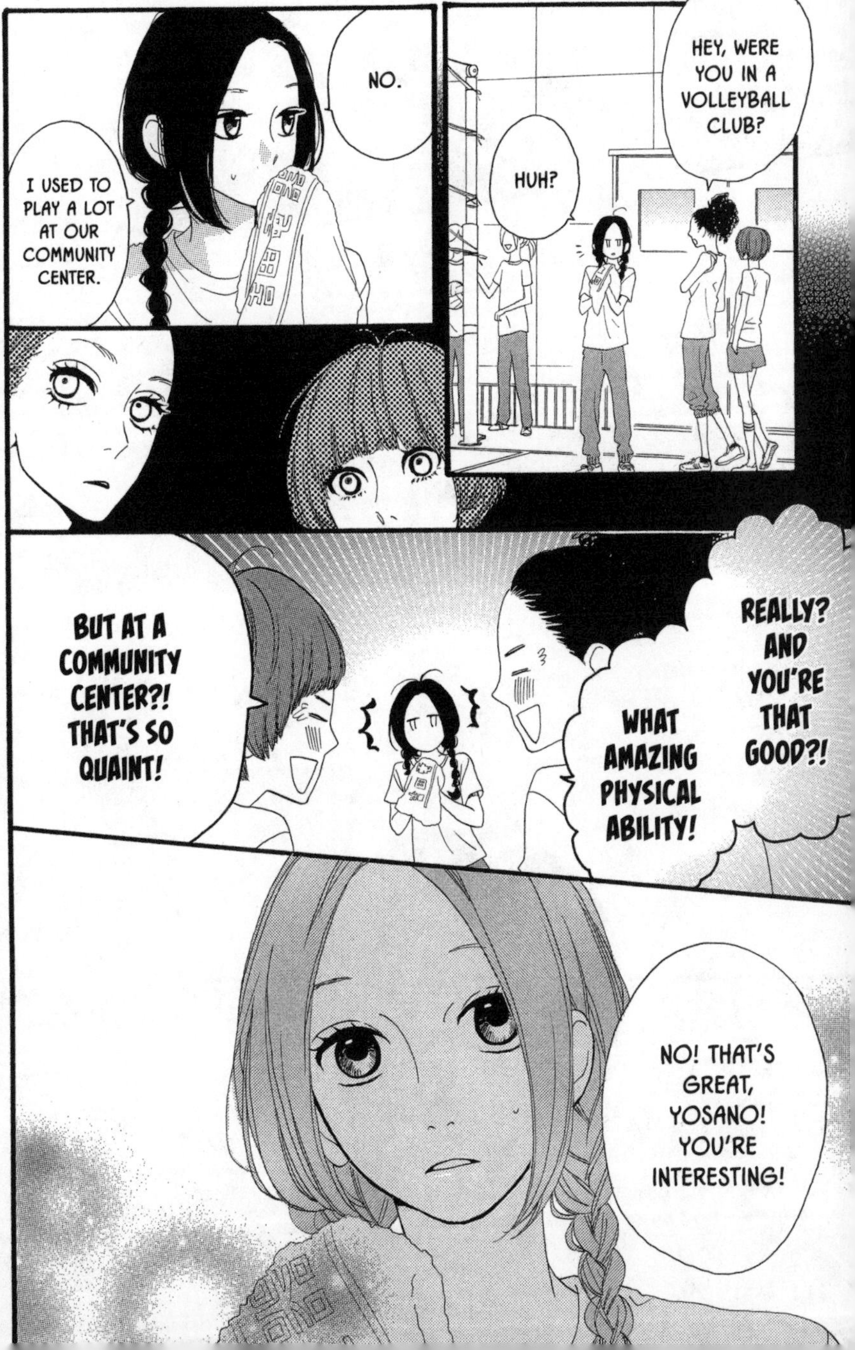
HEY, WERE YOU IN A VOLLEYBALL CLUB?
HUH?
NO.
I USED TO PLAY A LOT AT OUR COMMUNITY CENTER.
REALLY? AND YOU'RE THAT GOOD?!
WHAT AMAZING PHYSICAL ABILITY!
BUT AT A COMMUNITY CENTER?! THAT'S SO QUAINT!
NO! THAT'S GREAT, YOSANO! YOU'RE INTERESTING!

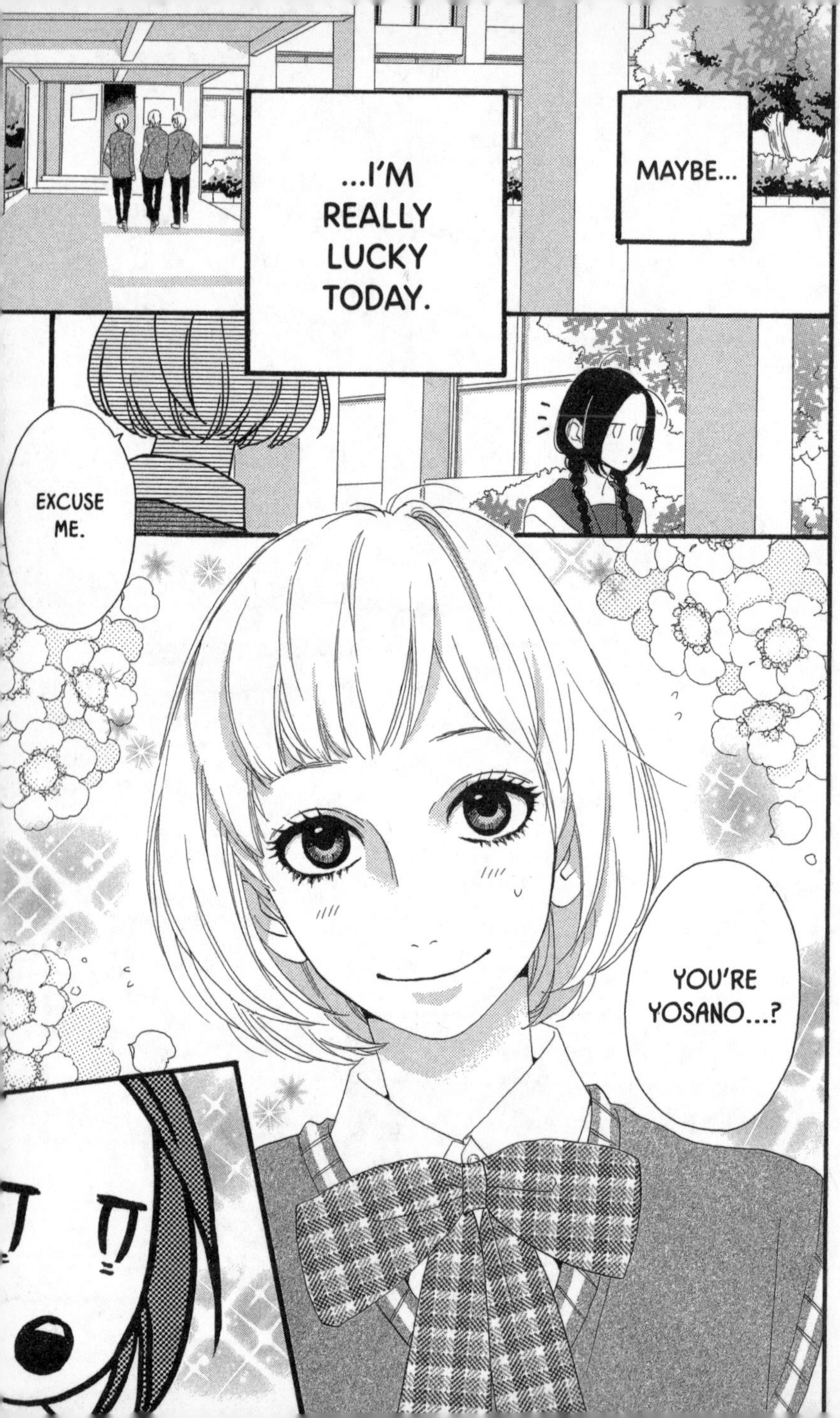
MAYBE...
...I'M REALLY LUCKY TODAY.
EXCUSE ME.
YOU'RE YOSANO...?

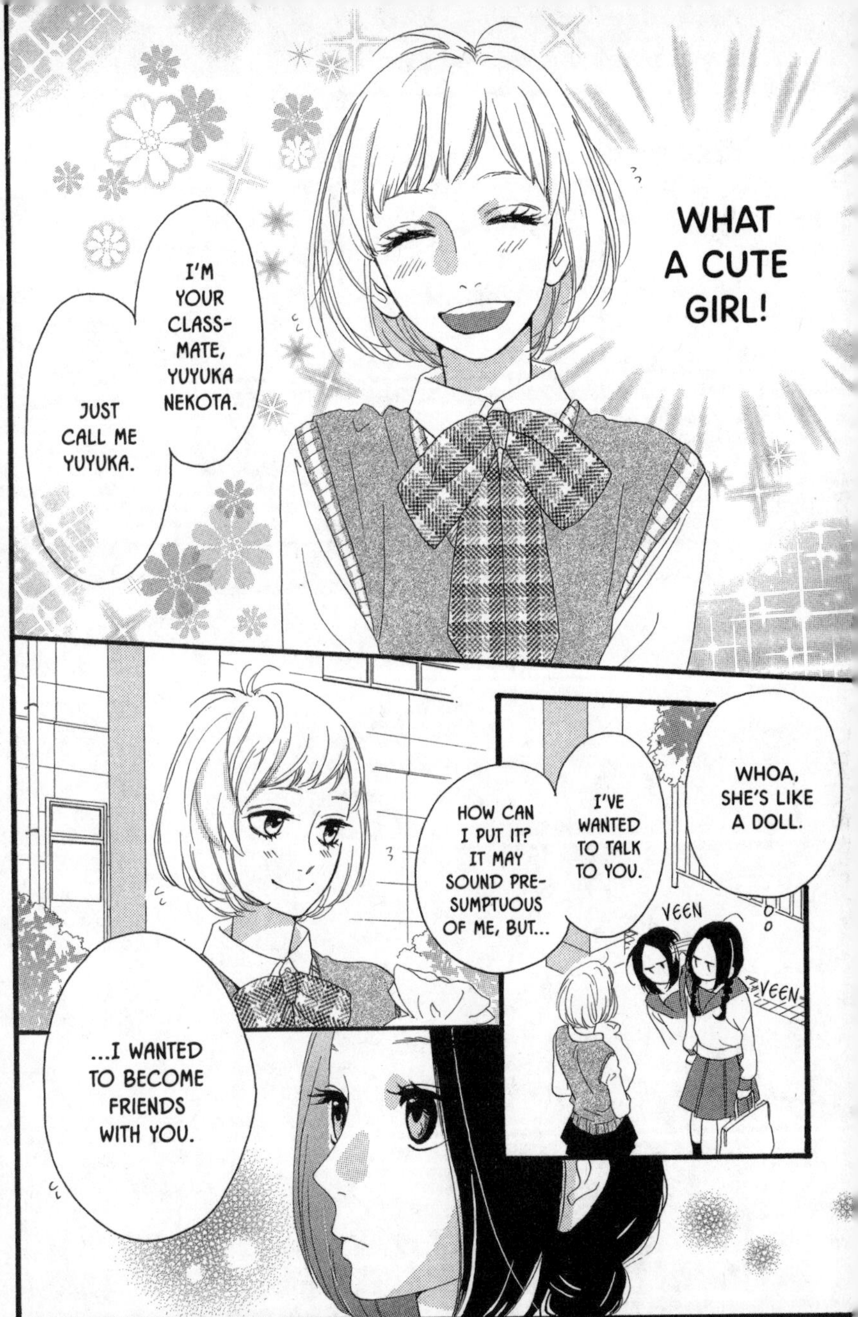
WHAT A CUTE GIRL!
I'M YOUR CLASS-MATE, YUYUKA NEKOTA.
JUST CALL ME YUYUKA.
WHOA, SHE'S LIKE A DOLL.
VEEN
VEEN
I'VE WANTED TO TALK TO YOU.
HOW CAN I PUT IT? IT MAY SOUND PRE-SUMPTUOUS OF ME, BUT...
...I WANTED TO BECOME FRIENDS WITH YOU.

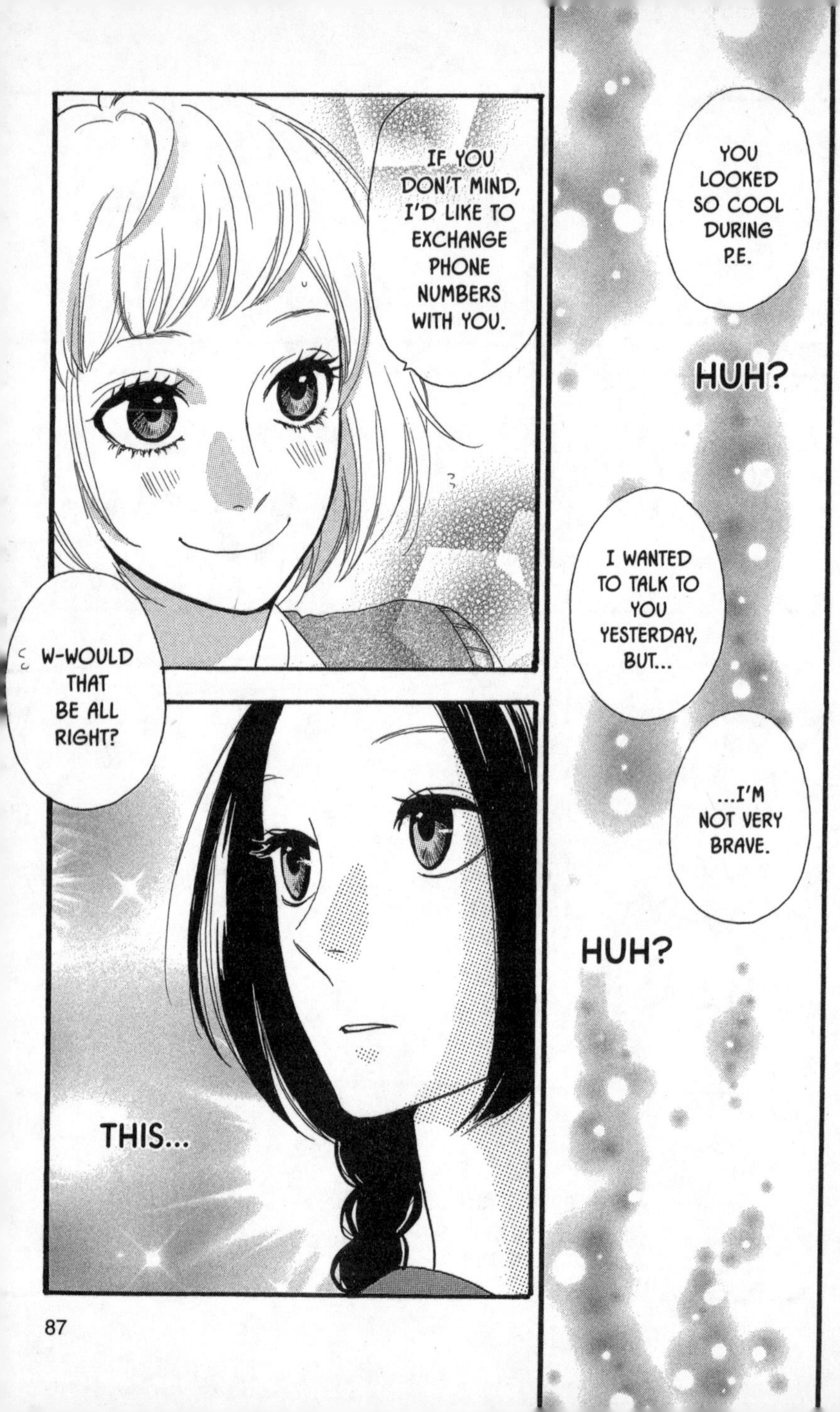
YOU LOOKED SO COOL DURING P.E.
HUH?
I WANTED TO TALK TO YOU YESTERDAY, BUT...
...I'M NOT VERY BRAVE.
HUH?
IF YOU DON'T MIND, I'D LIKE TO EXCHANGE PHONE NUMBERS WITH YOU.
W-WOULD THAT BE ALL RIGHT?
THIS...

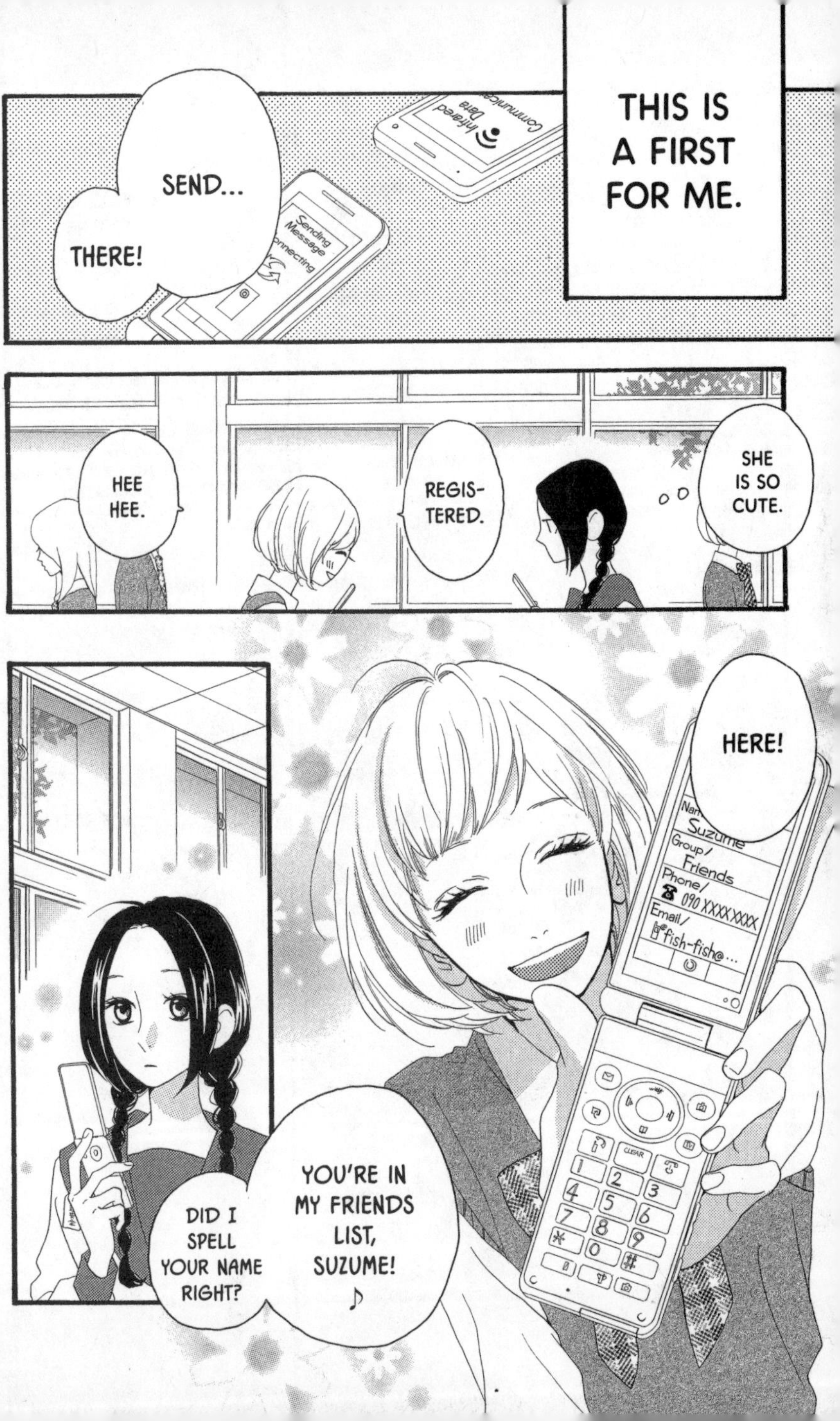
THIS IS A FIRST FOR ME.
Infrared Data
SEND...
Sending Message
THERE!
SHE IS SO CUTE.
REGIS-TERED.
HEE HEE.
HERE!
Suzume
Group/ Friends
Phone/ 090 XXXX XXXX
Email/ fish-fish@...
CLEAR
YOU'RE IN MY FRIENDS LIST, SUZUME! ♪
DID I SPELL YOUR NAME RIGHT?

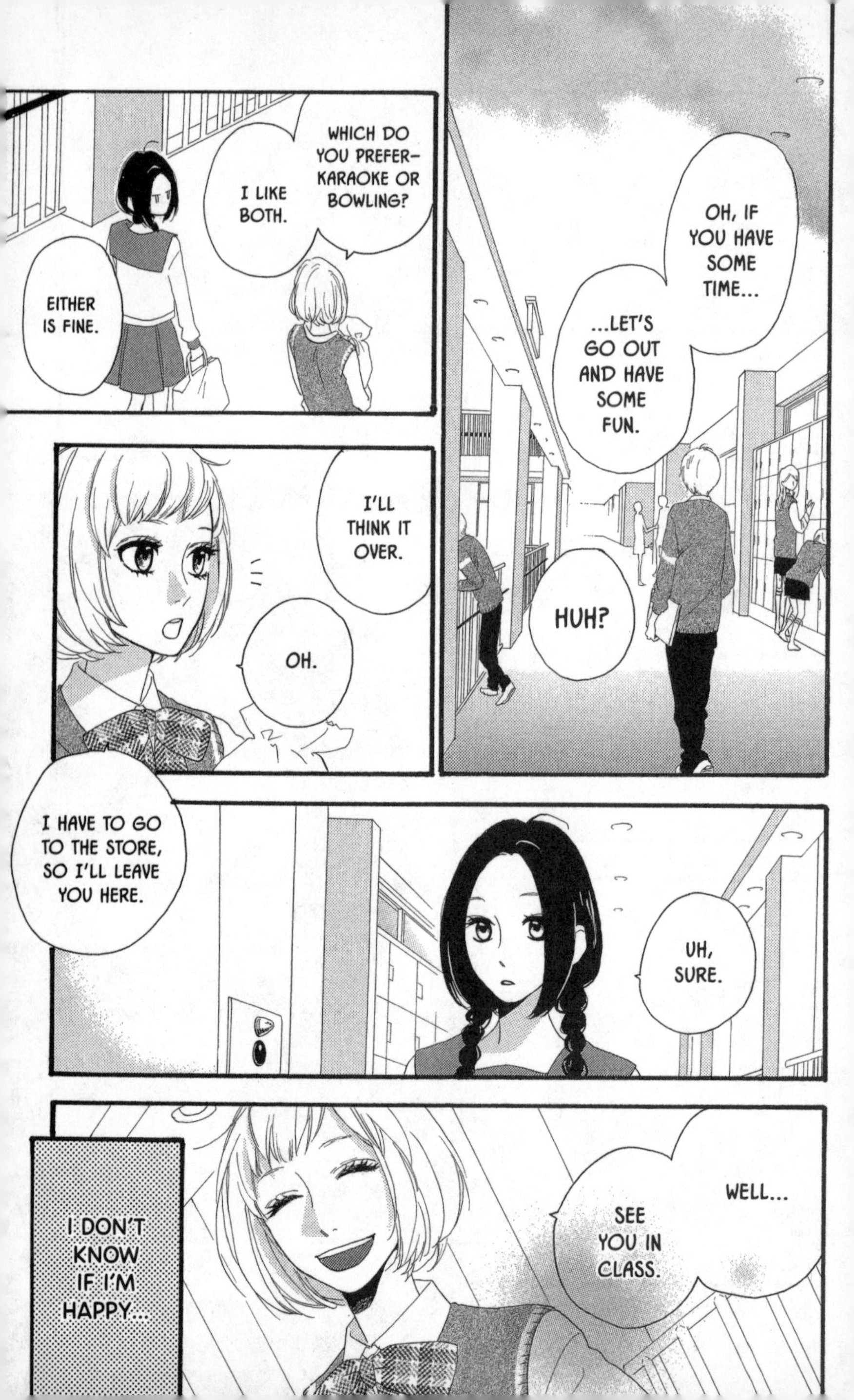
OH, IF YOU HAVE SOME TIME...
...LET'S GO OUT AND HAVE SOME FUN.
HUH?
WHICH DO YOU PREFER—KARAOKE OR BOWLING?
I LIKE BOTH.
EITHER IS FINE.
I'LL THINK IT OVER.
OH.
I HAVE TO GO TO THE STORE, SO I'LL LEAVE YOU HERE.
UH, SURE.
WELL...
SEE YOU IN CLASS.
I DON'T KNOW IF I'M HAPPY...

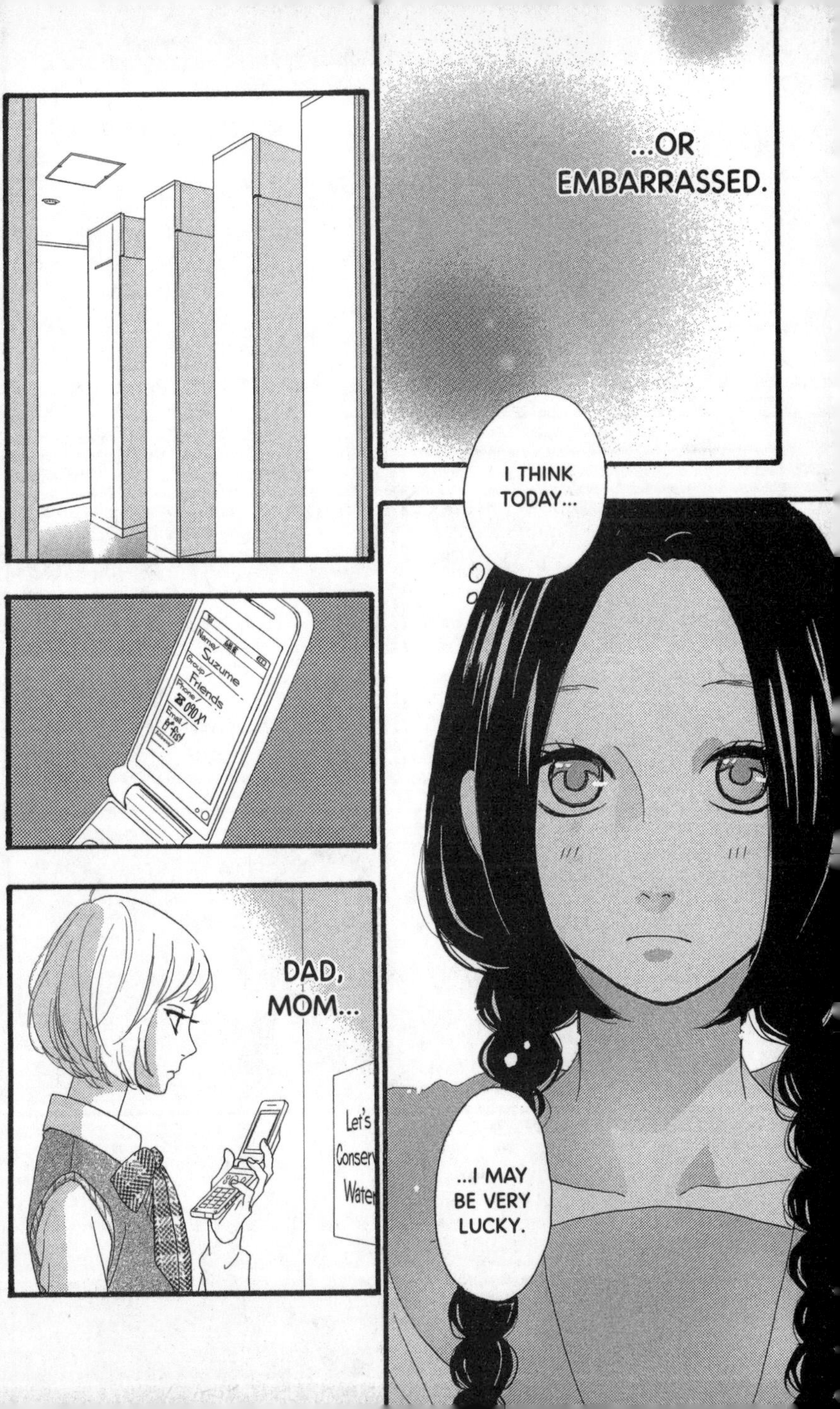
...OR EMBARRASSED.
I THINK TODAY...
...I MAY BE VERY LUCKY.
Name/ Suzume
Group/ Friends
Phone/
Email/
DAD, MOM...
Let's Conserv Wate

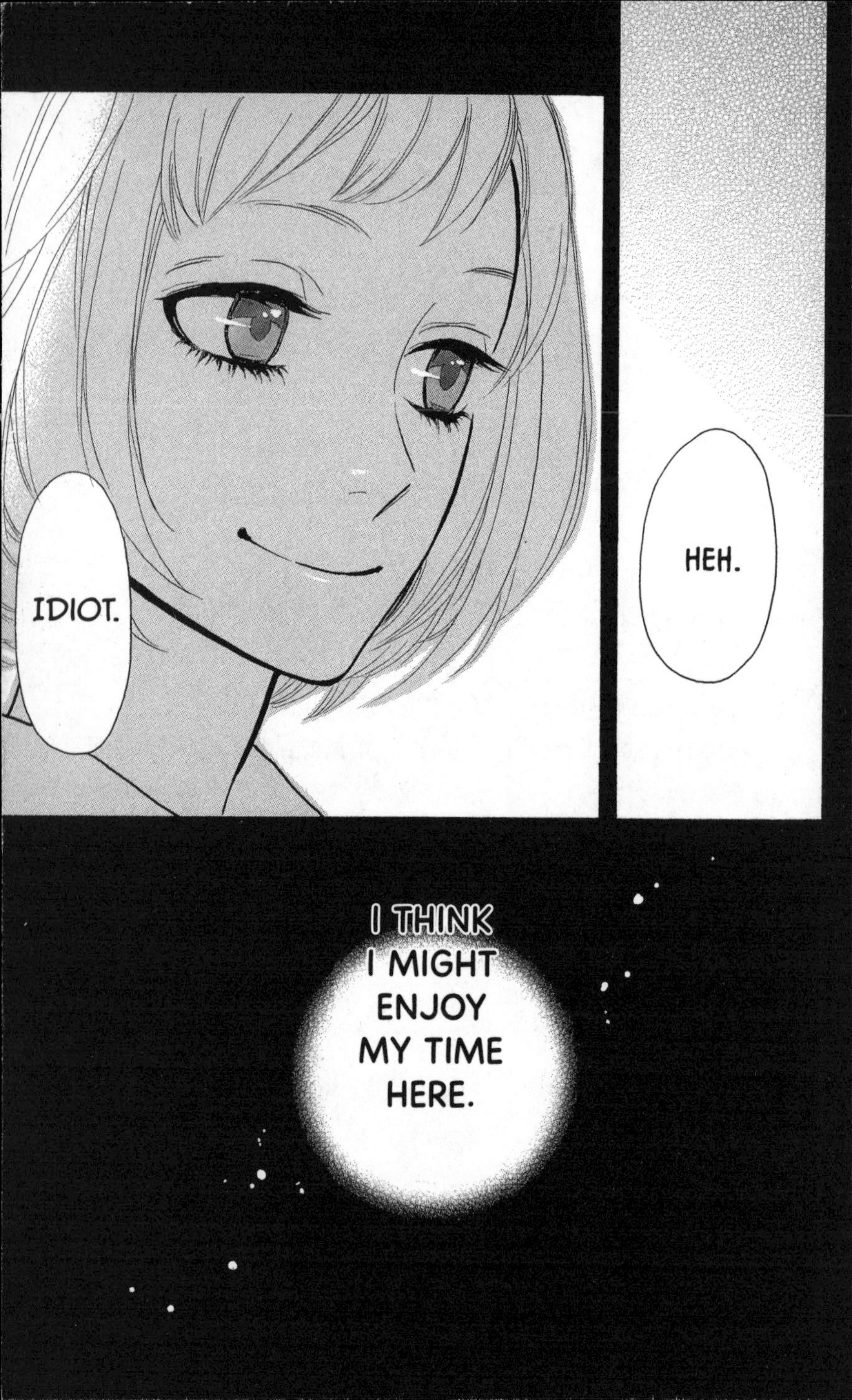
HEH.
IDIOT.
I THINK I MIGHT ENJOY MY TIME HERE.

A Little Apology...

In my afterword at the end of *Sugars,* I said I would reply to your fan letters "when I get a little time." However, I haven't answered a single one. Yikes! I'm sorry! I'm afraid I'm Japan's worst "all talk and no action" person!! I've written some responses, but I haven't sent them out yet. There are a lot in that category. (I thought it might be best to send them all at once... *mmbl mmbl*)

And so, when you send me a fan letter, please don't expect much in terms of a reply.

But your letters always fuel my energy! I've kept all your presents and drawings. ♪ Thank you very much! I sometimes end up crying out loud.

I'm sorry.

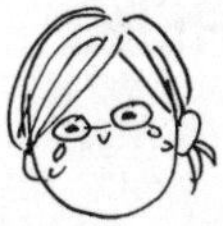

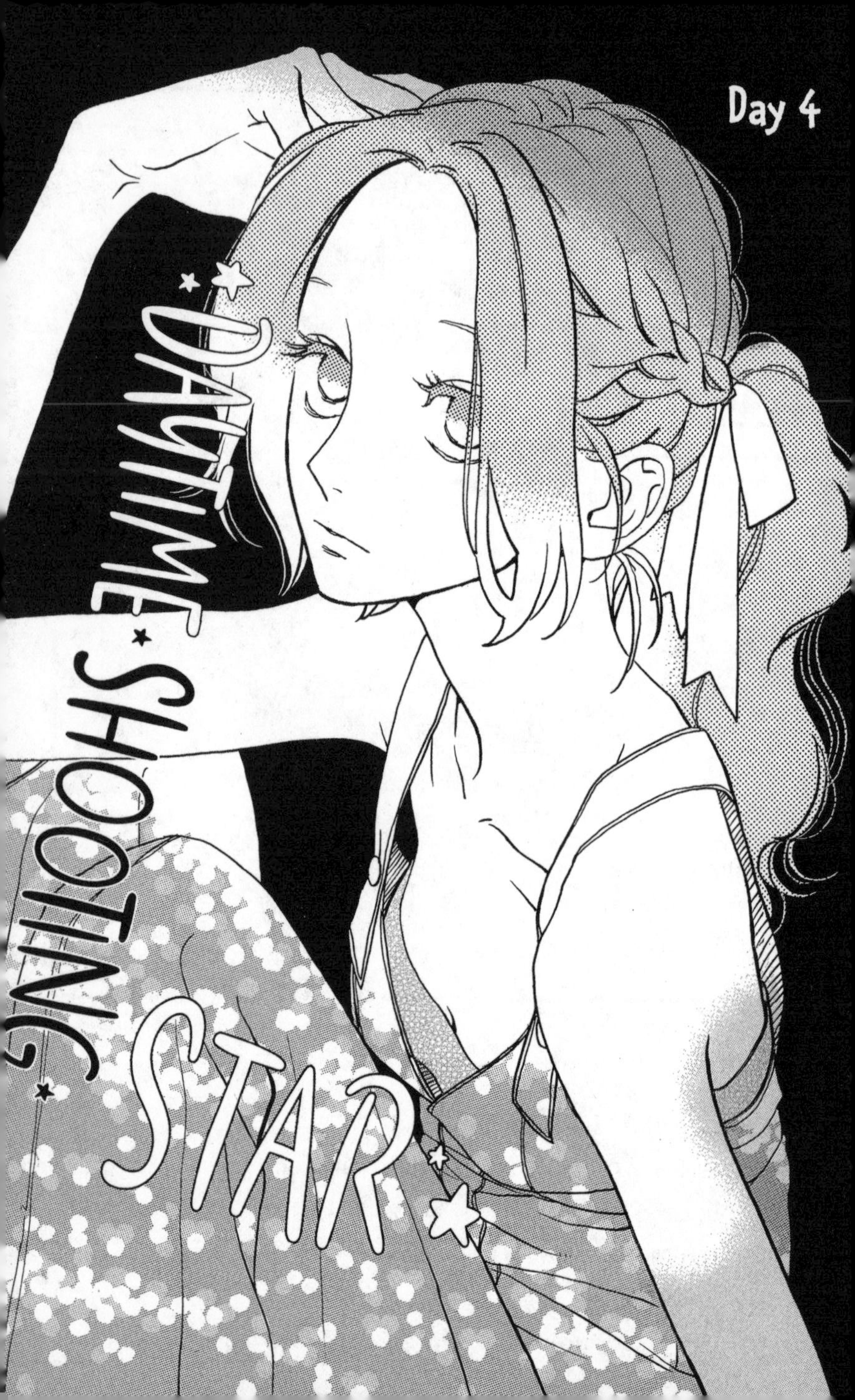
Day 4
DAYTIME SHOOTING STAR

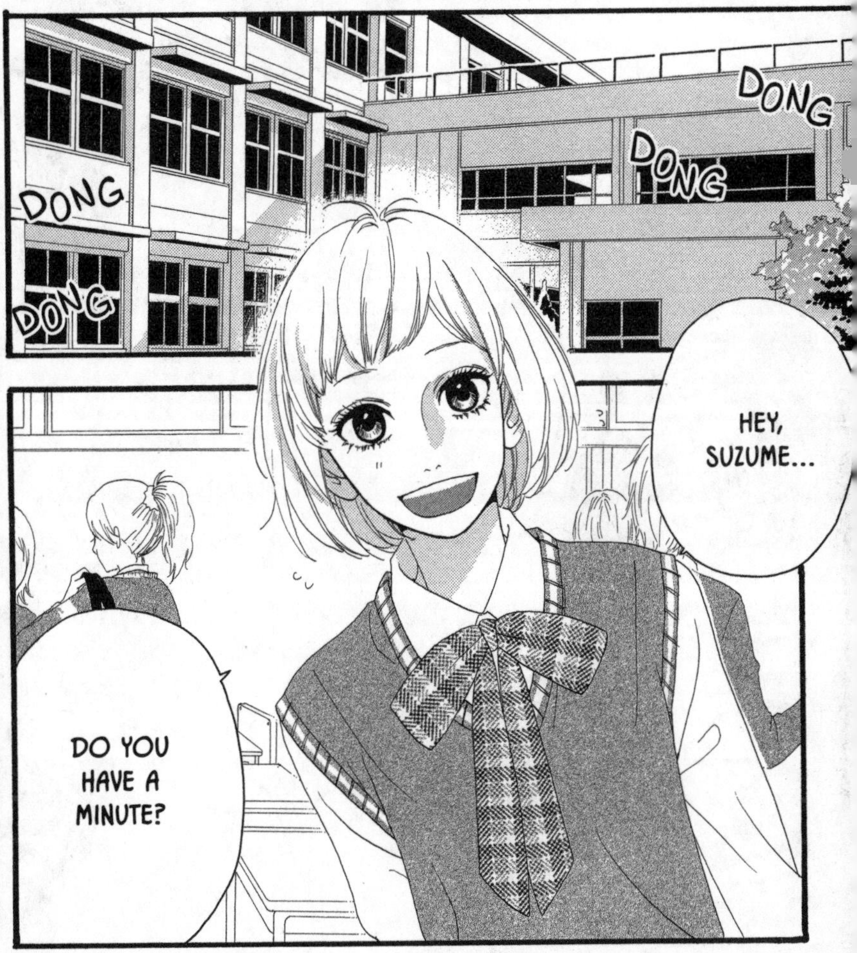
DONG
DONG
DONG
DONG
HEY, SUZUME...
DO YOU HAVE A MINUTE?

Shishio 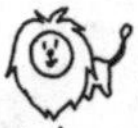 Strange, isn't this?

Birthday: October 3
Height: 5'10"
Weight: 147 lbs
Blood Type: O

① Umaibo. Katsudon.
② Smoker. Collects smooth-writing pens.
③ Suffers hangovers easily.

**Shishi* means "lion."

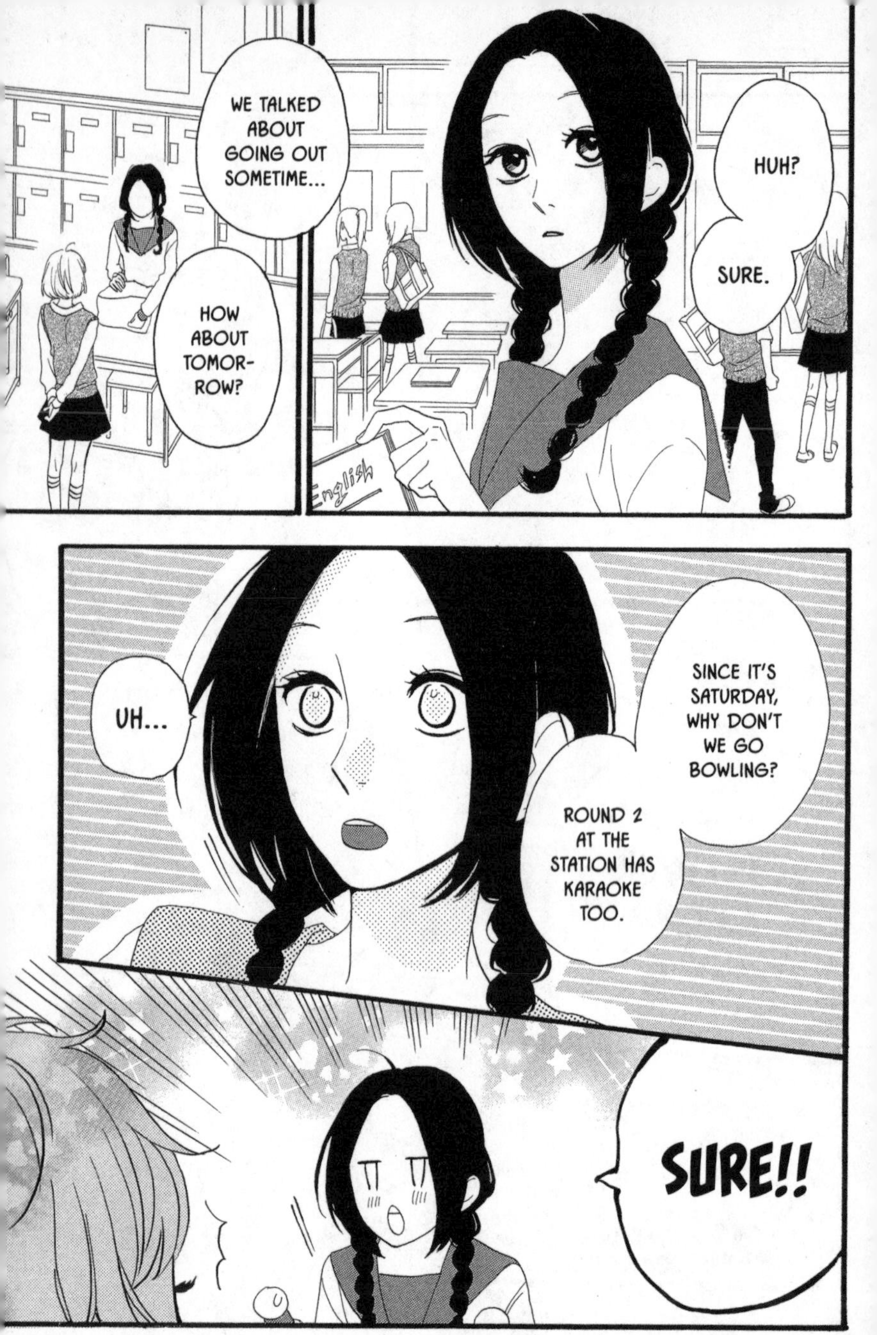
HUH?
SURE.
WE TALKED ABOUT GOING OUT SOMETIME...
HOW ABOUT TOMORROW?
SINCE IT'S SATURDAY, WHY DON'T WE GO BOWLING?
ROUND 2 AT THE STATION HAS KARAOKE TOO.
UH...
SURE!!

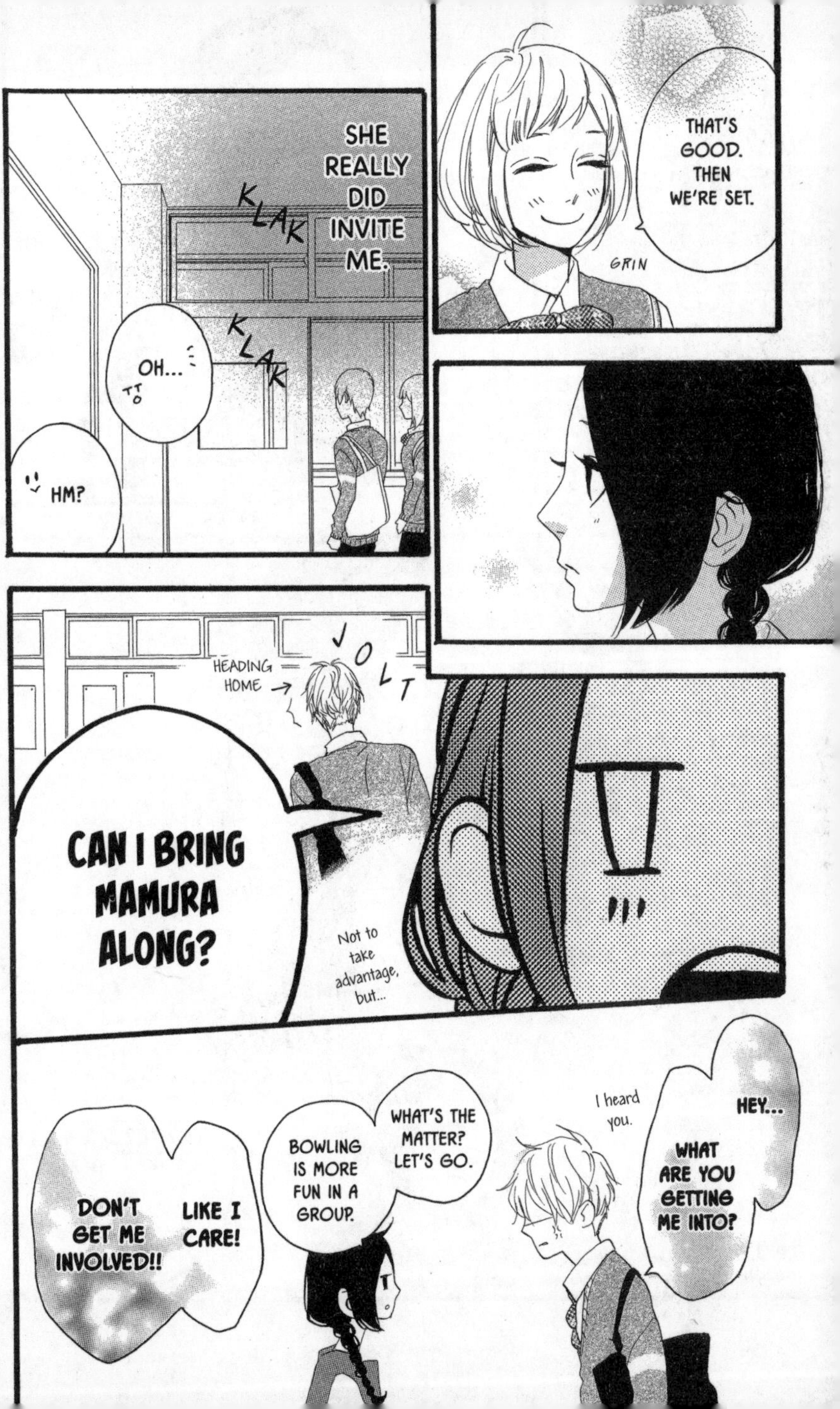
THAT'S GOOD. THEN WE'RE SET.
GRIN
SHE REALLY DID INVITE ME.
KLAK
KLAK
OH...
HM?
CAN I BRING MAMURA ALONG?
Not to take advantage, but...
HEADING HOME
JOLT
HEY...
WHAT ARE YOU GETTING ME INTO?
I heard you.
WHAT'S THE MATTER? LET'S GO.
BOWLING IS MORE FUN IN A GROUP.
LIKE I CARE!
DON'T GET ME INVOLVED!!

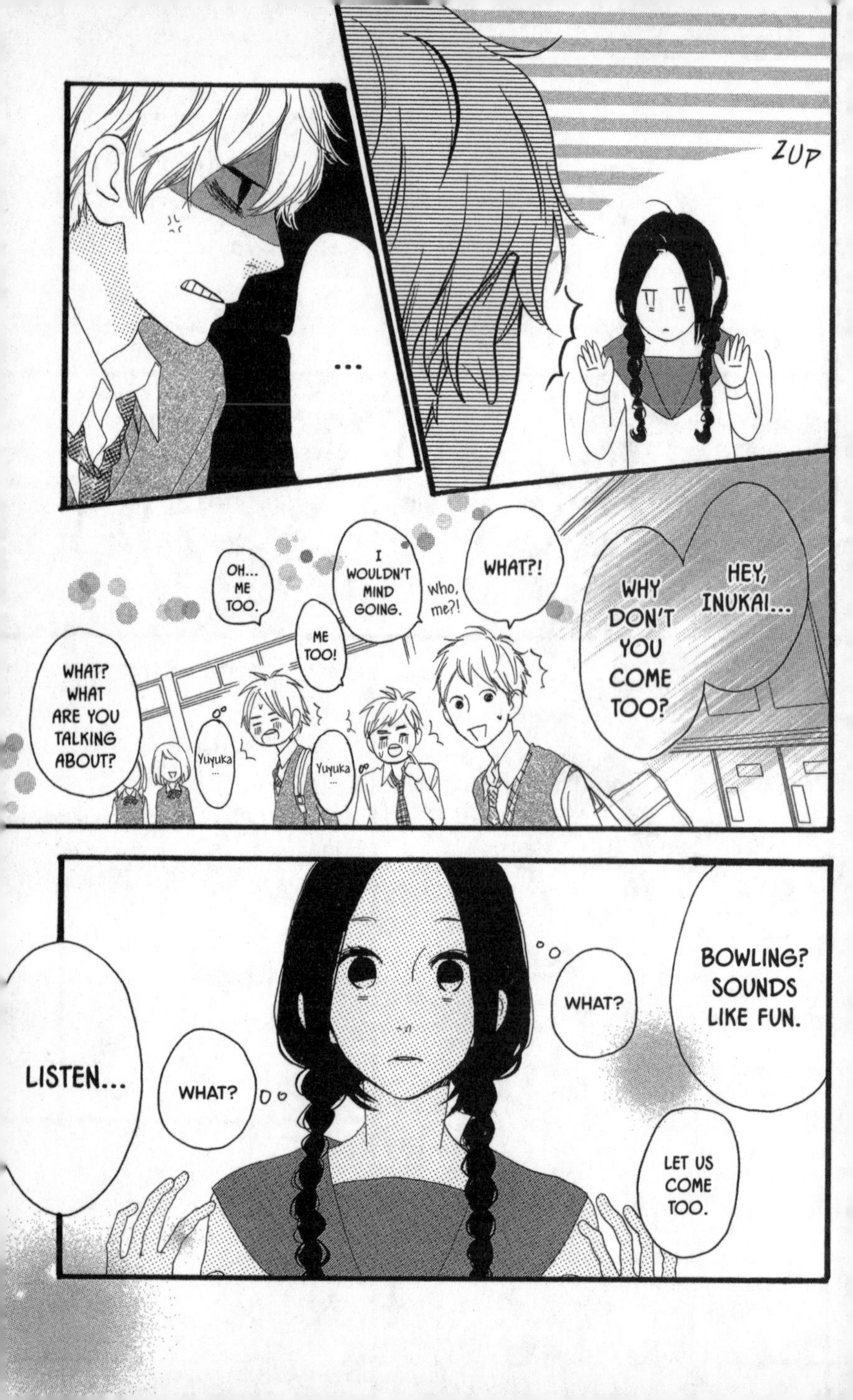
ZUP
...
HEY, INUKAI... WHY DON'T YOU COME TOO?
WHAT?!
Who, me?!
I WOULDN'T MIND GOING.
OH... ME TOO.
ME TOO!
Yuyuka...
Yuyuka...
WHAT? WHAT ARE YOU TALKING ABOUT?
BOWLING? SOUNDS LIKE FUN.
LET US COME TOO.
WHAT?
WHAT?
LISTEN...

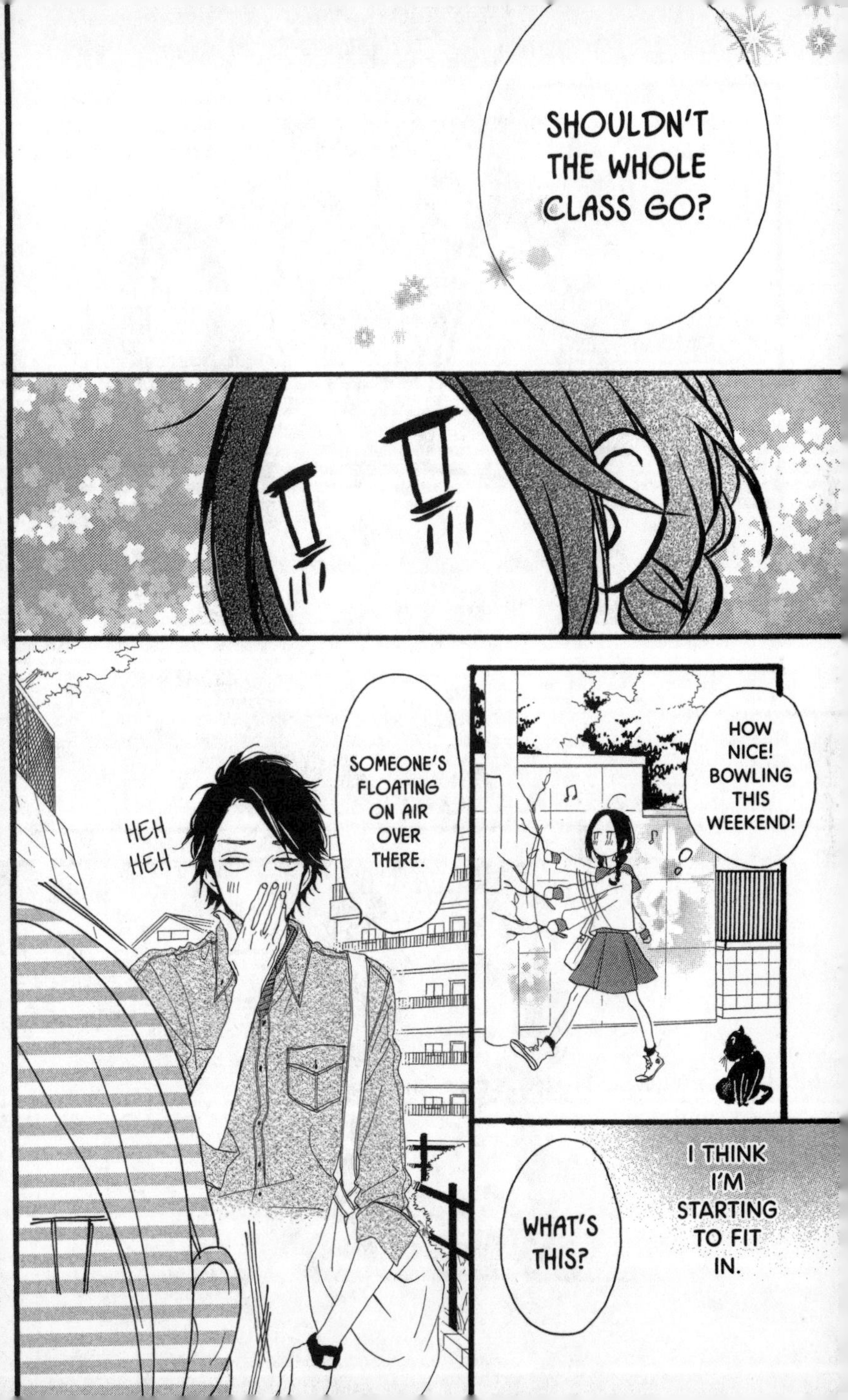
SHOULDN'T THE WHOLE CLASS GO?
HOW NICE! BOWLING THIS WEEKEND!
I THINK I'M STARTING TO FIT IN.
WHAT'S THIS?
SOMEONE'S FLOATING ON AIR OVER THERE.
HEH HEH

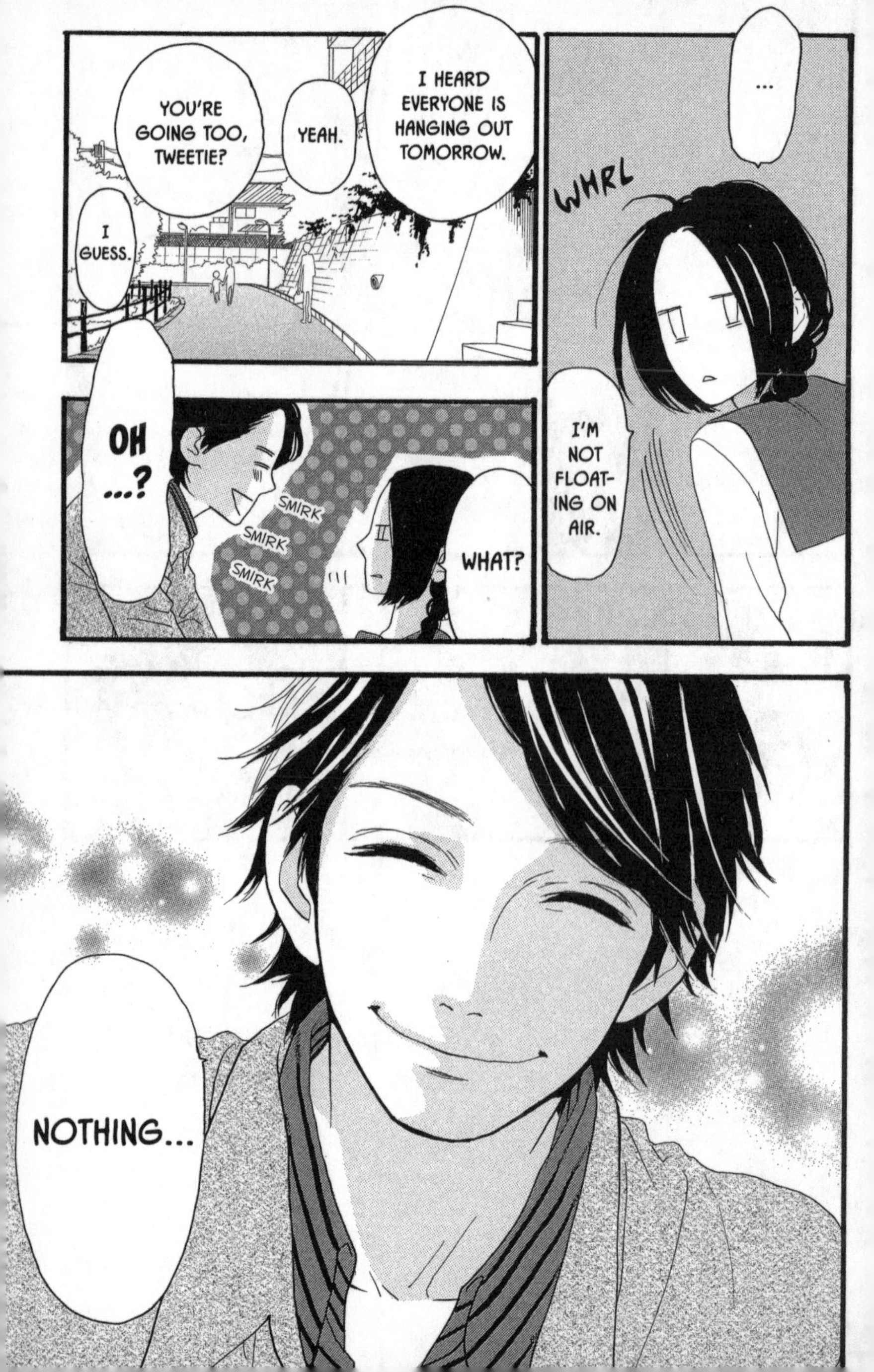
...
WHRL
I'M NOT FLOATING ON AIR.
I HEARD EVERYONE IS HANGING OUT TOMORROW.
YEAH.
YOU'RE GOING TOO, TWEETIE?
I GUESS.
WHAT?
SMIRK
SMIRK
SMIRK
OH ...?
NOTHING...

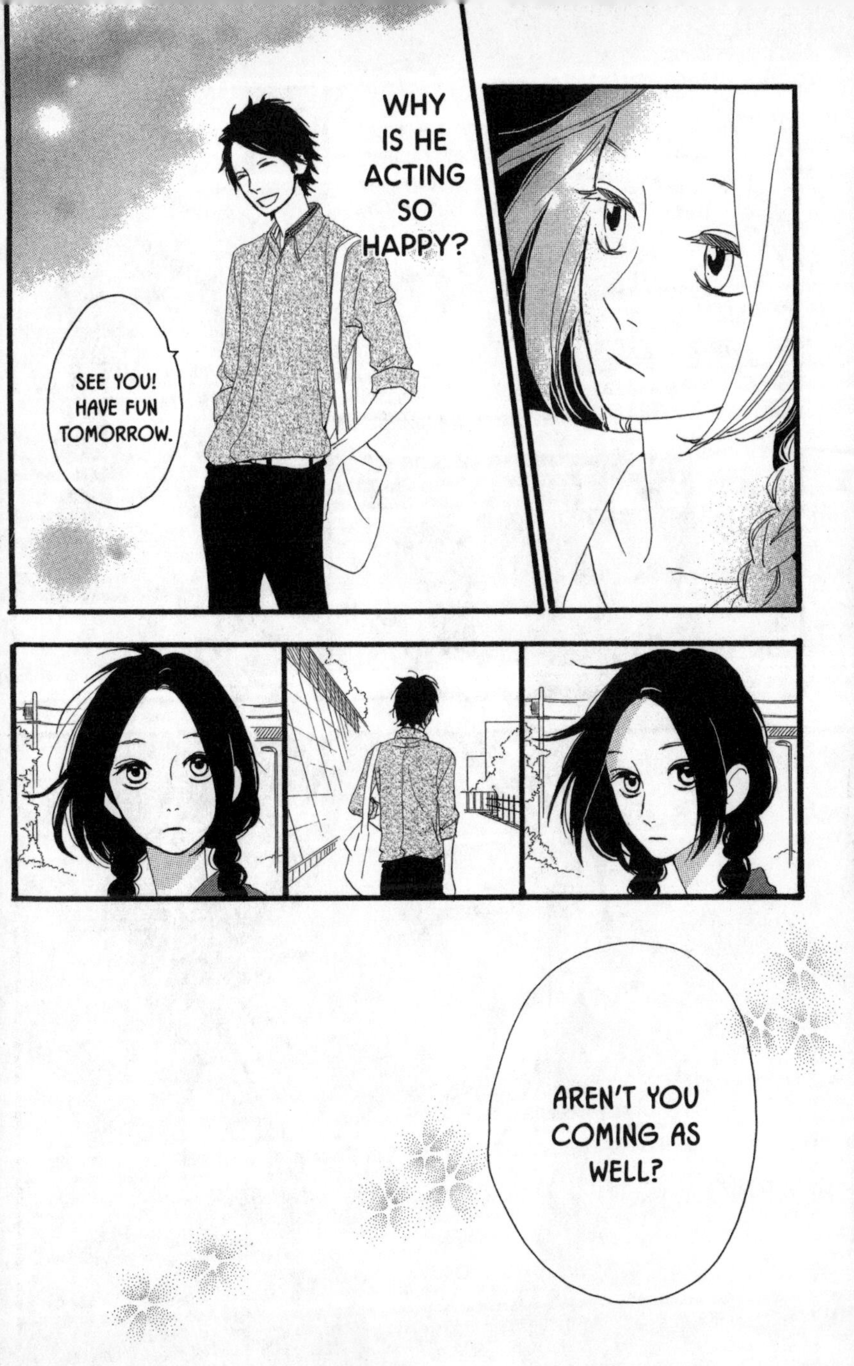
WHY IS HE ACTING SO HAPPY?
SEE YOU! HAVE FUN TOMORROW.
AREN'T YOU COMING AS WELL?

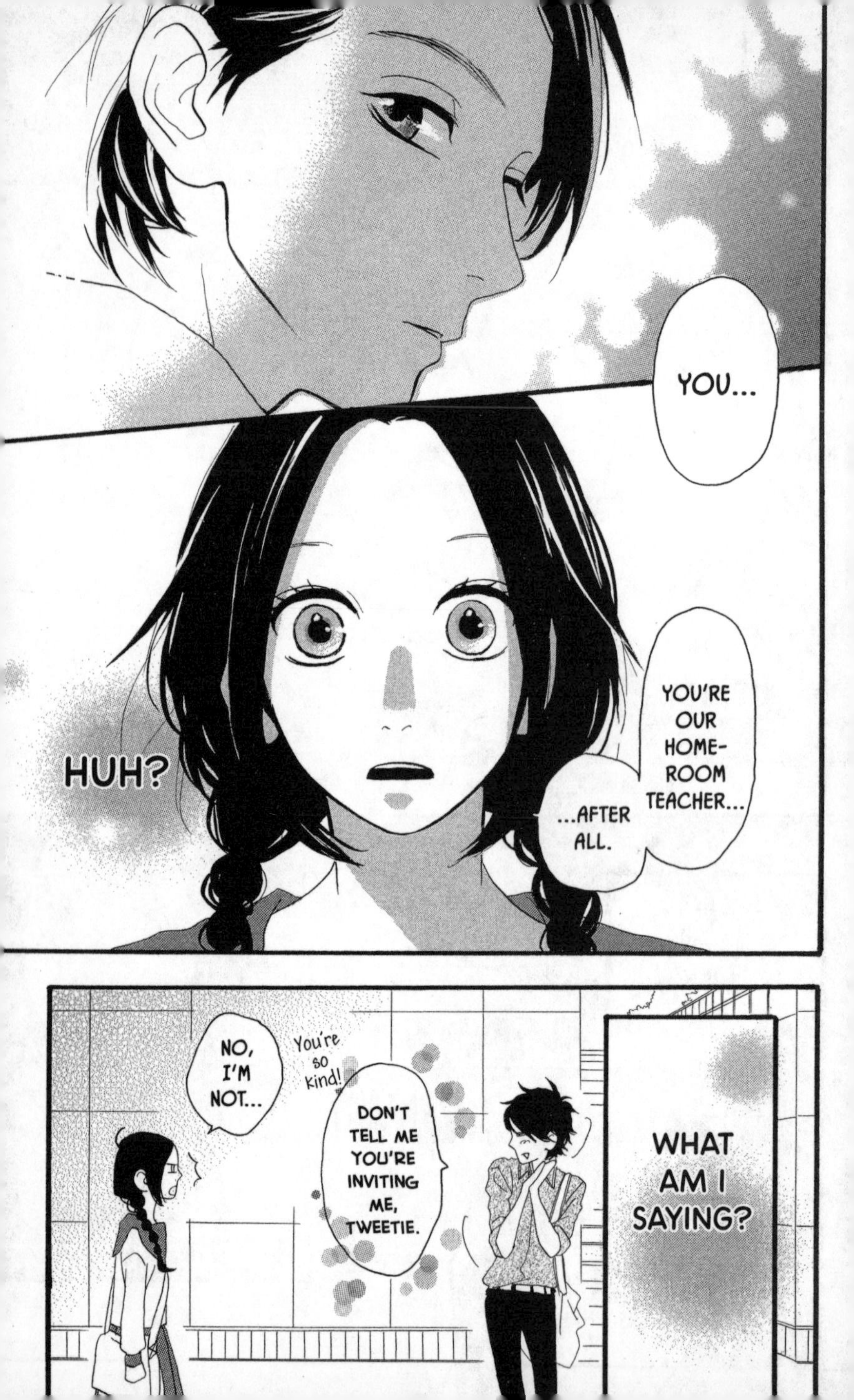

YOU...
YOU'RE OUR HOME-ROOM TEACHER...
...AFTER ALL.
HUH?
WHAT AM I SAYING?
DON'T TELL ME YOU'RE INVITING ME, TWEETIE.
You're so kind!
NO, I'M NOT...

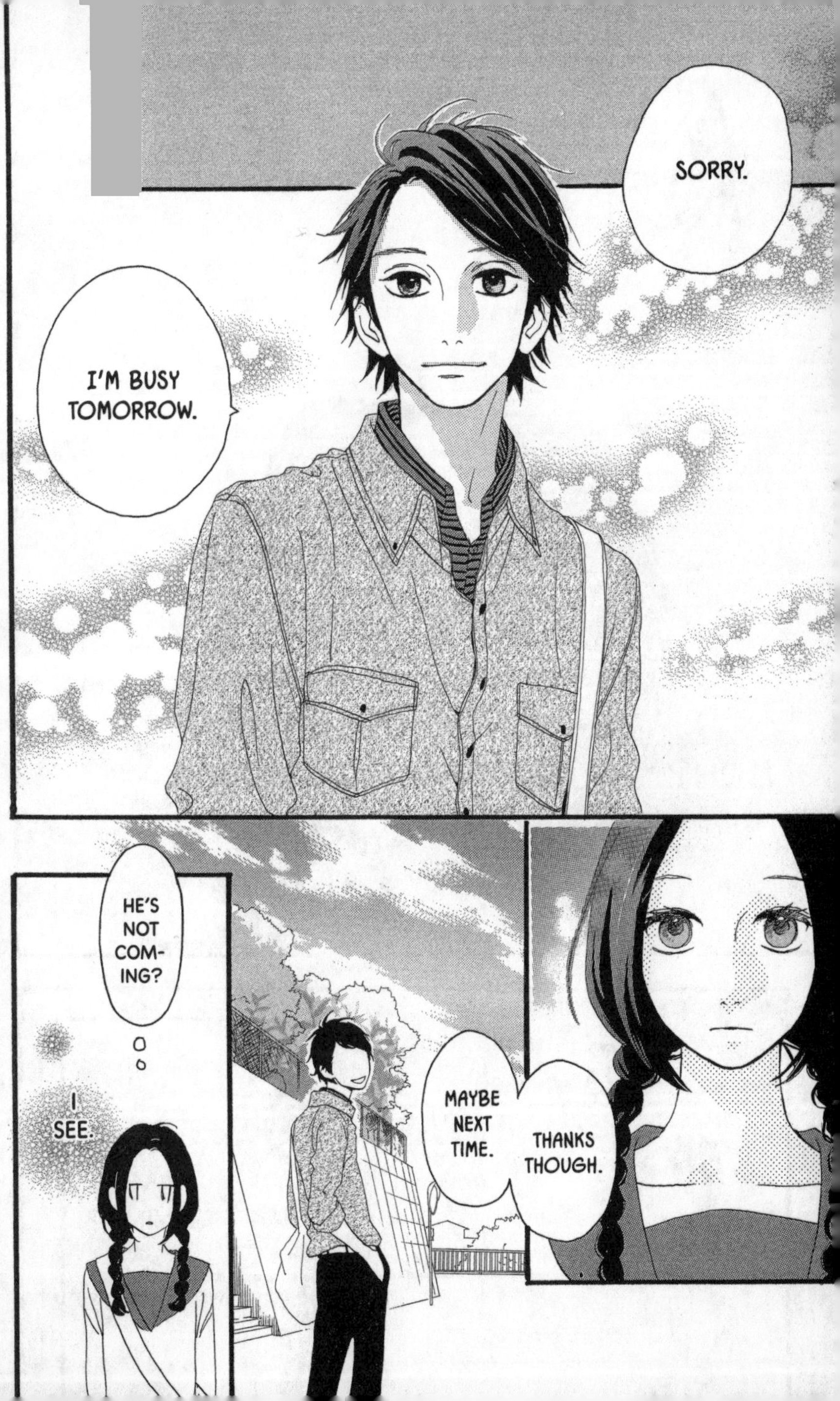
SORRY.
I'M BUSY TOMORROW.
MAYBE NEXT TIME. THANKS THOUGH.
HE'S NOT COMING?
I SEE.

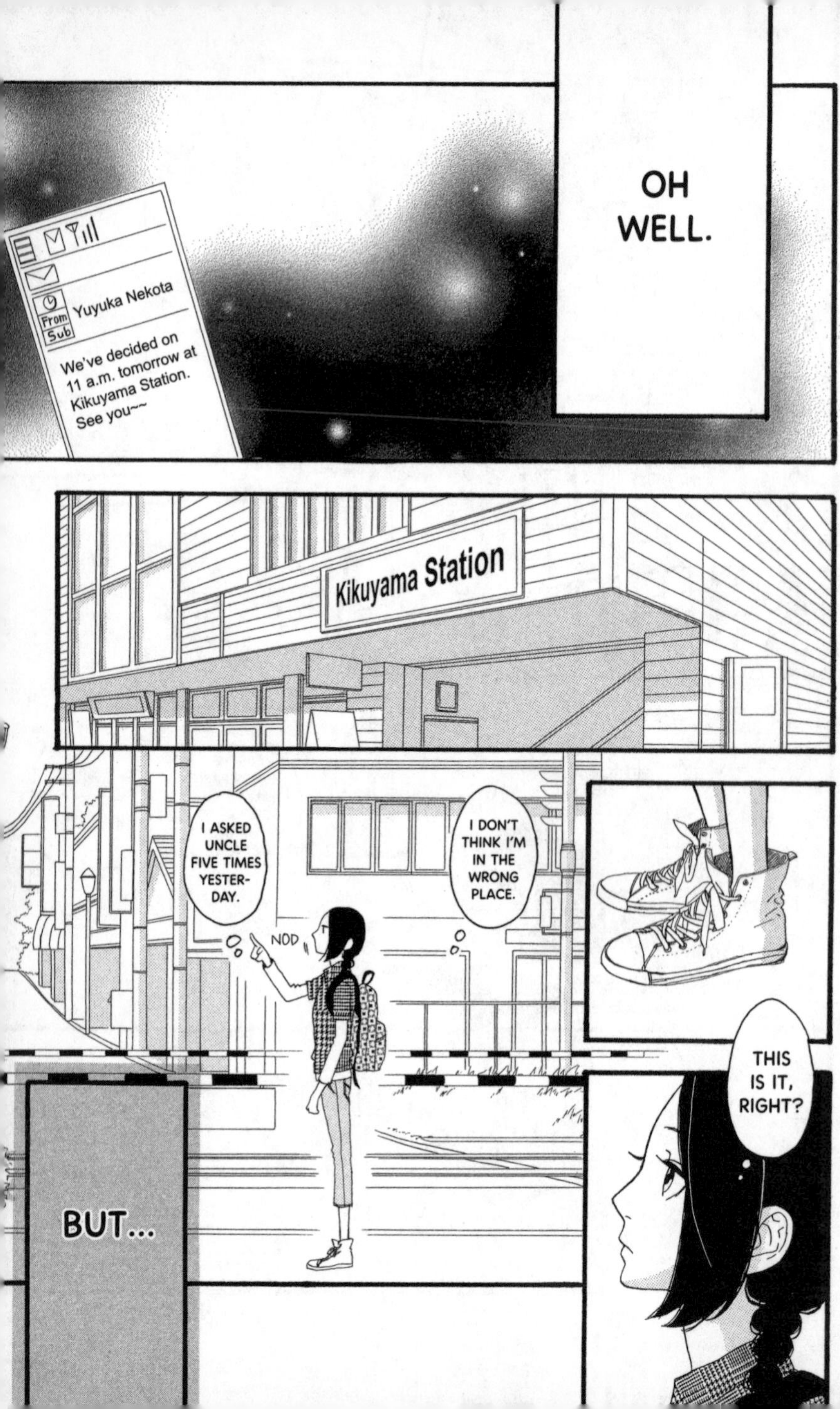

OH WELL.
Yuyuka Nekota
From
Sub
We've decided on 11 a.m. tomorrow at Kikuyama Station. See you~~
Kikuyama Station
THIS IS IT, RIGHT?
I DON'T THINK I'M IN THE WRONG PLACE.
NOD
I ASKED UNCLE FIVE TIMES YESTER-DAY.
BUT...

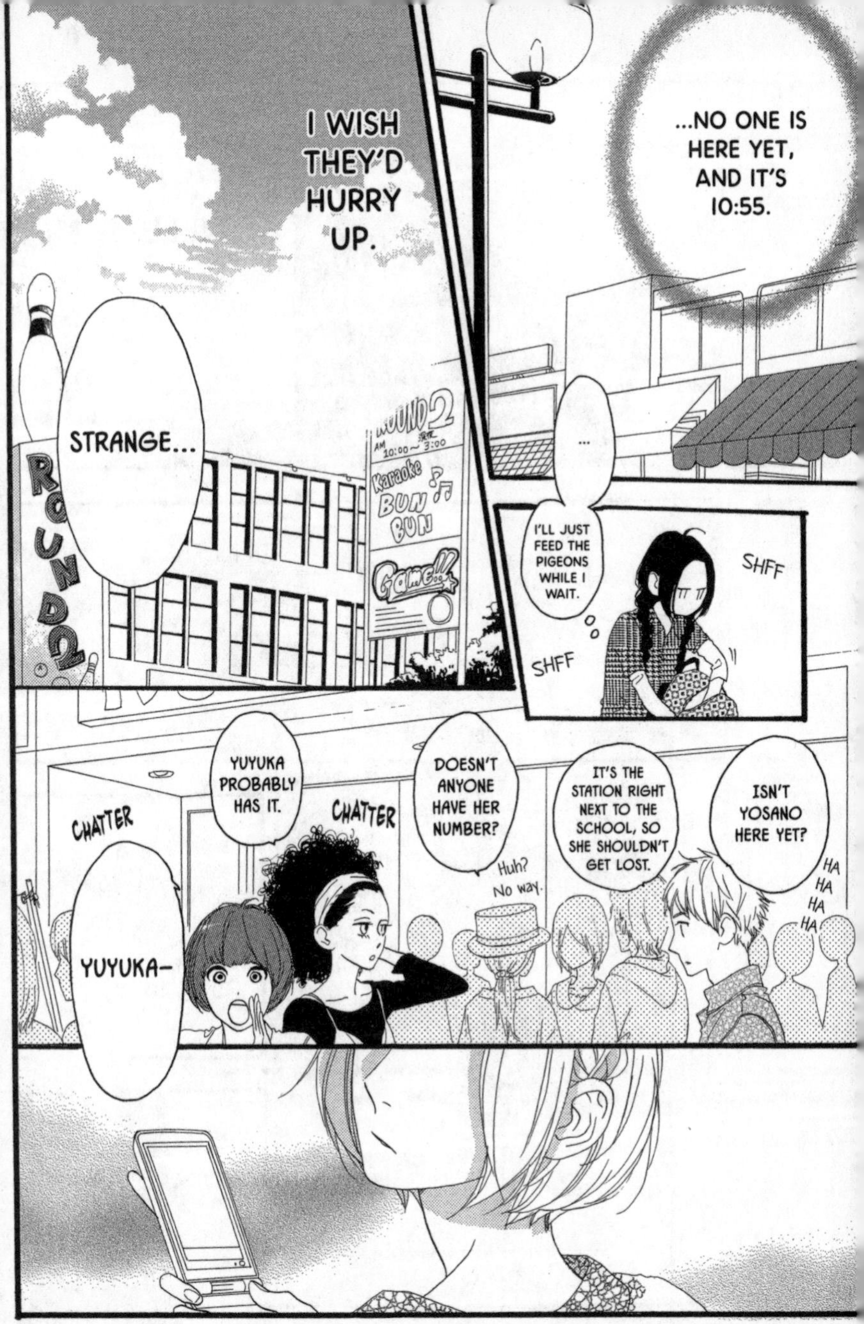

...NO ONE IS HERE YET, AND IT'S 10:55.
...
I'LL JUST FEED THE PIGEONS WHILE I WAIT.
SHFF
SHFF
I WISH THEY'D HURRY UP.
STRANGE...
ISN'T YOSANO HERE YET?
HA HA HA HA
IT'S THE STATION RIGHT NEXT TO THE SCHOOL, SO SHE SHOULDN'T GET LOST.
Huh? No way.
DOESN'T ANYONE HAVE HER NUMBER?
CHATTER
YUYUKA PROBABLY HAS IT.
CHATTER
YUYUKA–

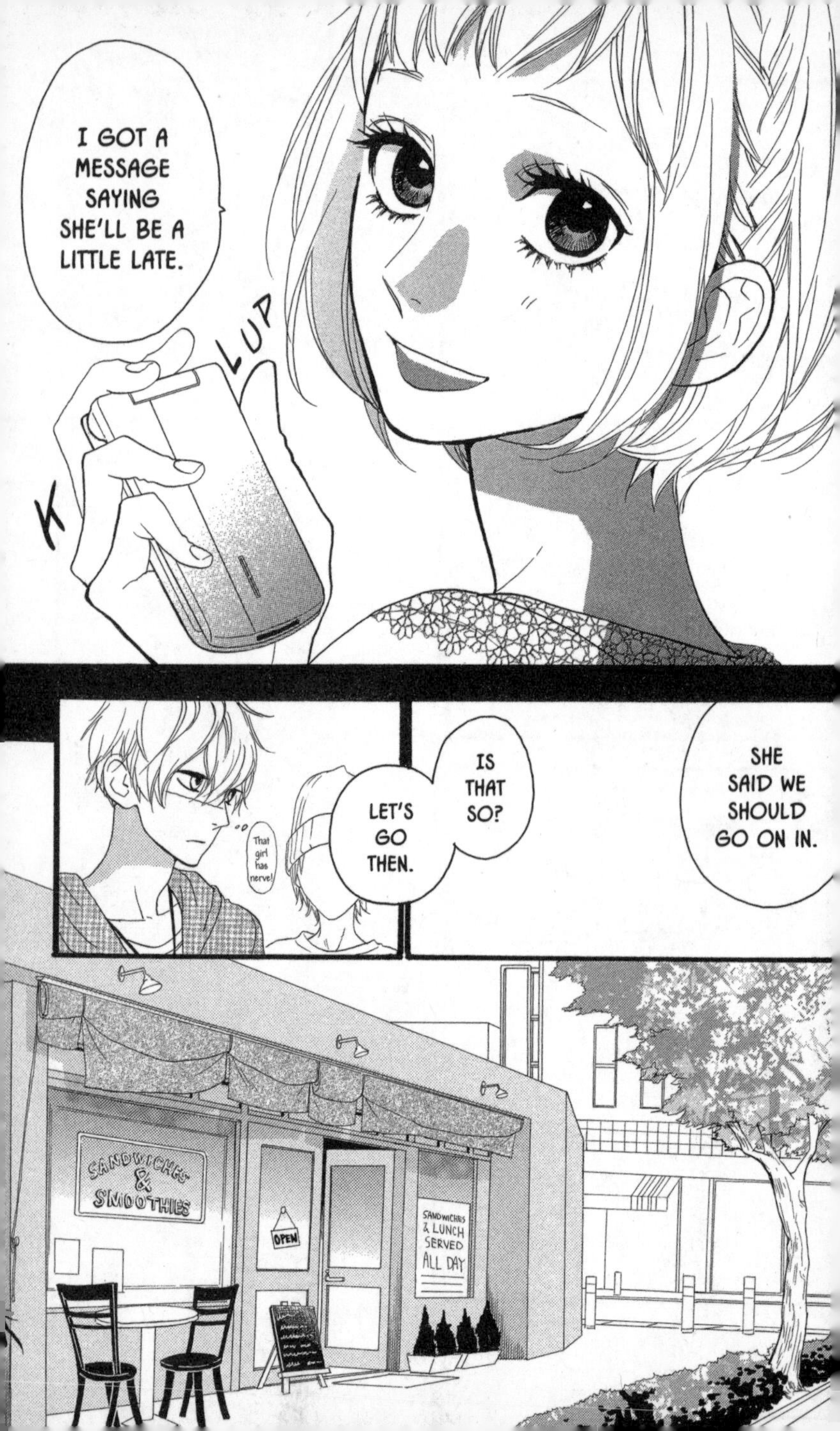
I GOT A MESSAGE SAYING SHE'LL BE A LITTLE LATE.
KLUP
SHE SAID WE SHOULD GO ON IN.
IS THAT SO?
LET'S GO THEN.
That girl has nerve!
SANDWICHES & SMOOTHIES
OPEN
SANDWICHES & LUNCH SERVED ALL DAY

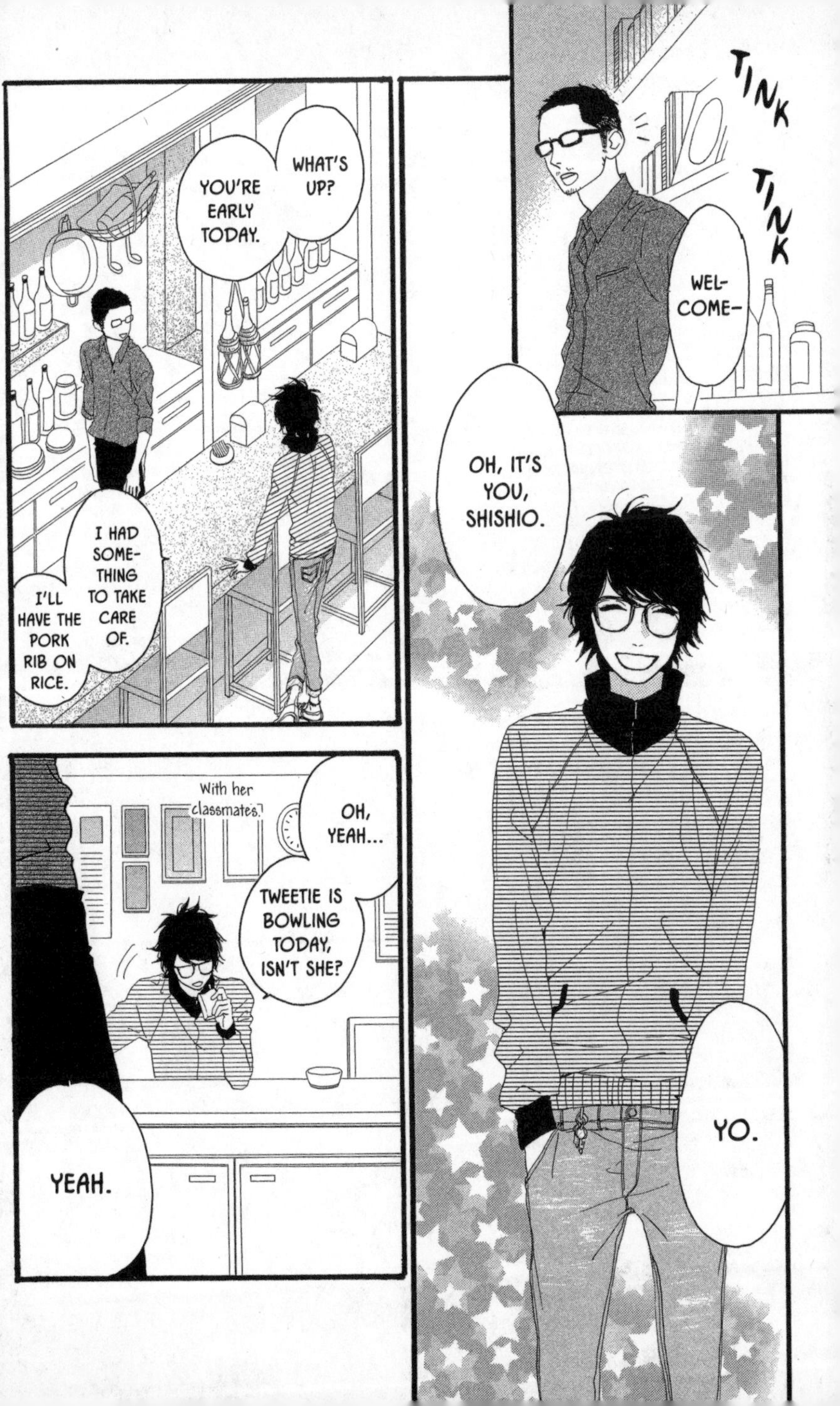
TINK
TINK
WEL-COME—
OH, IT'S YOU, SHISHIO.
YO.
WHAT'S UP?
YOU'RE EARLY TODAY.
I HAD SOME-THING TO TAKE CARE OF.
I'LL HAVE THE PORK RIB ON RICE.
OH, YEAH...
TWEETIE IS BOWLING TODAY, ISN'T SHE?
With her classmates.
YEAH.

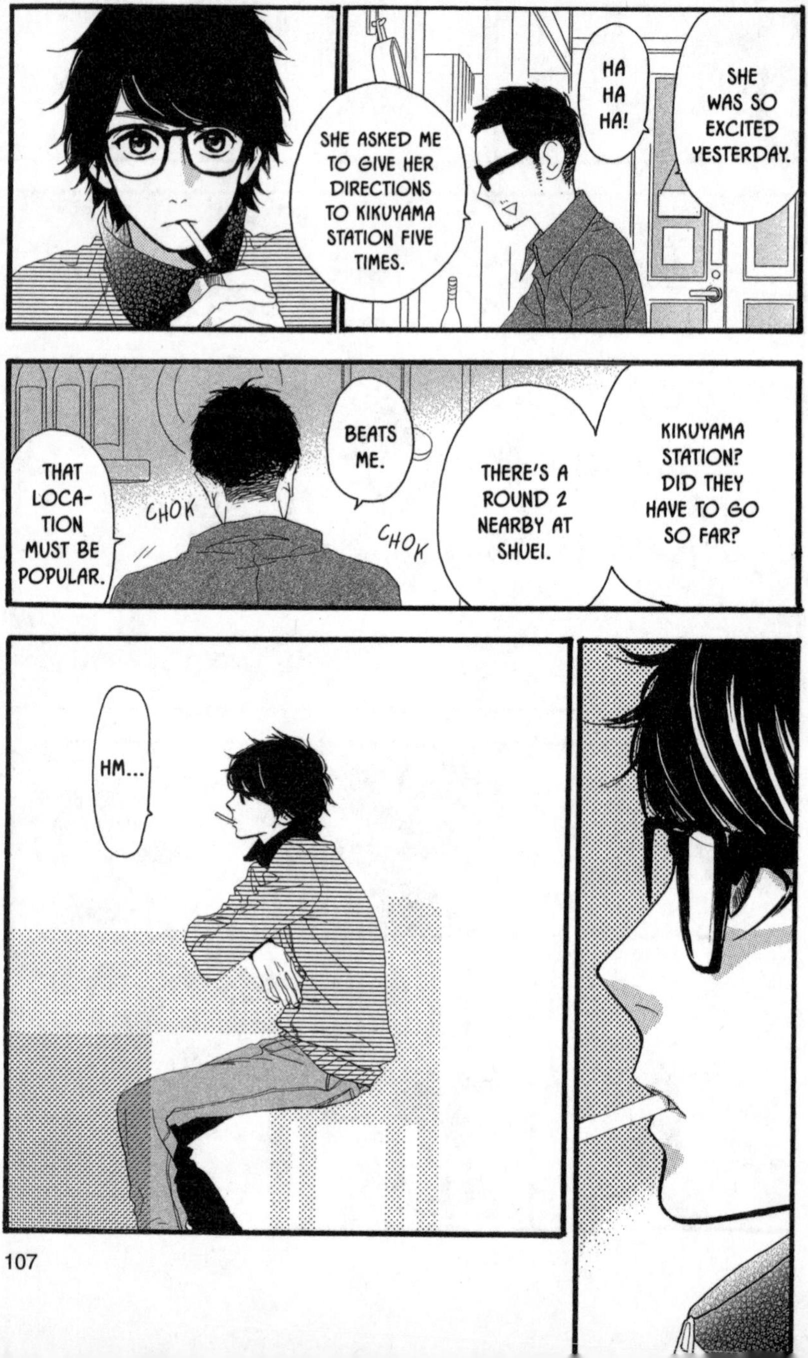
SHE WAS SO EXCITED YESTERDAY.
HA HA HA!
SHE ASKED ME TO GIVE HER DIRECTIONS TO KIKUYAMA STATION FIVE TIMES.
KIKUYAMA STATION? DID THEY HAVE TO GO SO FAR?
THERE'S A ROUND 2 NEARBY AT SHUEI.
CHOK
BEATS ME.
CHOK
THAT LOCATION MUST BE POPULAR.
HM...

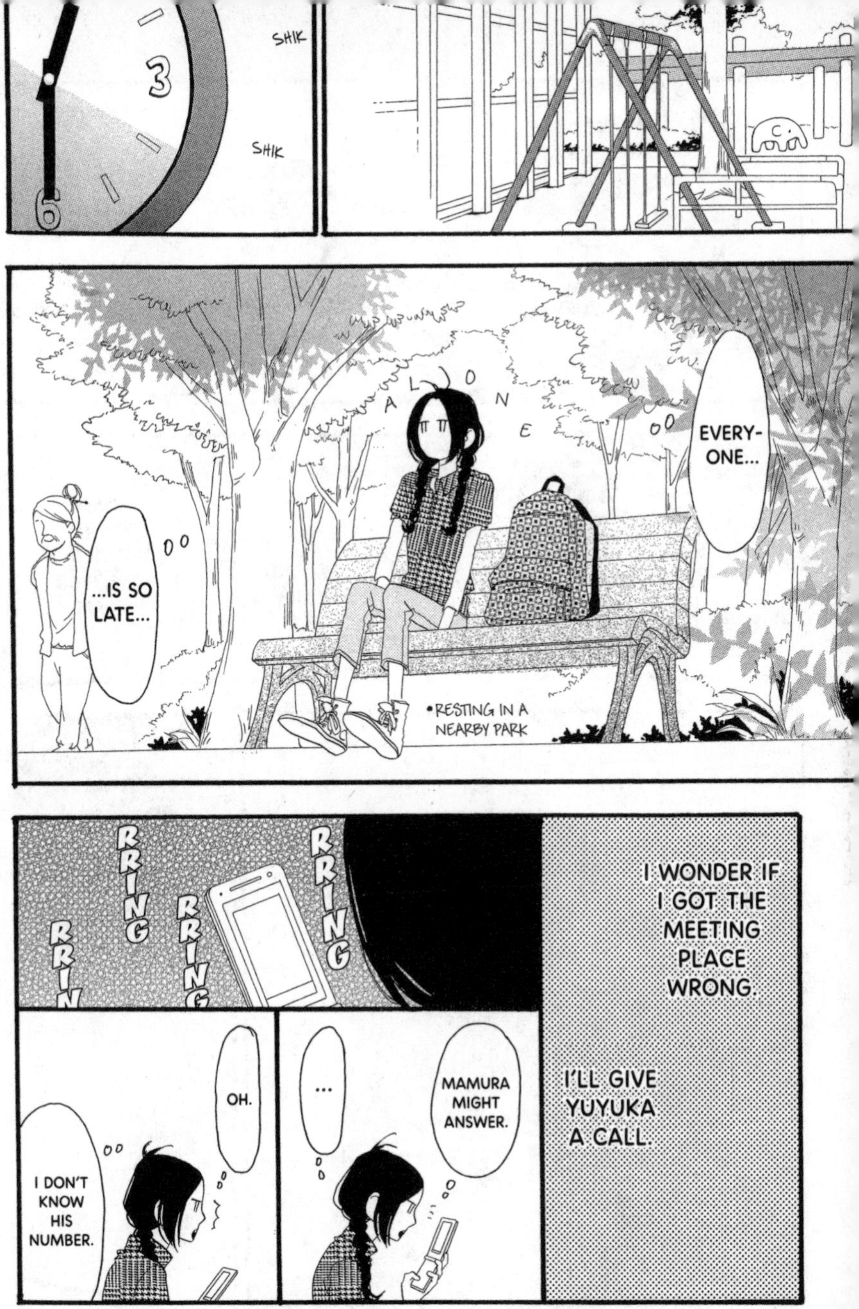
SHIK
SHIK
EVERY-ONE...
ALONE
...IS SO LATE...
•RESTING IN A NEARBY PARK
I WONDER IF I GOT THE MEETING PLACE WRONG.
I'LL GIVE YUYUKA A CALL.
RRING
RRING
RRING
RRIN
MAMURA MIGHT ANSWER.
...
OH.
I DON'T KNOW HIS NUMBER.

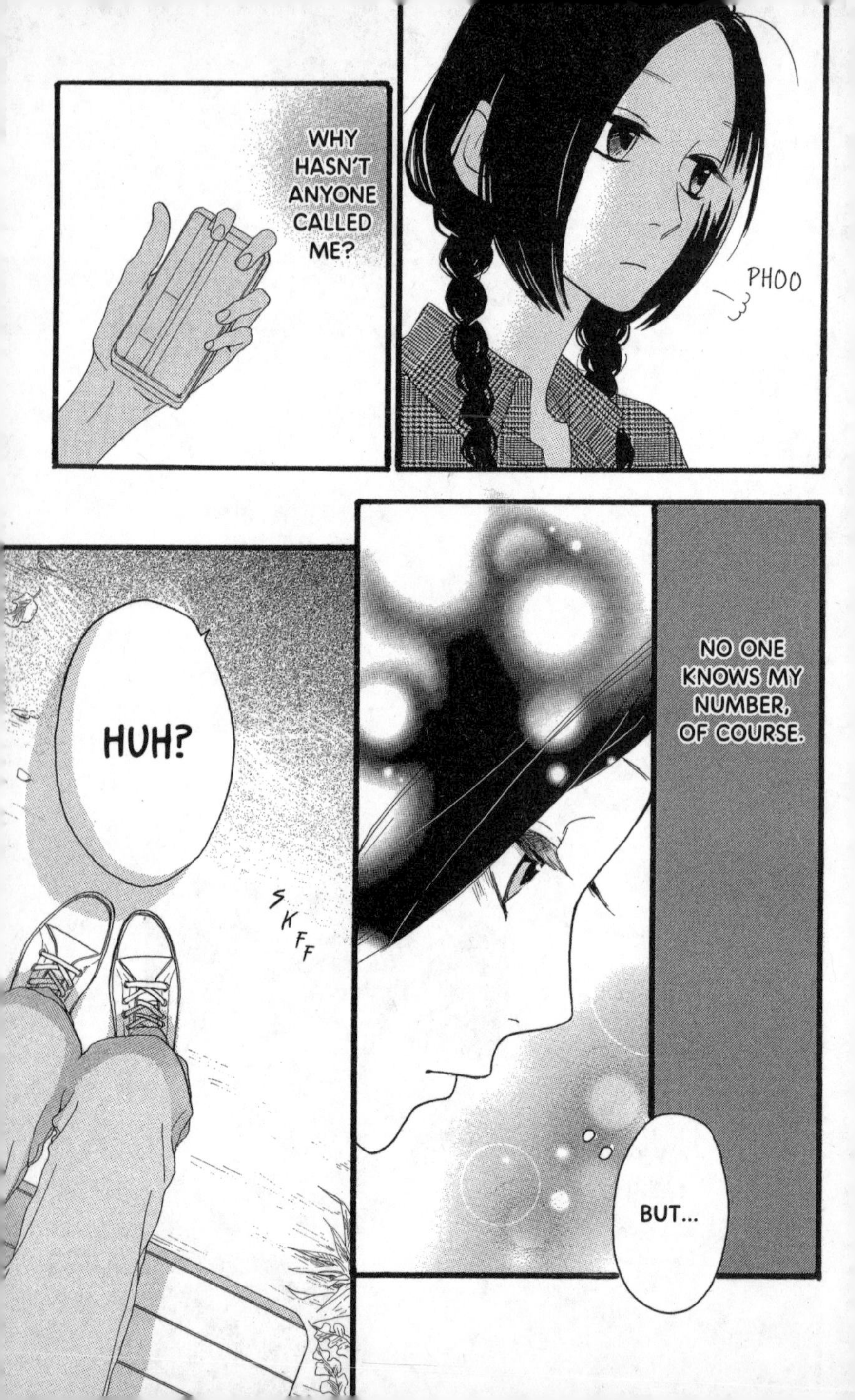
PHOO
WHY HASN'T ANYONE CALLED ME?
NO ONE KNOWS MY NUMBER, OF COURSE.
BUT...
HUH?
SKFF

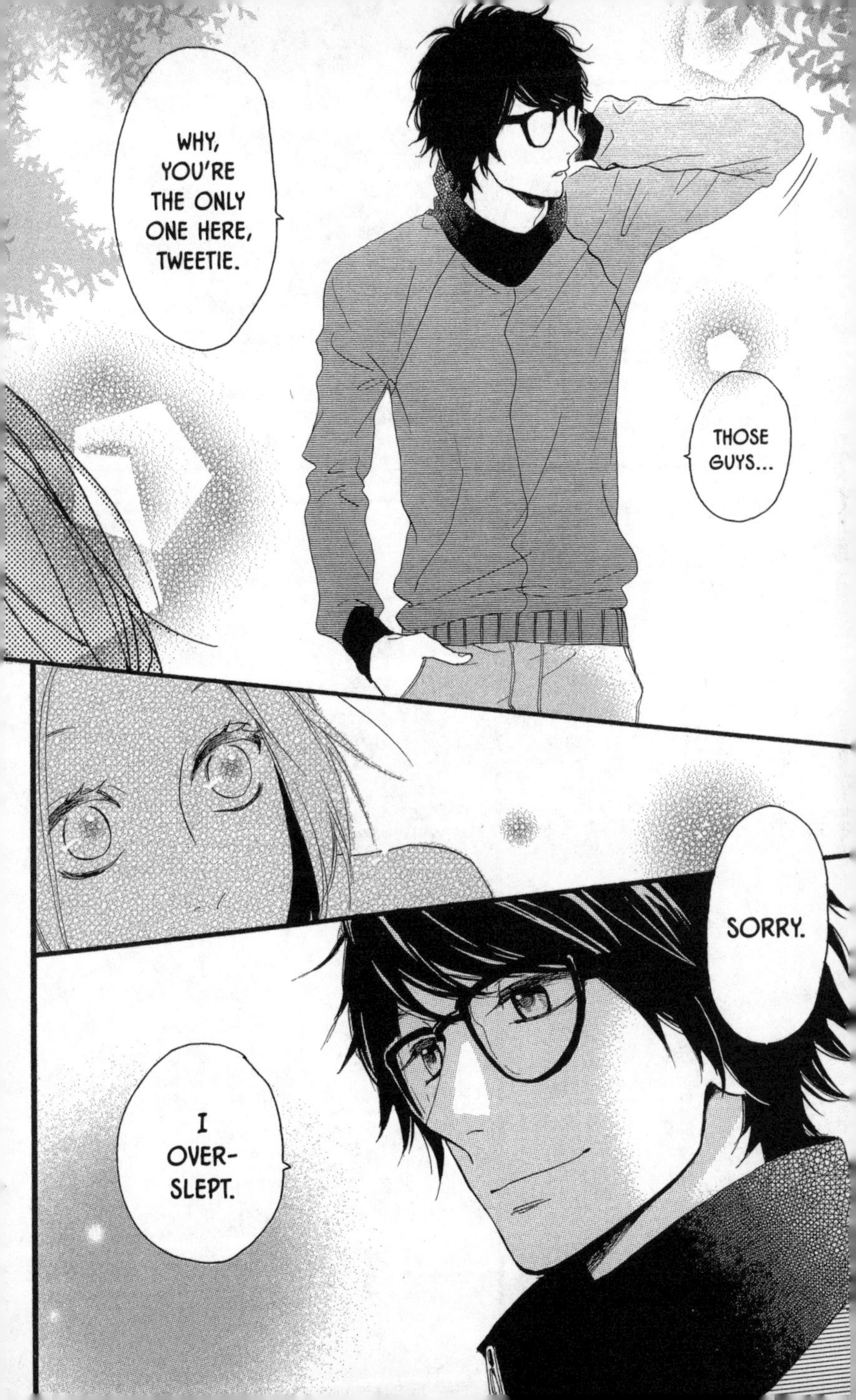
THOSE GUYS...
WHY, YOU'RE THE ONLY ONE HERE, TWEETIE.
SORRY.
I OVER-SLEPT.

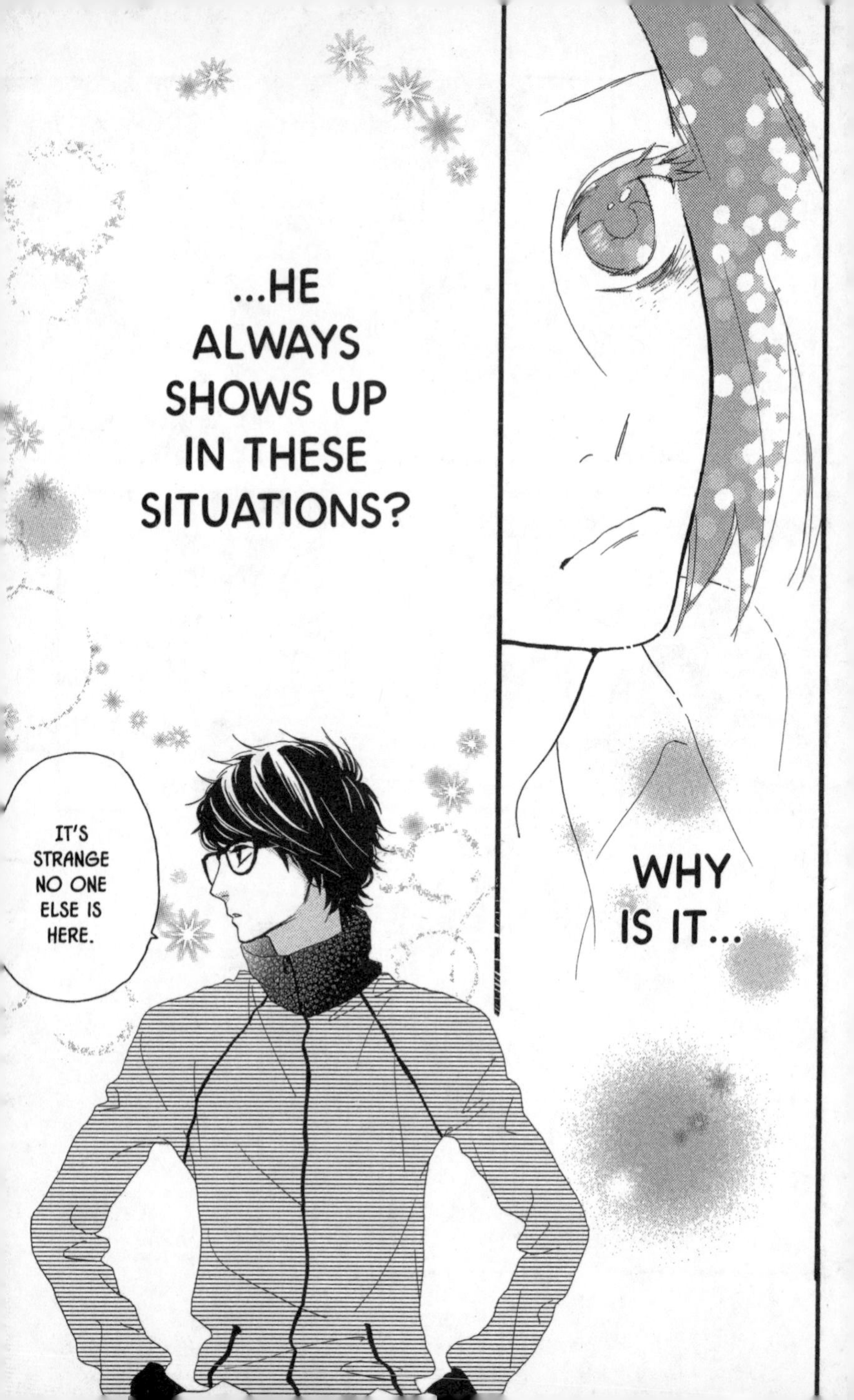
WHY IS IT...
...HE ALWAYS SHOWS UP IN THESE SITUATIONS?
IT'S STRANGE NO ONE ELSE IS HERE.

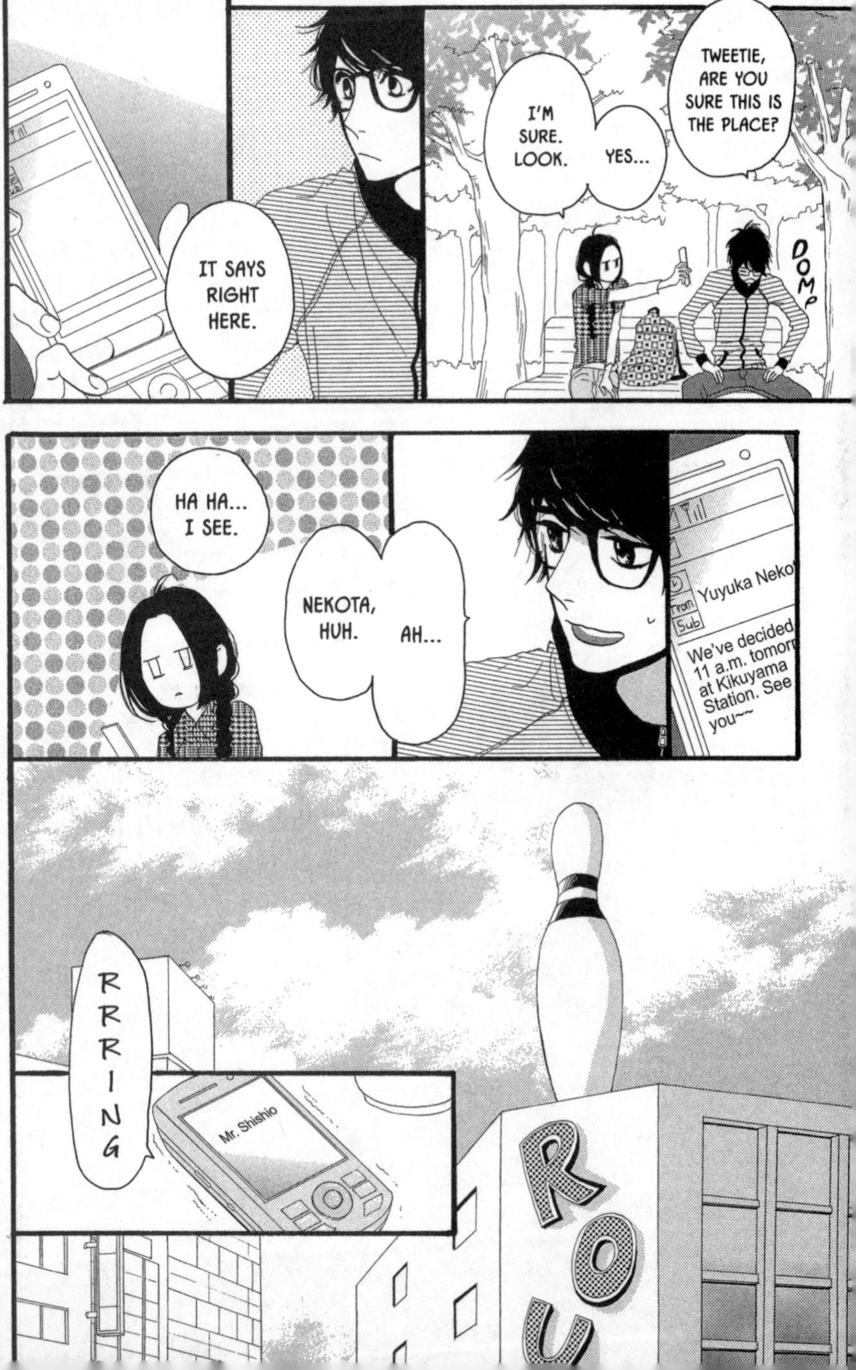
TWEETIE, ARE YOU SURE THIS IS THE PLACE?
YES...
I'M SURE. LOOK.
DOMP
IT SAYS RIGHT HERE.
From
Sub
Yuyuka Neko
We've decided 11 a.m. tomorr at Kikuyama Station. See you~~
AH...
NEKOTA, HUH.
HA HA... I SEE.
RRRING
Mr. Shishio

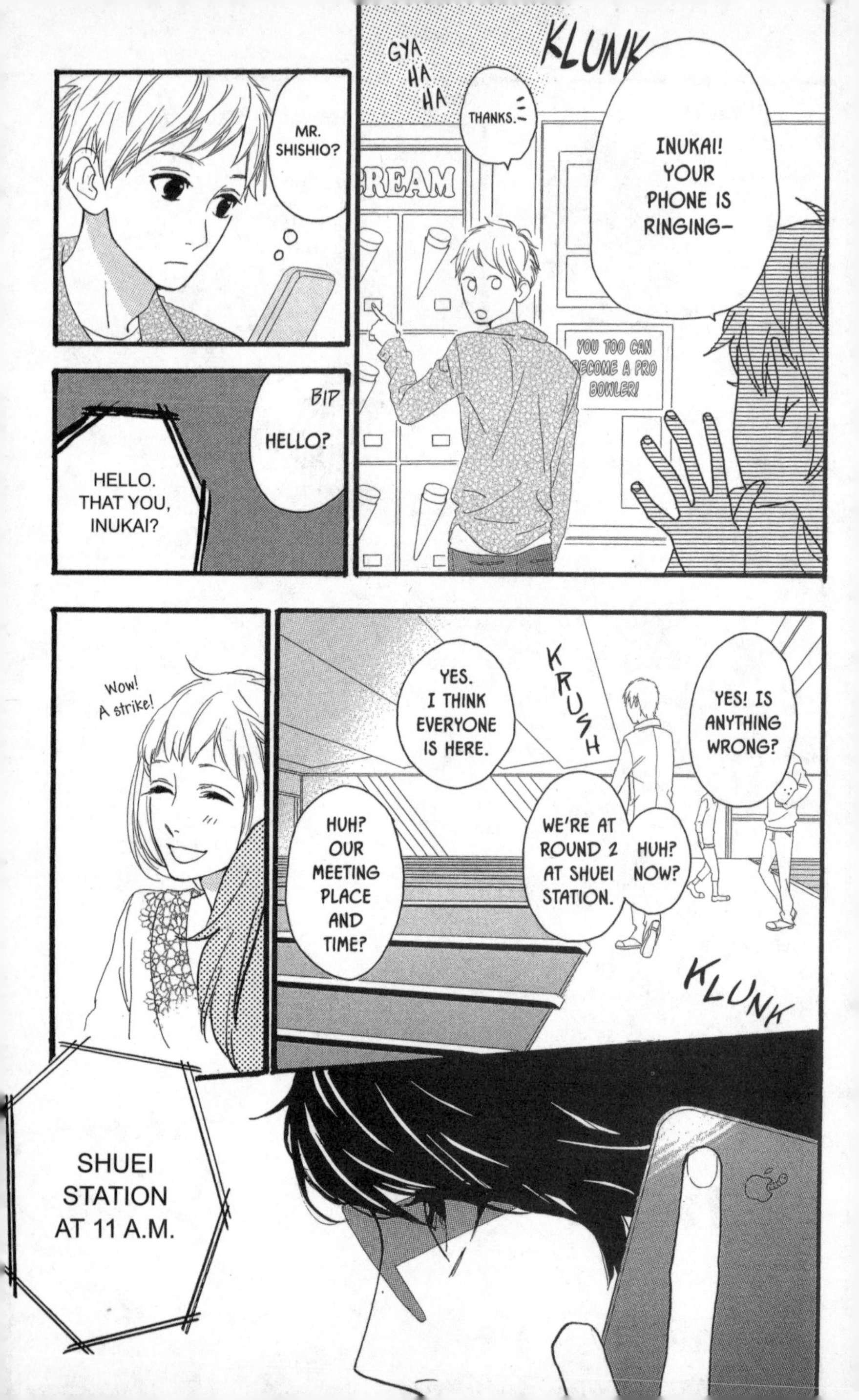
KLUNK
INUKAI! YOUR PHONE IS RINGING–
GYA HA HA
THANKS.
YOU TOO CAN BECOME A PRO BOWLER!
MR. SHISHIO?
BIP
HELLO?
HELLO. THAT YOU, INUKAI?
YES! IS ANYTHING WRONG?
KRUSH
YES. I THINK EVERYONE IS HERE.
HUH? NOW?
WE'RE AT ROUND 2 AT SHUEI STATION.
HUH? OUR MEETING PLACE AND TIME?
KLUNK
Wow! A strike!
SHUEI STATION AT 11 A.M.

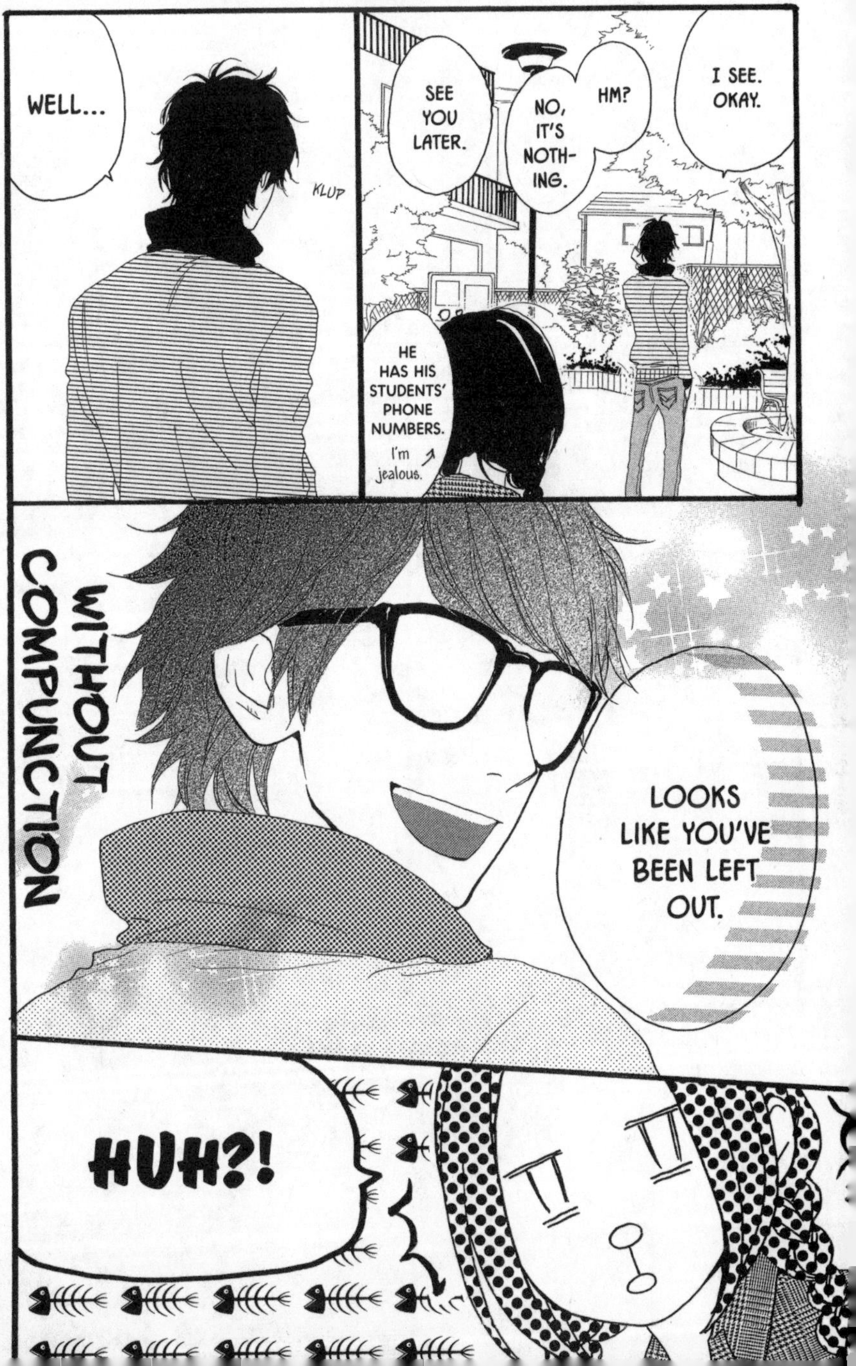
I SEE. OKAY.
HM?
NO, IT'S NOTHING.
SEE YOU LATER.
HE HAS HIS STUDENTS' PHONE NUMBERS.
I'm jealous.
WELL...
KLUP
LOOKS LIKE YOU'VE BEEN LEFT OUT.
WITHOUT COMPUNCTION
HUH?!

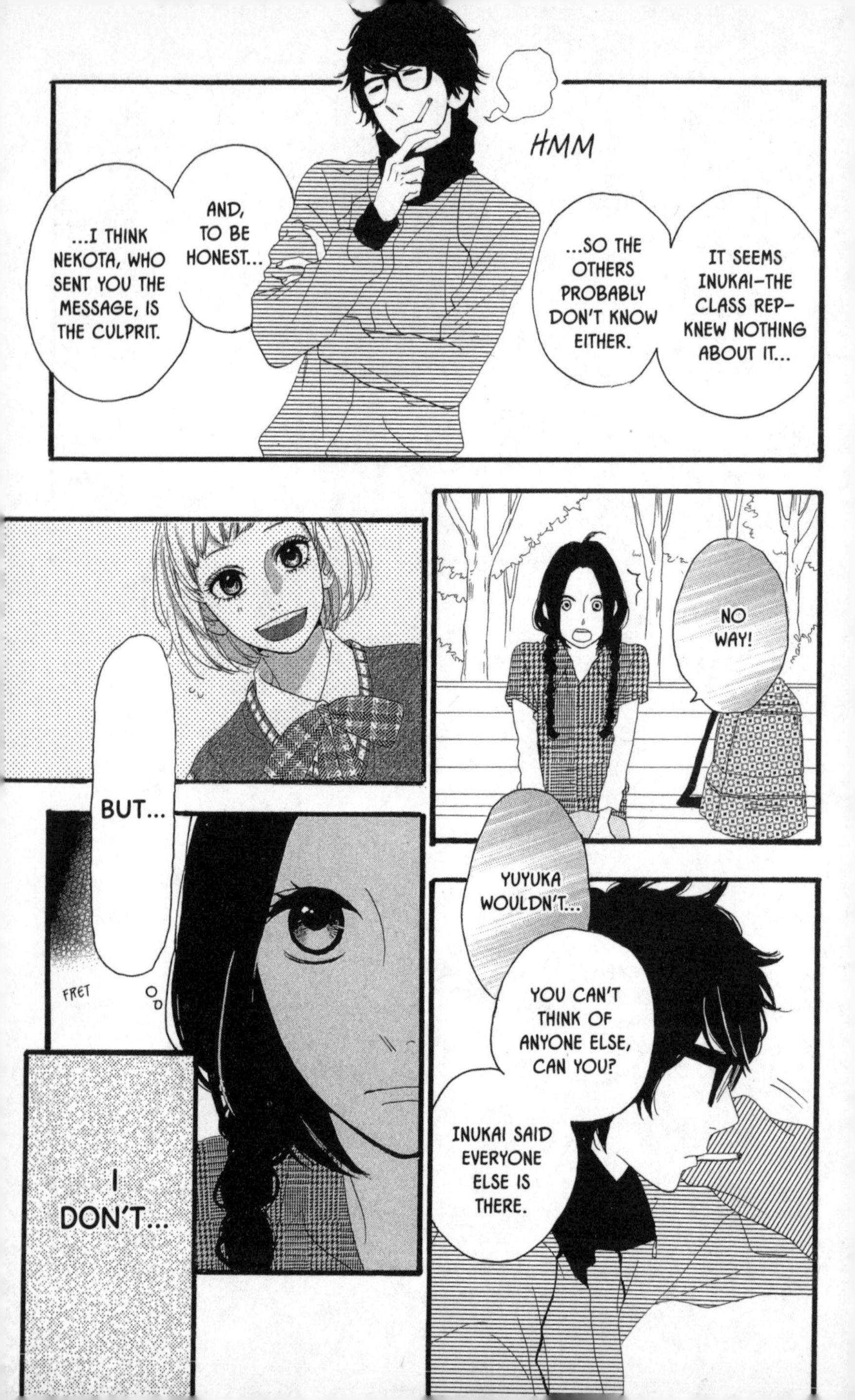

IT SEEMS INUKAI—THE CLASS REP—KNEW NOTHING ABOUT IT...
...SO THE OTHERS PROBABLY DON'T KNOW EITHER.
HMM
AND, TO BE HONEST...
...I THINK NEKOTA, WHO SENT YOU THE MESSAGE, IS THE CULPRIT.
NO WAY!
YUYUKA WOULDN'T...
BUT...
YOU CAN'T THINK OF ANYONE ELSE, CAN YOU?
INUKAI SAID EVERYONE ELSE IS THERE.
FRET
I DON'T...

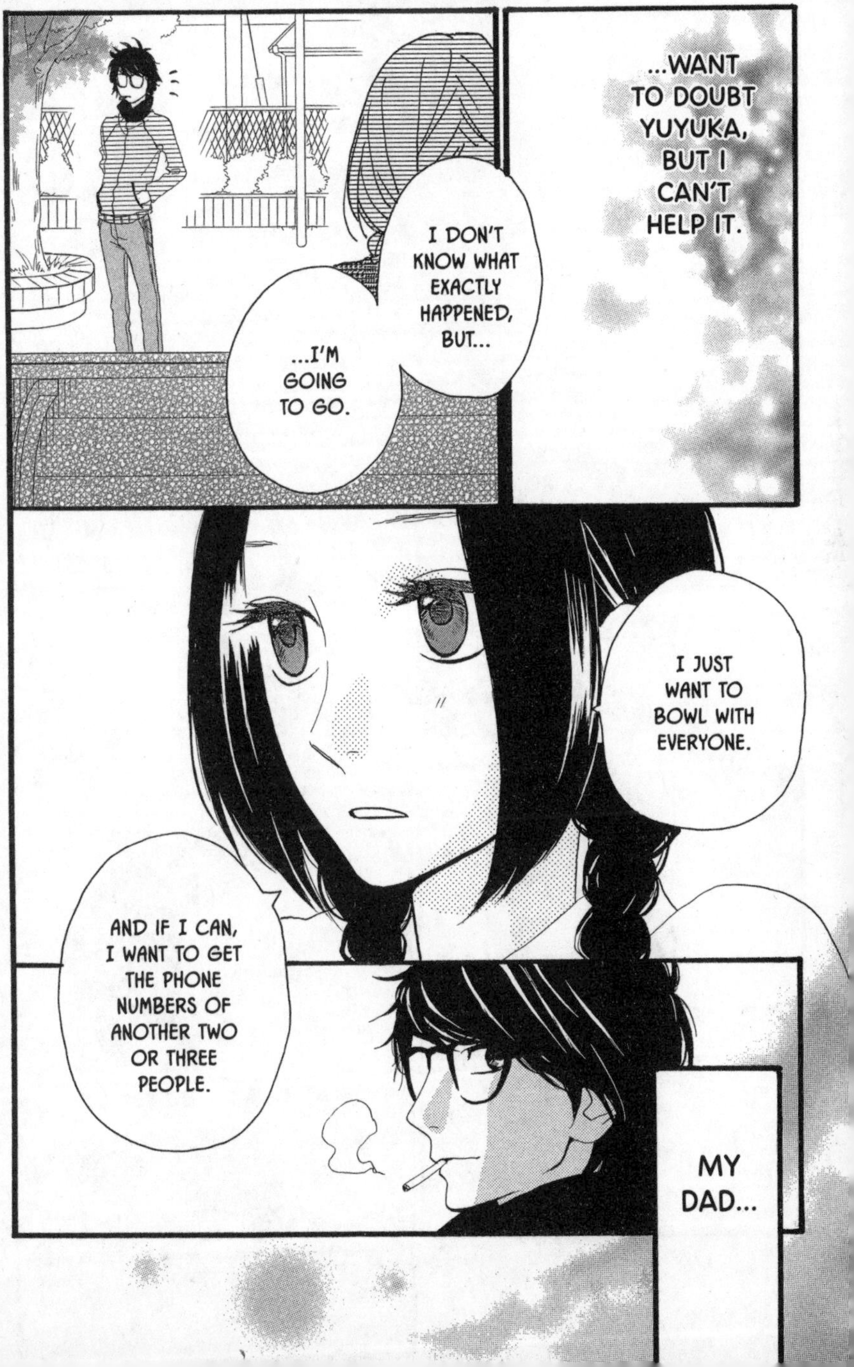
...WANT TO DOUBT YUYUKA, BUT I CAN'T HELP IT.
I DON'T KNOW WHAT EXACTLY HAPPENED, BUT...
...I'M GOING TO GO.
I JUST WANT TO BOWL WITH EVERYONE.
AND IF I CAN, I WANT TO GET THE PHONE NUMBERS OF ANOTHER TWO OR THREE PEOPLE.
MY DAD...

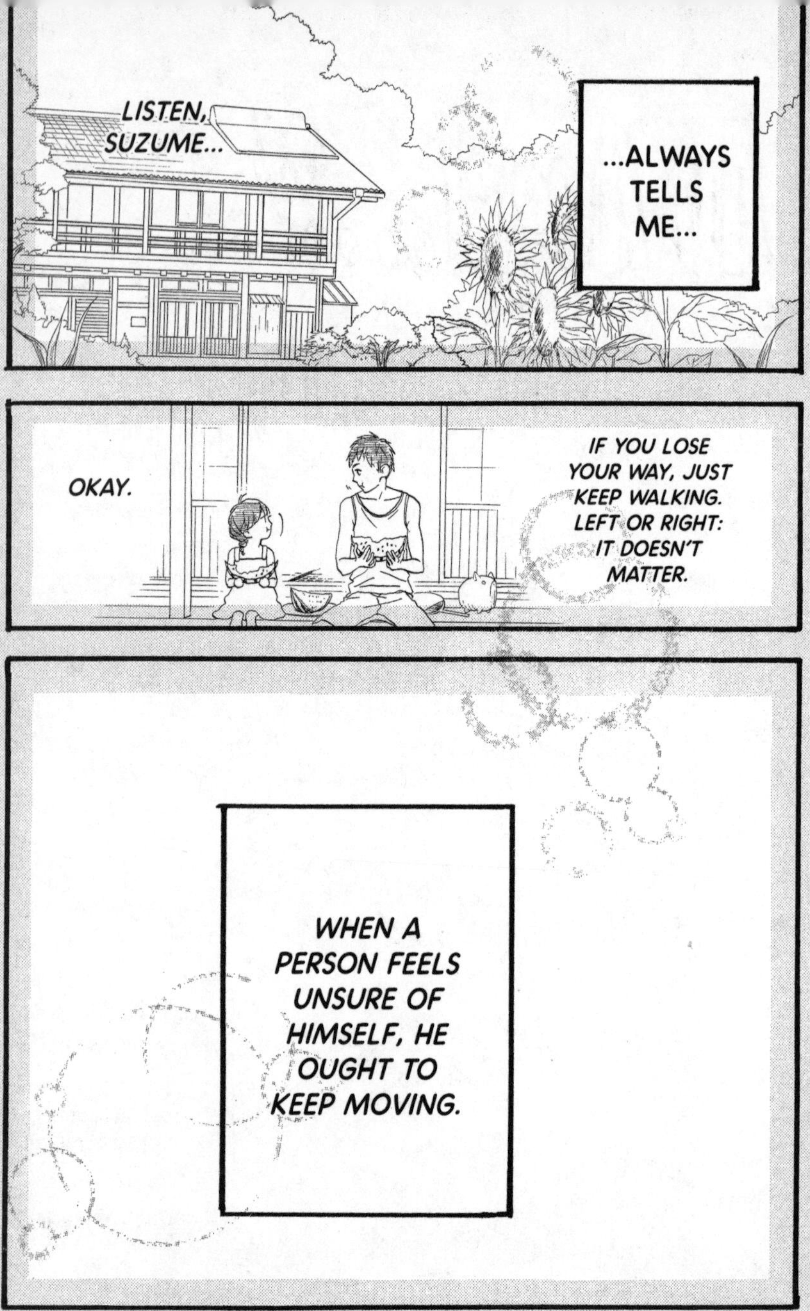
...ALWAYS TELLS ME...
LISTEN, SUZUME...
IF YOU LOSE YOUR WAY, JUST KEEP WALKING. LEFT OR RIGHT: IT DOESN'T MATTER.
OKAY.
WHEN A PERSON FEELS UNSURE OF HIMSELF, HE OUGHT TO KEEP MOVING.

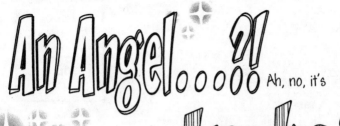

An Angel.∘∘∘?!

Ah, no, it's

Inukai

I fell in love with him the first time I saw him. His big, round eyes...his simple appearance... I love everything about him!!!

When will you have a special on Inukai? I'm tired of waiting. If Inukai said to me...

> You forgot your book? Do you want to share mine?

...I would have no regrets in life. Is this all right? Will people question your reputation for hiring someone like me, Yamamori-san? Your appetite is just a bit better than that of others. I'm the only one who's weird.

Sachie Noborio

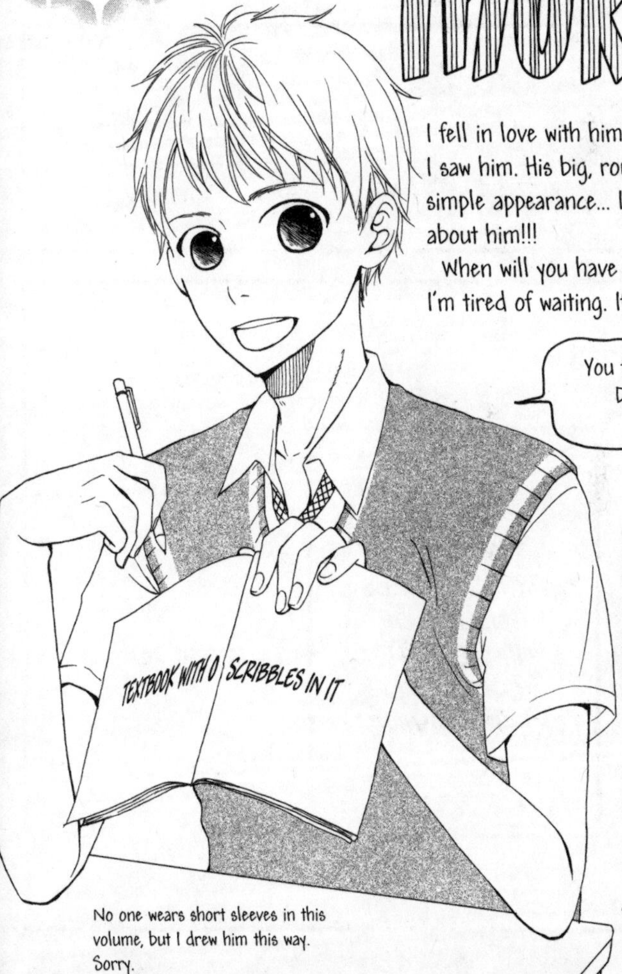

TEXTBOOK WITH 0 SCRIBBLES IN IT

No one wears short sleeves in this volume, but I drew him this way. Sorry.

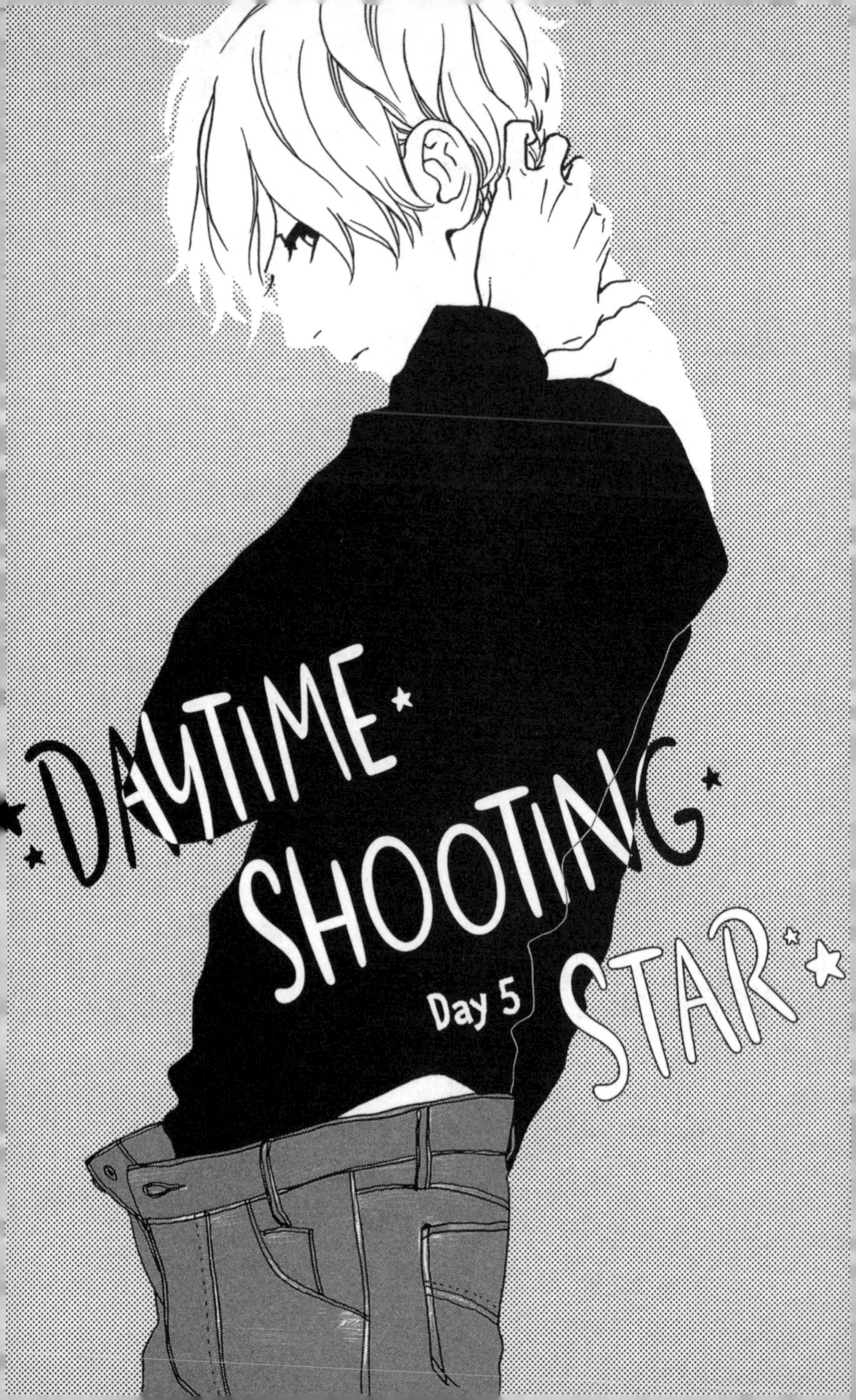
DAYTIME SHOOTING STAR
Day 5

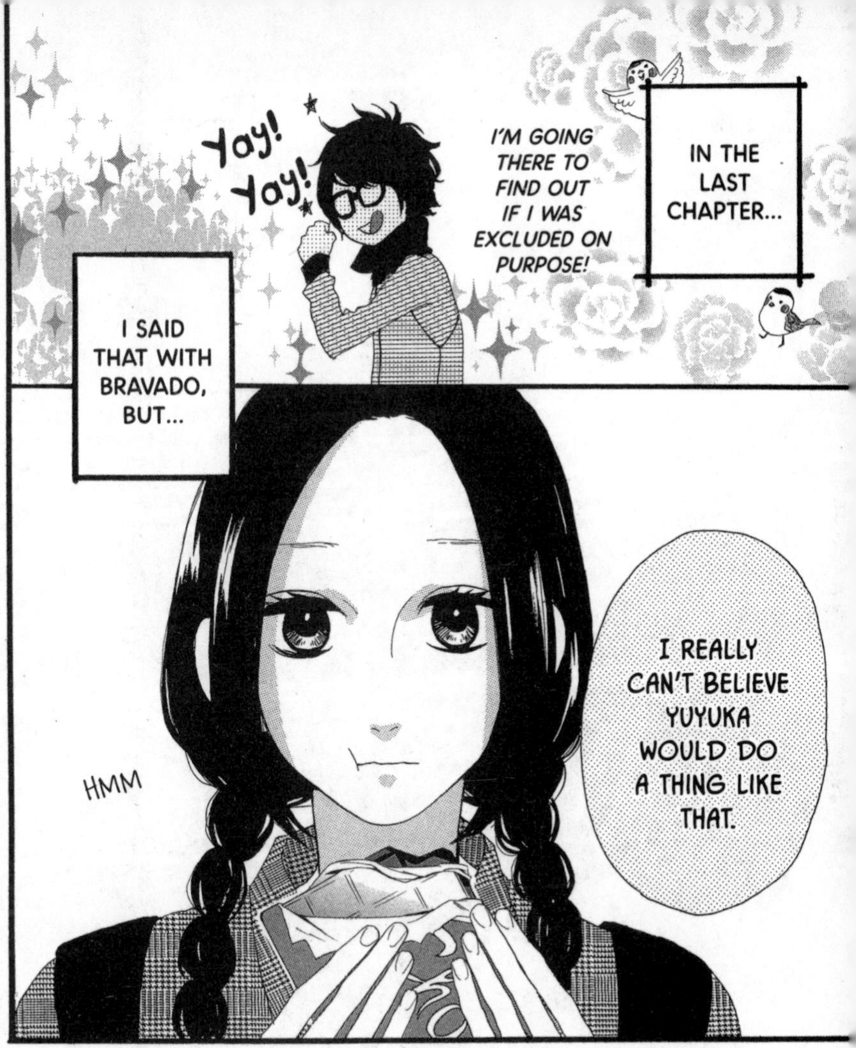
IN THE LAST CHAPTER...
I'M GOING THERE TO FIND OUT IF I WAS EXCLUDED ON PURPOSE!
Yay! Yay!
I SAID THAT WITH BRAVADO, BUT...
I REALLY CAN'T BELIEVE YUYUKA WOULD DO A THING LIKE THAT.
HMM

Mamura 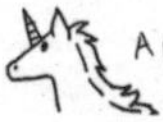 A unicorn!

Birthday: February 10
Height: 5'9"
Weight: 130 lbs
Blood Type: A

① Anything with cheese on it.
② Collecting toys packaged with candy.
③ The girl sitting at the next desk next to me is weird.

**Ma* means "horse."

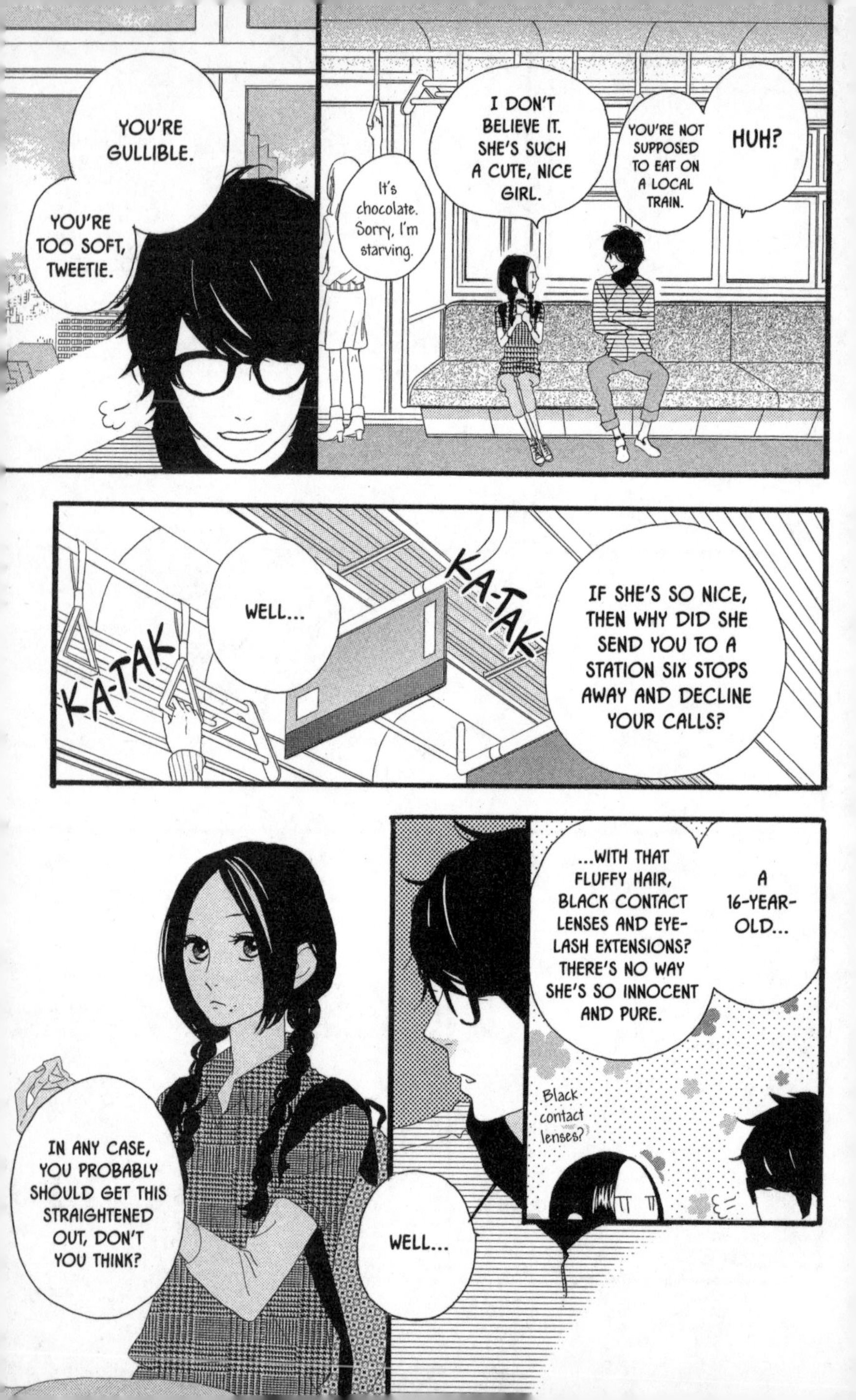
HUH?
YOU'RE NOT SUPPOSED TO EAT ON A LOCAL TRAIN.
I DON'T BELIEVE IT. SHE'S SUCH A CUTE, NICE GIRL.
It's chocolate. Sorry, I'm starving.
YOU'RE GULLIBLE.
YOU'RE TOO SOFT, TWEETIE.
IF SHE'S SO NICE, THEN WHY DID SHE SEND YOU TO A STATION SIX STOPS AWAY AND DECLINE YOUR CALLS?
KA-TAK
WELL...
KA-TAK
A 16-YEAR-OLD...
...WITH THAT FLUFFY HAIR, BLACK CONTACT LENSES AND EYE-LASH EXTENSIONS? THERE'S NO WAY SHE'S SO INNOCENT AND PURE.
Black contact lenses?
WELL...
IN ANY CASE, YOU PROBABLY SHOULD GET THIS STRAIGHTENED OUT, DON'T YOU THINK?

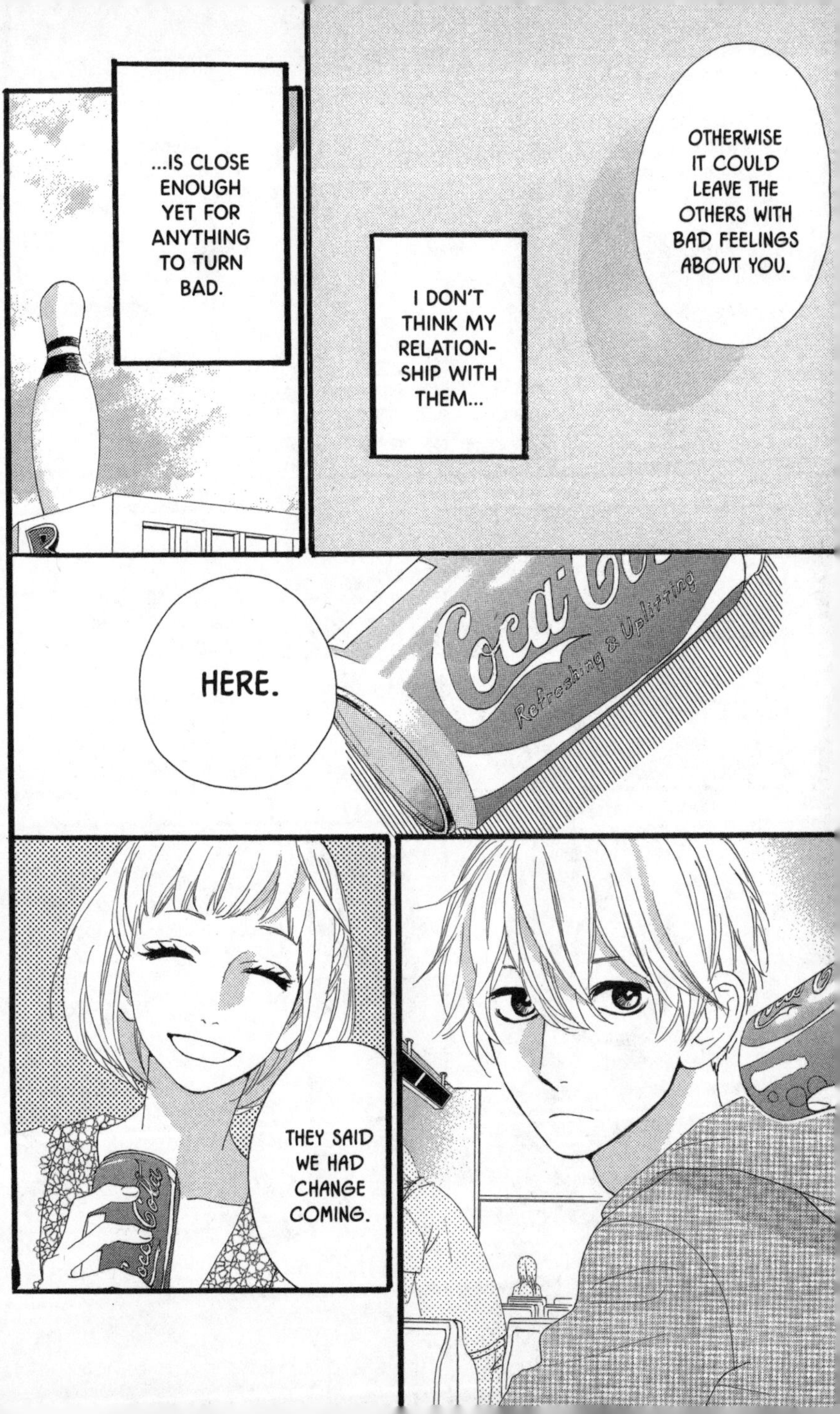
OTHERWISE IT COULD LEAVE THE OTHERS WITH BAD FEELINGS ABOUT YOU.
I DON'T THINK MY RELATION-SHIP WITH THEM...
...IS CLOSE ENOUGH YET FOR ANYTHING TO TURN BAD.
Refreshing & Uplifting
HERE.
THEY SAID WE HAD CHANGE COMING.

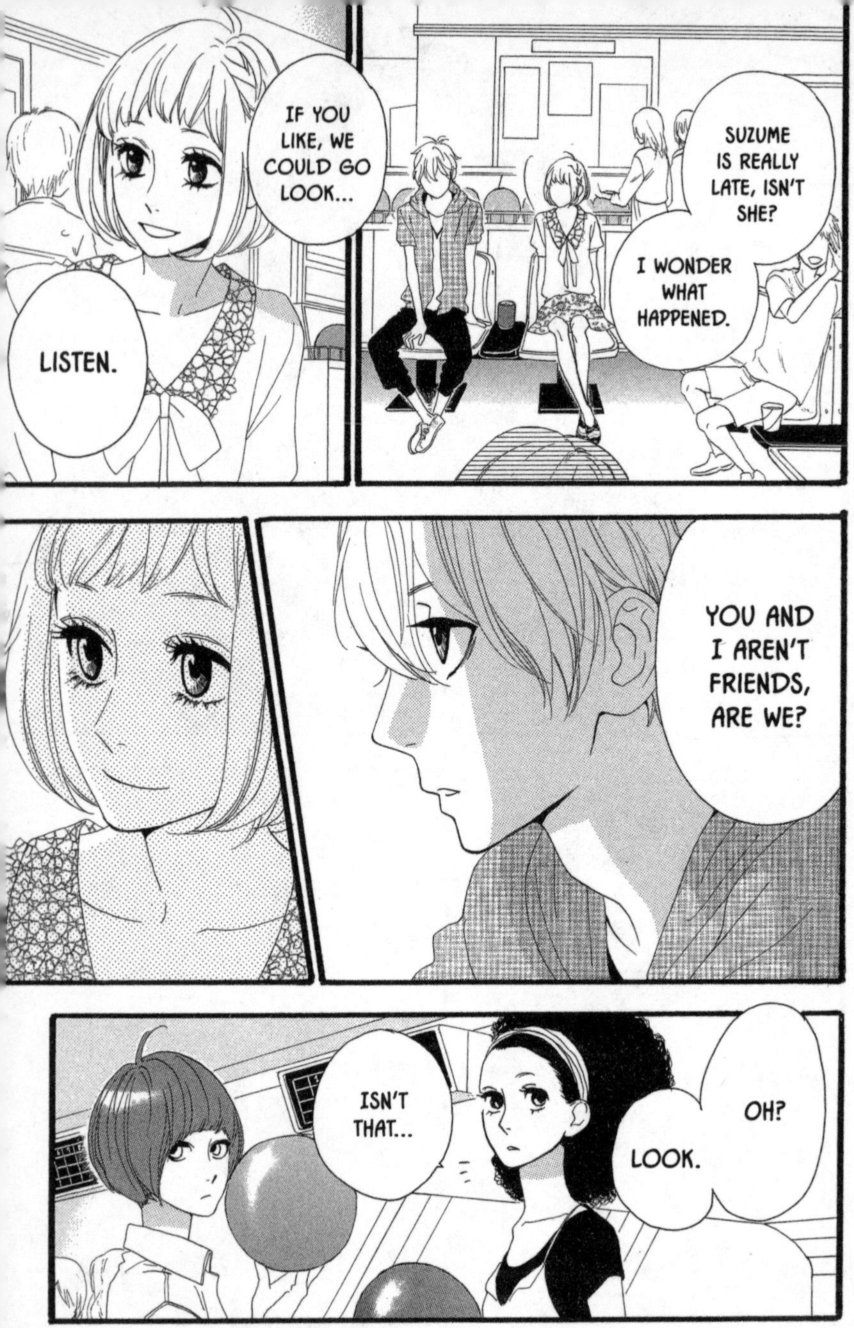
SUZUME IS REALLY LATE, ISN'T SHE?
I WONDER WHAT HAPPENED.
IF YOU LIKE, WE COULD GO LOOK...
LISTEN.
YOU AND I AREN'T FRIENDS, ARE WE?
OH?
LOOK.
ISN'T THAT...

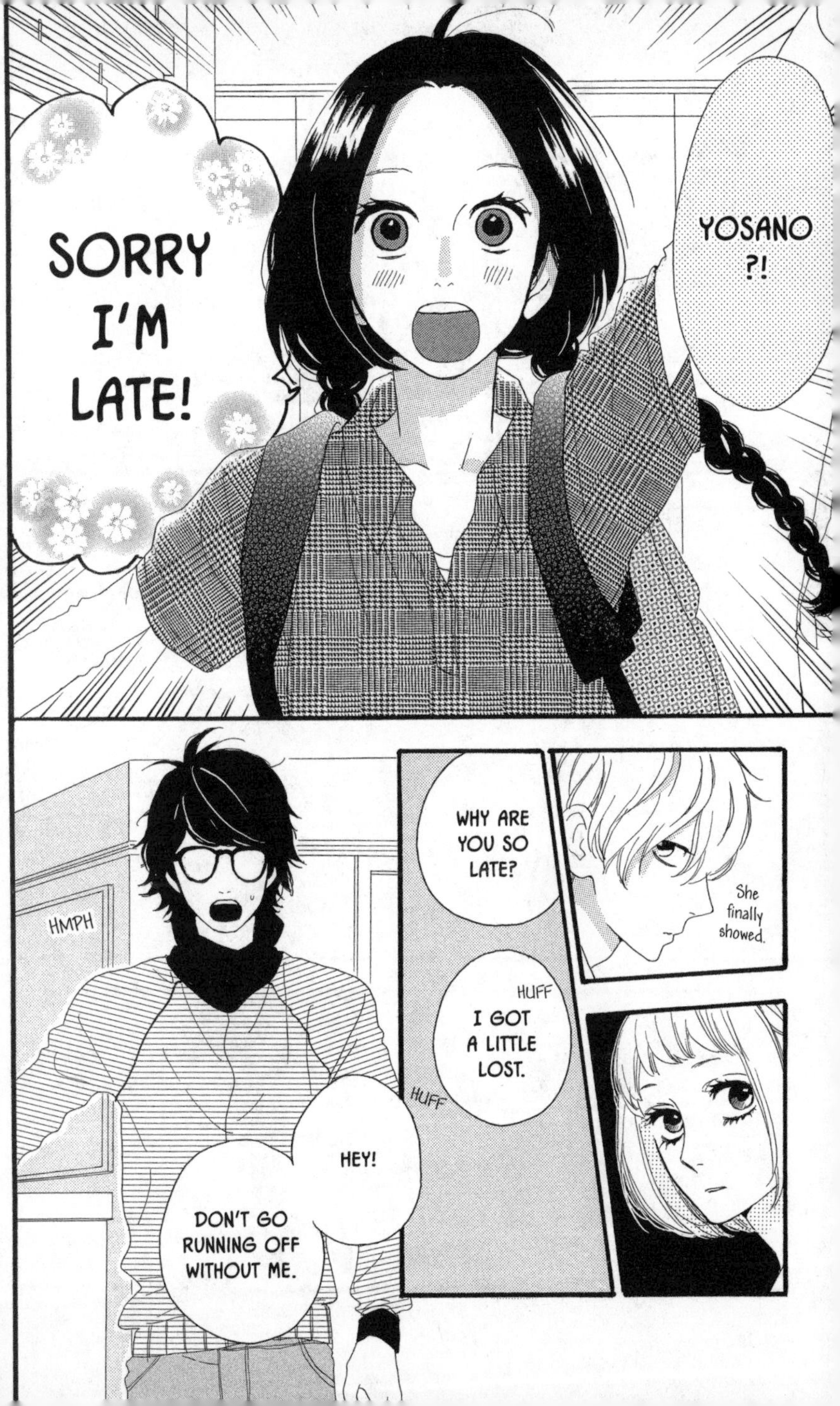
YOSANO ?!
SORRY I'M LATE!
She finally showed.
WHY ARE YOU SO LATE?
HUFF
I GOT A LITTLE LOST.
HUFF
HEY!
DON'T GO RUNNING OFF WITHOUT ME.
HMPH

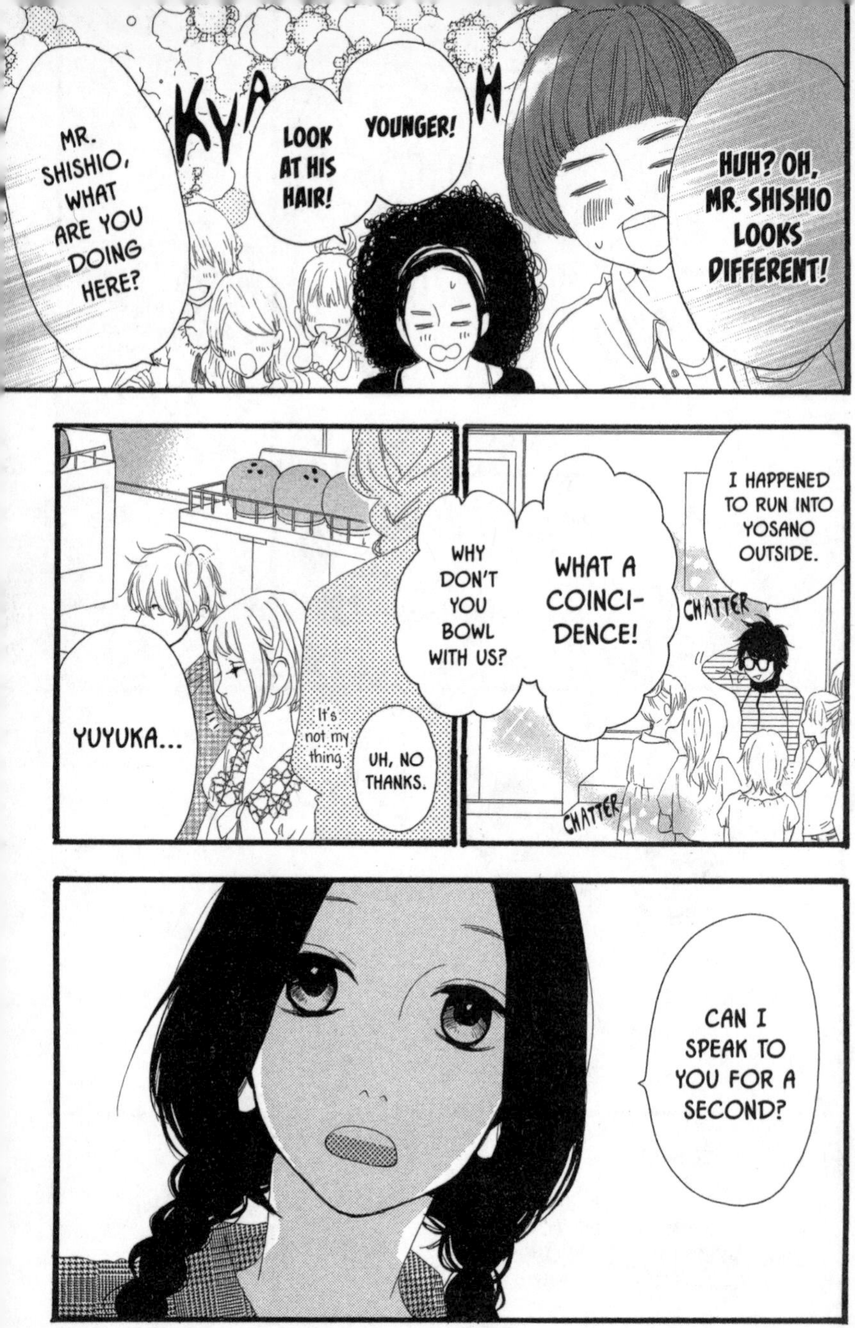
HUH? OH, MR. SHISHIO LOOKS DIFFERENT!
KYA H
YOUNGER!
LOOK AT HIS HAIR!
MR. SHISHIO, WHAT ARE YOU DOING HERE?
I HAPPENED TO RUN INTO YOSANO OUTSIDE.
CHATTER
WHAT A COINCIDENCE!
WHY DON'T YOU BOWL WITH US?
CHATTER
UH, NO THANKS.
It's not my thing.
YUYUKA...
CAN I SPEAK TO YOU FOR A SECOND?

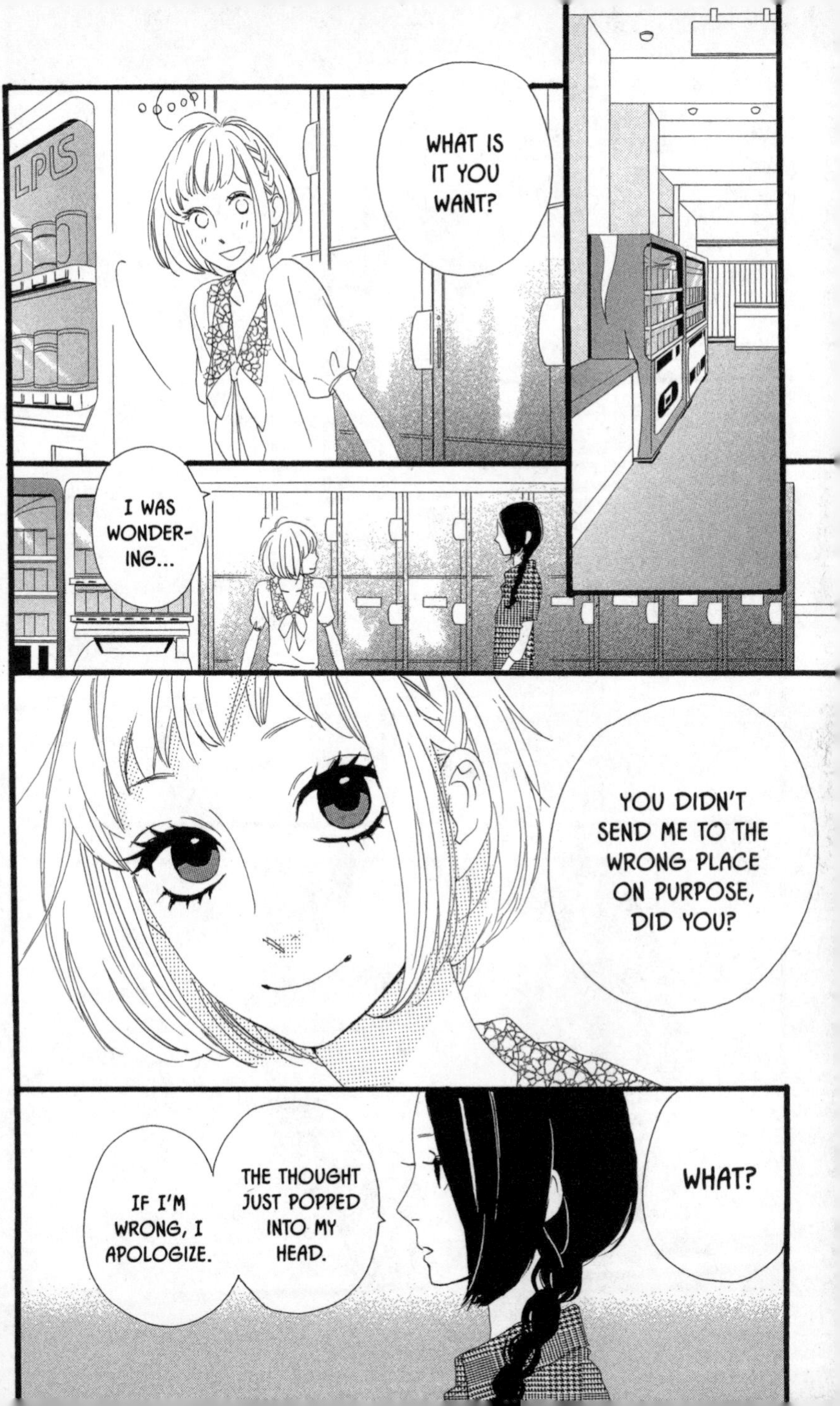
WHAT IS IT YOU WANT?
I WAS WONDER-ING...
YOU DIDN'T SEND ME TO THE WRONG PLACE ON PURPOSE, DID YOU?
WHAT?
THE THOUGHT JUST POPPED INTO MY HEAD.
IF I'M WRONG, I APOLOGIZE.

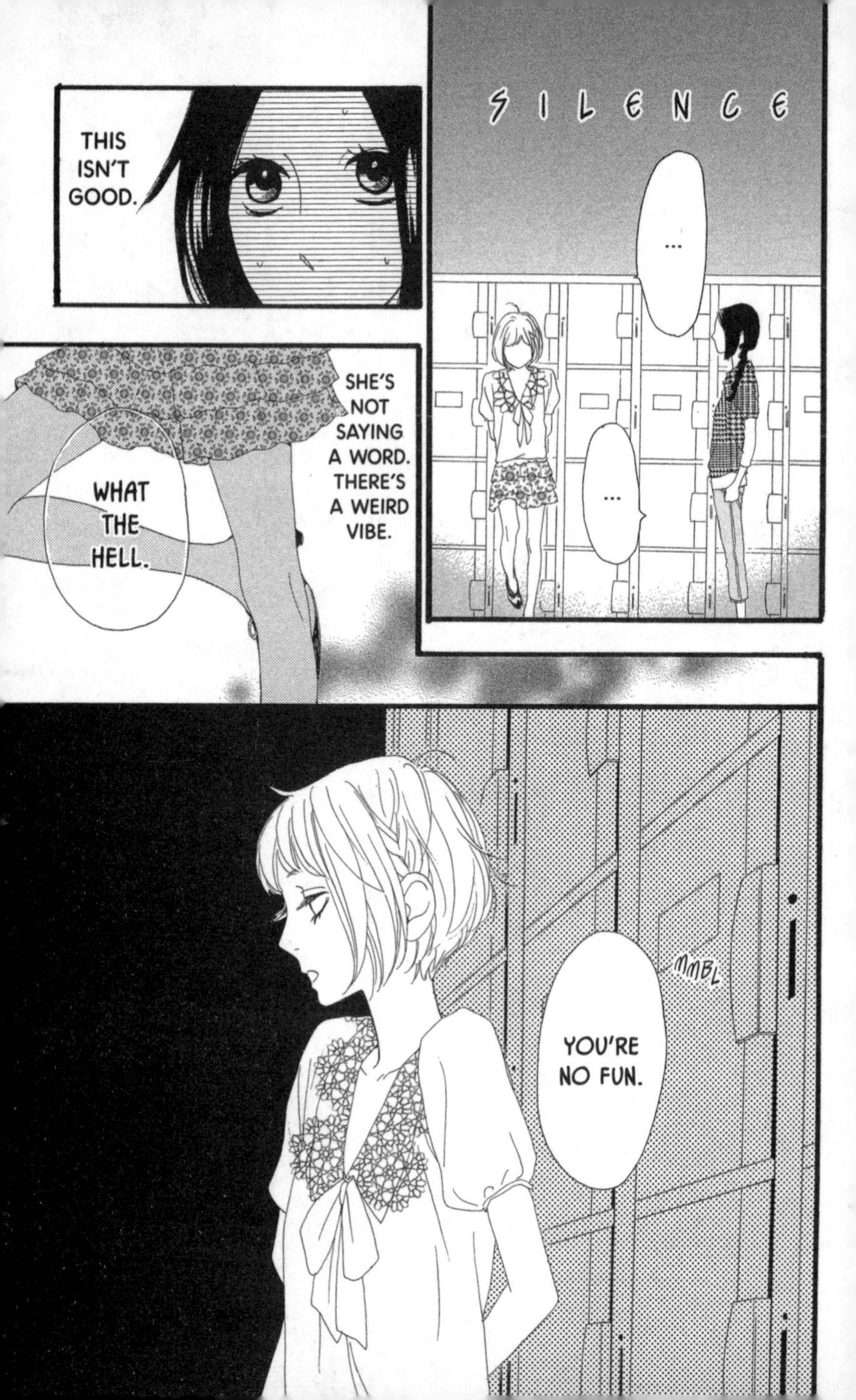
SILENCE
...
...
THIS ISN'T GOOD.
SHE'S NOT SAYING A WORD. THERE'S A WEIRD VIBE.
WHAT THE HELL.
MMBL
YOU'RE NO FUN.

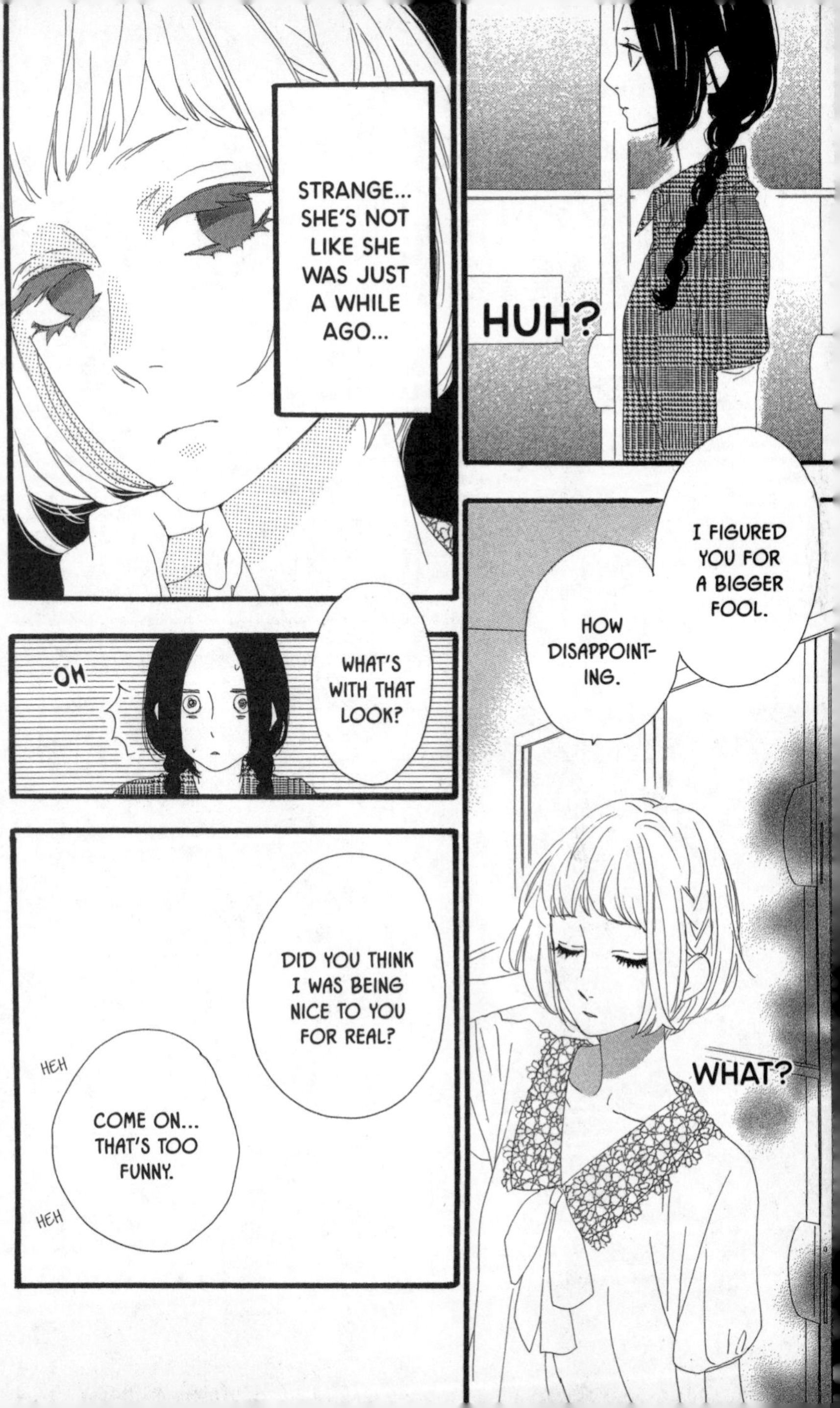
HUH?
I FIGURED YOU FOR A BIGGER FOOL.
HOW DISAPPOINTING.
WHAT?
STRANGE... SHE'S NOT LIKE SHE WAS JUST A WHILE AGO...
WHAT'S WITH THAT LOOK?
OH
DID YOU THINK I WAS BEING NICE TO YOU FOR REAL?
HEH
COME ON... THAT'S TOO FUNNY.
HEH

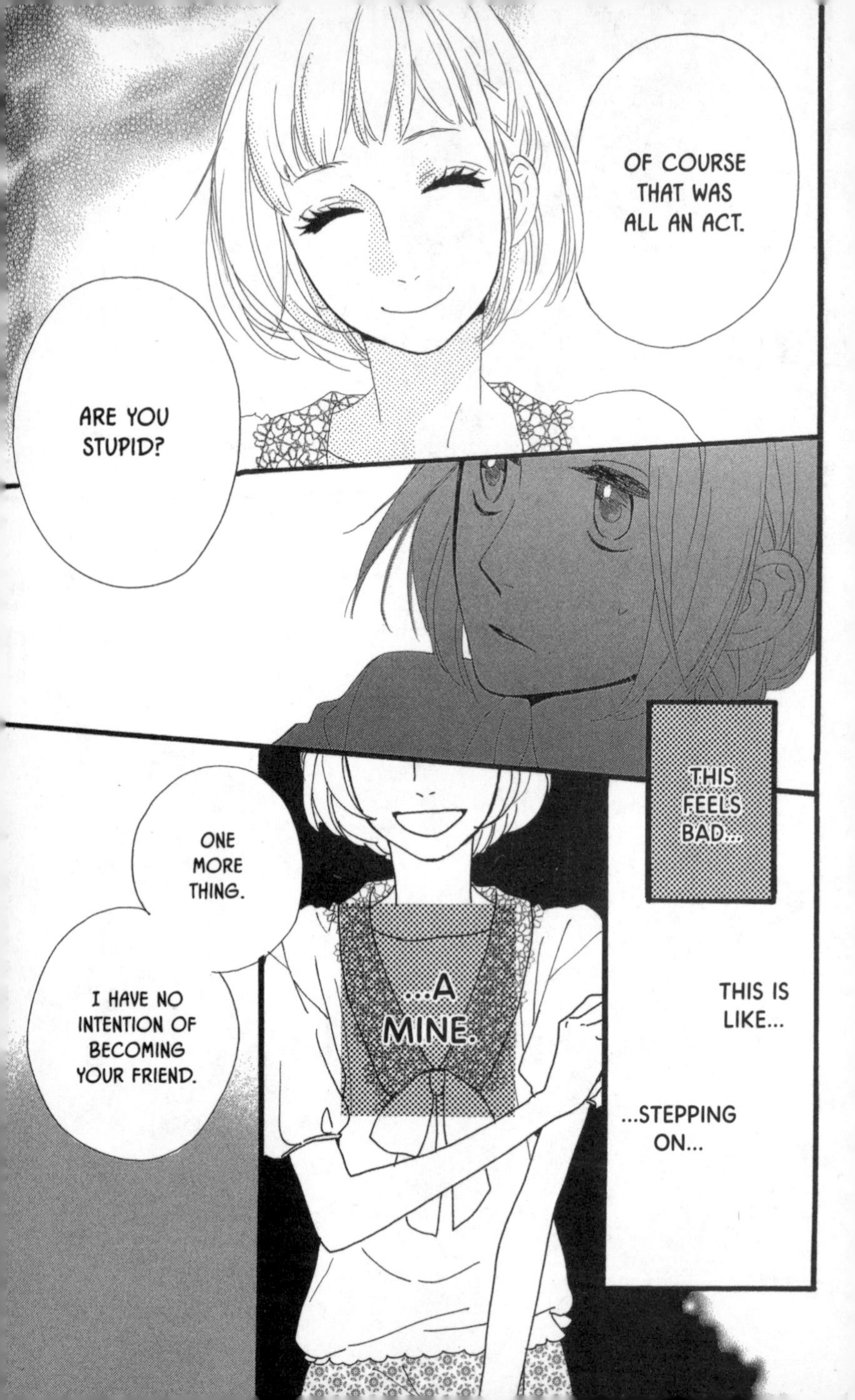
OF COURSE THAT WAS ALL AN ACT.
ARE YOU STUPID?
THIS FEELS BAD...
ONE MORE THING.
I HAVE NO INTENTION OF BECOMING YOUR FRIEND.
THIS IS LIKE...
...STEPPING ON...
...A MINE.

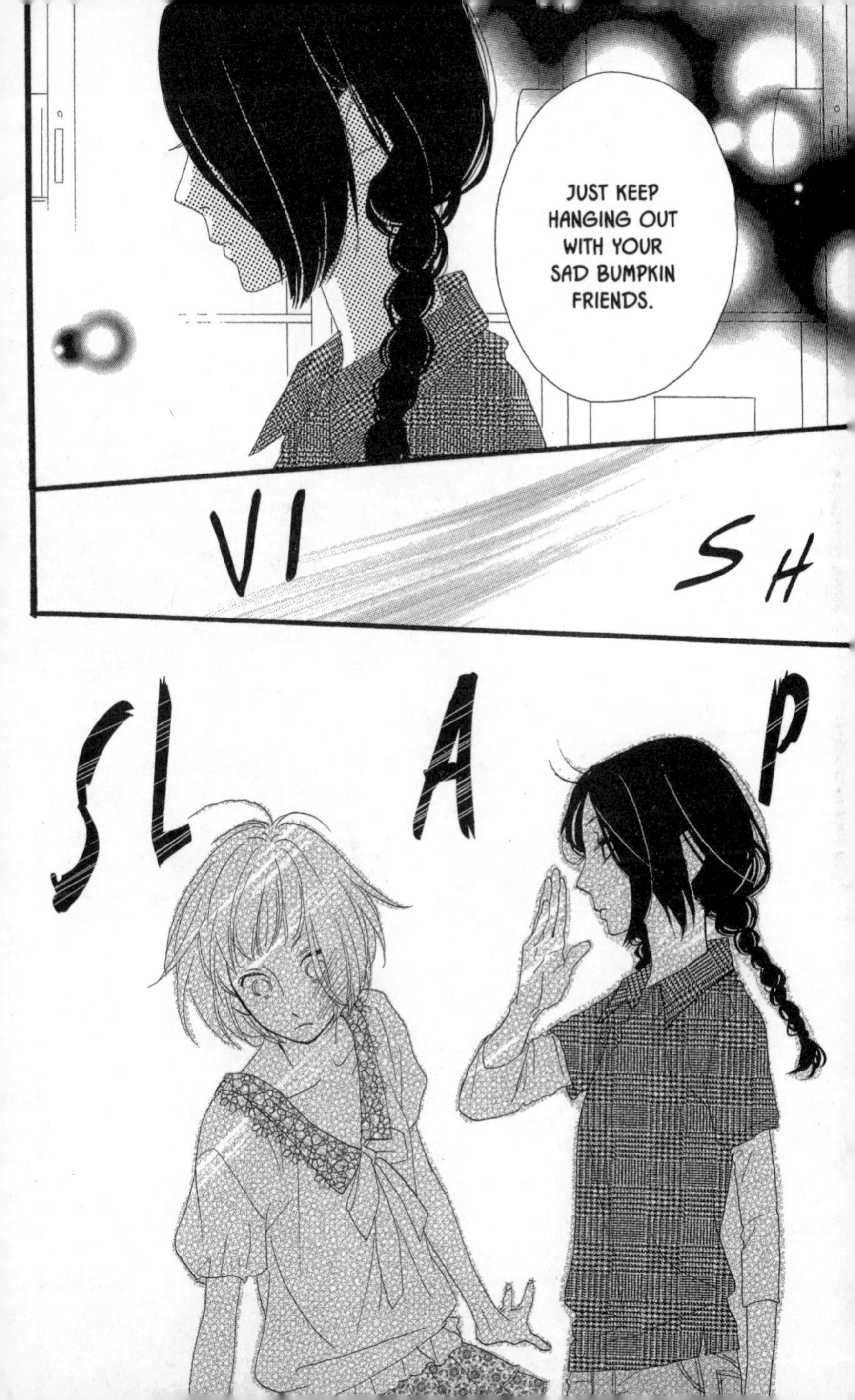
JUST KEEP HANGING OUT WITH YOUR SAD BUMPKIN FRIENDS.
VI SH
SLAP

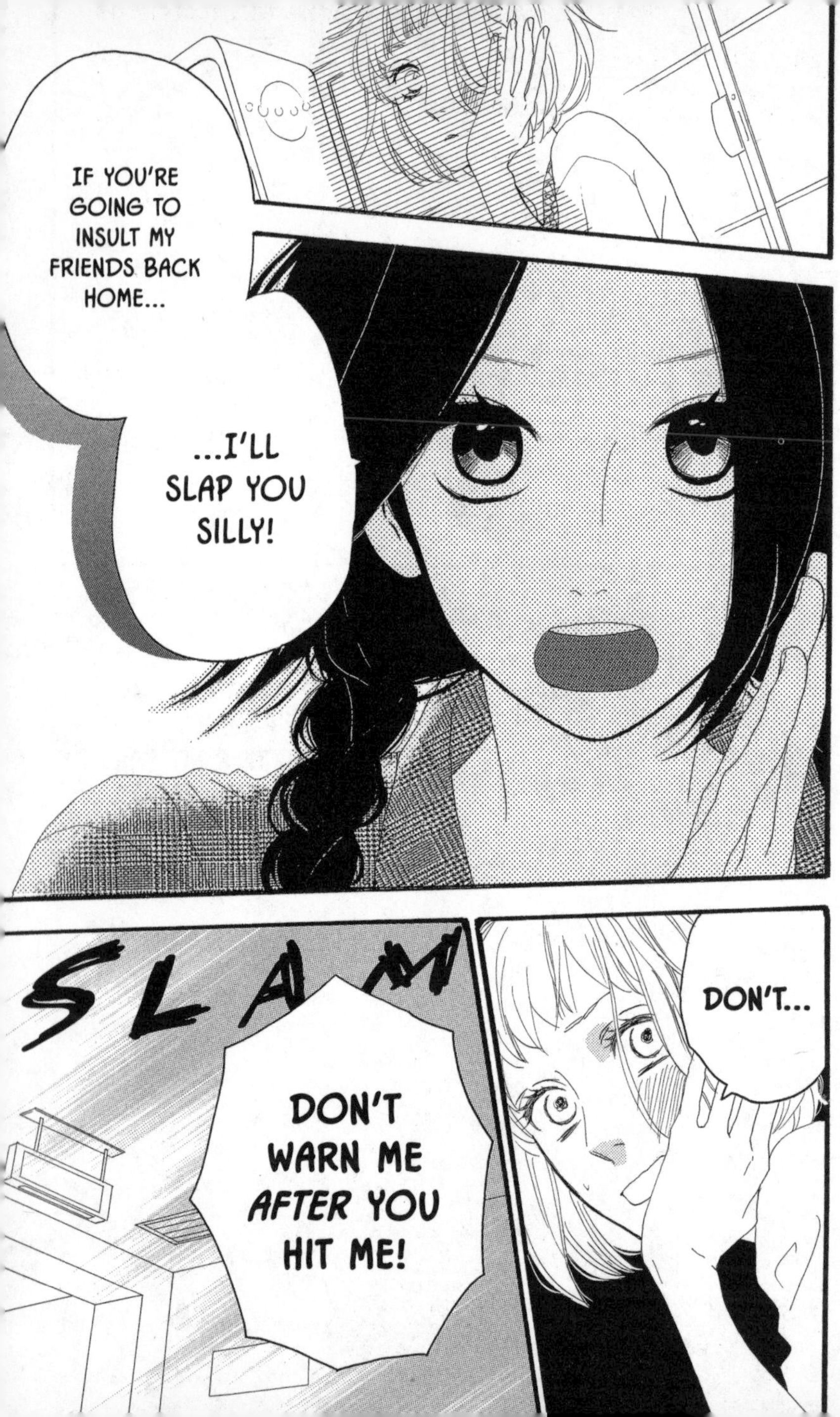
IF YOU'RE GOING TO INSULT MY FRIENDS BACK HOME...
...I'LL SLAP YOU SILLY!
DON'T...
SLAM
DON'T WARN ME AFTER YOU HIT ME!

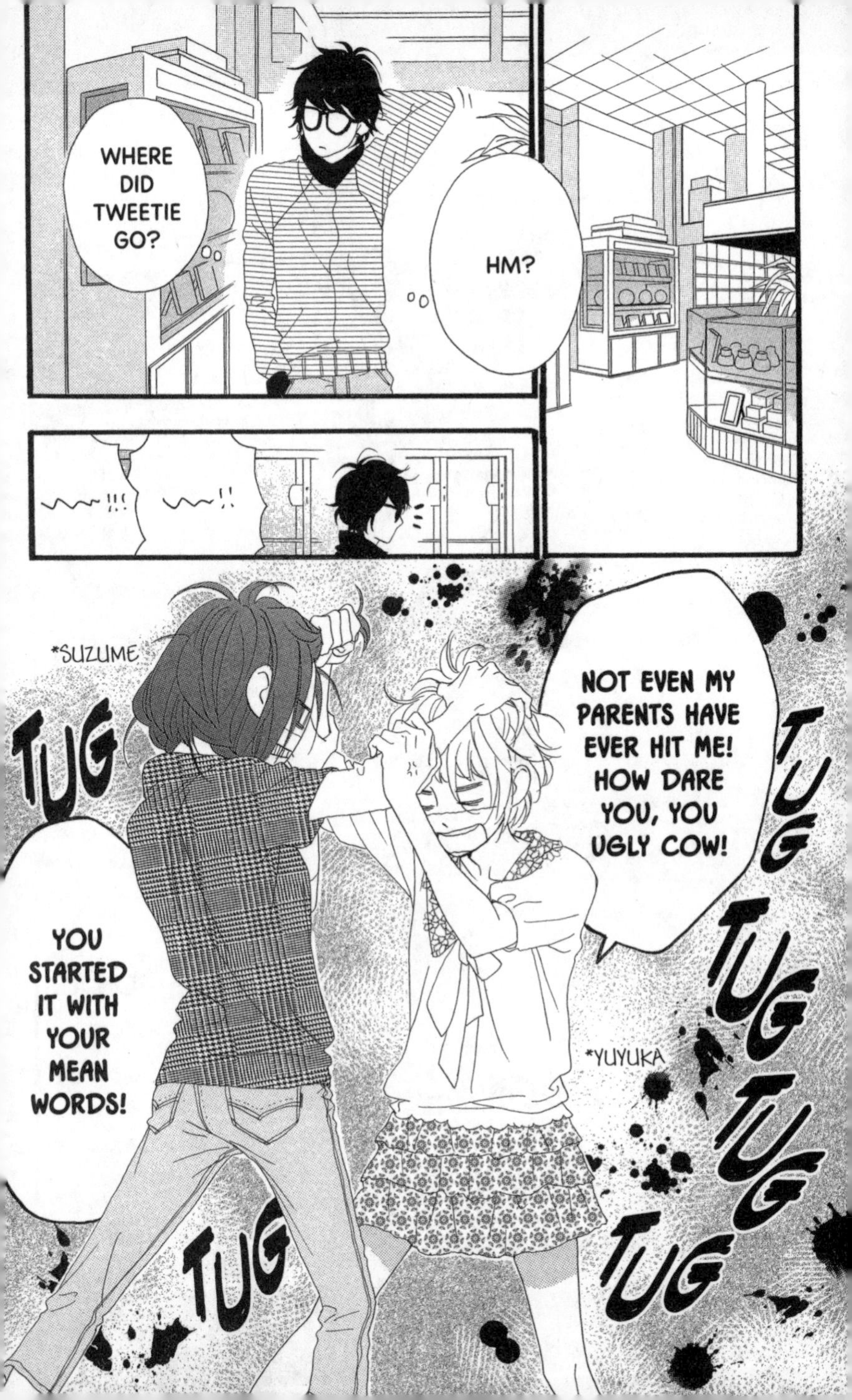

WHERE DID TWEETIE GO?
HM?
NOT EVEN MY PARENTS HAVE EVER HIT ME! HOW DARE YOU, YOU UGLY COW!
TUG TUG TUG TUG TUG
*YUYUKA
*SUZUME
TUG
YOU STARTED IT WITH YOUR MEAN WORDS!
TUG

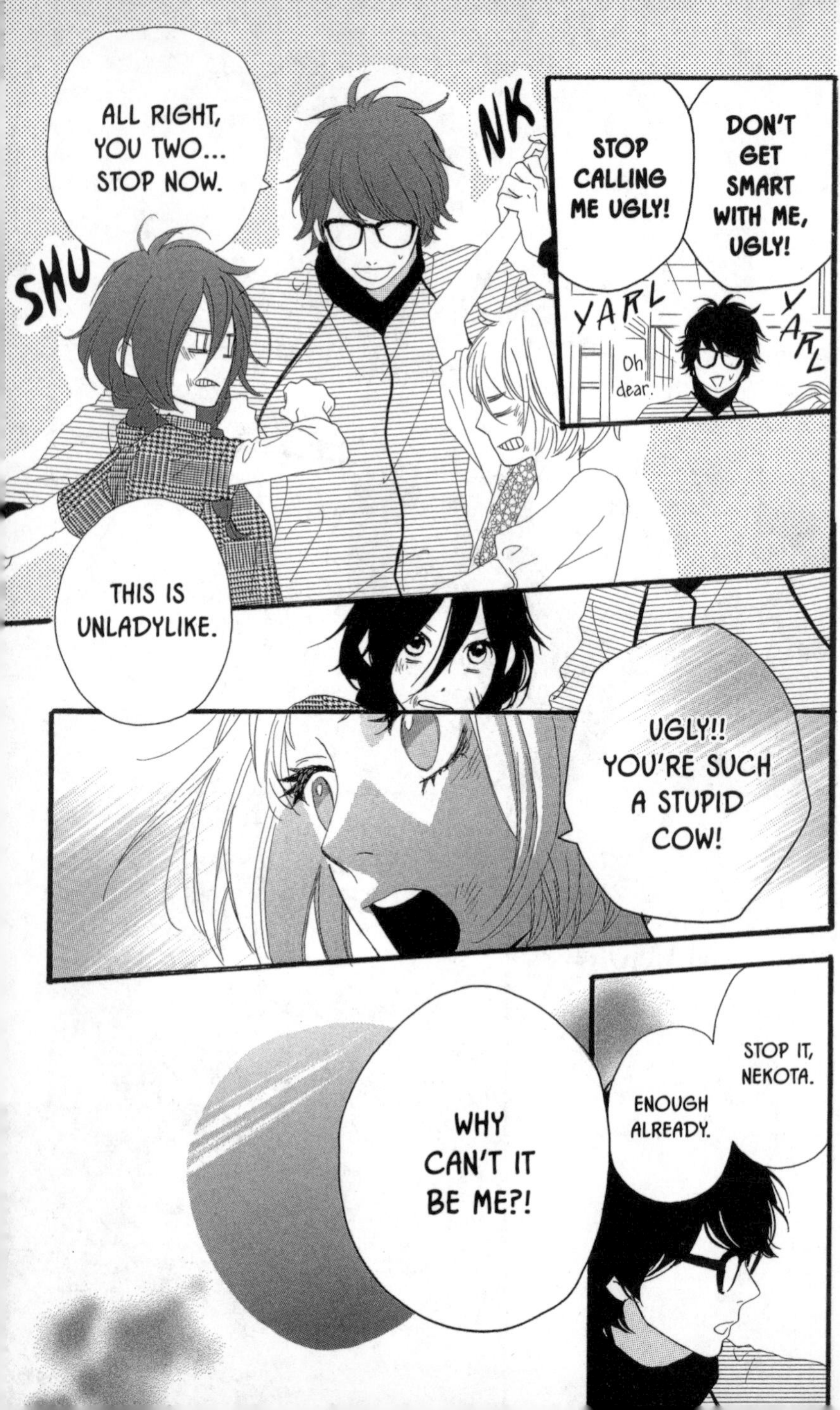
DON'T GET SMART WITH ME, UGLY!
STOP CALLING ME UGLY!
YARL
YARL
Oh dear.
NK
ALL RIGHT, YOU TWO... STOP NOW.
SHU
THIS IS UNLADYLIKE.
UGLY!! YOU'RE SUCH A STUPID COW!
STOP IT, NEKOTA.
ENOUGH ALREADY.
WHY CAN'T IT BE ME?!

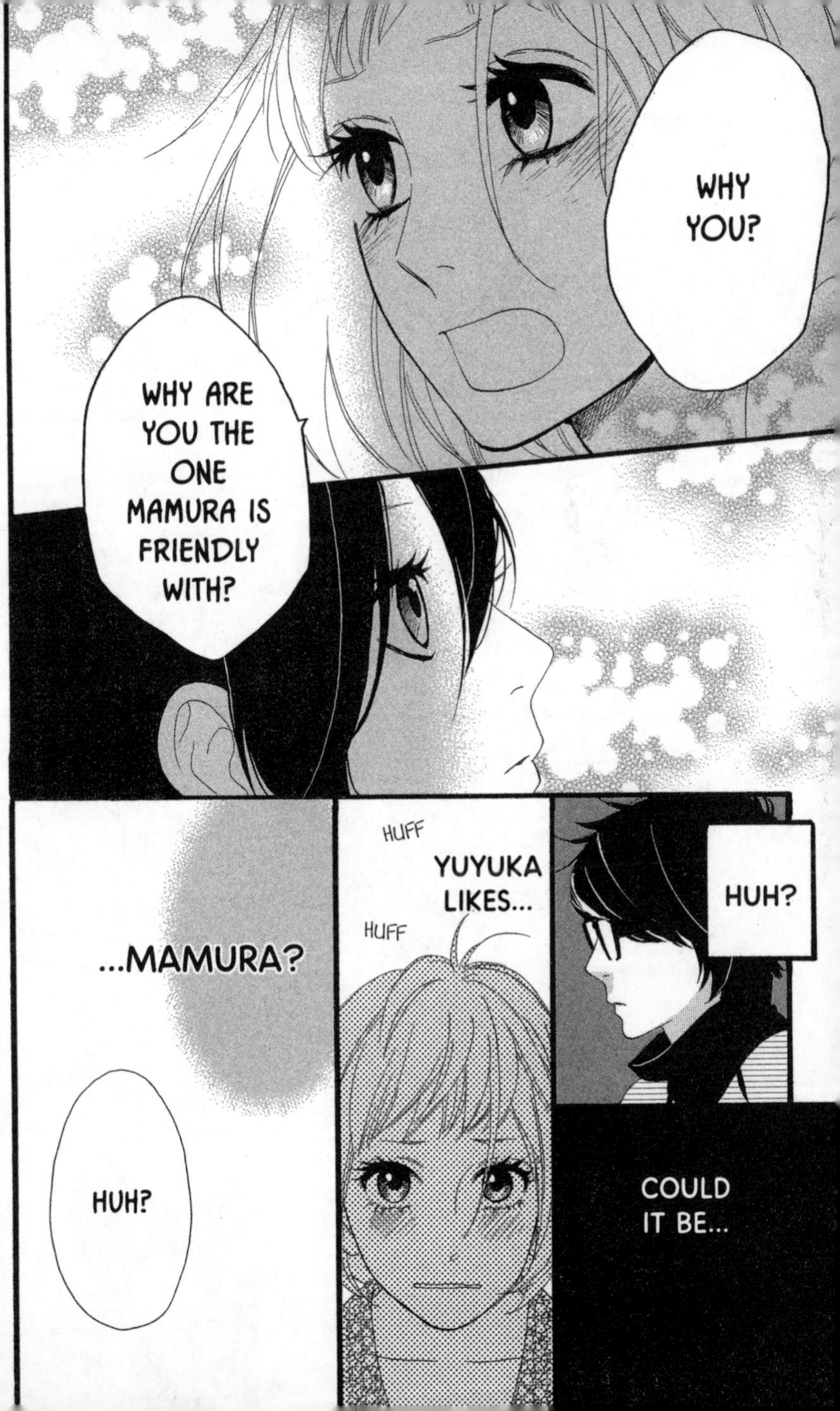

WHY YOU?
WHY ARE YOU THE ONE MAMURA IS FRIENDLY WITH?
HUH?
COULD IT BE...
HUFF
YUYUKA LIKES...
HUFF
...MAMURA?
HUH?

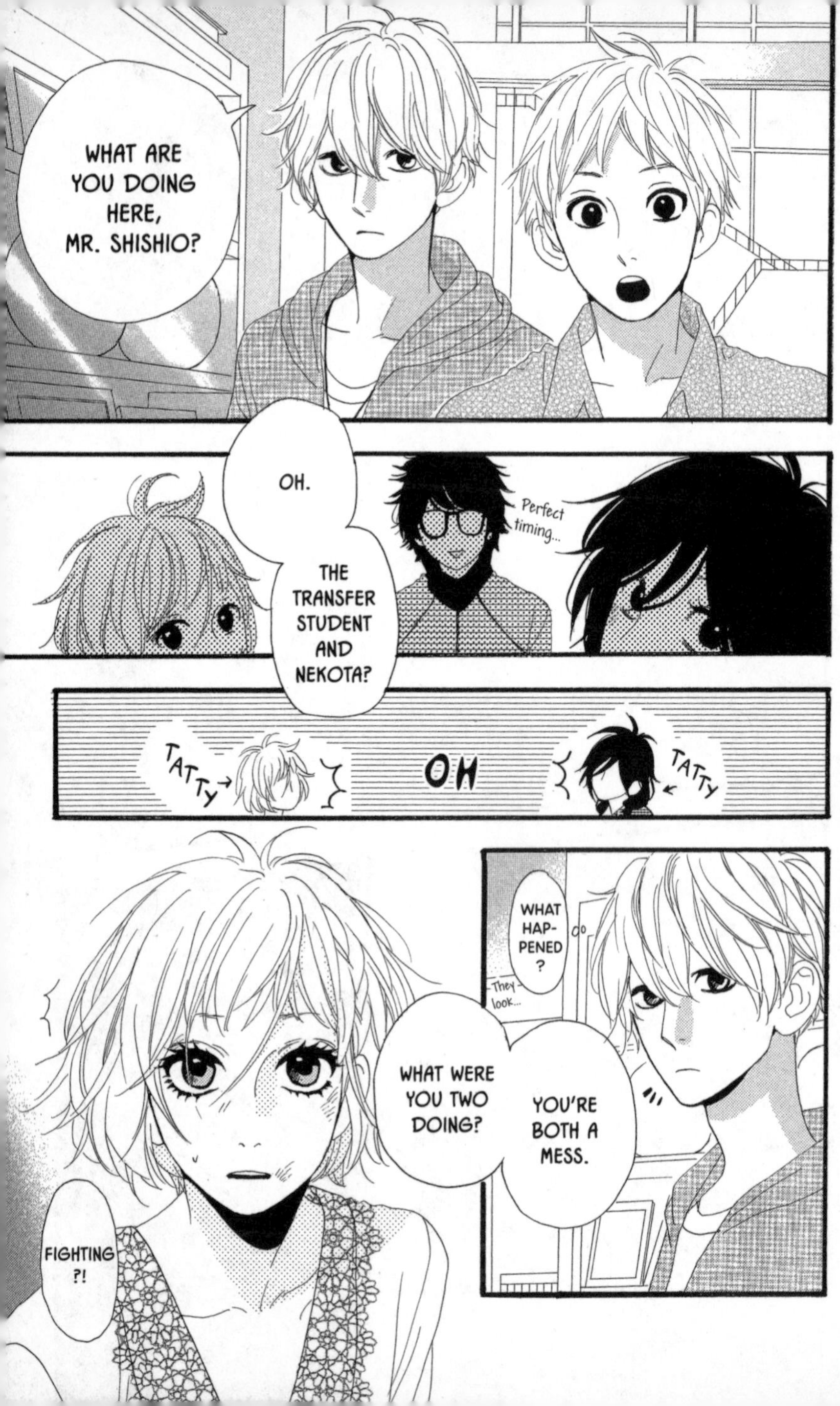
WHAT ARE YOU DOING HERE, MR. SHISHIO?
Perfect timing...
OH.
THE TRANSFER STUDENT AND NEKOTA?
TATTY
OH
TATTY
WHAT HAPPENED?
They look...
YOU'RE BOTH A MESS.
WHAT WERE YOU TWO DOING?
FIGHTING?!

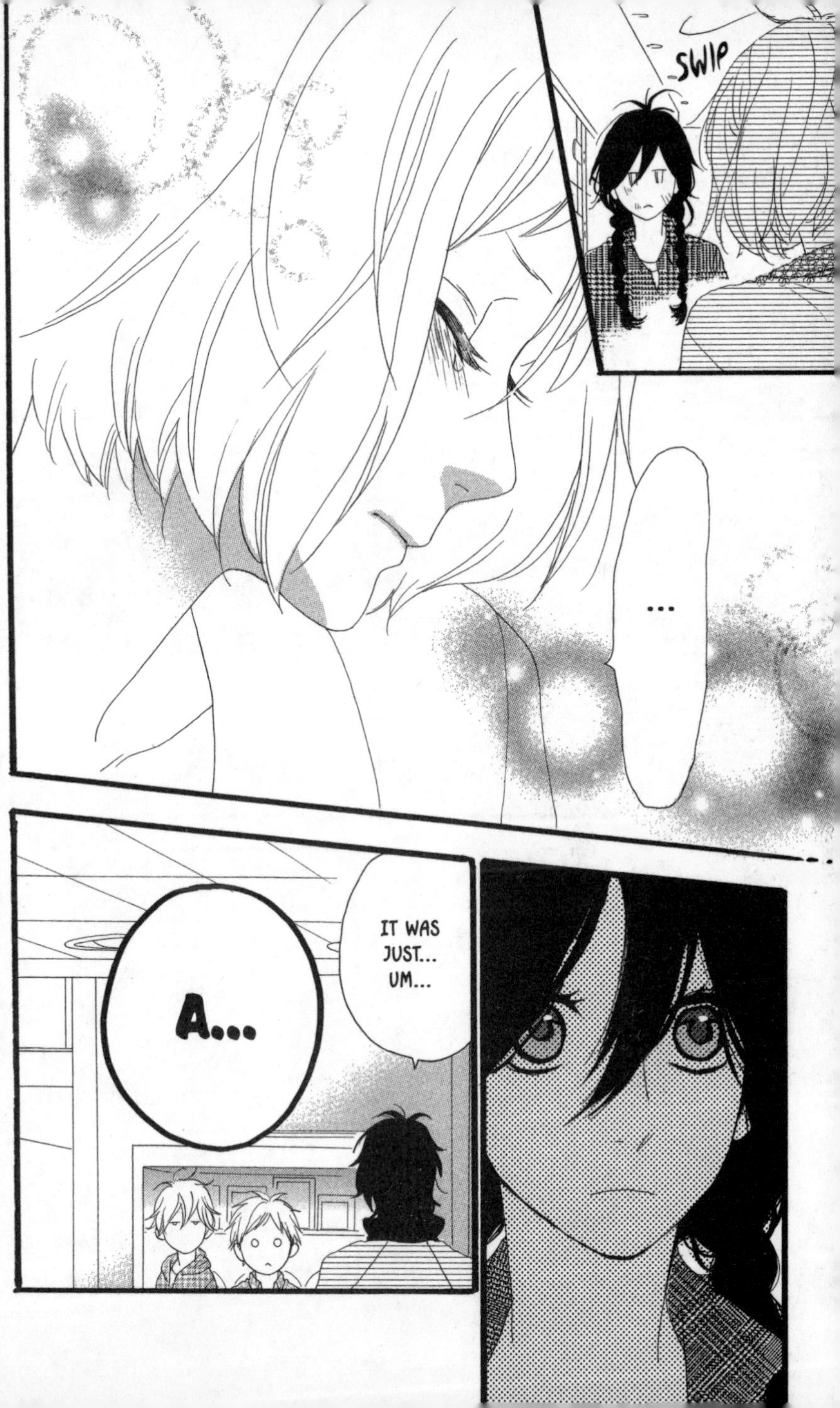
SWIP
...
IT WAS JUST... UM...
A...

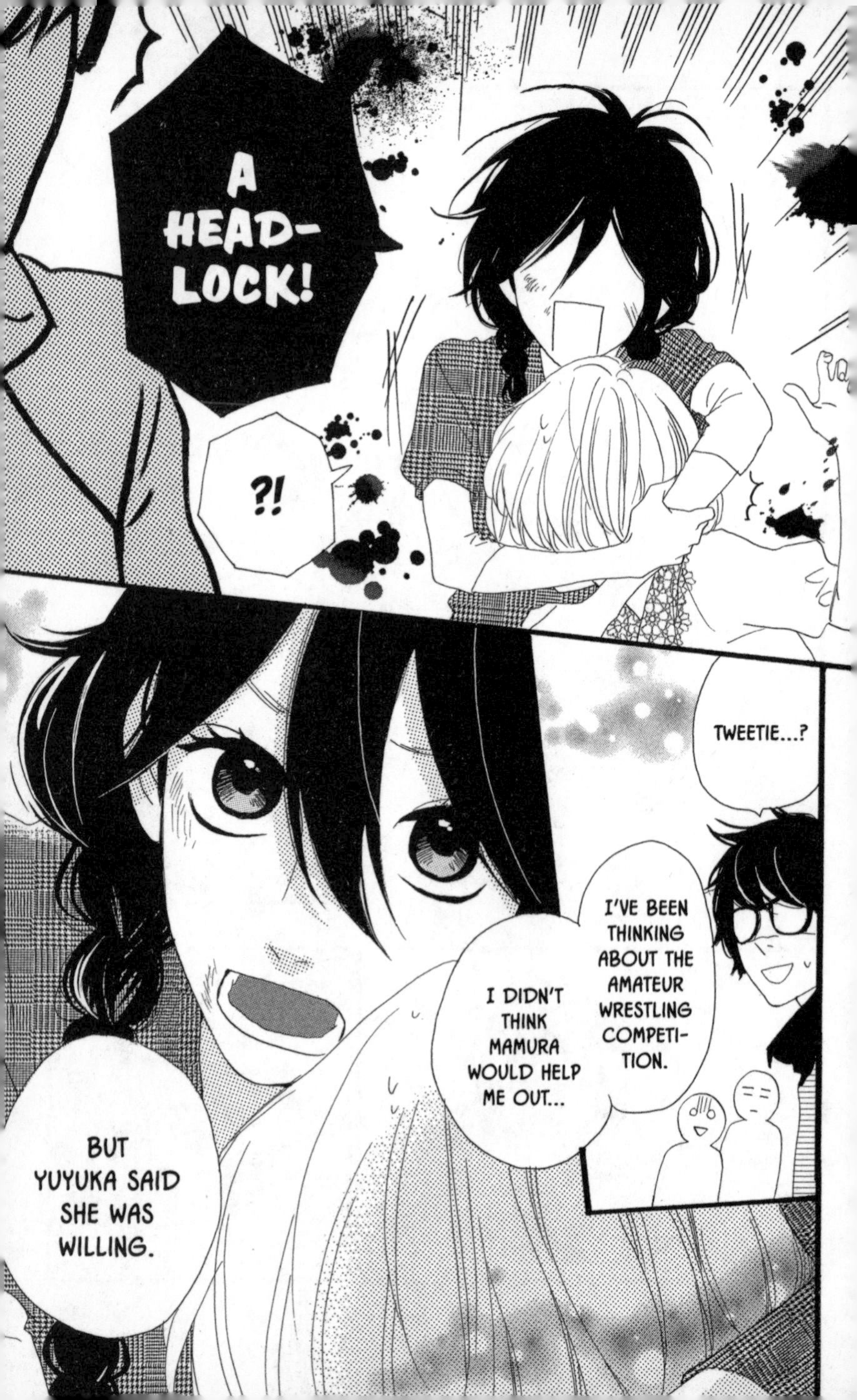
A HEAD-LOCK!
?!
TWEETIE...?
I'VE BEEN THINKING ABOUT THE AMATEUR WRESTLING COMPETITION.
I DIDN'T THINK MAMURA WOULD HELP ME OUT...
BUT YUYUKA SAID SHE WAS WILLING.

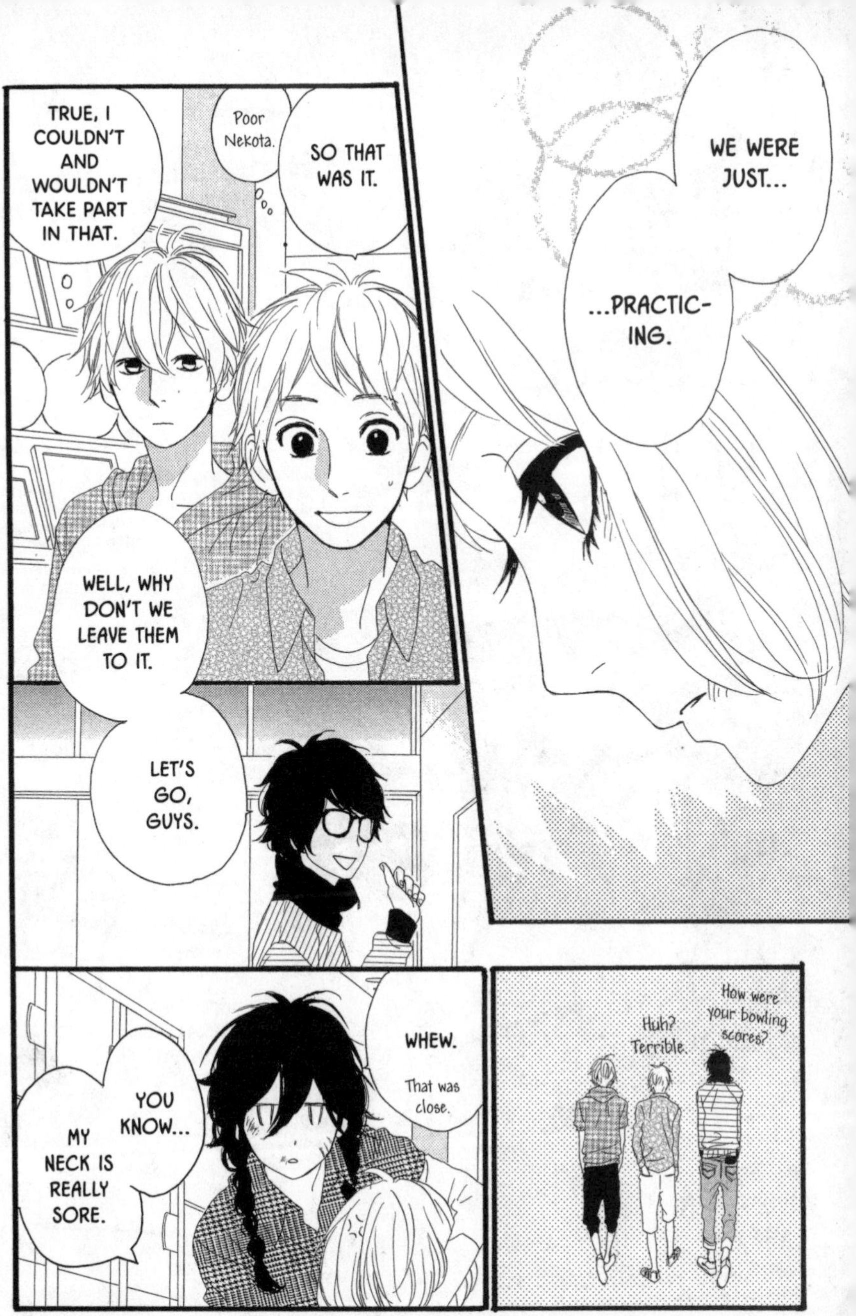
WE WERE JUST...
...PRACTIC-ING.
SO THAT WAS IT.
Poor Nekota.
TRUE, I COULDN'T AND WOULDN'T TAKE PART IN THAT.
WELL, WHY DON'T WE LEAVE THEM TO IT.
LET'S GO, GUYS.
How were your bowling scores?
Huh? Terrible.
WHEW.
That was close.
YOU KNOW...
MY NECK IS REALLY SORE.

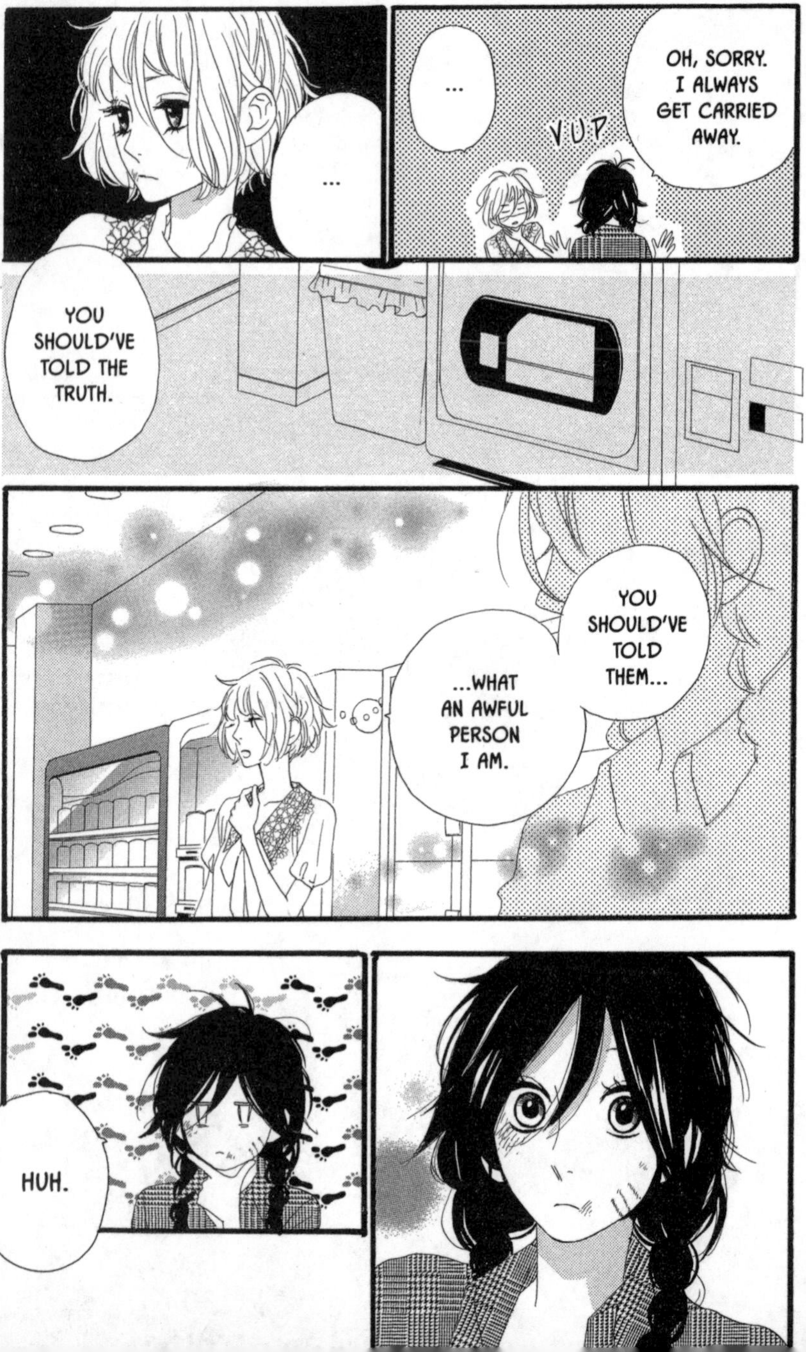
OH, SORRY. I ALWAYS GET CARRIED AWAY.
...
VUP
...
YOU SHOULD'VE TOLD THE TRUTH.
YOU SHOULD'VE TOLD THEM...
...WHAT AN AWFUL PERSON I AM.
HUH.

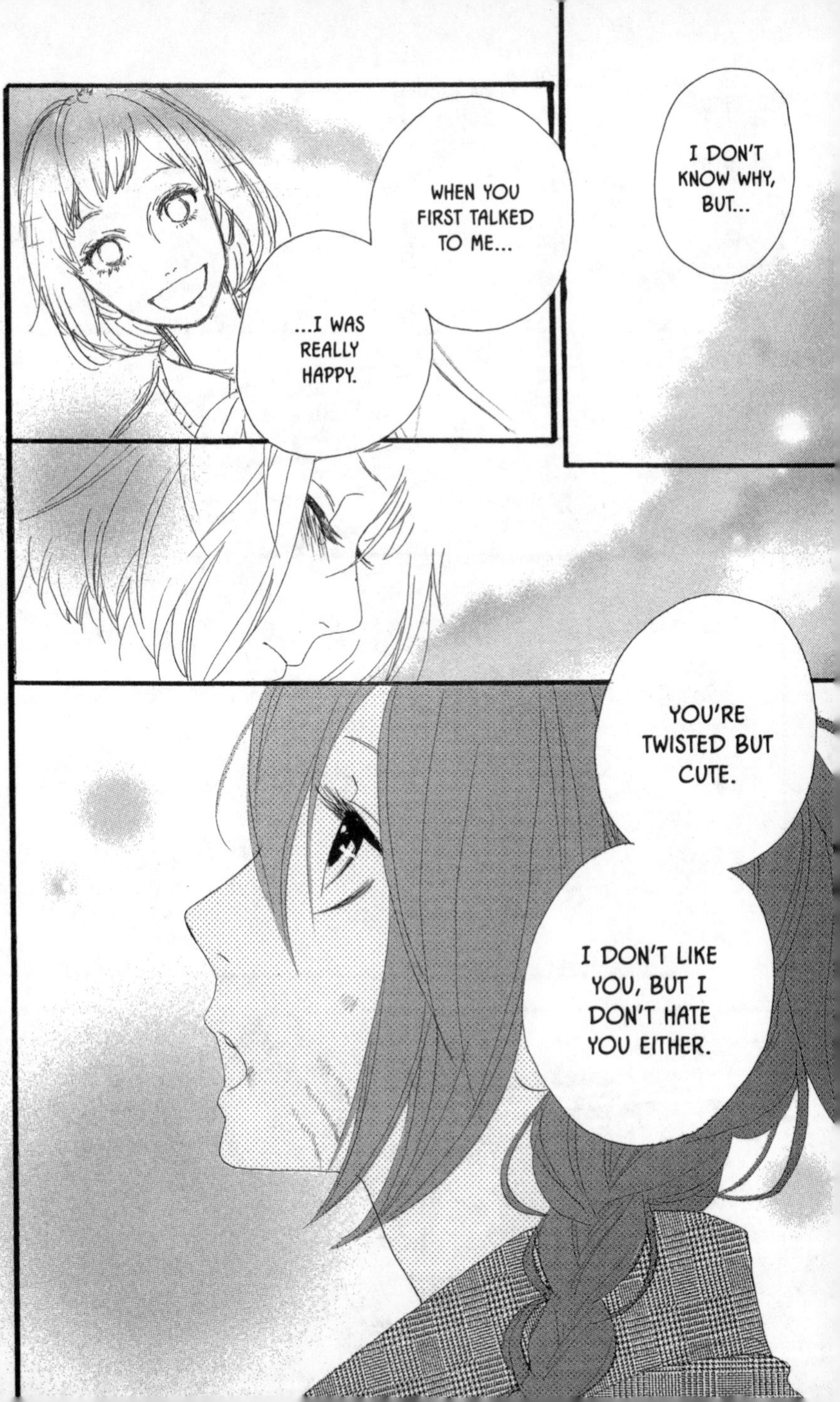
I DON'T KNOW WHY, BUT...
WHEN YOU FIRST TALKED TO ME...
...I WAS REALLY HAPPY.
YOU'RE TWISTED BUT CUTE.
I DON'T LIKE YOU, BUT I DON'T HATE YOU EITHER.

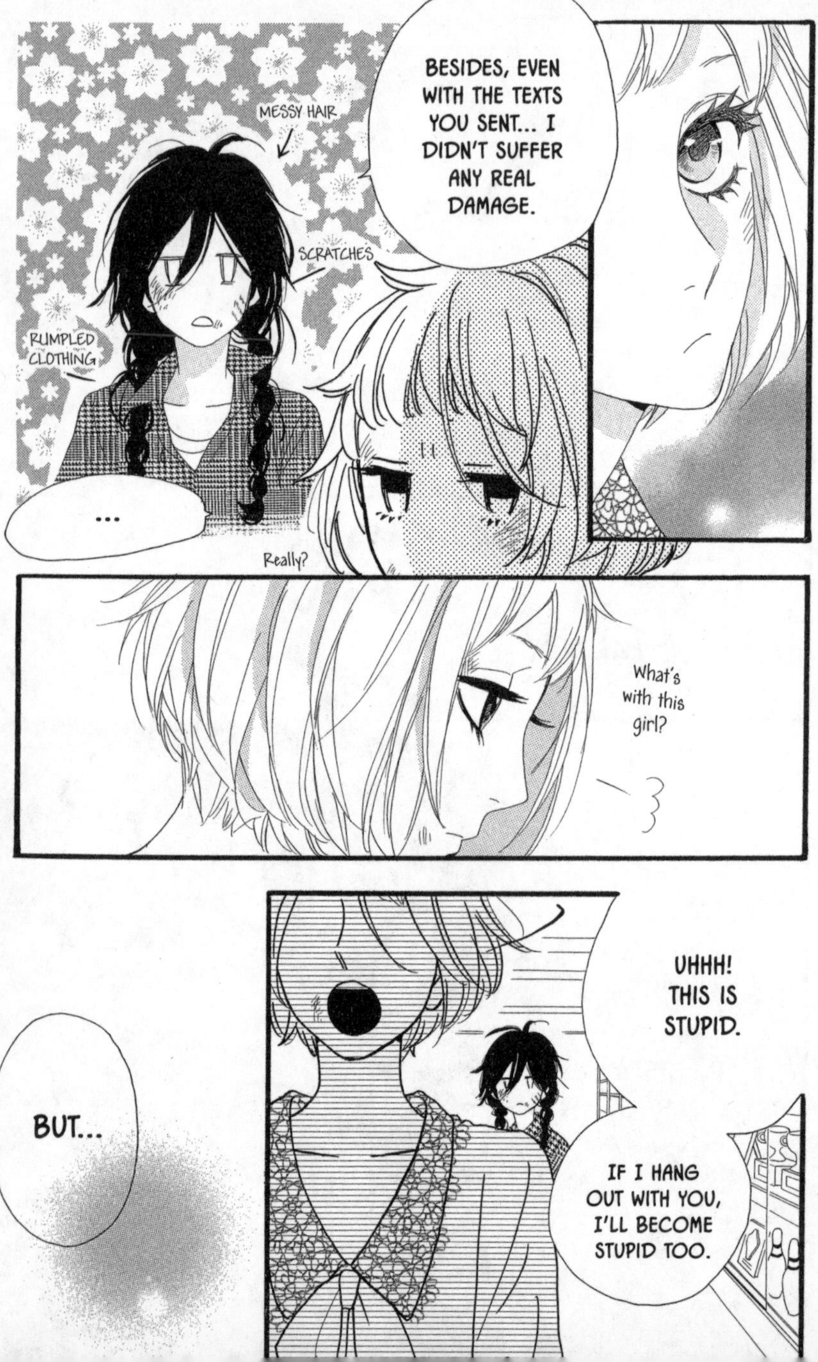
BESIDES, EVEN WITH THE TEXTS YOU SENT... I DIDN'T SUFFER ANY REAL DAMAGE.
Really?
MESSY HAIR
SCRATCHES
RUMPLED CLOTHING
...
What's with this girl?
UHHH! THIS IS STUPID.
IF I HANG OUT WITH YOU, I'LL BECOME STUPID TOO.
BUT...

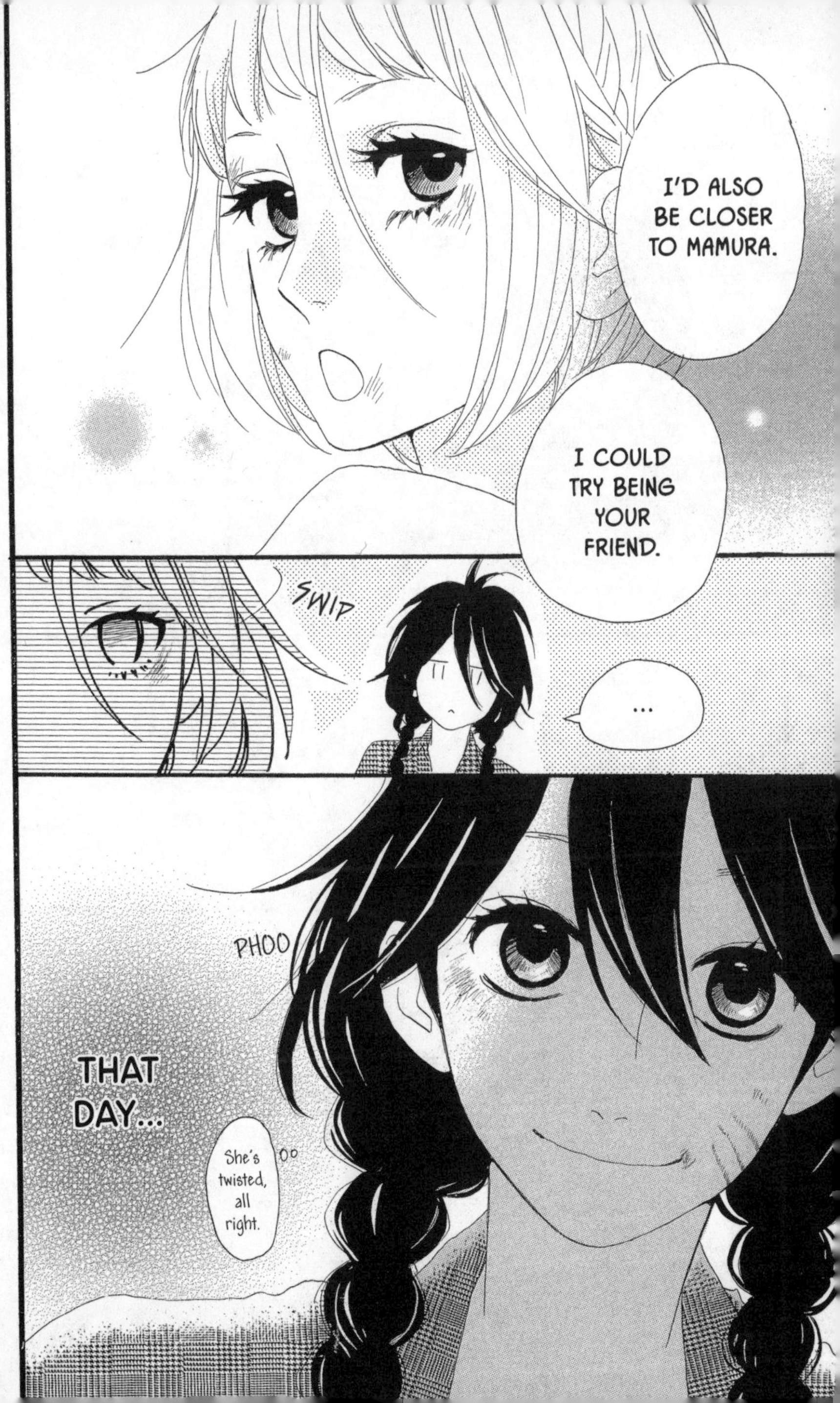
I'D ALSO BE CLOSER TO MAMURA.
I COULD TRY BEING YOUR FRIEND.
...
SWIP
PHOO
She's twisted, all right.
THAT DAY...

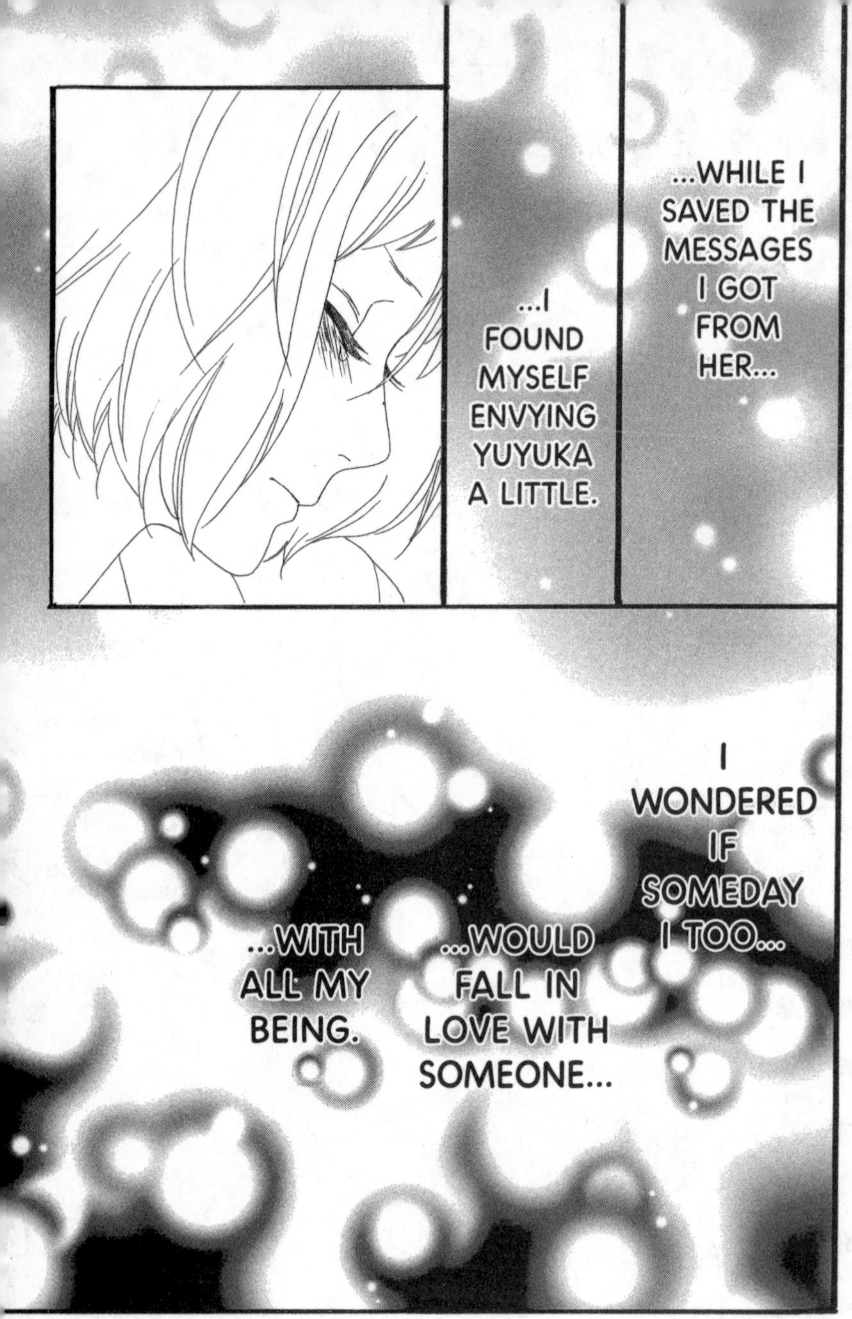
...WHILE I SAVED THE MESSAGES I GOT FROM HER...
...I FOUND MYSELF ENVYING YUYUKA A LITTLE.
I WONDERED IF SOMEDAY I TOO...
...WOULD FALL IN LOVE WITH SOMEONE...
...WITH ALL MY BEING.

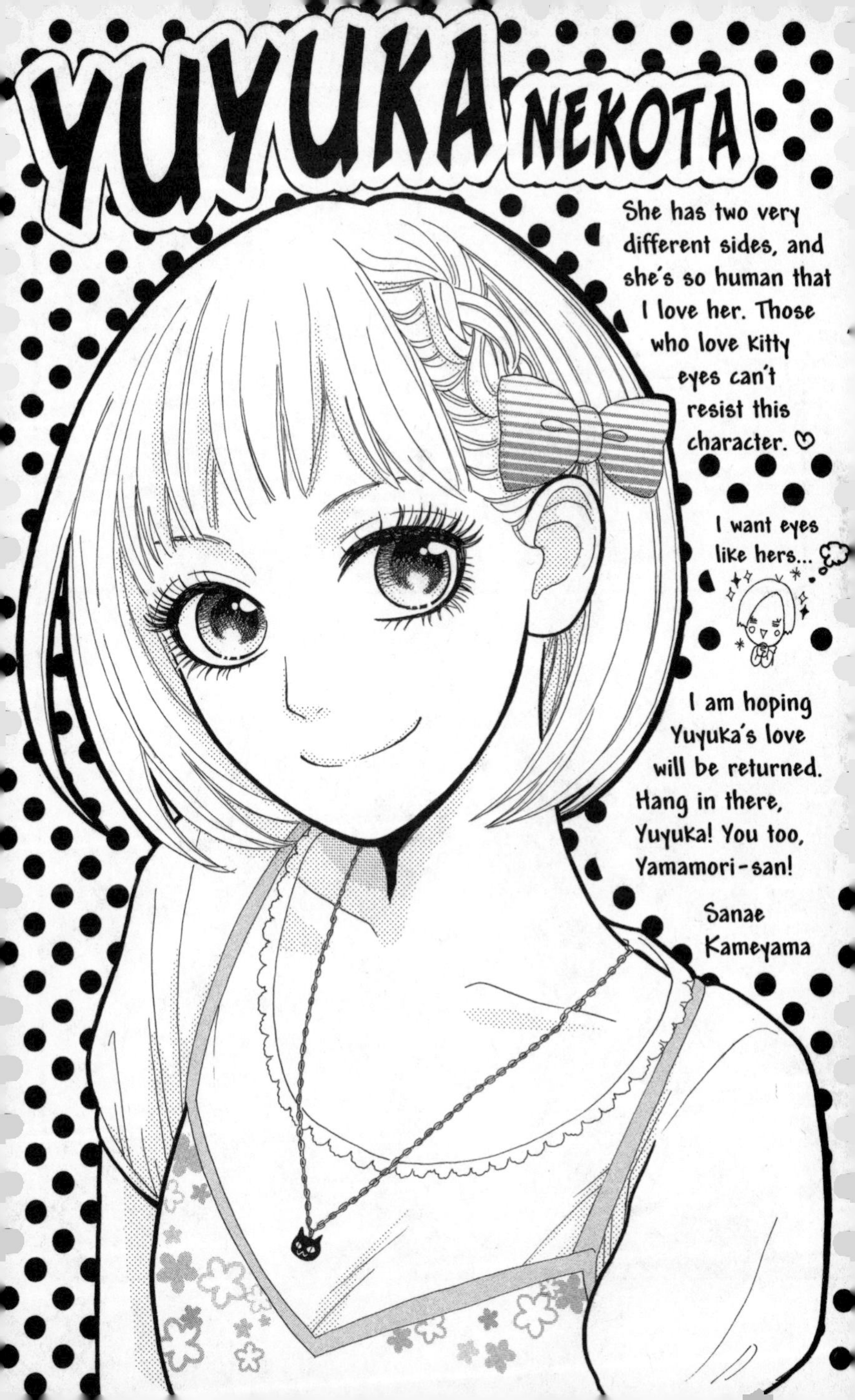
YUYUKA NEKOTA
She has two very different sides, and she's so human that I love her. Those who love kitty eyes can't resist this character. ♡
I want eyes like hers...
I am hoping Yuyuka's love will be returned. Hang in there, Yuyuka! You too, Yamamori-san!
Sanae Kameyama

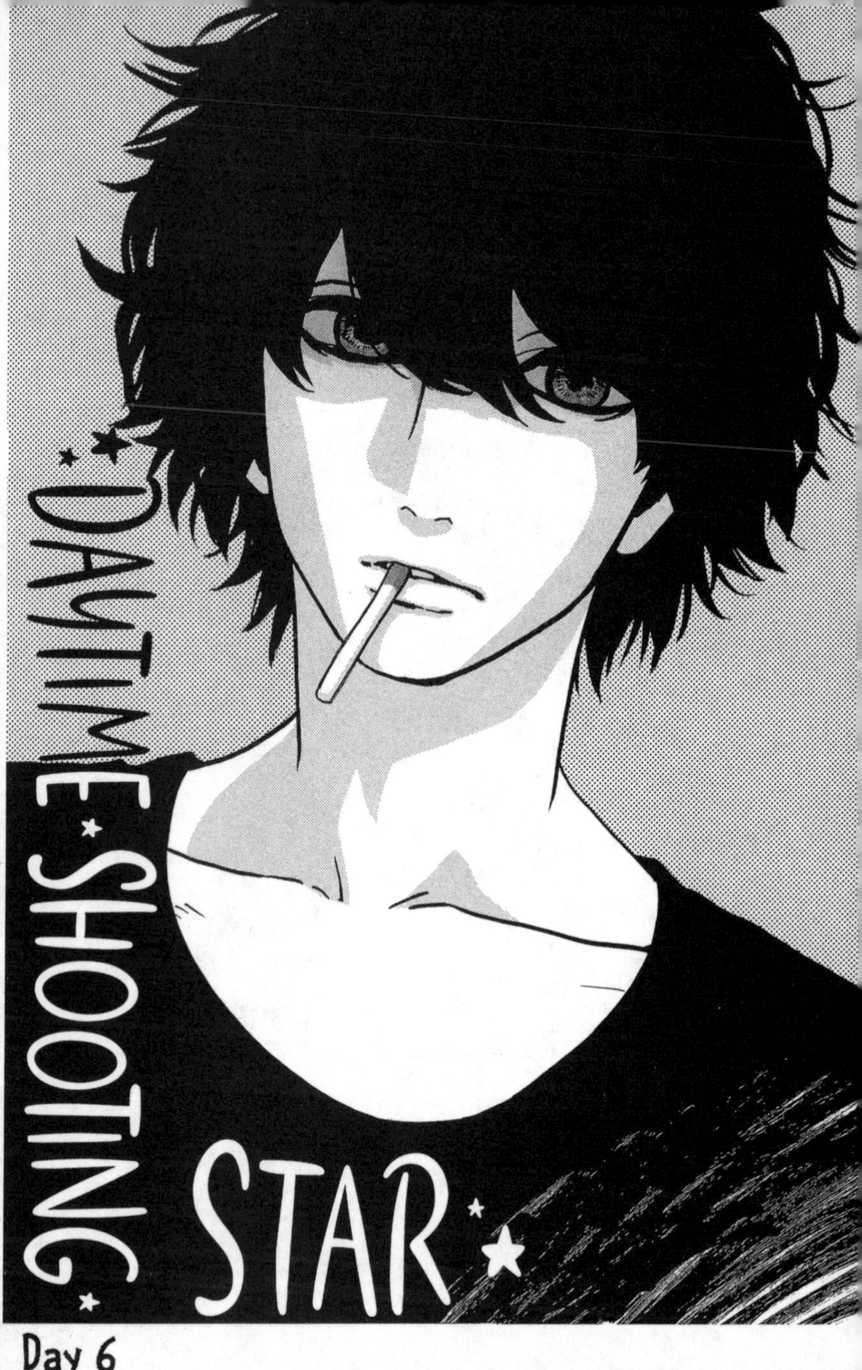
DAYTIME SHOOTING STAR

Day 6

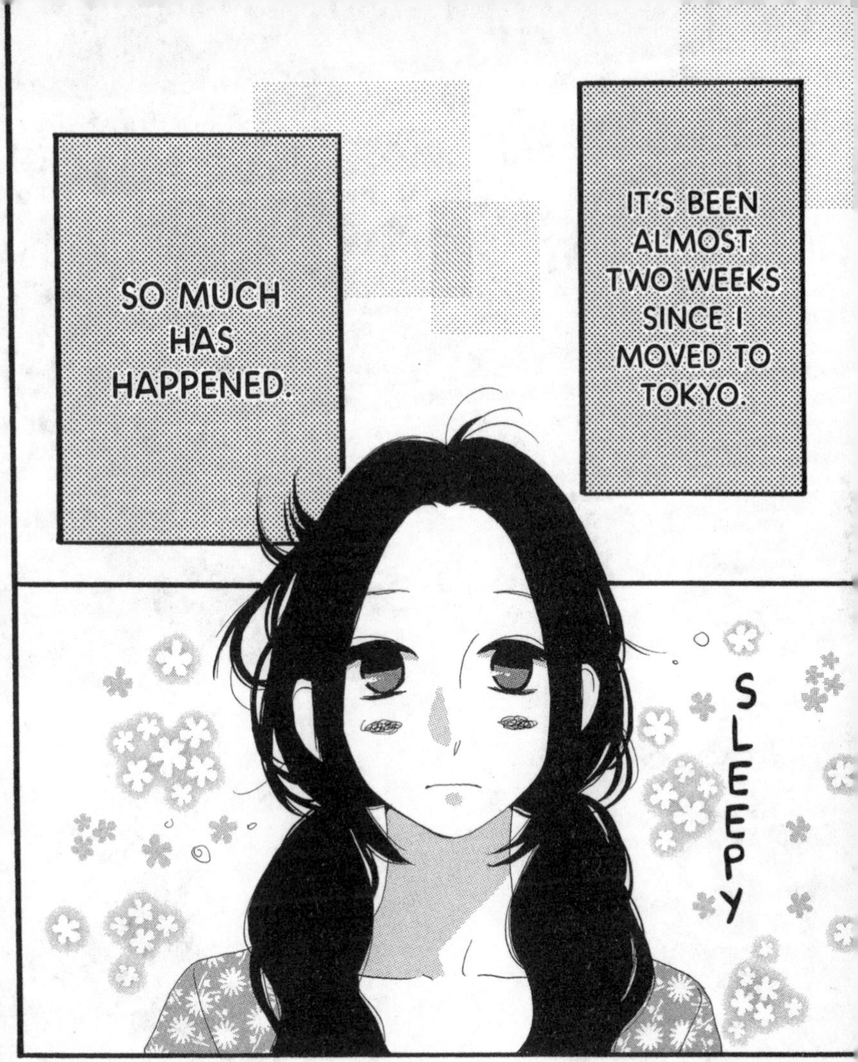
IT'S BEEN ALMOST TWO WEEKS SINCE I MOVED TO TOKYO.
SO MUCH HAS HAPPENED.
SLEEPY

Yuyuka Nekota

Birthday: August 30
Height: 5'1"
Weight: 95 lbs
Blood Type: AB

① Pies. Anything powdery.
② Fingernails. Makeup.
③ Her phone battery dies quickly.

*Neko means "cat."

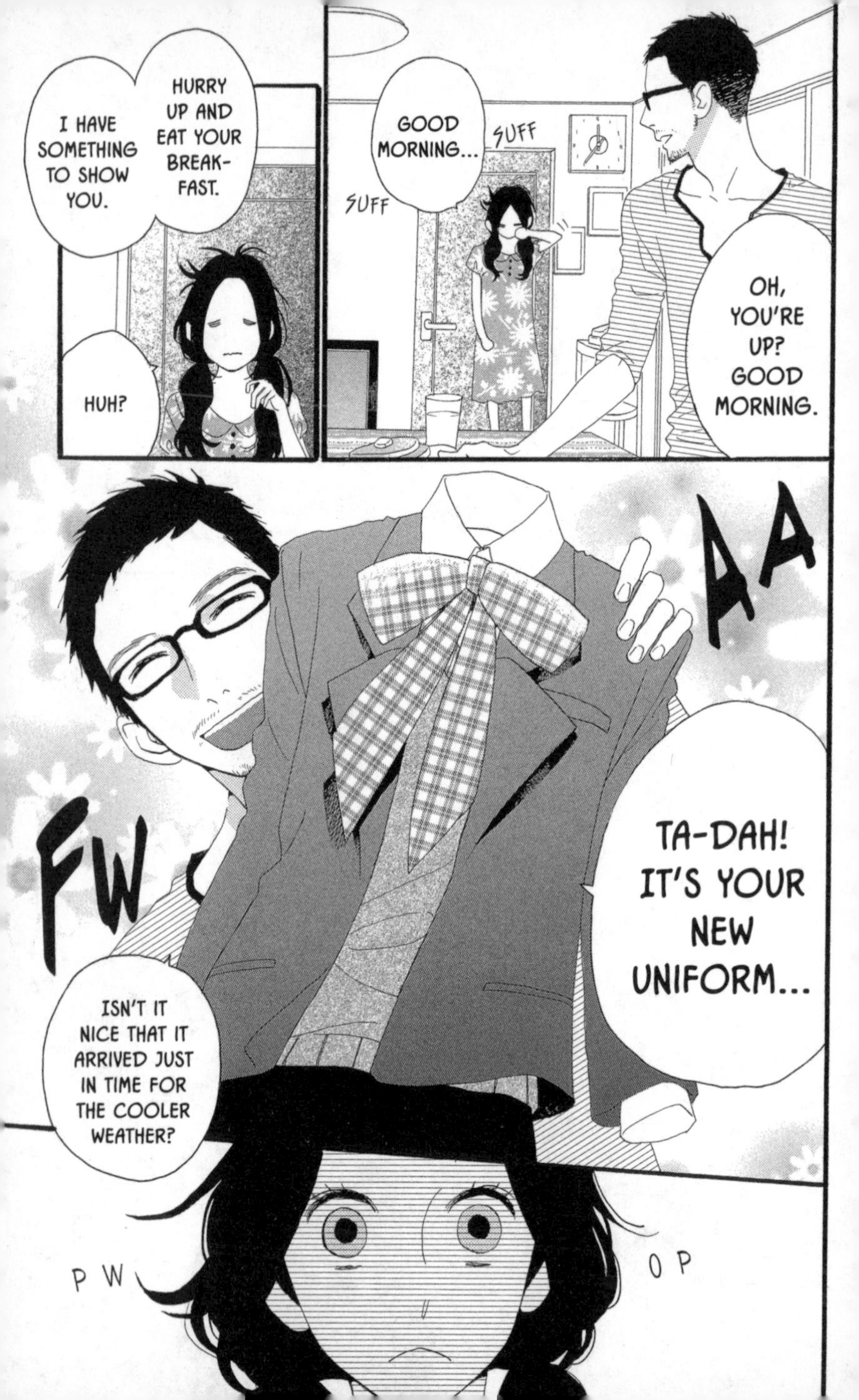
GOOD MORNING...
SUFF
SUFF
OH, YOU'RE UP? GOOD MORNING.
HURRY UP AND EAT YOUR BREAKFAST.
I HAVE SOMETHING TO SHOW YOU.
HUH?
FWAA
TA-DAH! IT'S YOUR NEW UNIFORM...
ISN'T IT NICE THAT IT ARRIVED JUST IN TIME FOR THE COOLER WEATHER?
PWOP

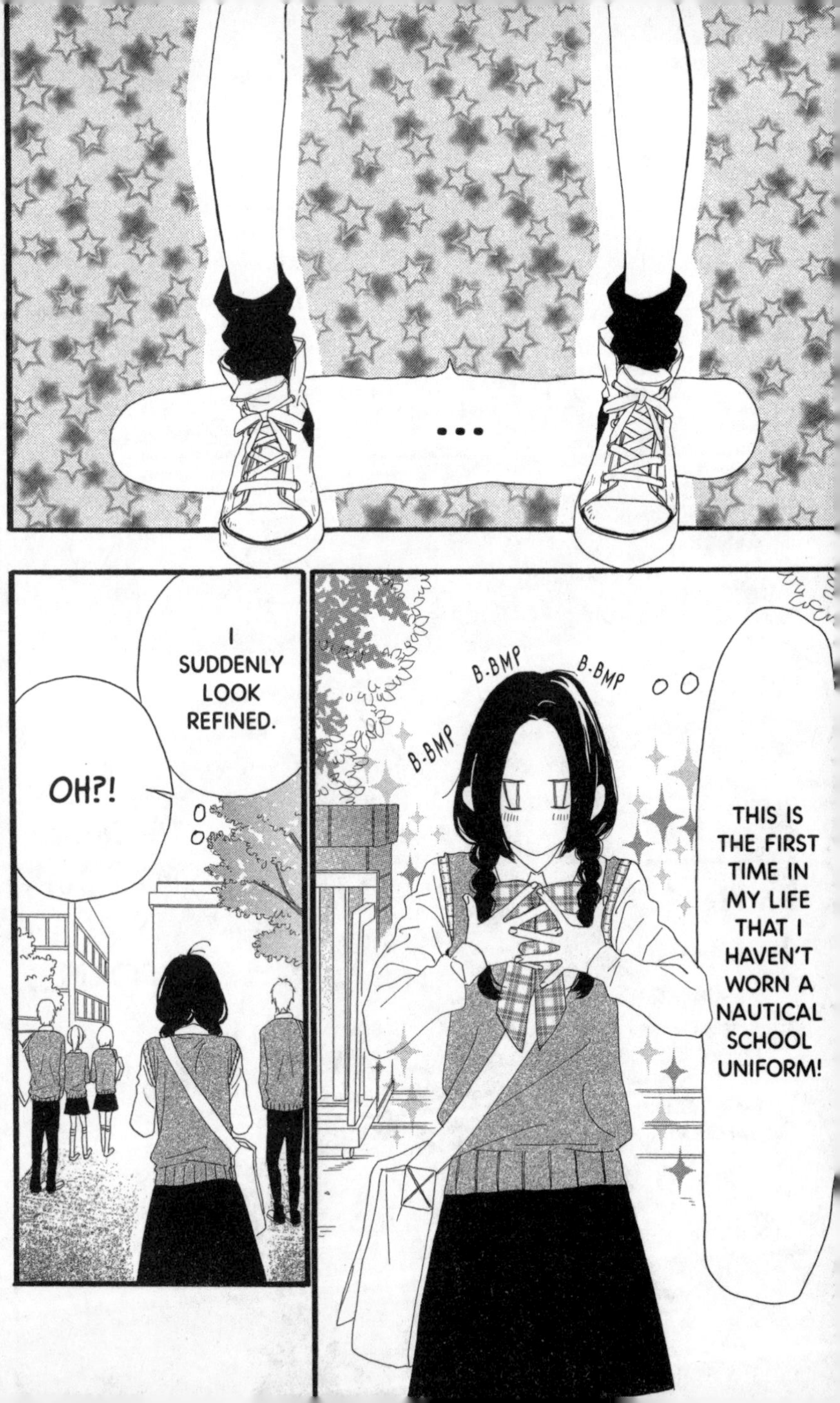
...
THIS IS THE FIRST TIME IN MY LIFE THAT I HAVEN'T WORN A NAUTICAL SCHOOL UNIFORM!
B-BMP
B-BMP
B-BMP
I SUDDENLY LOOK REFINED.
OH?!

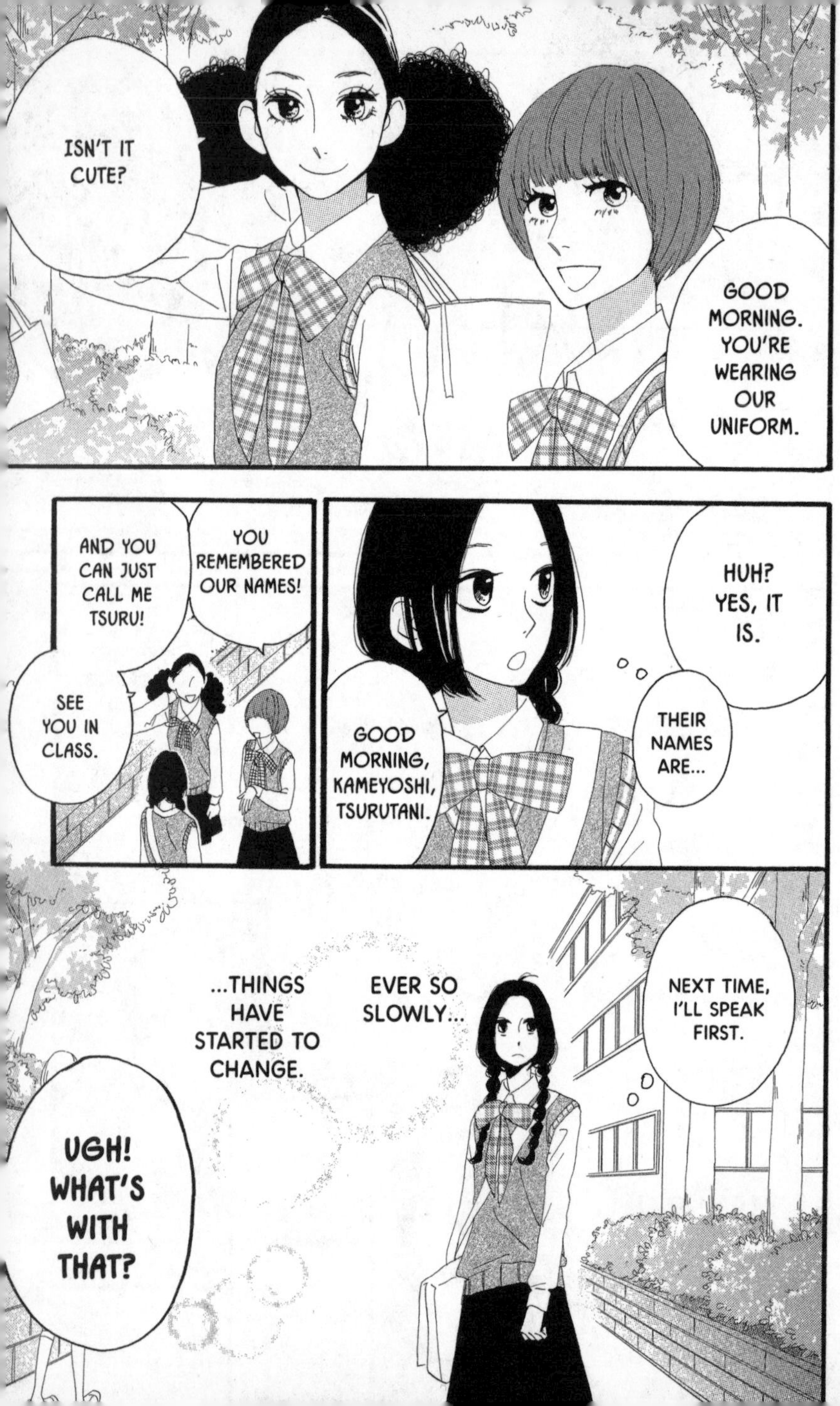
GOOD MORNING. YOU'RE WEARING OUR UNIFORM.
ISN'T IT CUTE?
HUH? YES, IT IS.
THEIR NAMES ARE...
GOOD MORNING, KAMEYOSHI, TSURUTANI.
YOU REMEMBERED OUR NAMES!
AND YOU CAN JUST CALL ME TSURU!
SEE YOU IN CLASS.
NEXT TIME, I'LL SPEAK FIRST.
EVER SO SLOWLY...
...THINGS HAVE STARTED TO CHANGE.
UGH! WHAT'S WITH THAT?

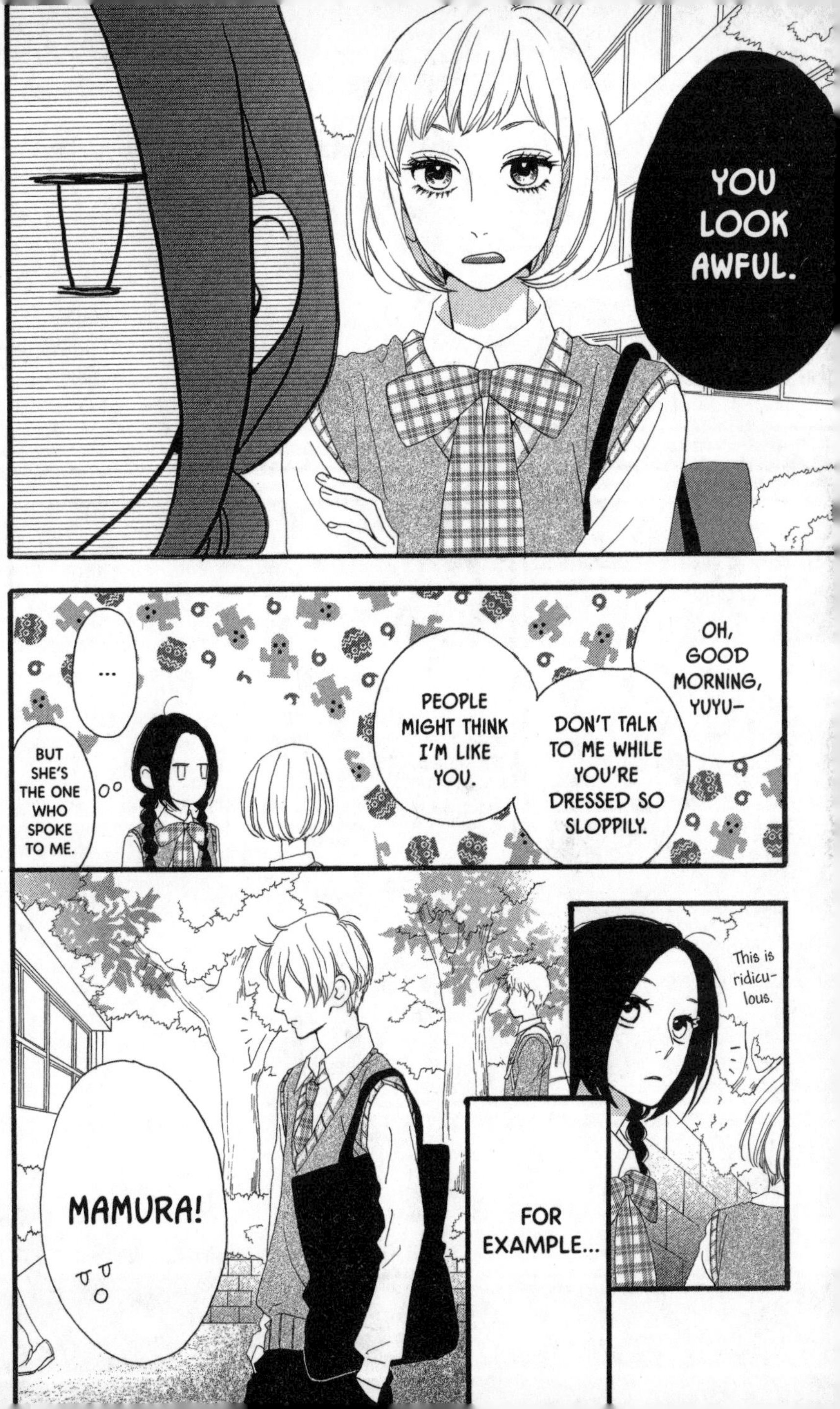
YOU LOOK AWFUL.
OH, GOOD MORNING, YUYU–
DON'T TALK TO ME WHILE YOU'RE DRESSED SO SLOPPILY.
PEOPLE MIGHT THINK I'M LIKE YOU.
...
BUT SHE'S THE ONE WHO SPOKE TO ME.
This is ridicu-lous.
FOR EXAMPLE...
MAMURA!

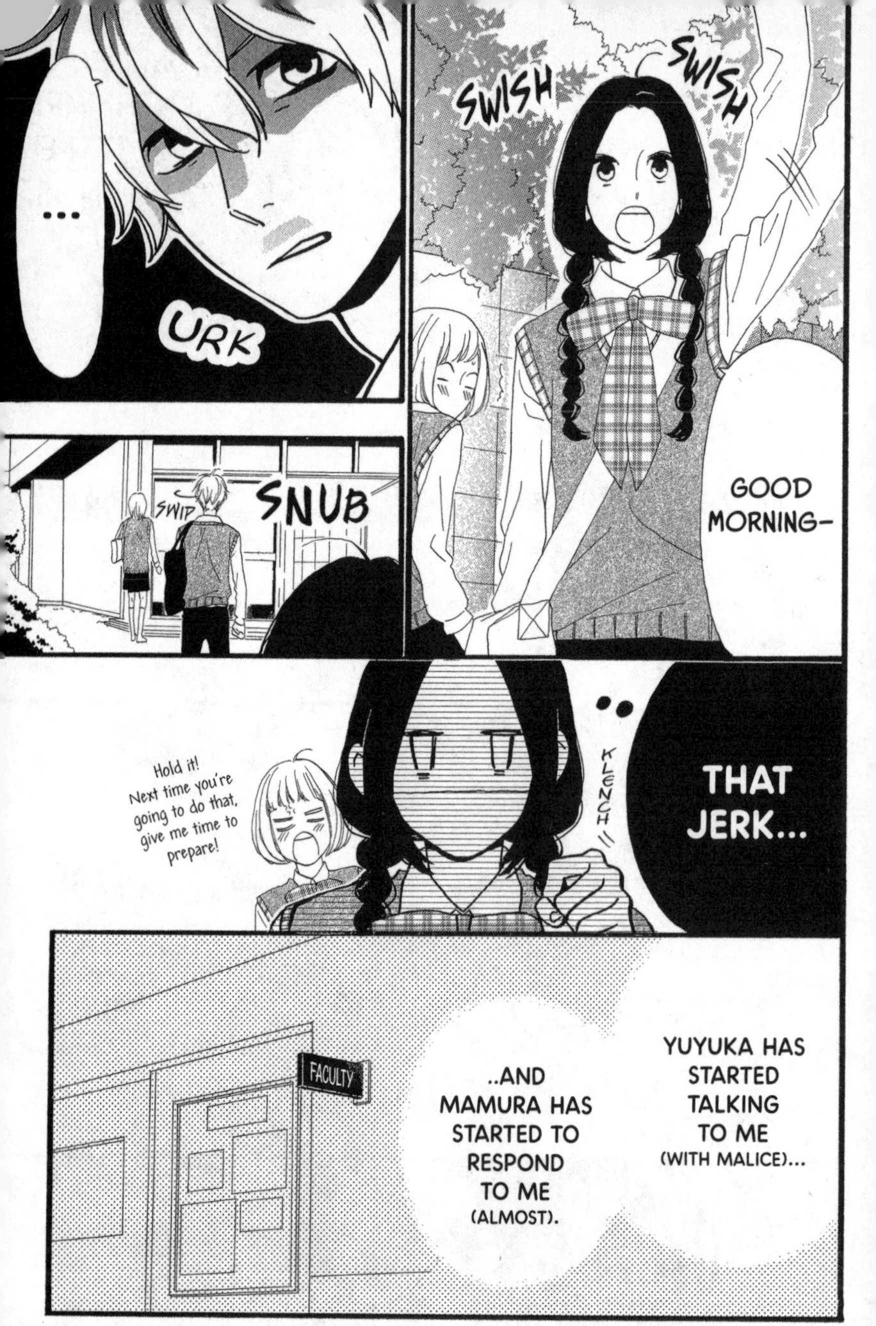
SWISH
SWISH
GOOD MORNING-
...
URK
SWIP
SNUB
••
THAT JERK...
KLENCH
Hold it! Next time you're going to do that, give me time to prepare!
YUYUKA HAS STARTED TALKING TO ME (WITH MALICE)...
..AND MAMURA HAS STARTED TO RESPOND TO ME (ALMOST).
FACULTY

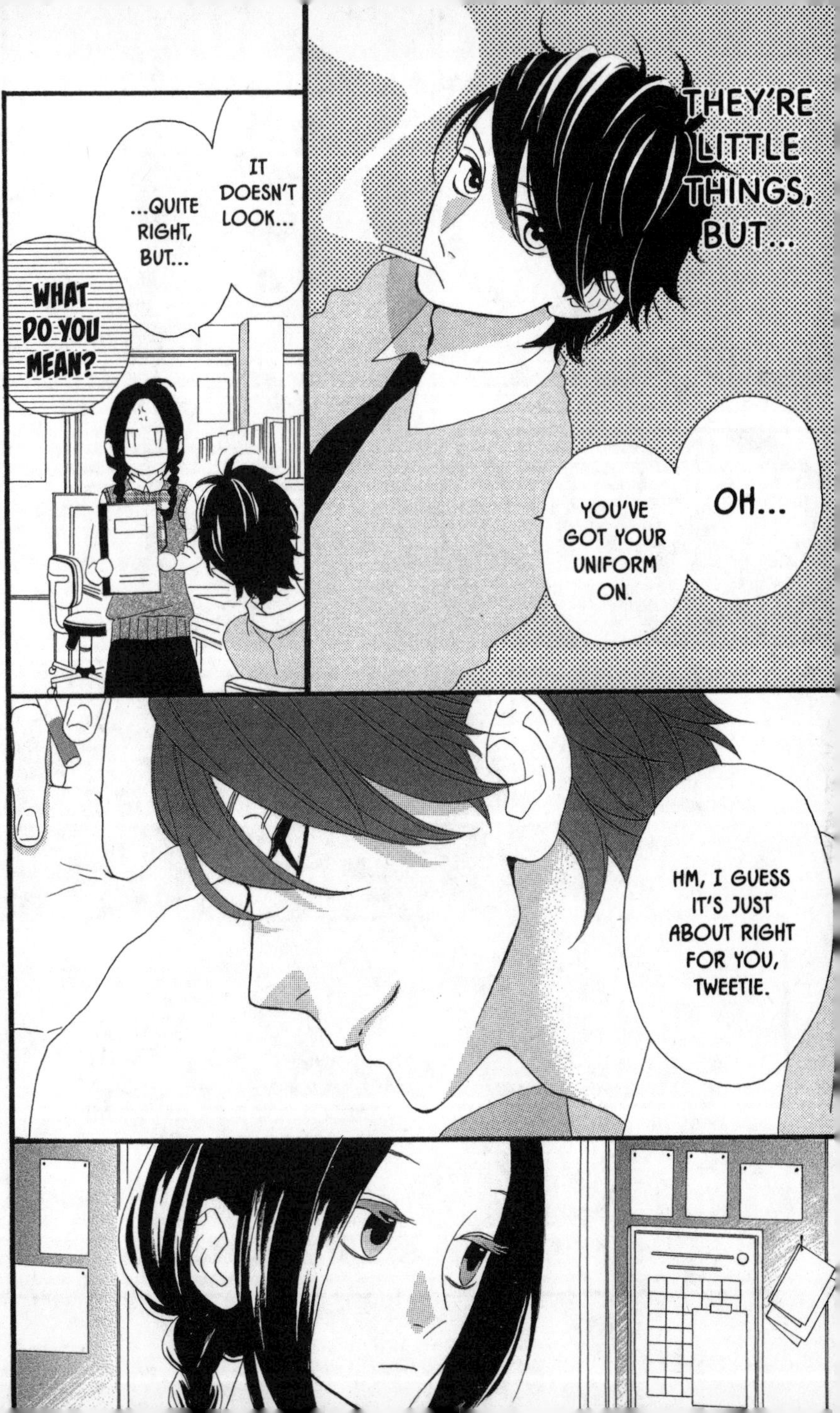
THEY'RE LITTLE THINGS, BUT...
OH...
YOU'VE GOT YOUR UNIFORM ON.
IT DOESN'T LOOK...
...QUITE RIGHT, BUT...
WHAT DO YOU MEAN?
HM, I GUESS IT'S JUST ABOUT RIGHT FOR YOU, TWEETIE.

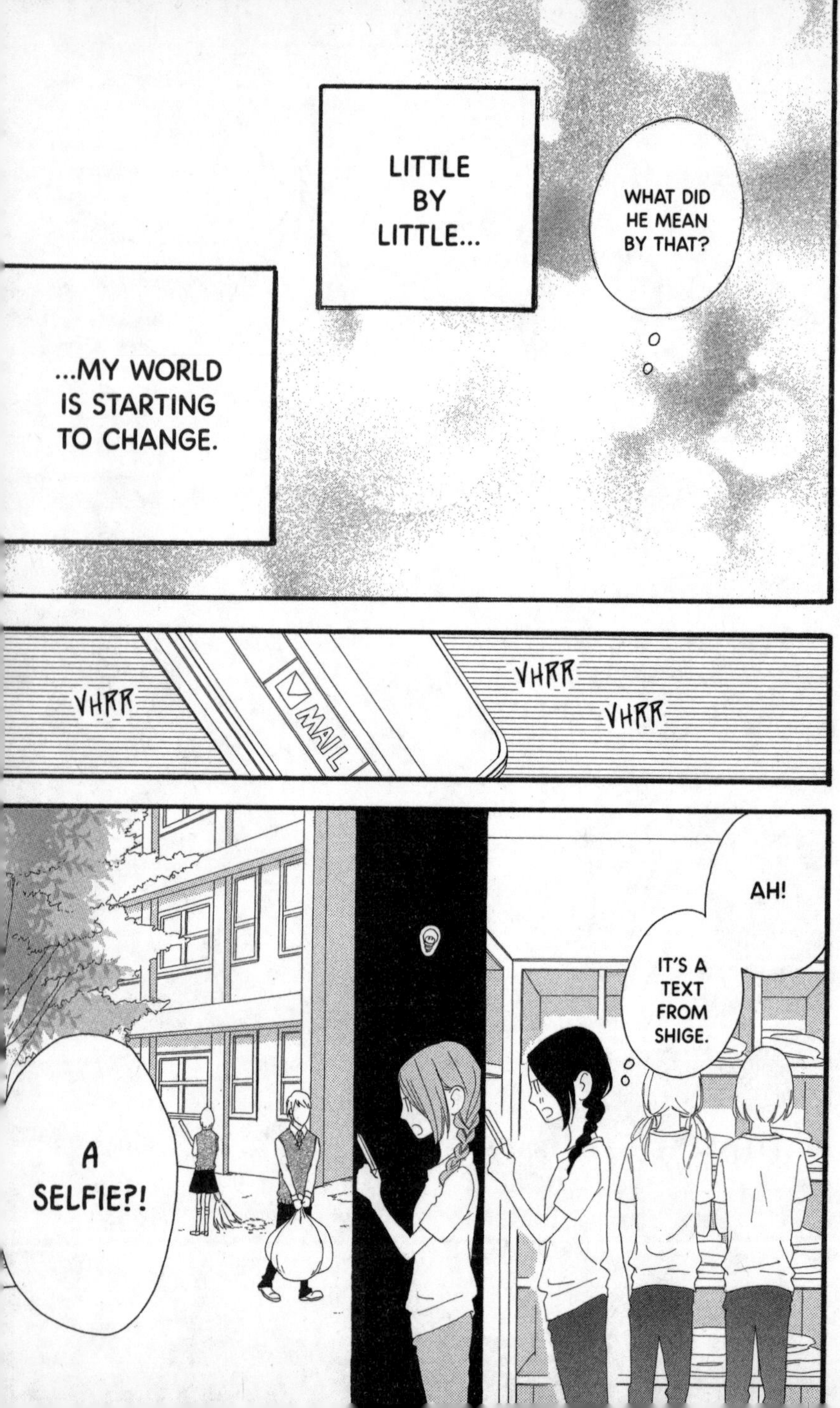
WHAT DID HE MEAN BY THAT?
LITTLE BY LITTLE...
...MY WORLD IS STARTING TO CHANGE.
VHRR
VHRR
MAIL
VHRR
AH!
IT'S A TEXT FROM SHIGE.
A SELFIE?!

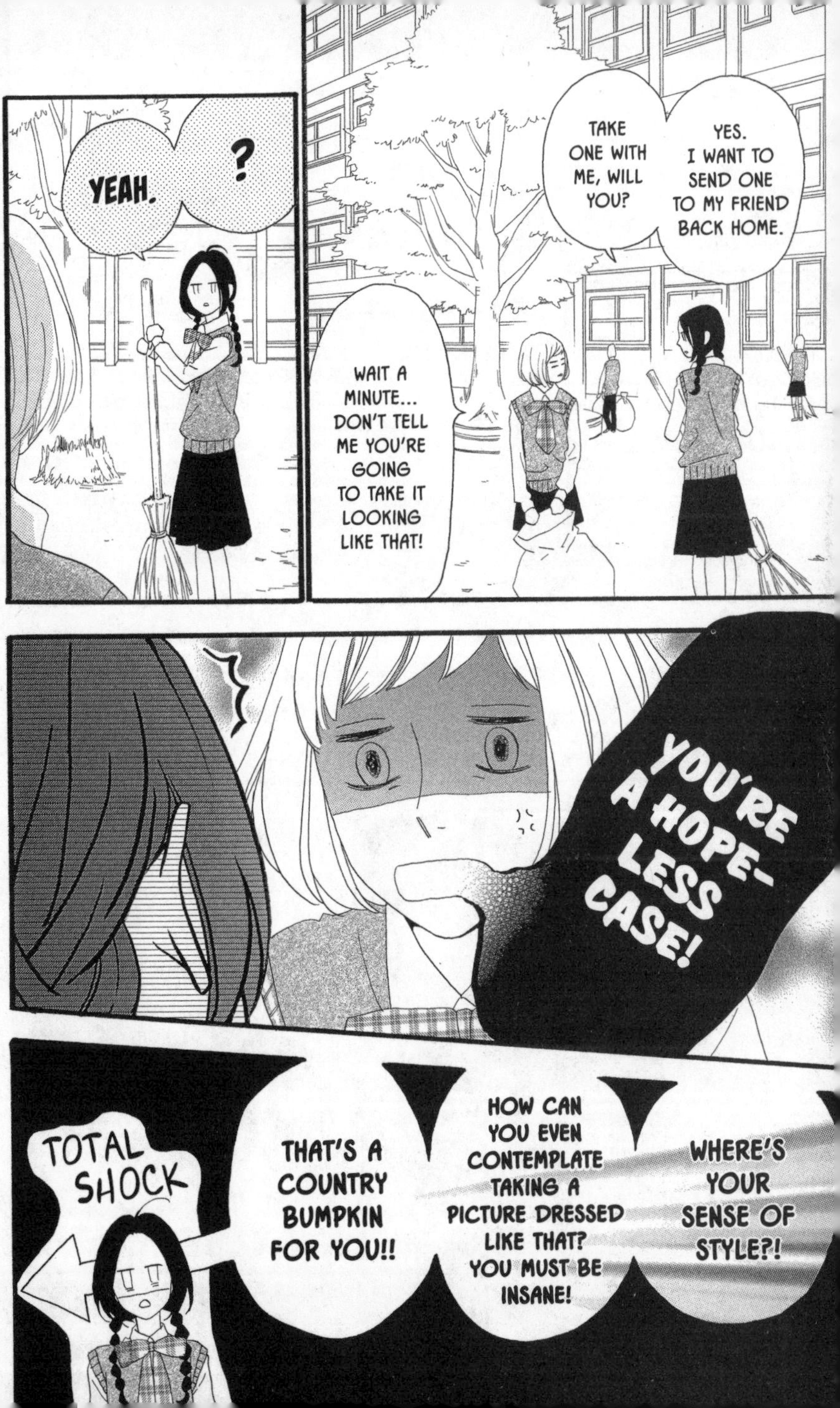
YES. I WANT TO SEND ONE TO MY FRIEND BACK HOME.
TAKE ONE WITH ME, WILL YOU?
WAIT A MINUTE... DON'T TELL ME YOU'RE GOING TO TAKE IT LOOKING LIKE THAT!
?
YEAH.
YOU'RE A HOPE-LESS CASE!
WHERE'S YOUR SENSE OF STYLE?!
HOW CAN YOU EVEN CONTEMPLATE TAKING A PICTURE DRESSED LIKE THAT? YOU MUST BE INSANE!
THAT'S A COUNTRY BUMPKIN FOR YOU!!
TOTAL SHOCK

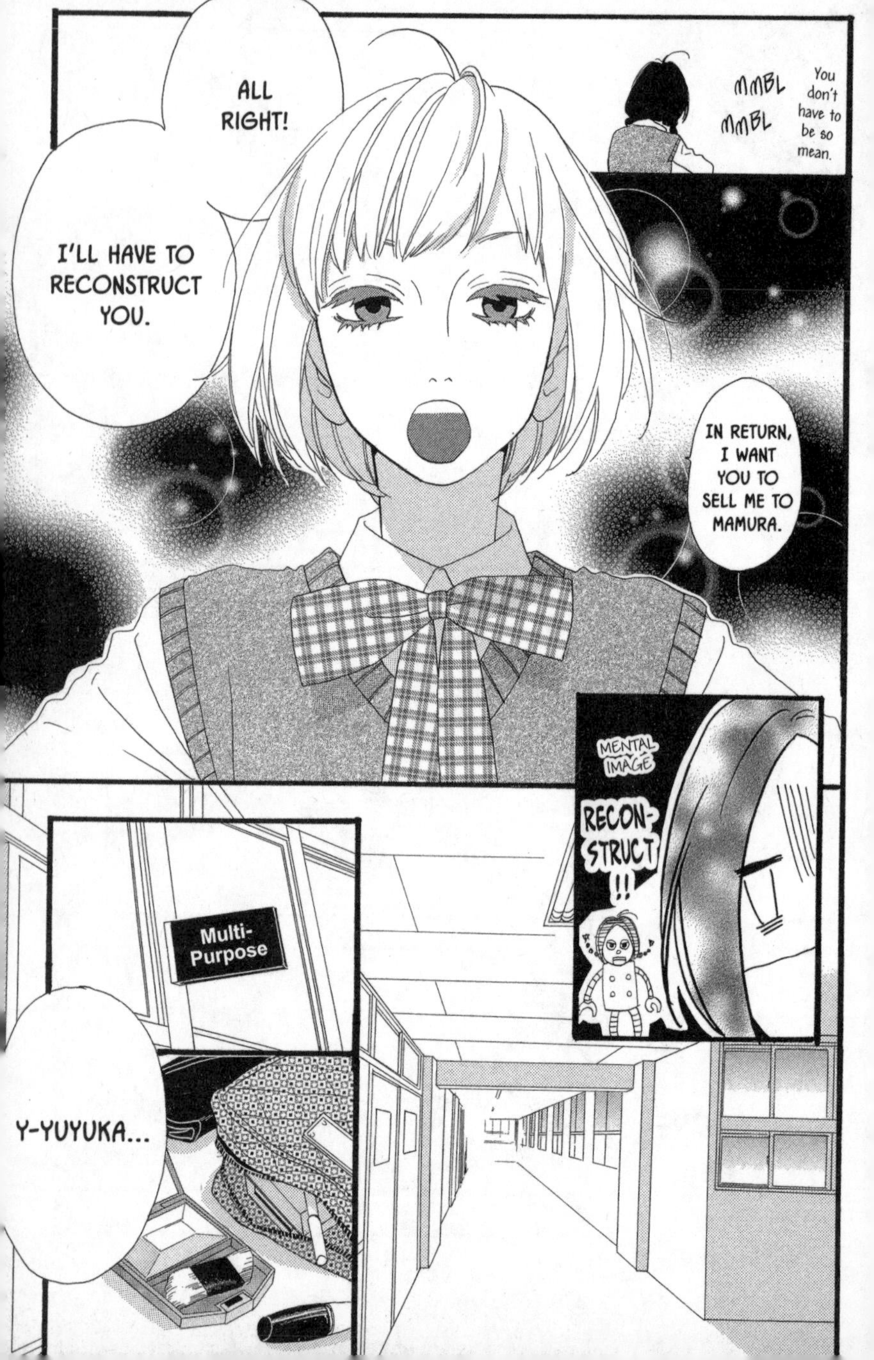
MMBL
MMBL
You don't have to be so mean.
ALL RIGHT!
I'LL HAVE TO RECONSTRUCT YOU.
IN RETURN, I WANT YOU TO SELL ME TO MAMURA.
MENTAL IMAGE
RECON-STRUCT !!
Multi-Purpose
Y-YUYUKA...

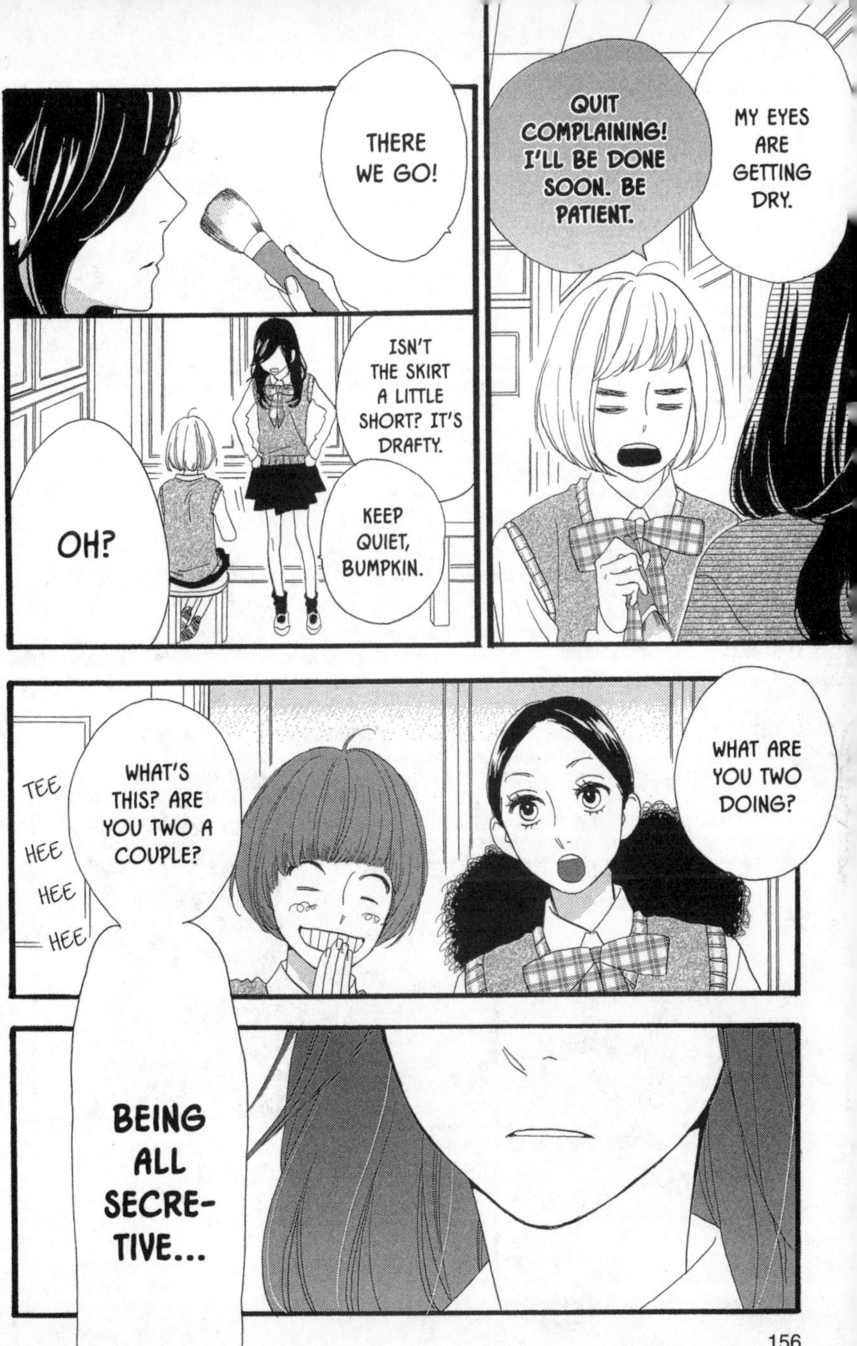
MY EYES ARE GETTING DRY.
QUIT COMPLAINING! I'LL BE DONE SOON. BE PATIENT.
THERE WE GO!
ISN'T THE SKIRT A LITTLE SHORT? IT'S DRAFTY.
KEEP QUIET, BUMPKIN.
OH?
WHAT ARE YOU TWO DOING?
WHAT'S THIS? ARE YOU TWO A COUPLE?
TEE HEE HEE HEE
BEING ALL SECRE-TIVE...

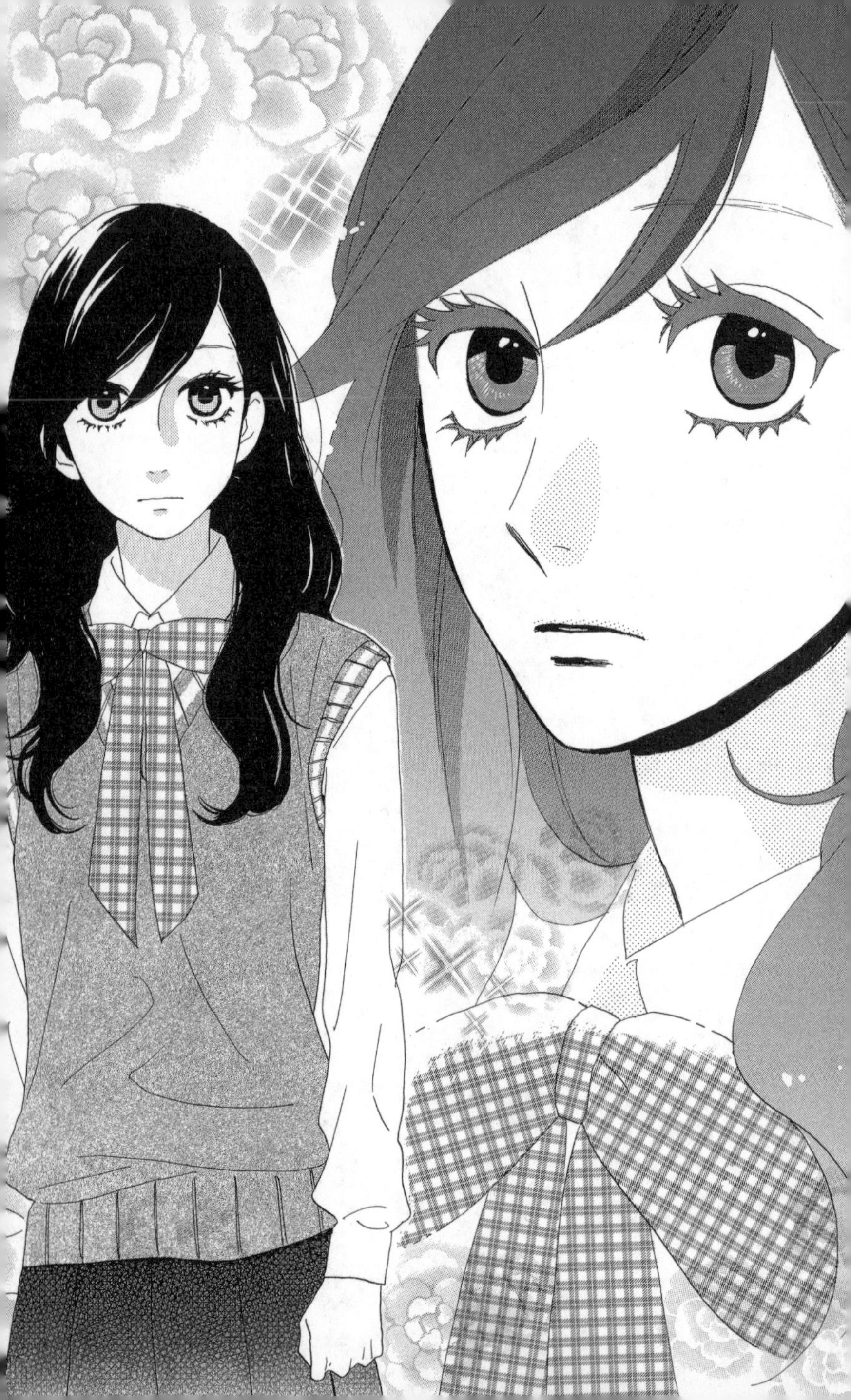

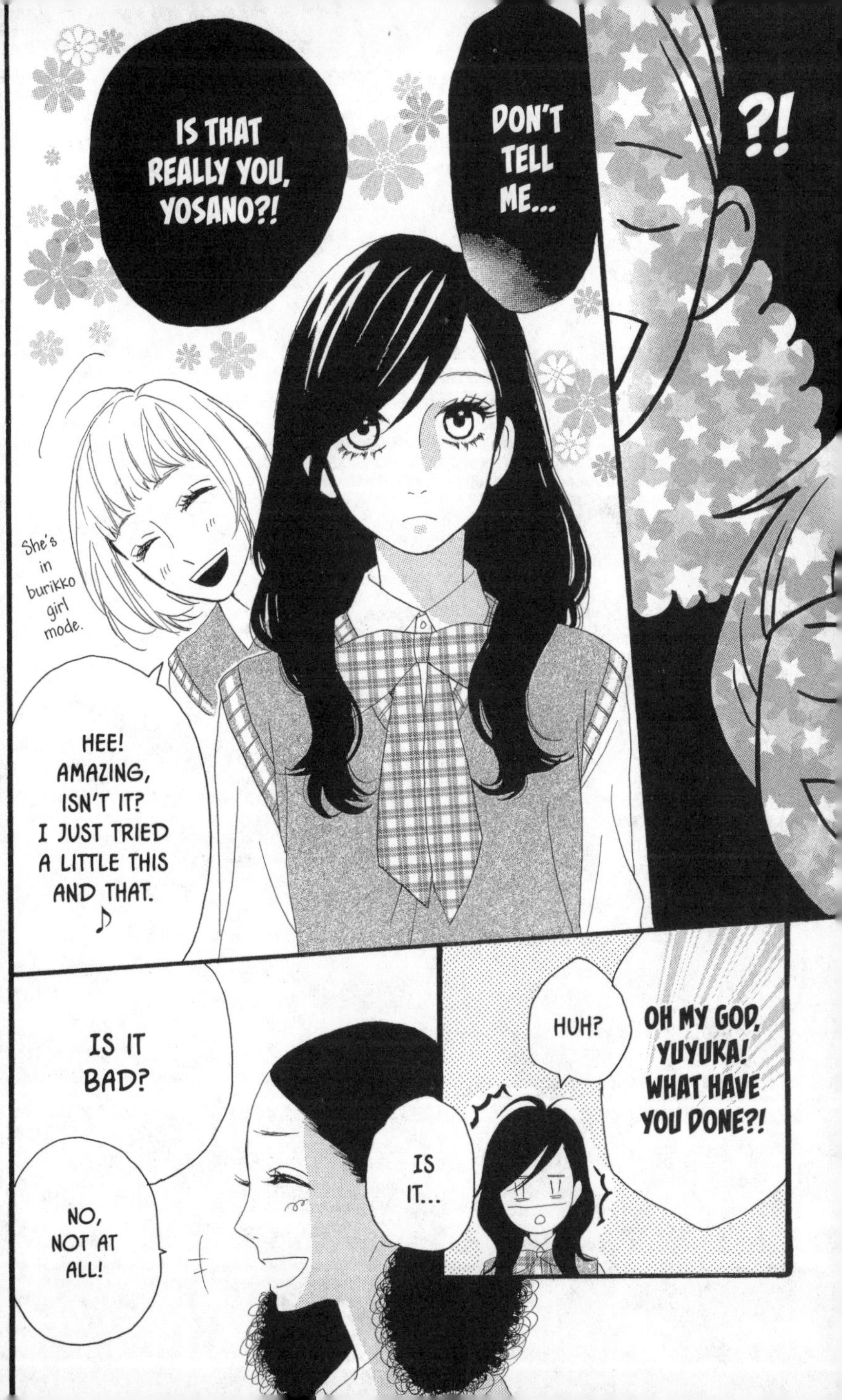
?!
DON'T TELL ME...
IS THAT REALLY YOU, YOSANO?!
She's in burikko girl mode.
HEE! AMAZING, ISN'T IT? I JUST TRIED A LITTLE THIS AND THAT. ♪
OH MY GOD, YUYUKA! WHAT HAVE YOU DONE?!
HUH?
IS IT...
IS IT BAD?
NO, NOT AT ALL!

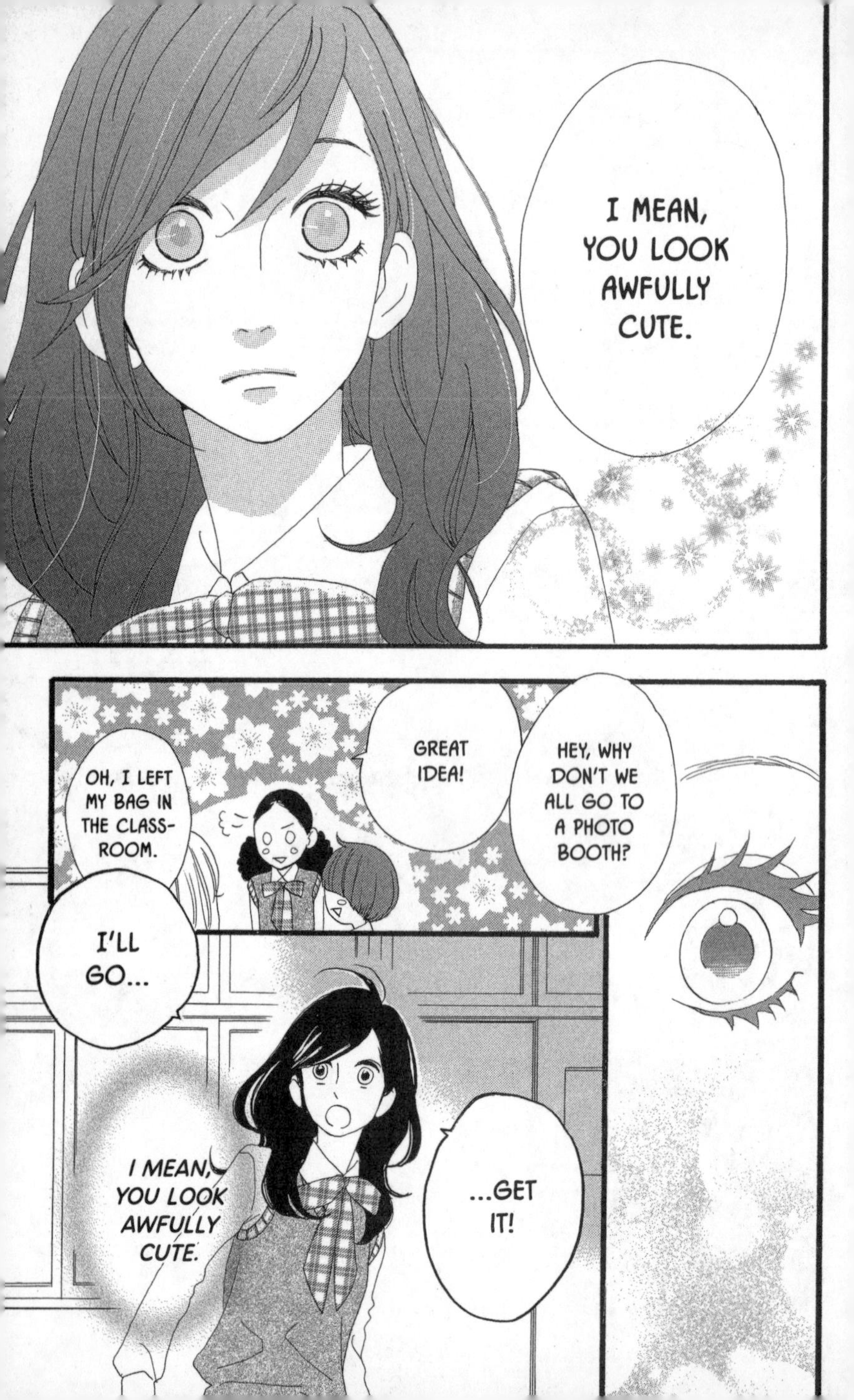
I MEAN, YOU LOOK AWFULLY CUTE.
HEY, WHY DON'T WE ALL GO TO A PHOTO BOOTH?
GREAT IDEA!
OH, I LEFT MY BAG IN THE CLASS-ROOM.
I'LL GO...
...GET IT!
I MEAN, YOU LOOK AWFULLY CUTE.

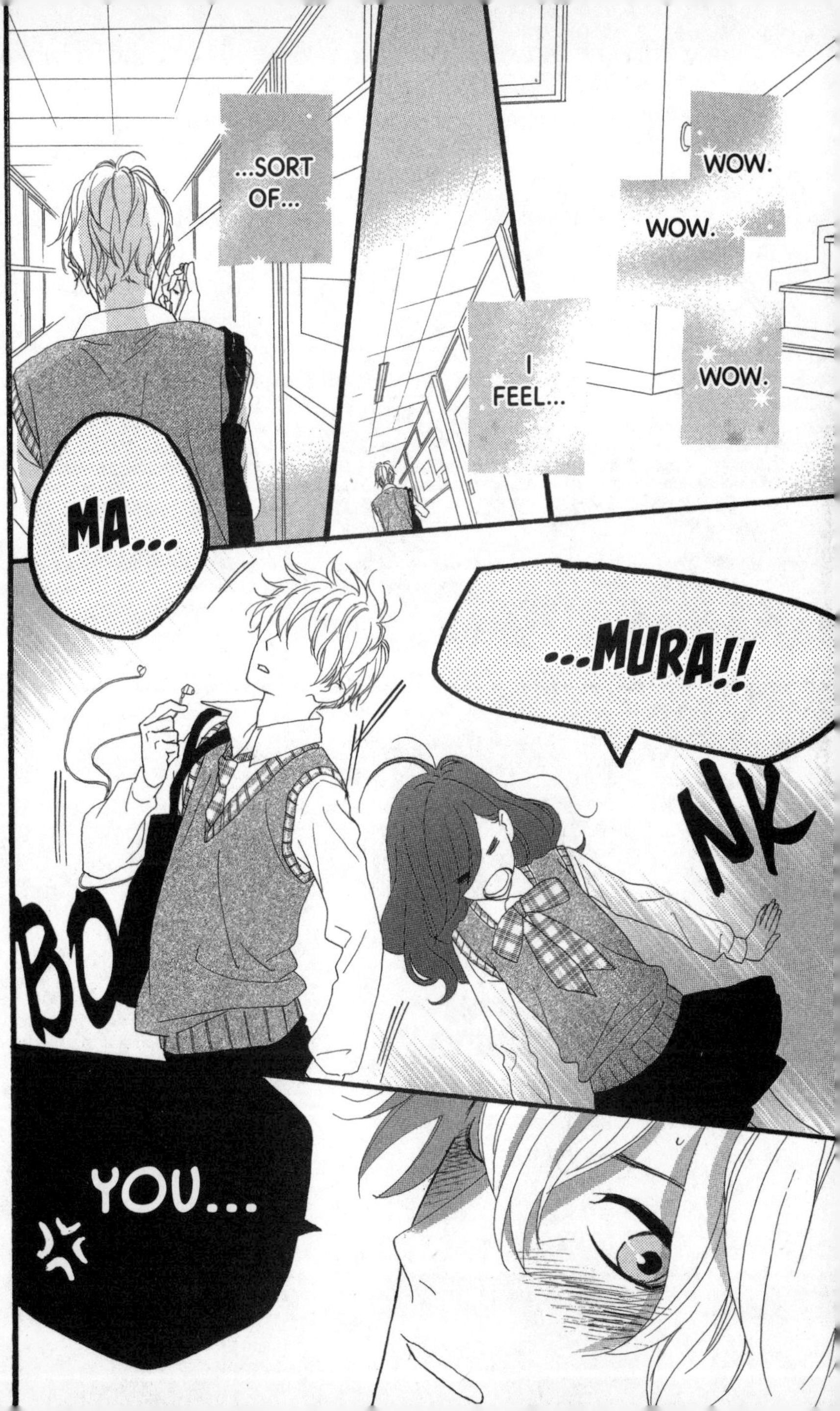
WOW.
WOW.
WOW.
I FEEL...
...SORT OF...
MA...
...MURA!!
BO
NK
YOU...

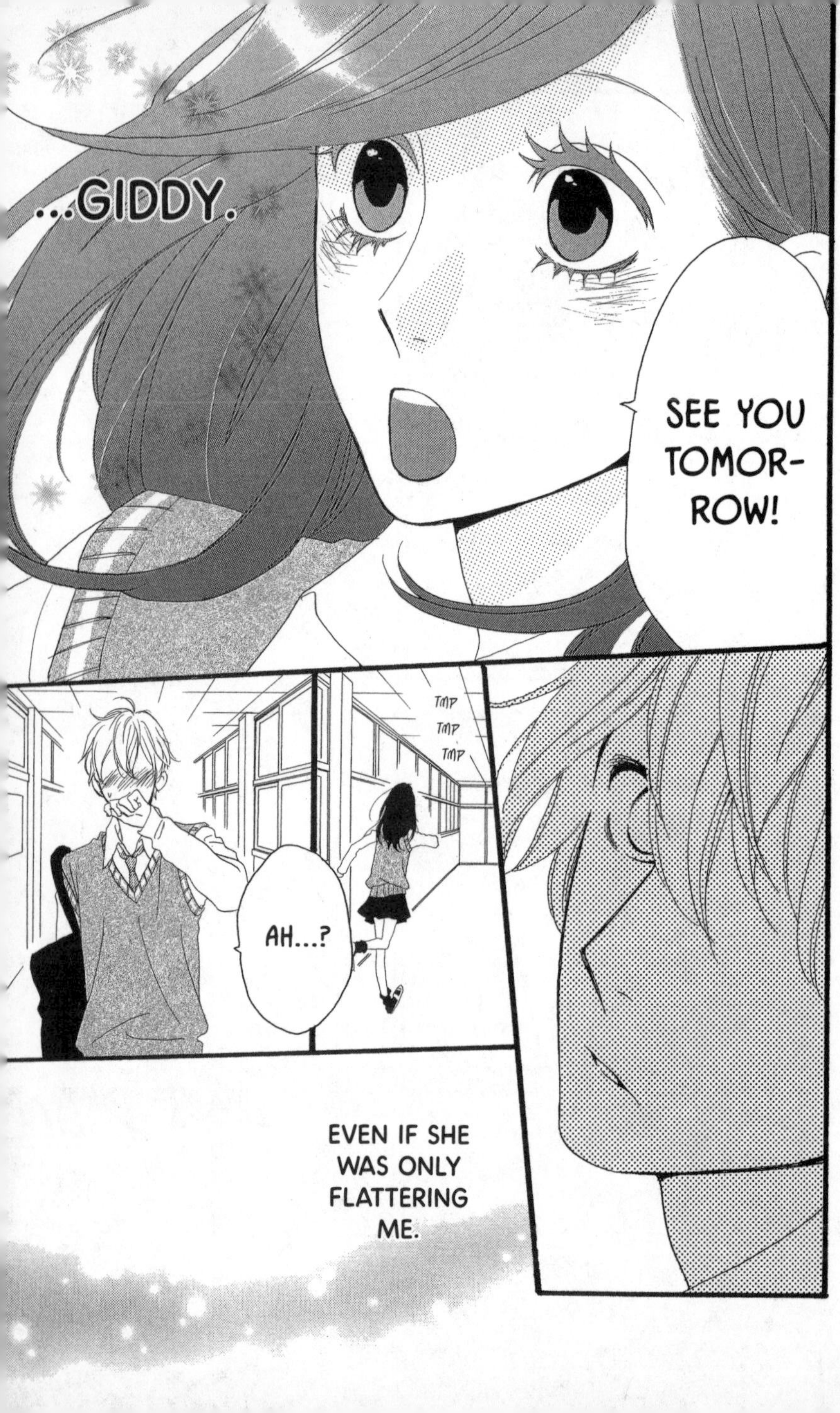
...GIDDY.
SEE YOU TOMORROW!
TMP TMP TMP
AH...?
EVEN IF SHE WAS ONLY FLATTERING ME.

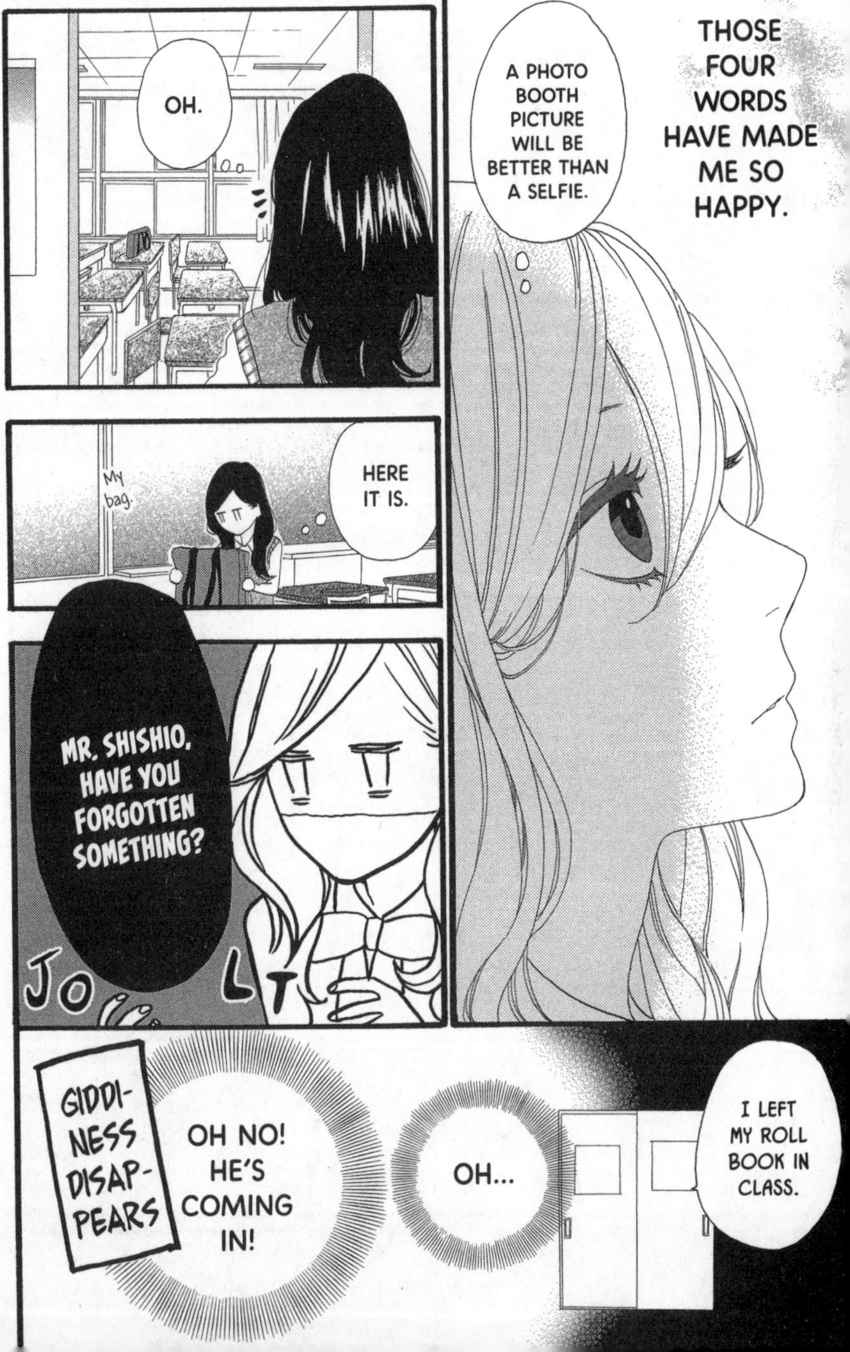
THOSE FOUR WORDS HAVE MADE ME SO HAPPY.
A PHOTO BOOTH PICTURE WILL BE BETTER THAN A SELFIE.
OH.
HERE IT IS.
My bag.
MR. SHISHIO, HAVE YOU FORGOTTEN SOMETHING?
JOLT
I LEFT MY ROLL BOOK IN CLASS.
OH...
OH NO! HE'S COMING IN!
GIDDI-NESS DISAP-PEARS

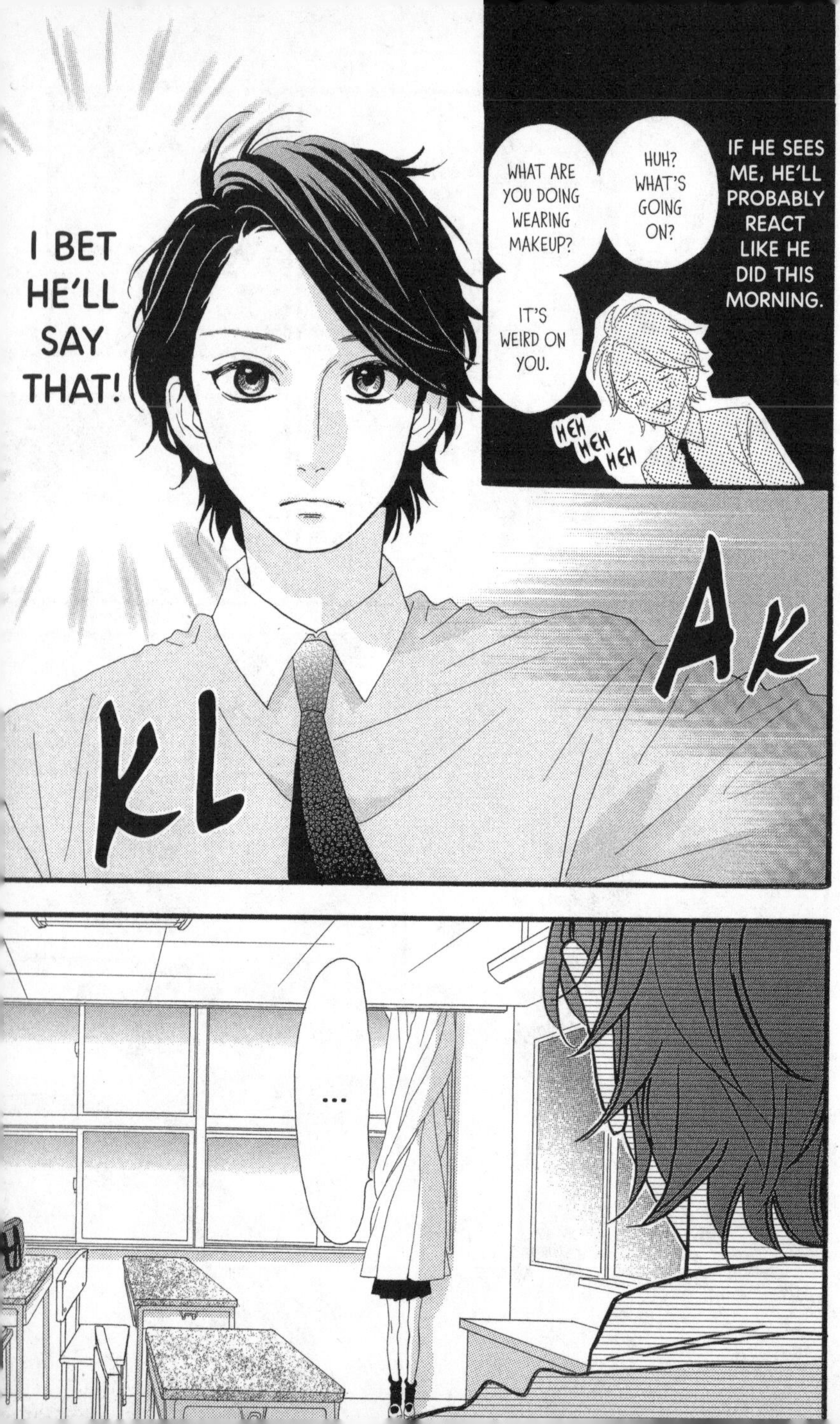
IF HE SEES ME, HE'LL PROBABLY REACT LIKE HE DID THIS MORNING.
HUH? WHAT'S GOING ON?
WHAT ARE YOU DOING WEARING MAKEUP?
IT'S WEIRD ON YOU.
HEH HEH HEH
I BET HE'LL SAY THAT!
AK
KL
...

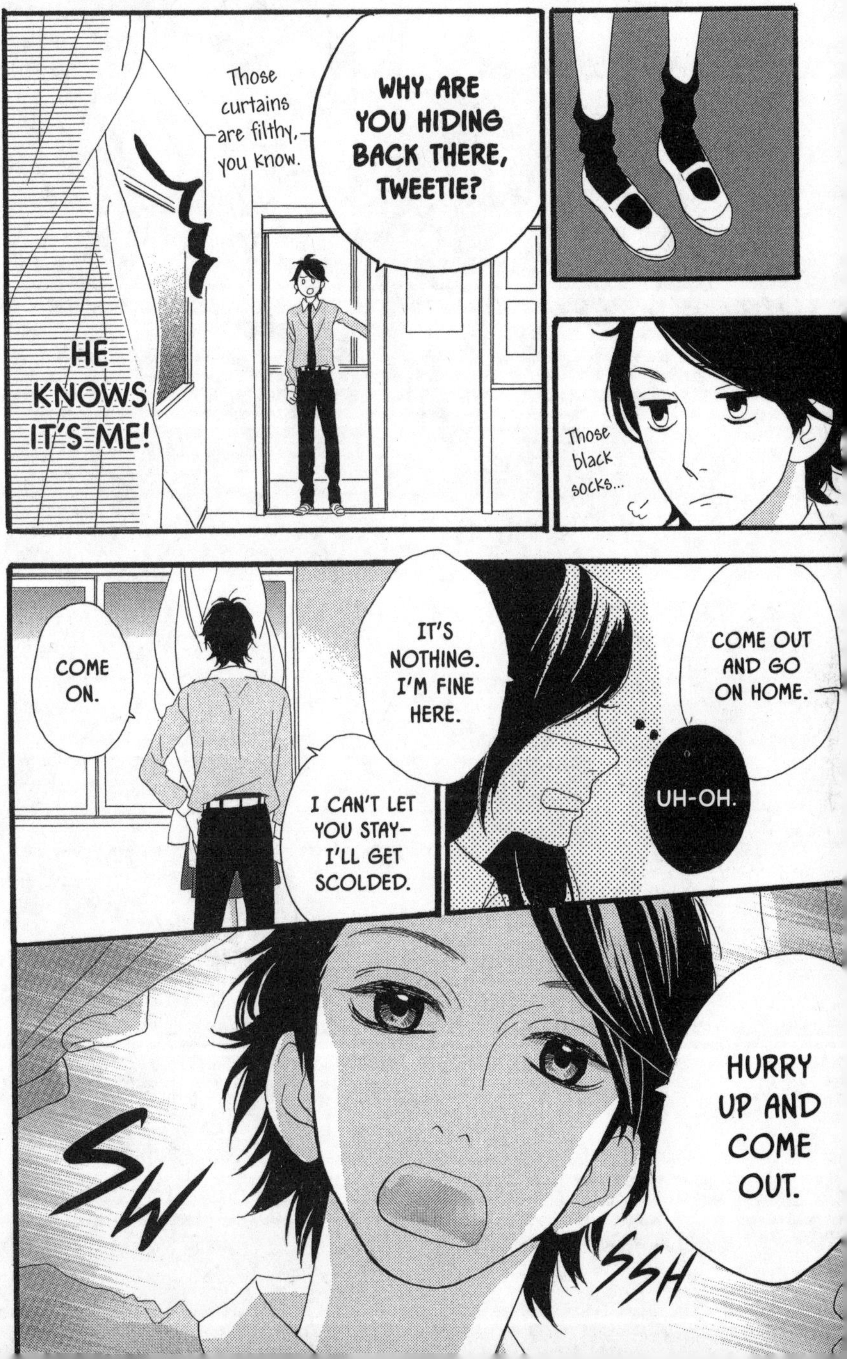
Those black socks...
WHY ARE YOU HIDING BACK THERE, TWEETIE?
Those curtains are filthy, you know.
HE KNOWS IT'S ME!
COME OUT AND GO ON HOME.
IT'S NOTHING. I'M FINE HERE.
UH-OH.
COME ON.
I CAN'T LET YOU STAY— I'LL GET SCOLDED.
HURRY UP AND COME OUT.
SWSSH

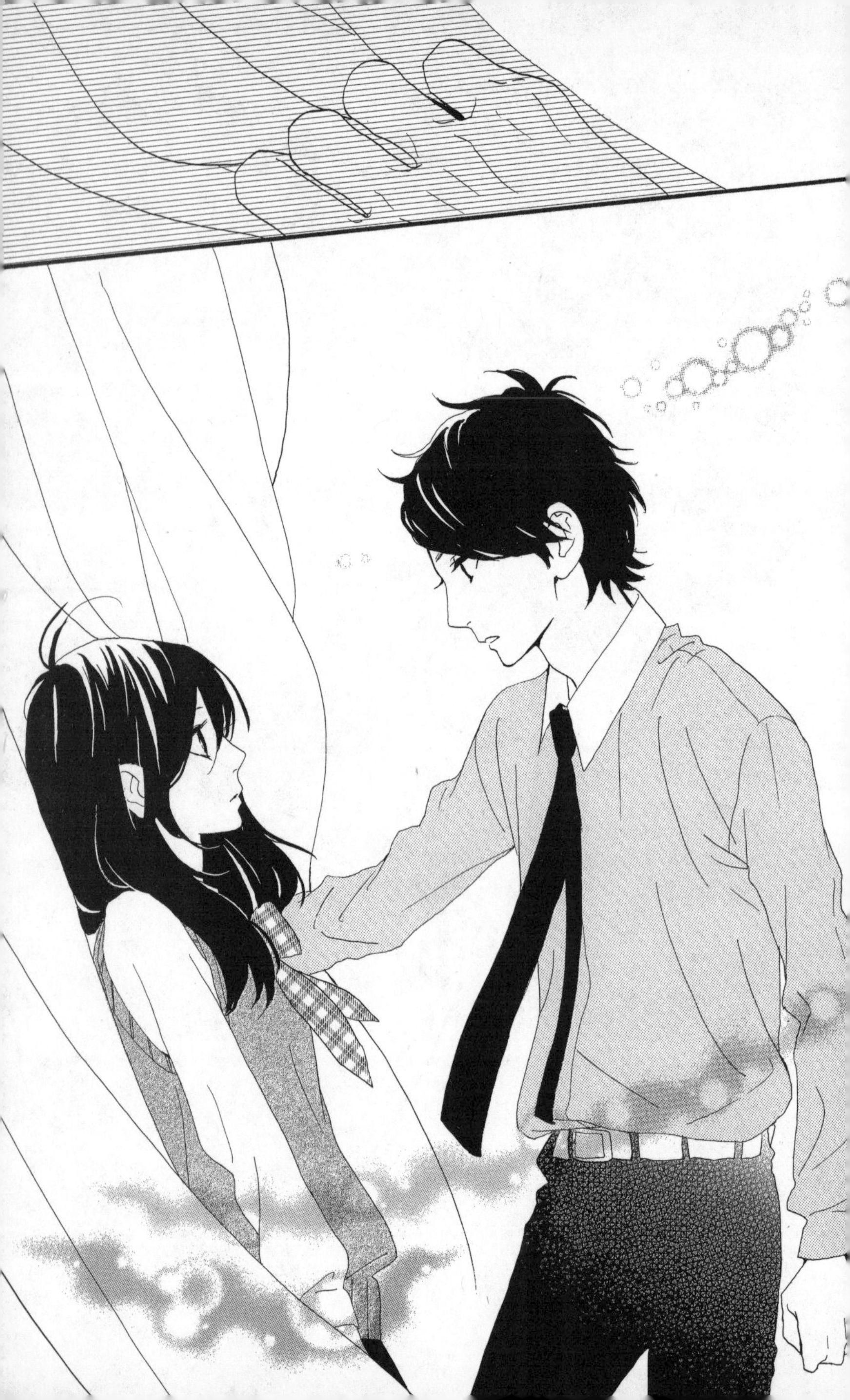

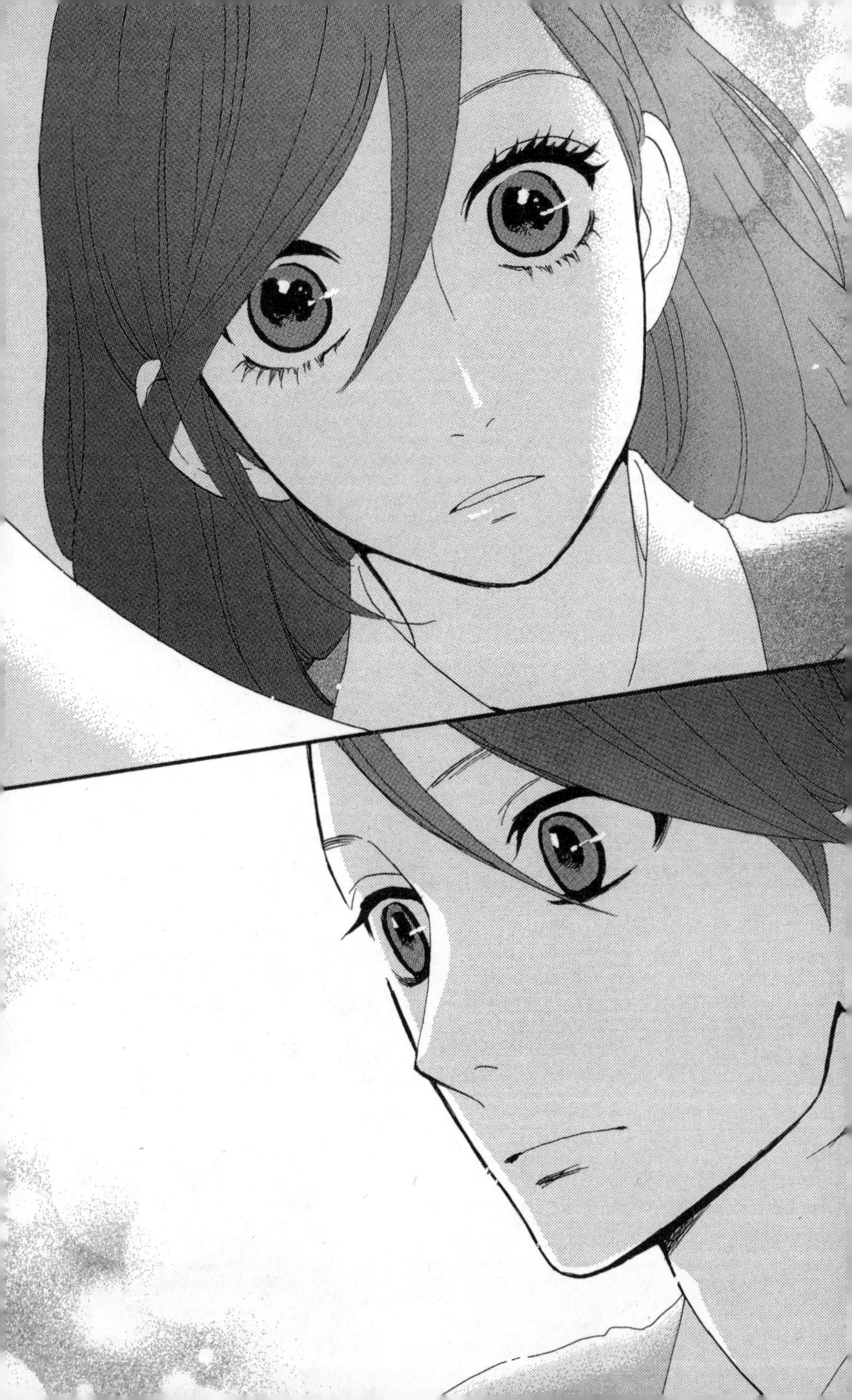

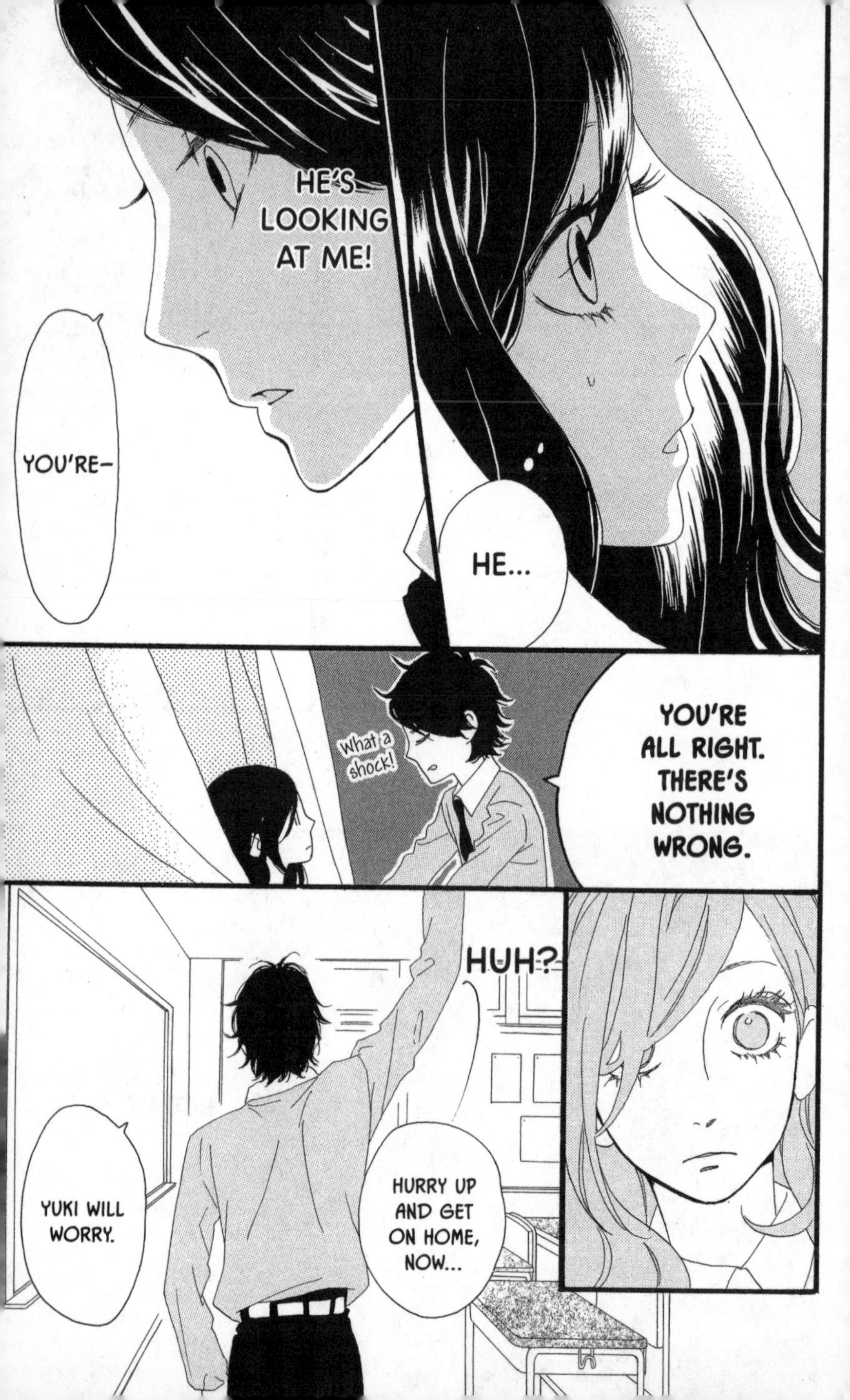
HE...
HE'S LOOKING AT ME!
YOU'RE–
YOU'RE ALL RIGHT. THERE'S NOTHING WRONG.
What a shock!
HUH?
HURRY UP AND GET ON HOME, NOW...
YUKI WILL WORRY.

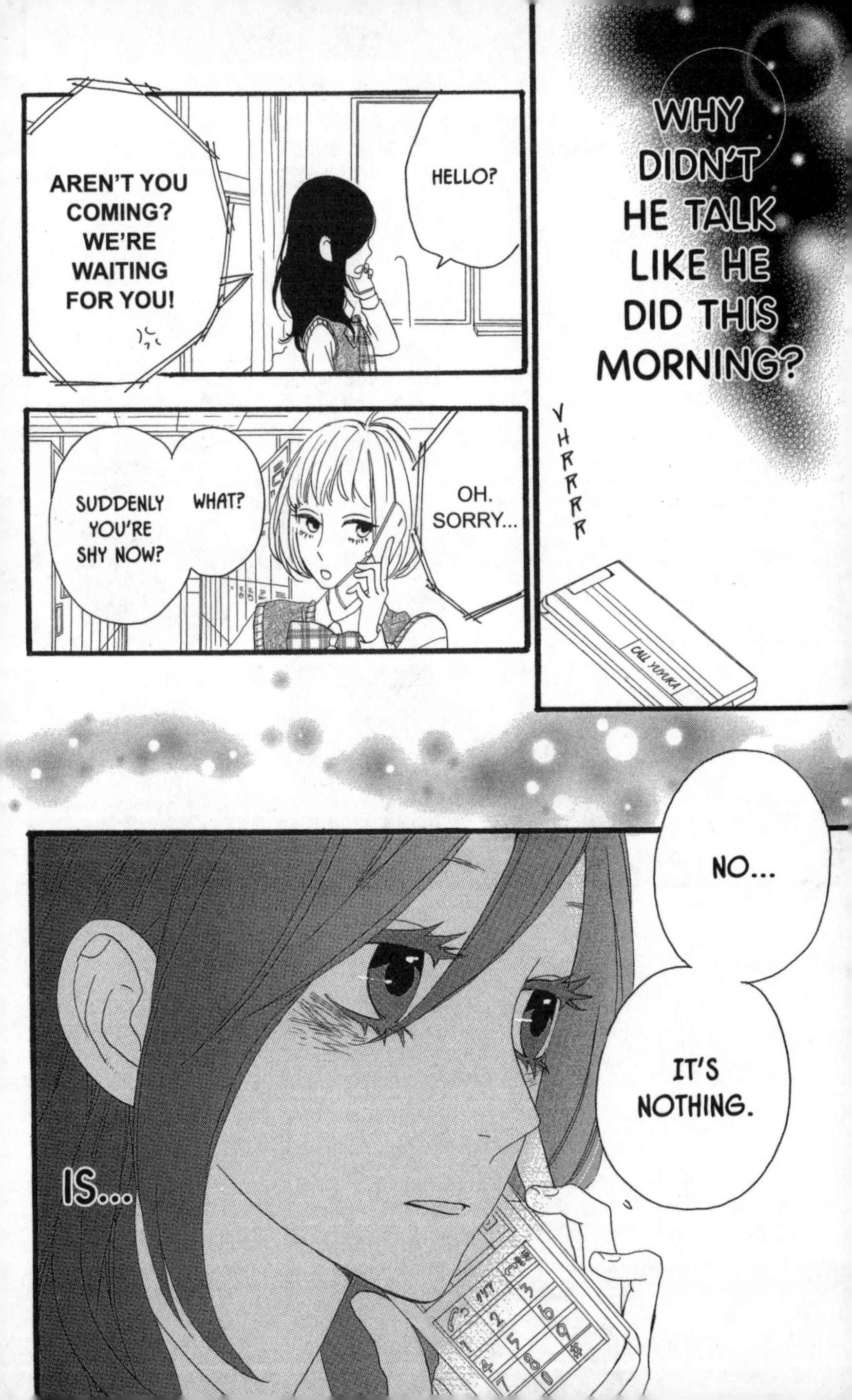
WHY DIDN'T HE TALK LIKE HE DID THIS MORNING?
VHRRRR
CALL YUYUKA
HELLO?
AREN'T YOU COMING? WE'RE WAITING FOR YOU!
OH. SORRY...
WHAT?
SUDDENLY YOU'RE SHY NOW?
NO...
IT'S NOTHING.
IS...

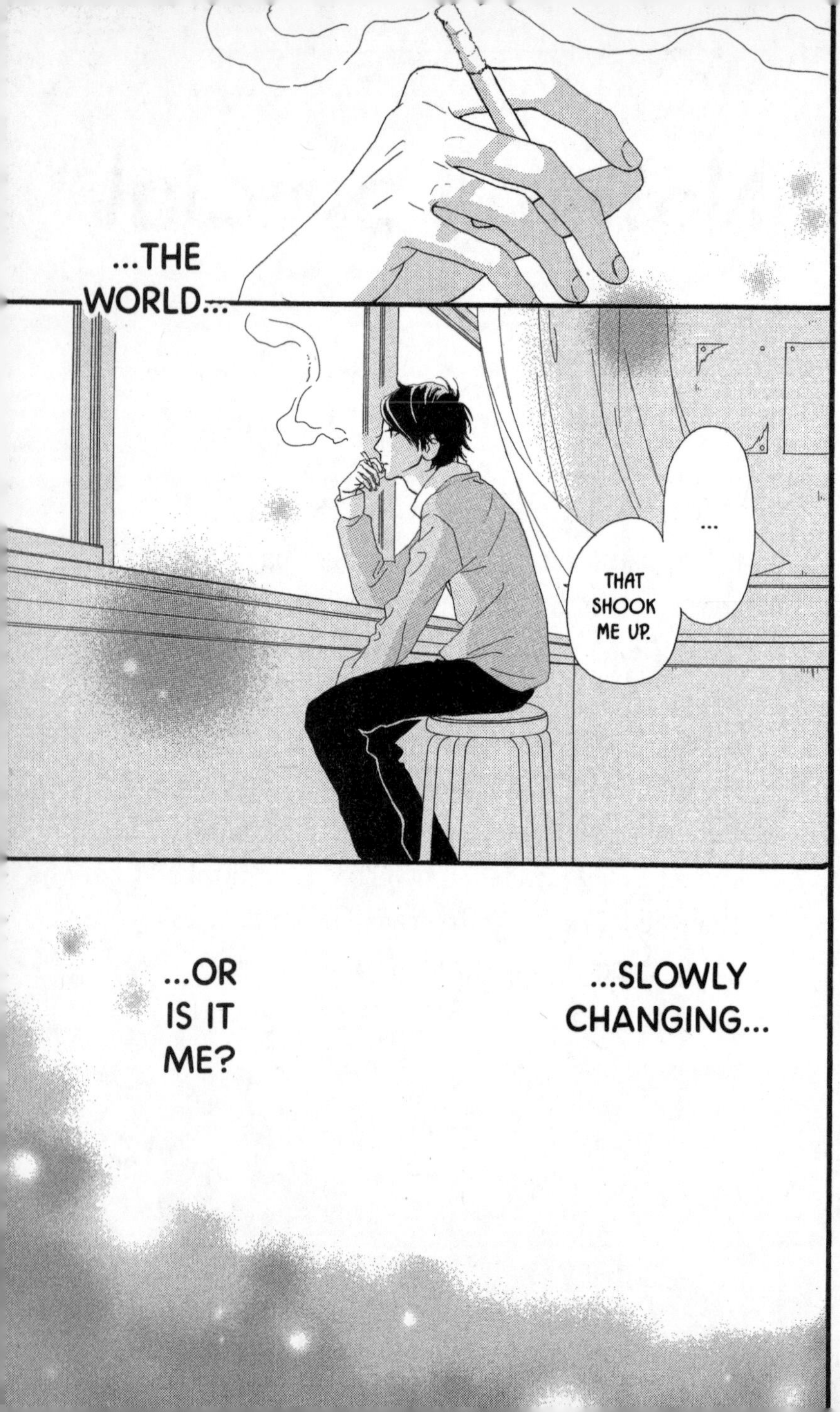
...THE WORLD...
...
THAT SHOOK ME UP.
...SLOWLY CHANGING...
...OR IS IT ME?

Nothing Special

Every character in this series has an animal as part of their name. I always have trouble deciding on names for my characters. I've changed some names two or three times. If they had some sort of distinguishing characteristic it helped me settle on a name, but deciding this always takes me so much time. I can't possibly use my readers' names without permission either.

Hm...

And so, in future, I may try to create some sort of special traits for new characters in the story. (Even with special traits I'll probably revise things two or three times.)

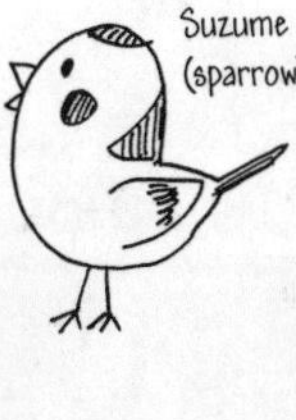
Suzume
(sparrow)?

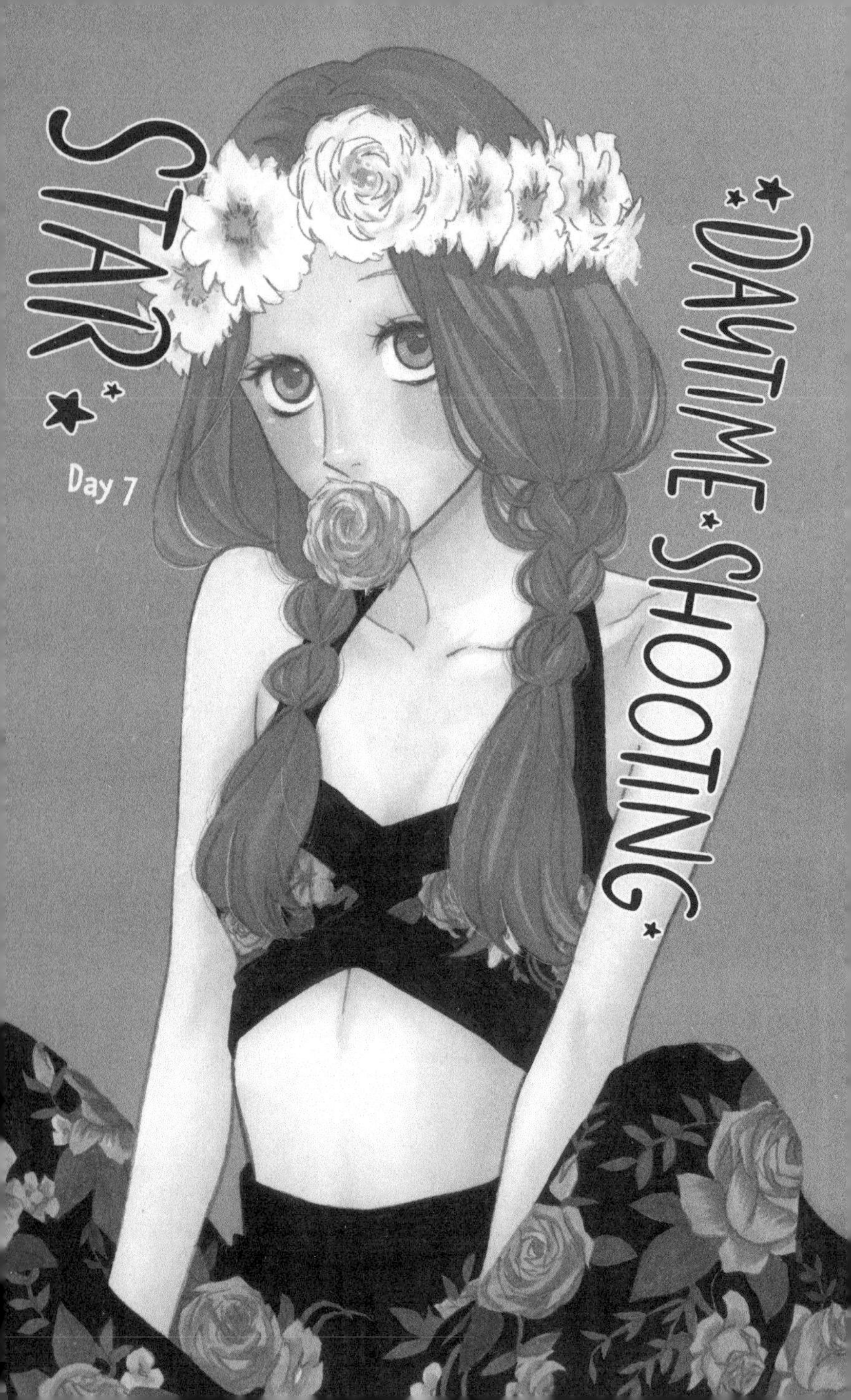

DAYTIME SHOOTING STAR
Day 7

Afterword

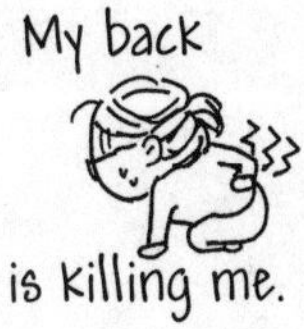
My back
is killing me.

And here is my afterword.
Well, being that this series is a little different from what I am used to, I'm sure it falls short in many areas, but I will do my best.

Many apologies to everyone who suffers because of me: my editor, the editorial department, the designer, the folks at the printer, and my assistants. I will try my very best!

And thanks very much to my loyal readers.
I hope to see you again in the next volume.

Fall 2011

Mika Yamamori

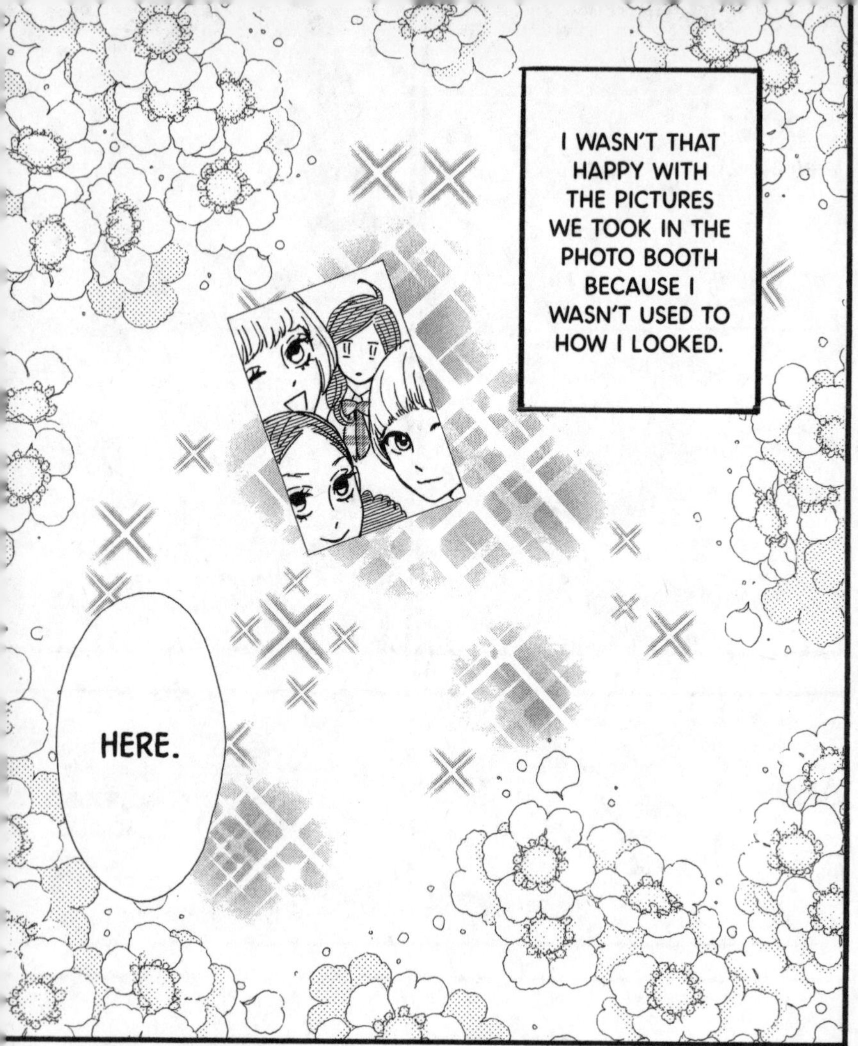
I WASN'T THAT HAPPY WITH THE PICTURES WE TOOK IN THE PHOTO BOOTH BECAUSE I WASN'T USED TO HOW I LOOKED.
HERE.

Yukichi Kumamoto Bear...?

Birthday: May 2
Height: 6'1"
Weight: 159 lbs
Blood Type: O

Kuma means "bear."

1. Anything.
2. Collects nightgowns for Suzume. Grows herbs.
3. I often get asked out by other men. (But I'm heterosexual.)

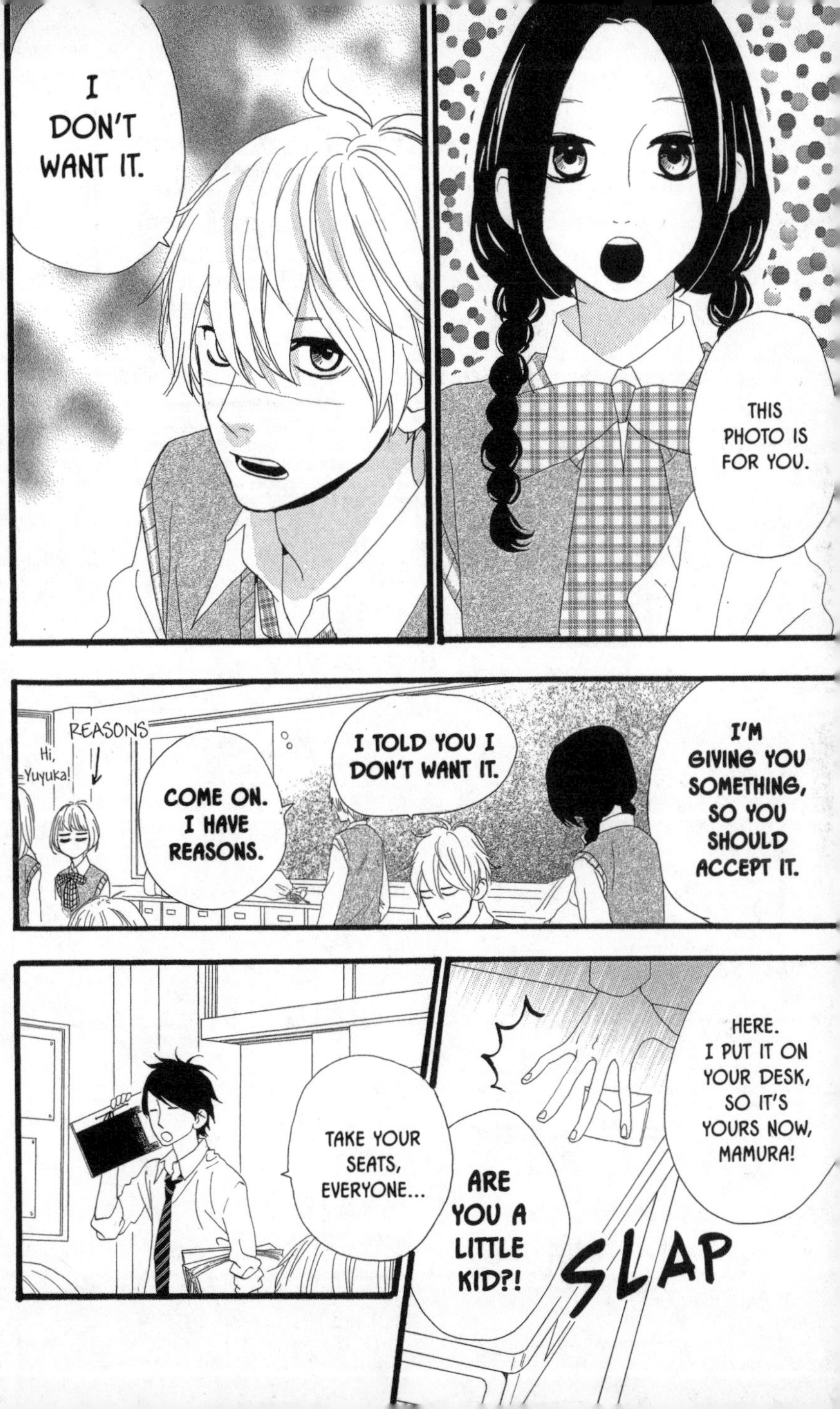
THIS PHOTO IS FOR YOU.
I DON'T WANT IT.
I'M GIVING YOU SOMETHING, SO YOU SHOULD ACCEPT IT.
I TOLD YOU I DON'T WANT IT.
COME ON. I HAVE REASONS.
REASONS
Hi, Yuyuka!
HERE. I PUT IT ON YOUR DESK, SO IT'S YOURS NOW, MAMURA!
SLAP
ARE YOU A LITTLE KID?!
TAKE YOUR SEATS, EVERYONE...

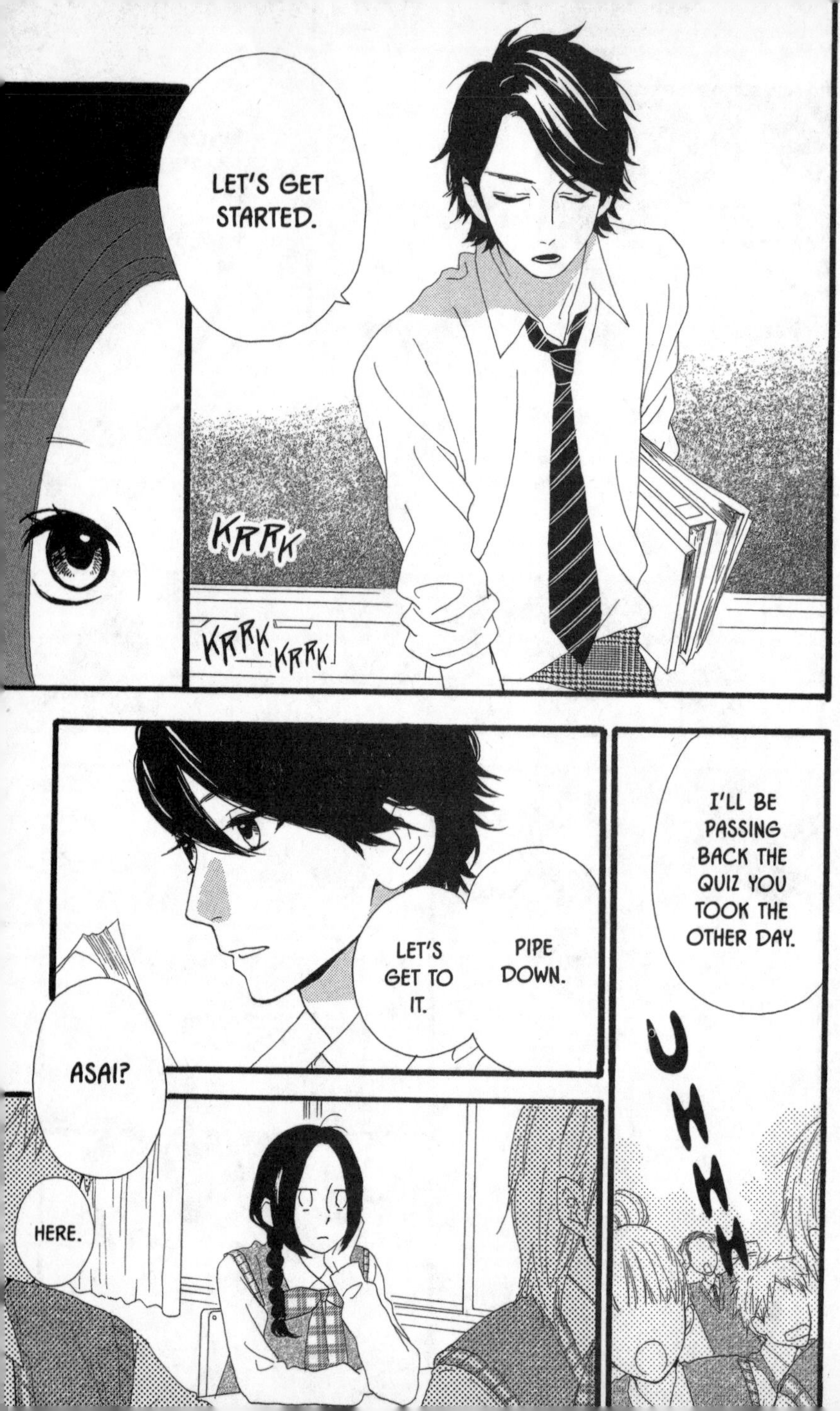
LET'S GET STARTED.
KRRRK
KRRK
KRRK
I'LL BE PASSING BACK THE QUIZ YOU TOOK THE OTHER DAY.
UHHHH
PIPE DOWN.
LET'S GET TO IT.
ASAI?
HERE.

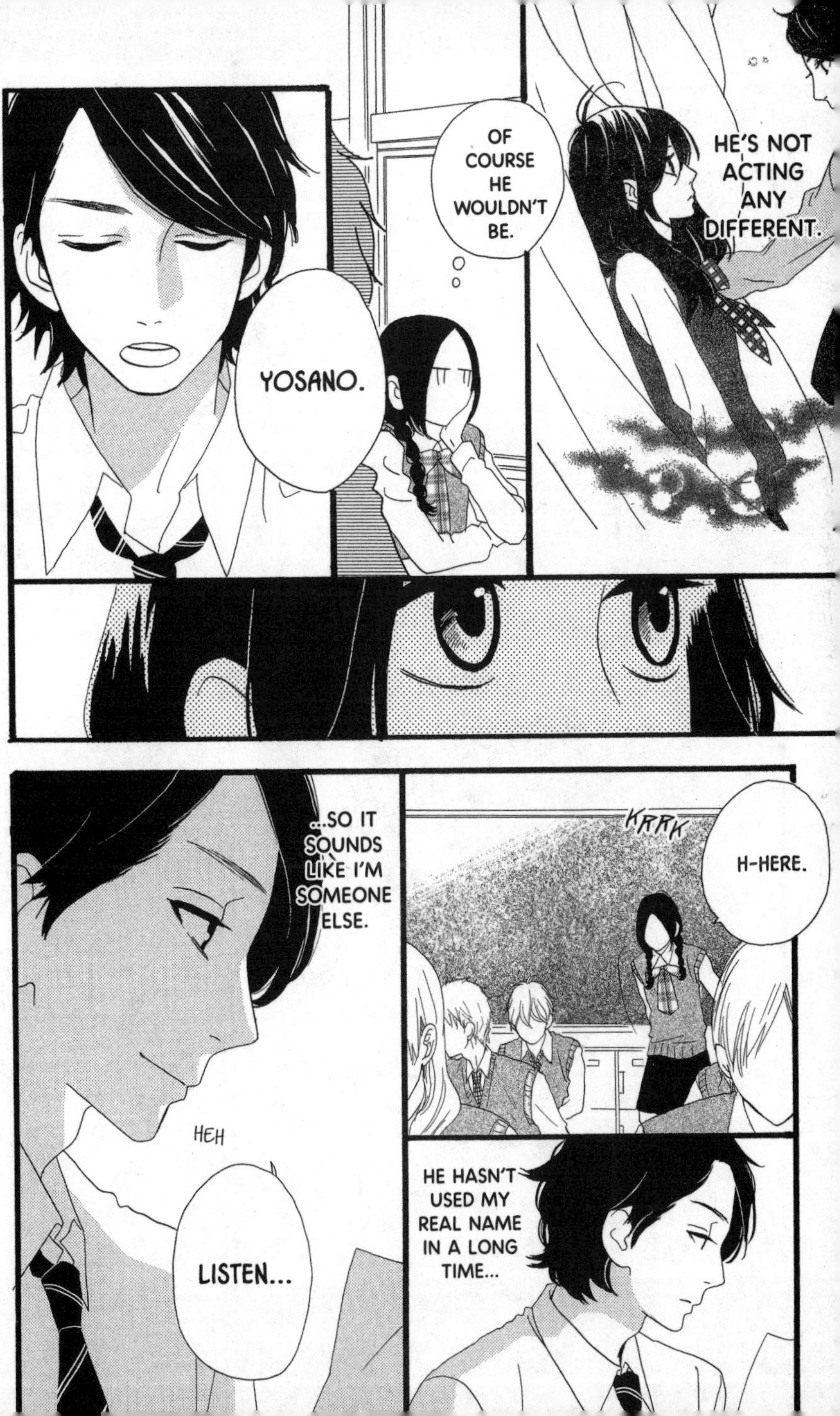
HE'S NOT ACTING ANY DIFFERENT.
OF COURSE HE WOULDN'T BE.
YOSANO.
KRRK
H-HERE.
HE HASN'T USED MY REAL NAME IN A LONG TIME...
...SO IT SOUNDS LIKE I'M SOMEONE ELSE.
HEH
LISTEN...

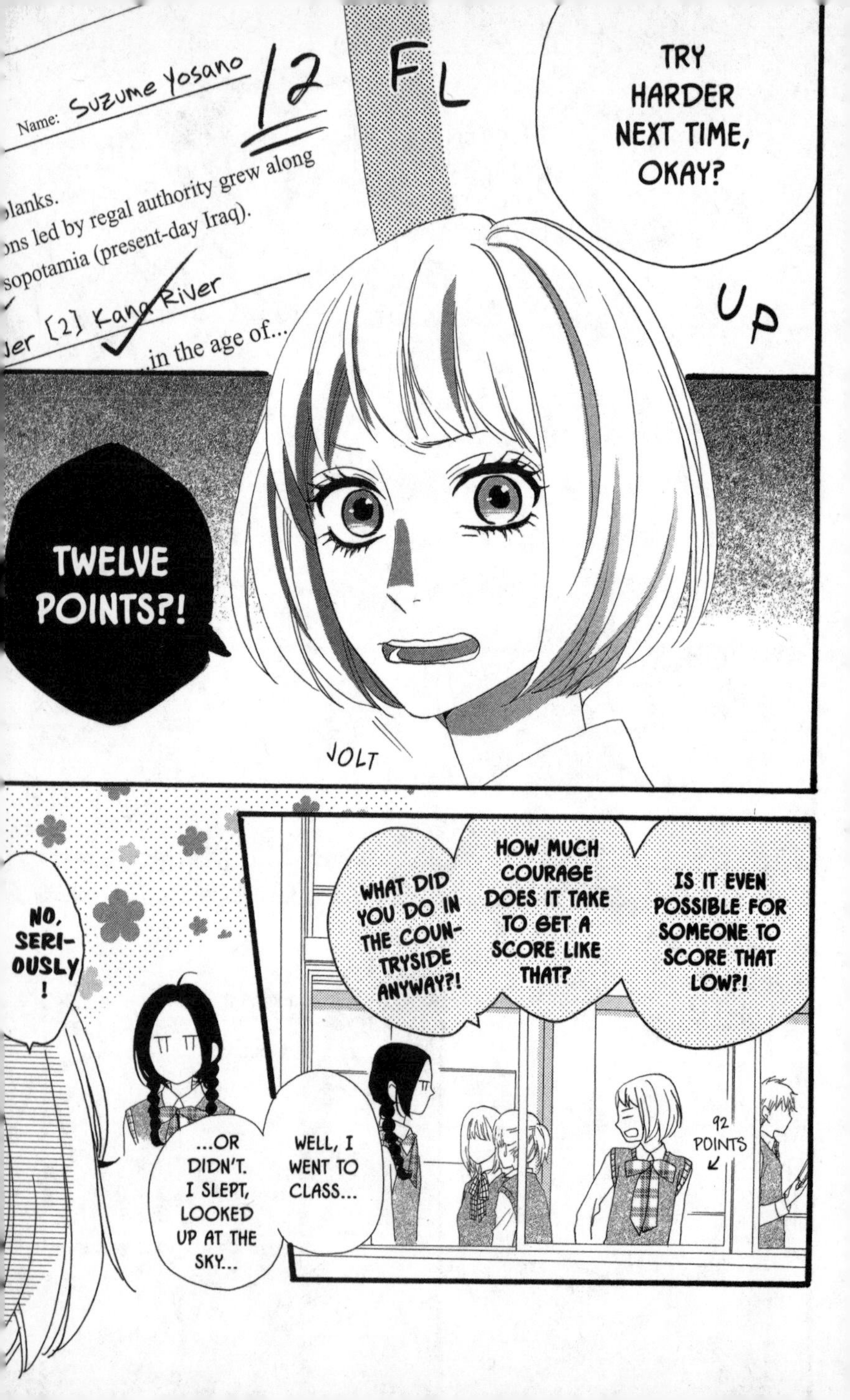

Name: Suzume Yosano
12
planks.
ons led by regal authority grew along
sopotamia (present-day Iraq).
ver [2] Kana River
...in the age of...
FL
UP
TRY HARDER NEXT TIME, OKAY?
TWELVE POINTS?!
JOLT
IS IT EVEN POSSIBLE FOR SOMEONE TO SCORE THAT LOW?!
HOW MUCH COURAGE DOES IT TAKE TO GET A SCORE LIKE THAT?
WHAT DID YOU DO IN THE COUN-TRYSIDE ANYWAY?!
92 POINTS
WELL, I WENT TO CLASS...
...OR DIDN'T. I SLEPT, LOOKED UP AT THE SKY...
NO, SERI-OUSLY!

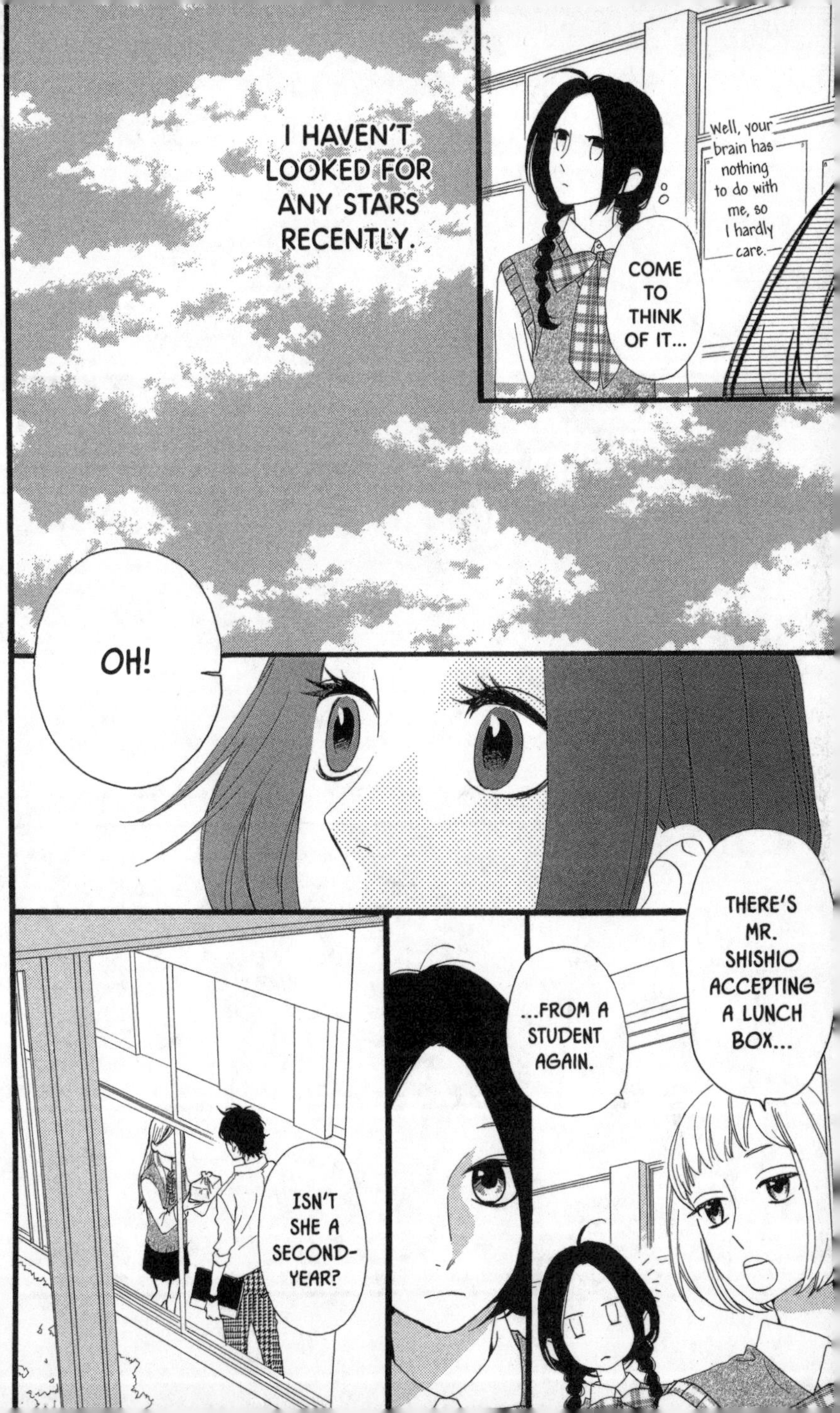

Well, your brain has nothing to do with me, so I hardly care.
COME TO THINK OF IT...
I HAVEN'T LOOKED FOR ANY STARS RECENTLY.
OH!
THERE'S MR. SHISHIO ACCEPTING A LUNCH BOX...
...FROM A STUDENT AGAIN.
ISN'T SHE A SECOND-YEAR?

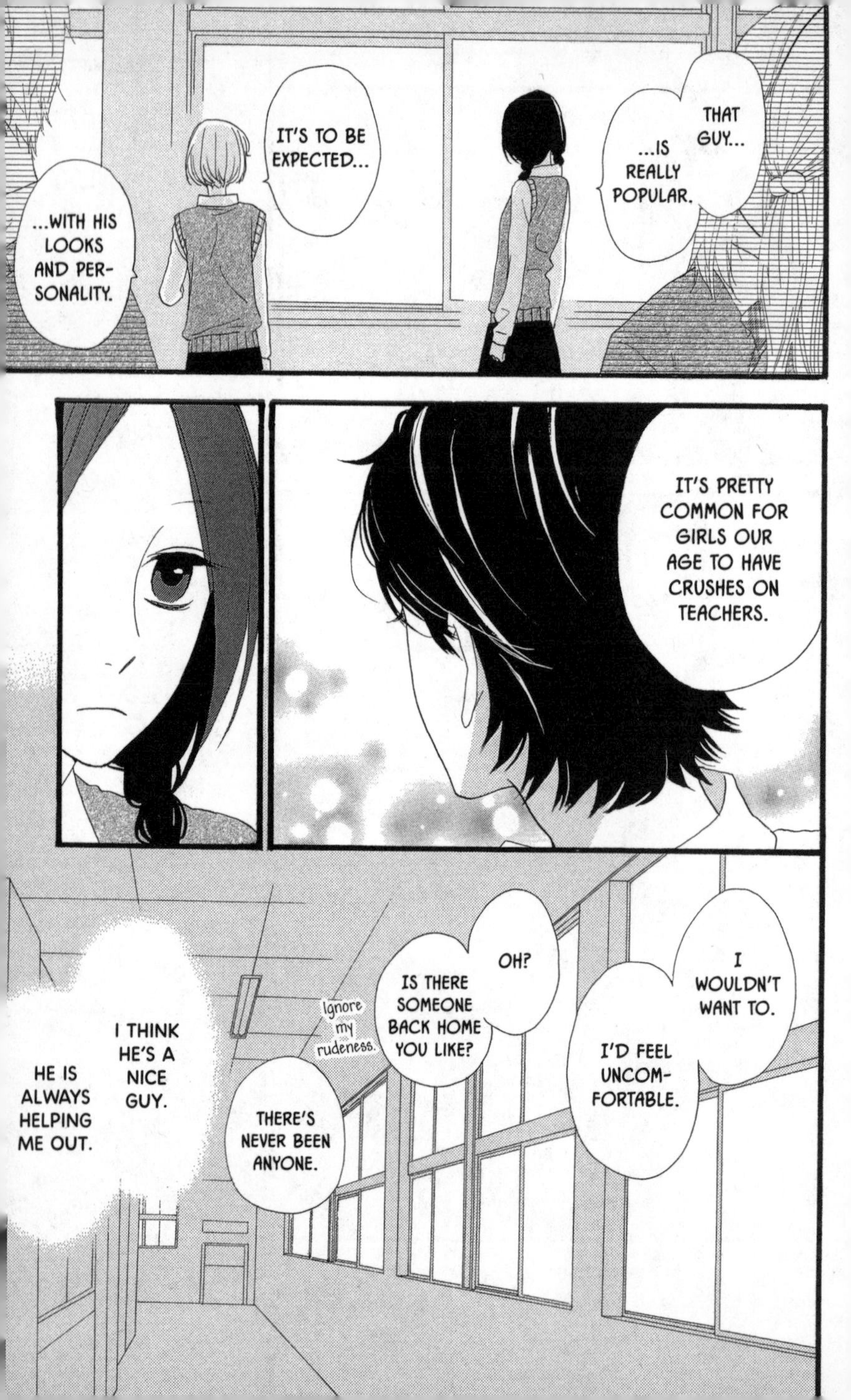
THAT GUY... ...IS REALLY POPULAR.
IT'S TO BE EXPECTED...
...WITH HIS LOOKS AND PER-SONALITY.
IT'S PRETTY COMMON FOR GIRLS OUR AGE TO HAVE CRUSHES ON TEACHERS.
I WOULDN'T WANT TO.
I'D FEEL UNCOM-FORTABLE.
OH?
IS THERE SOMEONE BACK HOME YOU LIKE?
Ignore my rudeness.
THERE'S NEVER BEEN ANYONE.
I THINK HE'S A NICE GUY.
HE IS ALWAYS HELPING ME OUT.

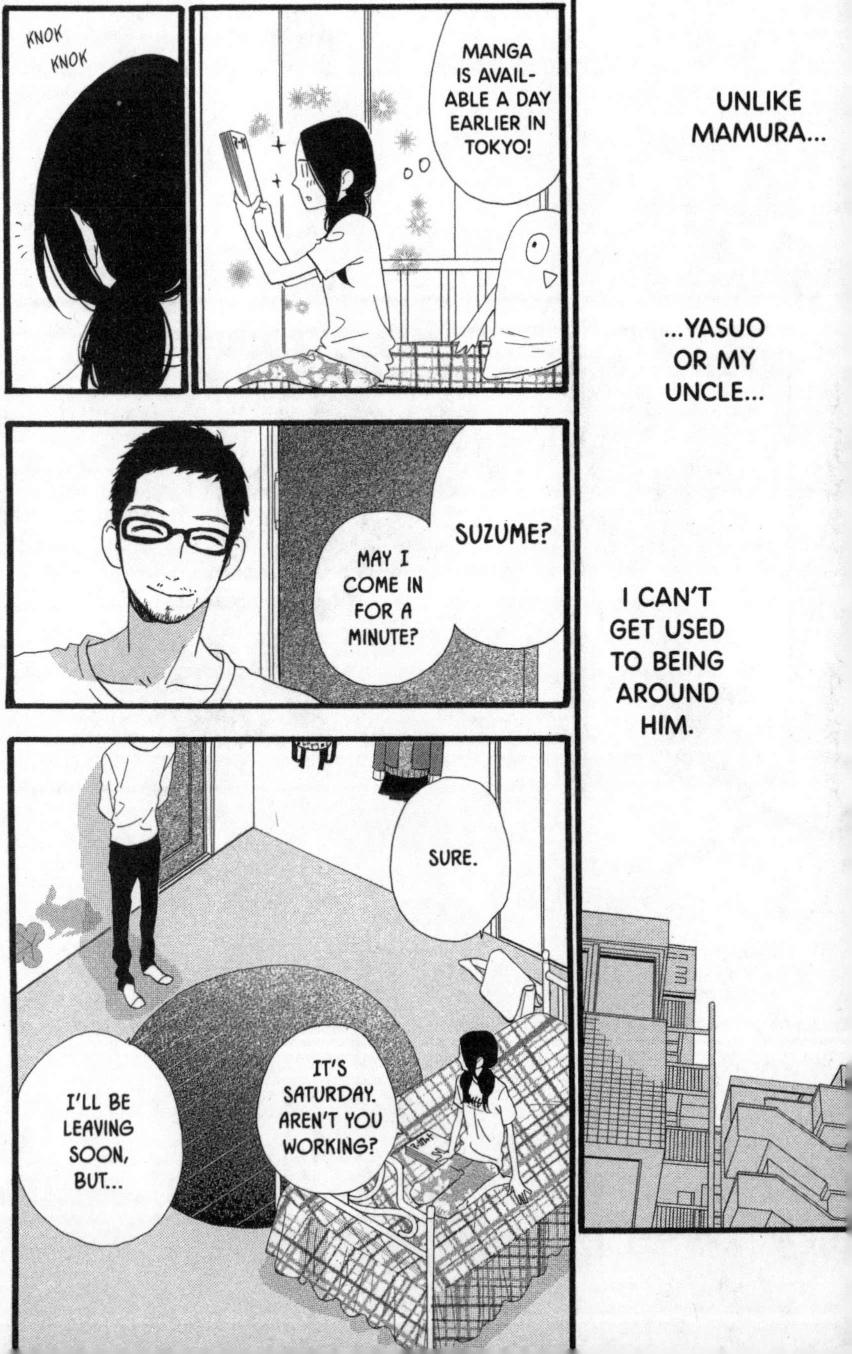
UNLIKE MAMURA...
...YASUO OR MY UNCLE...
I CAN'T GET USED TO BEING AROUND HIM.
MANGA IS AVAIL-ABLE A DAY EARLIER IN TOKYO!
KNOK KNOK
SUZUME?
MAY I COME IN FOR A MINUTE?
SURE.
IT'S SATURDAY. AREN'T YOU WORKING?
I'LL BE LEAVING SOON, BUT...

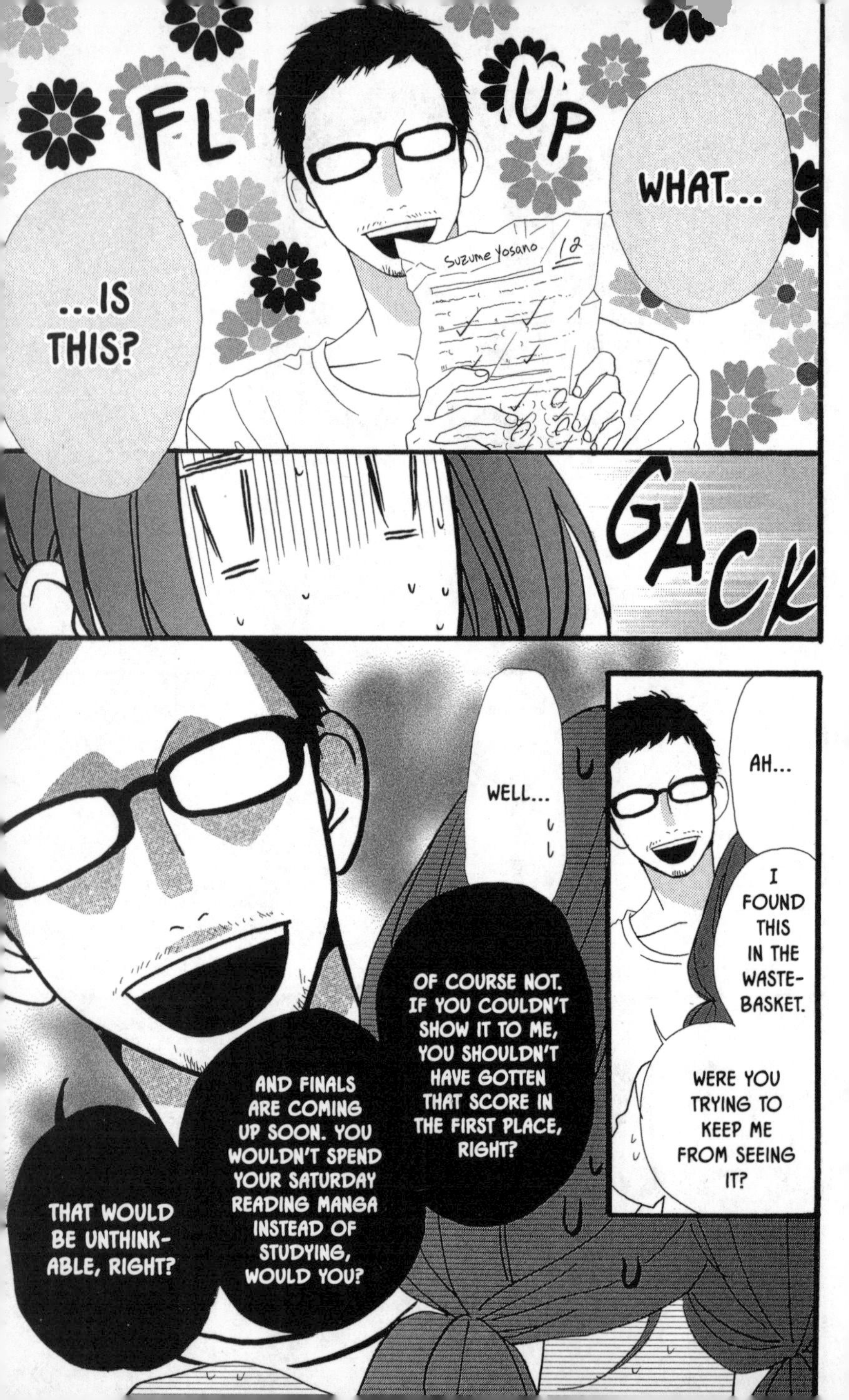
FL UP
WHAT...
...IS THIS?
Suzume Yosano 12
GACK
AH...
I FOUND THIS IN THE WASTE-BASKET.
WERE YOU TRYING TO KEEP ME FROM SEEING IT?
WELL...
OF COURSE NOT. IF YOU COULDN'T SHOW IT TO ME, YOU SHOULDN'T HAVE GOTTEN THAT SCORE IN THE FIRST PLACE, RIGHT?
AND FINALS ARE COMING UP SOON. YOU WOULDN'T SPEND YOUR SATURDAY READING MANGA INSTEAD OF STUDYING, WOULD YOU?
THAT WOULD BE UNTHINK-ABLE, RIGHT?

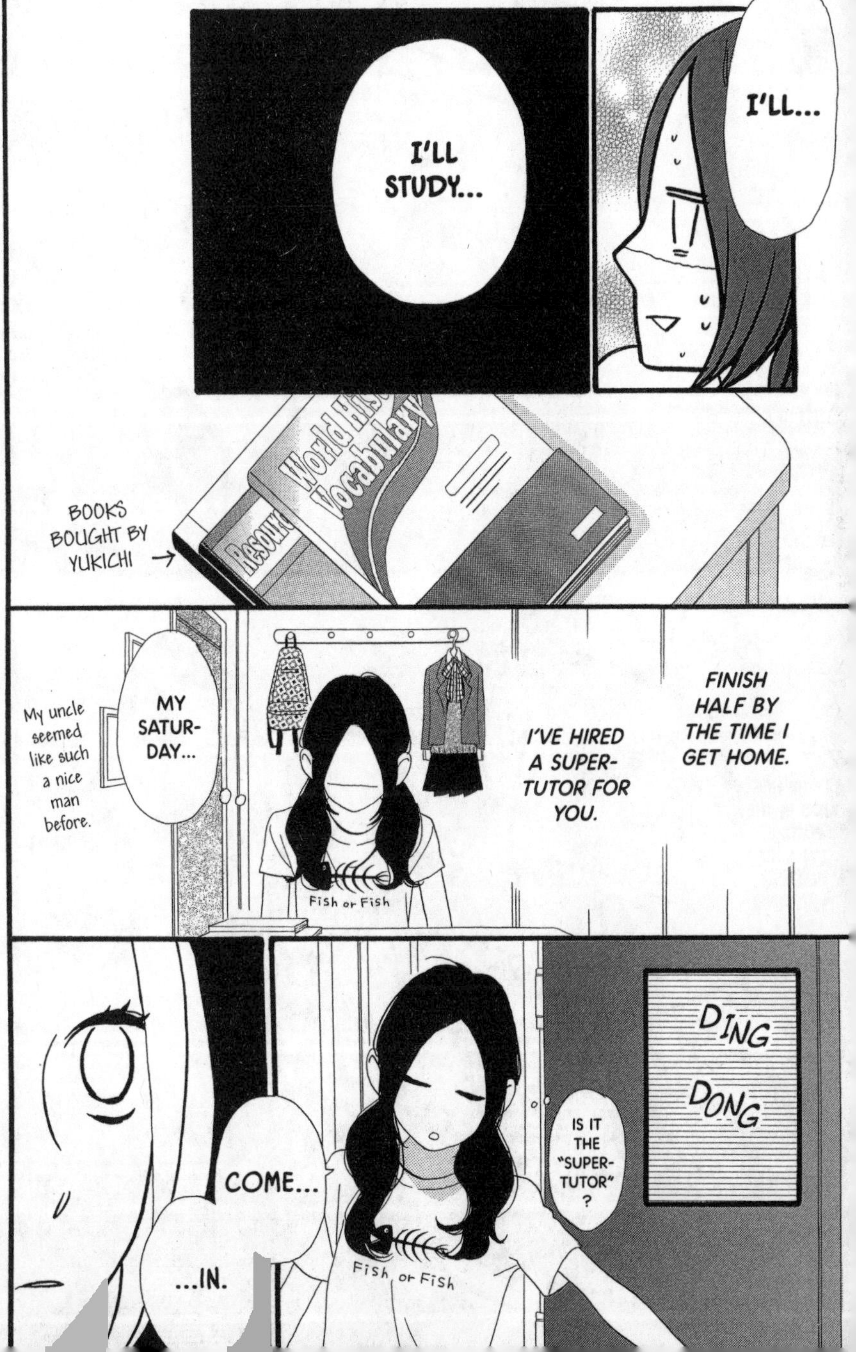
I'LL...
I'LL STUDY...
BOOKS BOUGHT BY YUKICHI →
World History Vocabulary
Resource
FINISH HALF BY THE TIME I GET HOME.
I'VE HIRED A SUPER-TUTOR FOR YOU.
MY SATURDAY...
My uncle seemed like such a nice man before.
Fish or Fish
DING DONG
IS IT THE "SUPER-TUTOR"?
Fish or Fish
COME...
...IN.

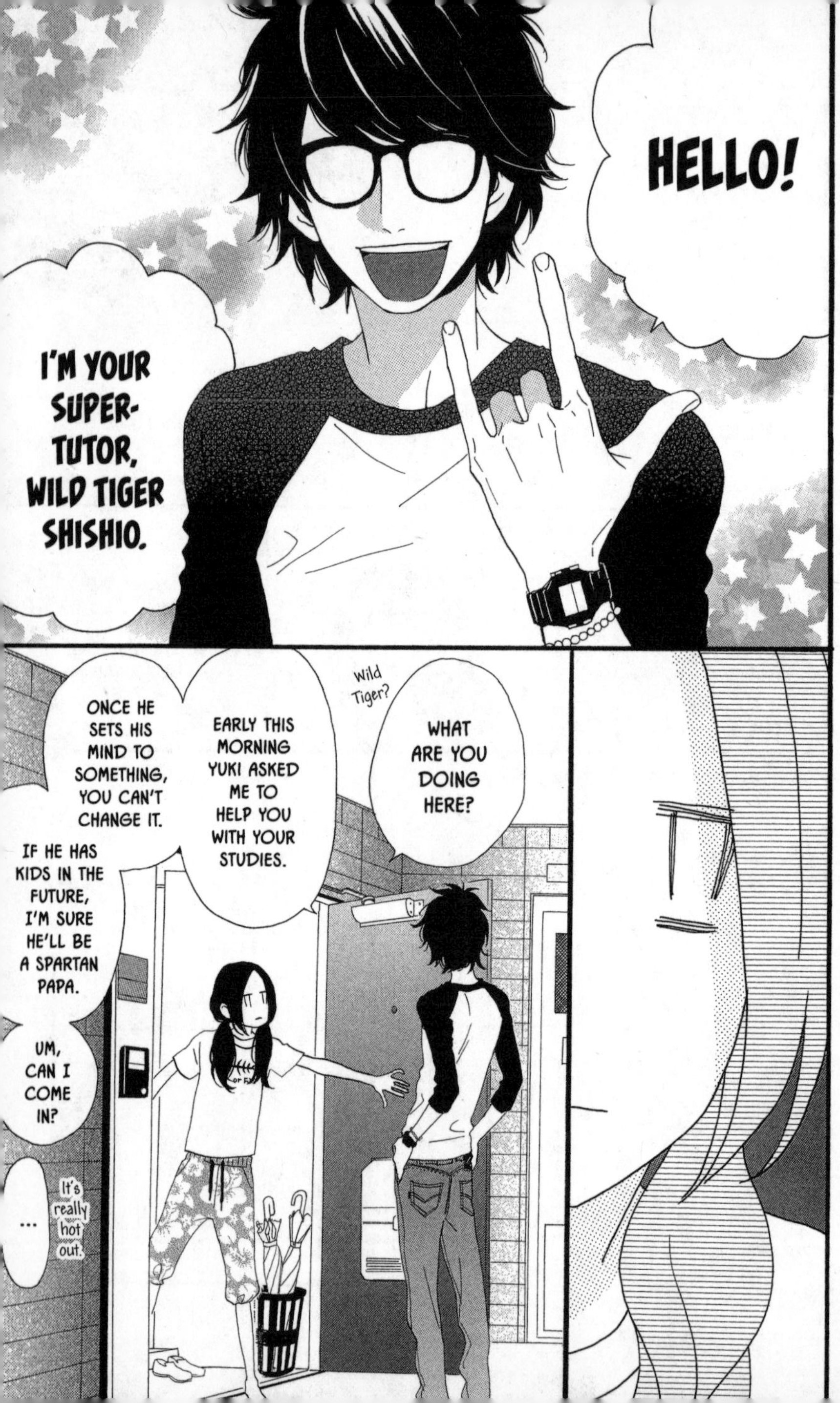
HELLO!
I'M YOUR SUPER-TUTOR, WILD TIGER SHISHIO.
Wild Tiger?
WHAT ARE YOU DOING HERE?
EARLY THIS MORNING YUKI ASKED ME TO HELP YOU WITH YOUR STUDIES.
ONCE HE SETS HIS MIND TO SOMETHING, YOU CAN'T CHANGE IT.
IF HE HAS KIDS IN THE FUTURE, I'M SURE HE'LL BE A SPARTAN PAPA.
UM, CAN I COME IN?
It's really hot out.
...

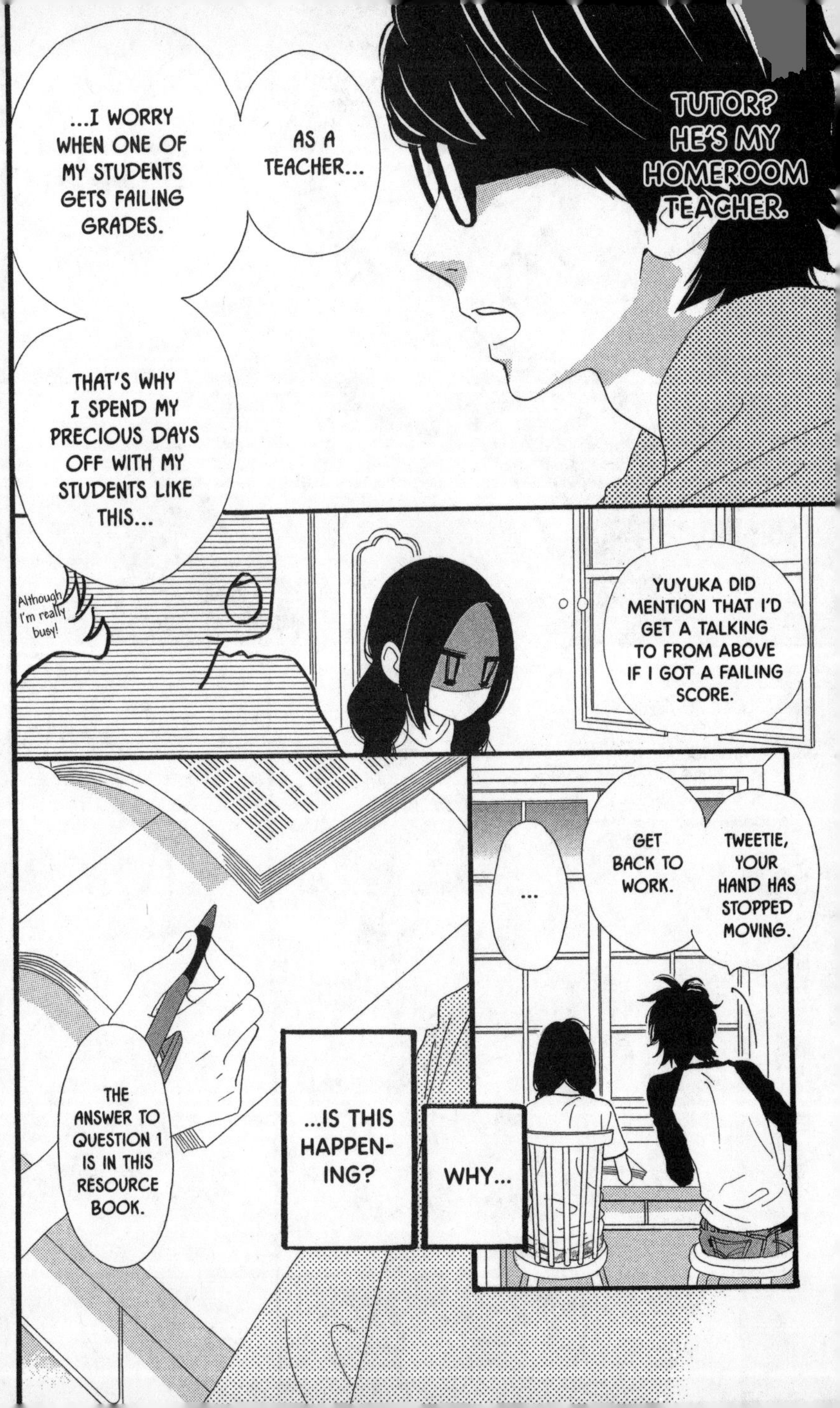
TUTOR? HE'S MY HOMEROOM TEACHER.
AS A TEACHER...
...I WORRY WHEN ONE OF MY STUDENTS GETS FAILING GRADES.
THAT'S WHY I SPEND MY PRECIOUS DAYS OFF WITH MY STUDENTS LIKE THIS...
Although I'm really busy!
YUYUKA DID MENTION THAT I'D GET A TALKING TO FROM ABOVE IF I GOT A FAILING SCORE.
TWEETIE, YOUR HAND HAS STOPPED MOVING.
GET BACK TO WORK.
...
WHY...
...IS THIS HAPPEN-ING?
THE ANSWER TO QUESTION 1 IS IN THIS RESOURCE BOOK.

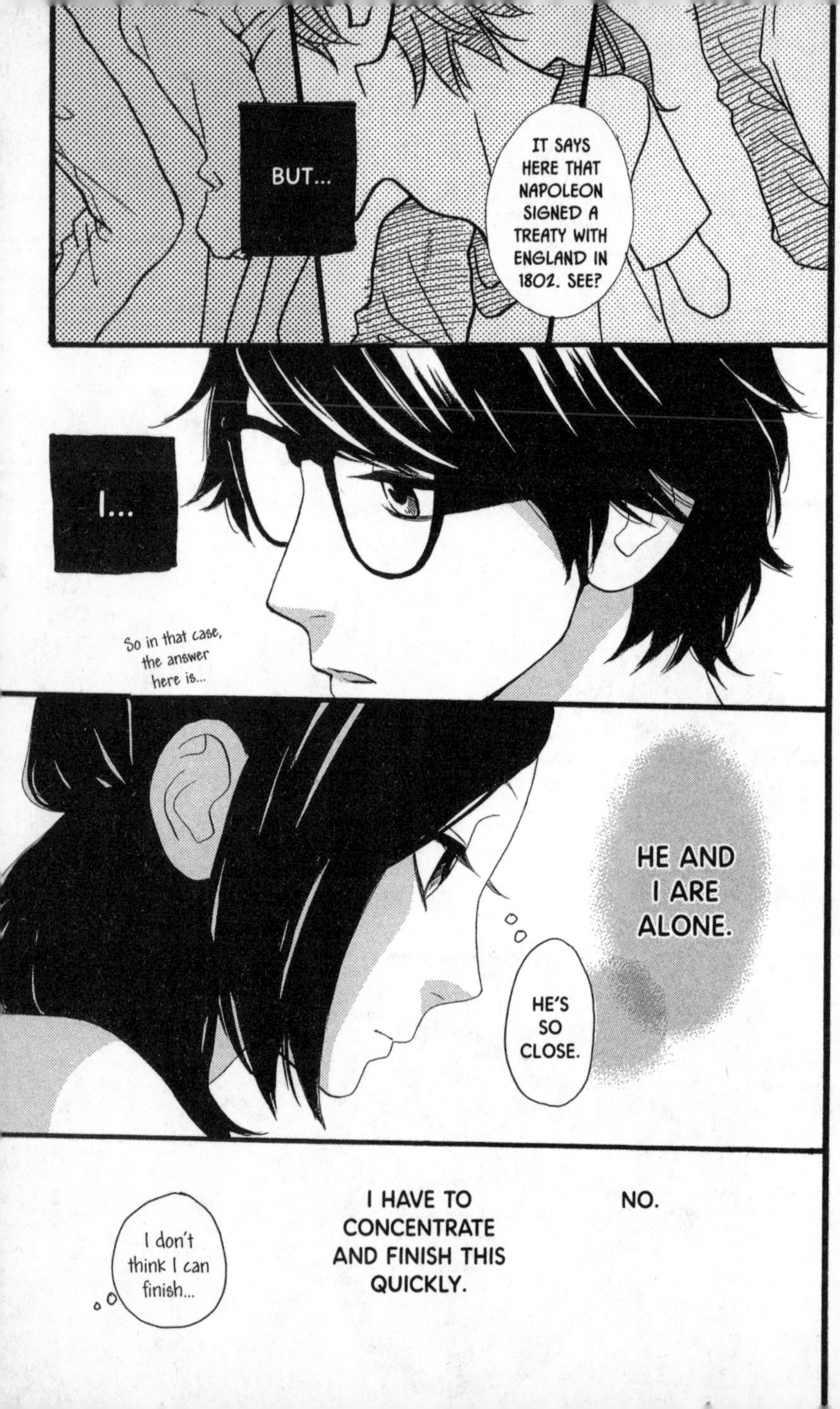
IT SAYS HERE THAT NAPOLEON SIGNED A TREATY WITH ENGLAND IN 1802. SEE?
BUT...
I...
So in that case, the answer here is...
HE AND I ARE ALONE.
HE'S SO CLOSE.
NO.
I HAVE TO CONCENTRATE AND FINISH THIS QUICKLY.
I don't think I can finish...

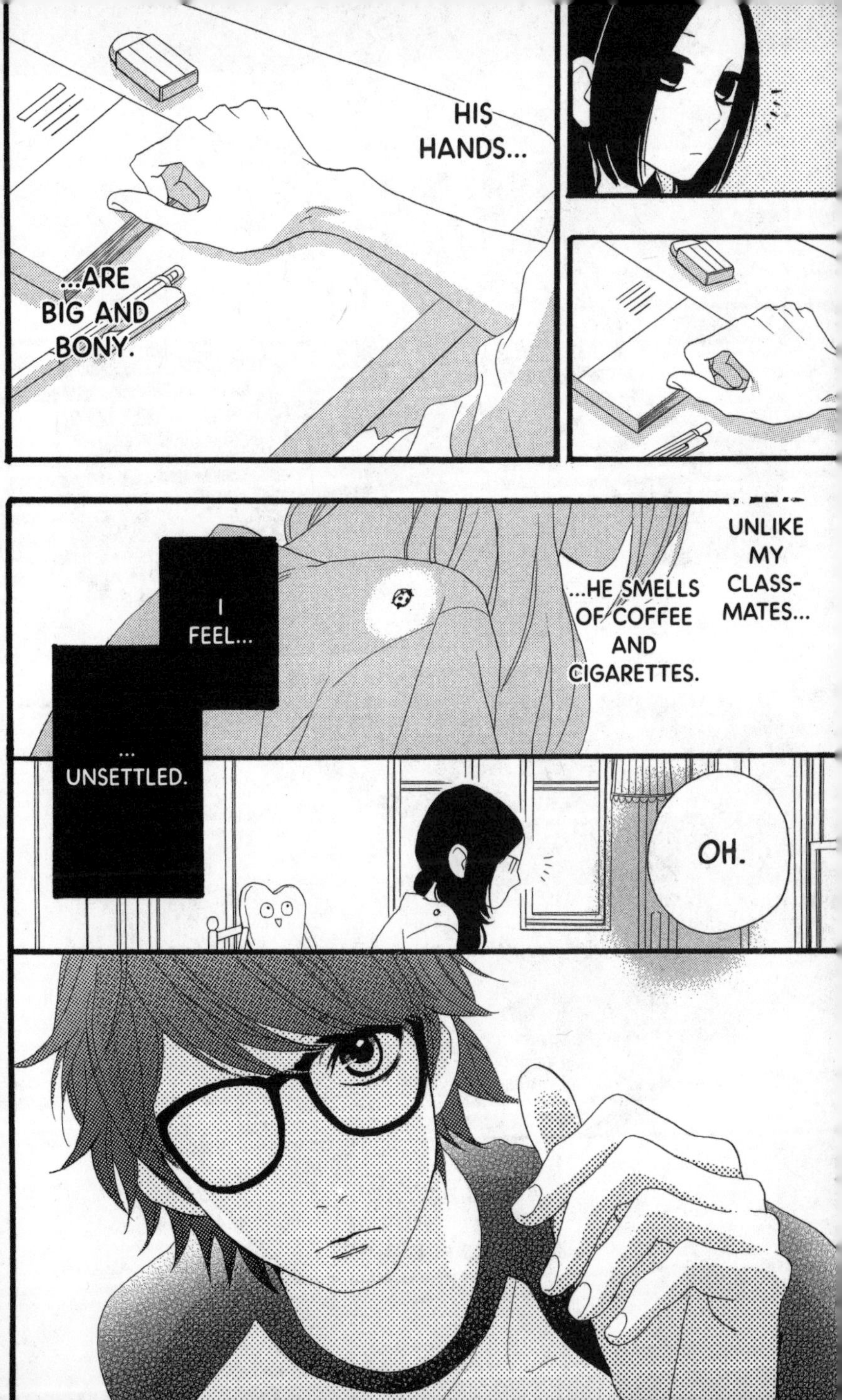
HIS HANDS...
...ARE BIG AND BONY.
UNLIKE MY CLASS-MATES...
...HE SMELLS OF COFFEE AND CIGARETTES.
I FEEL...
... UNSETTLED.
OH.

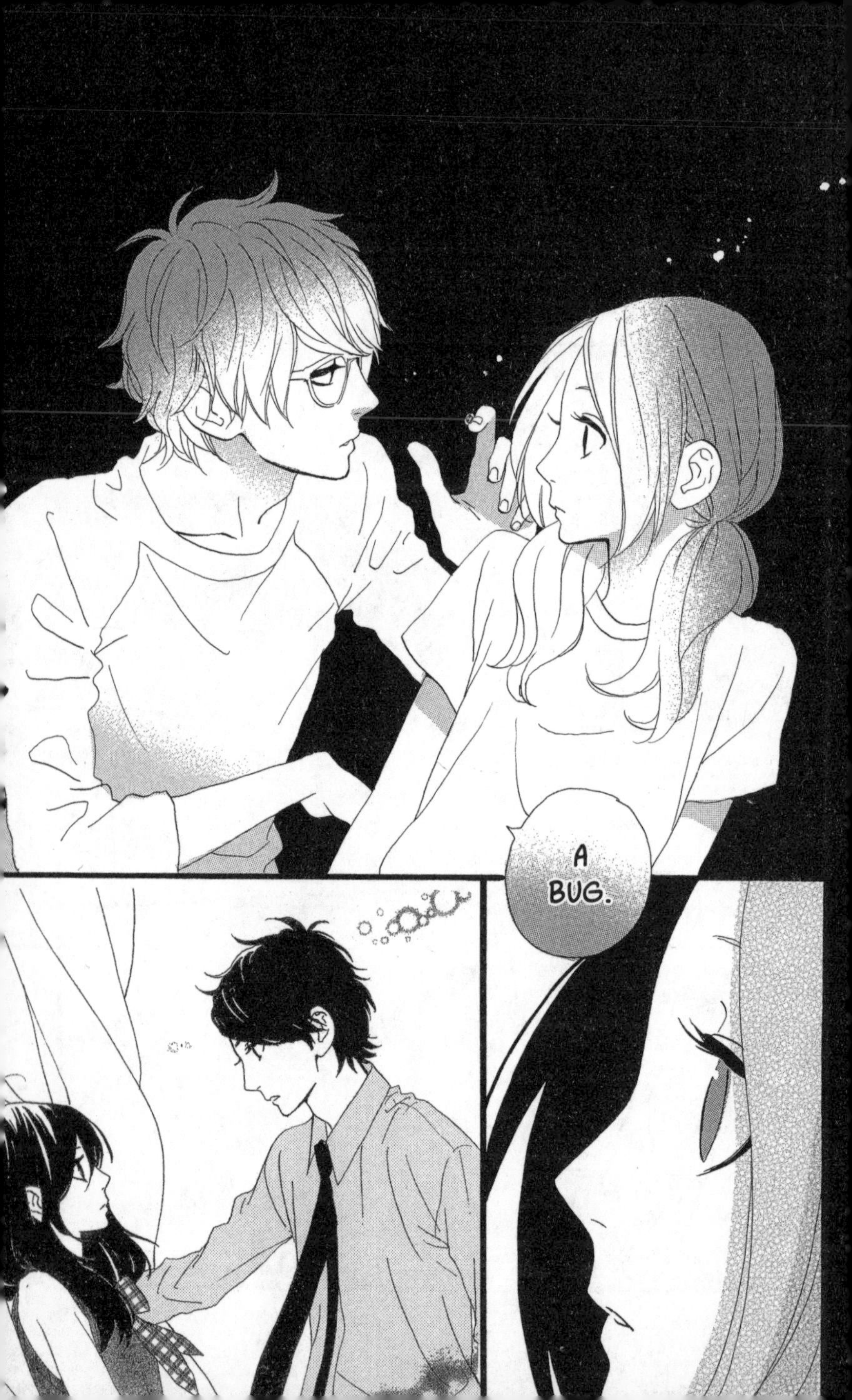
A BUG.

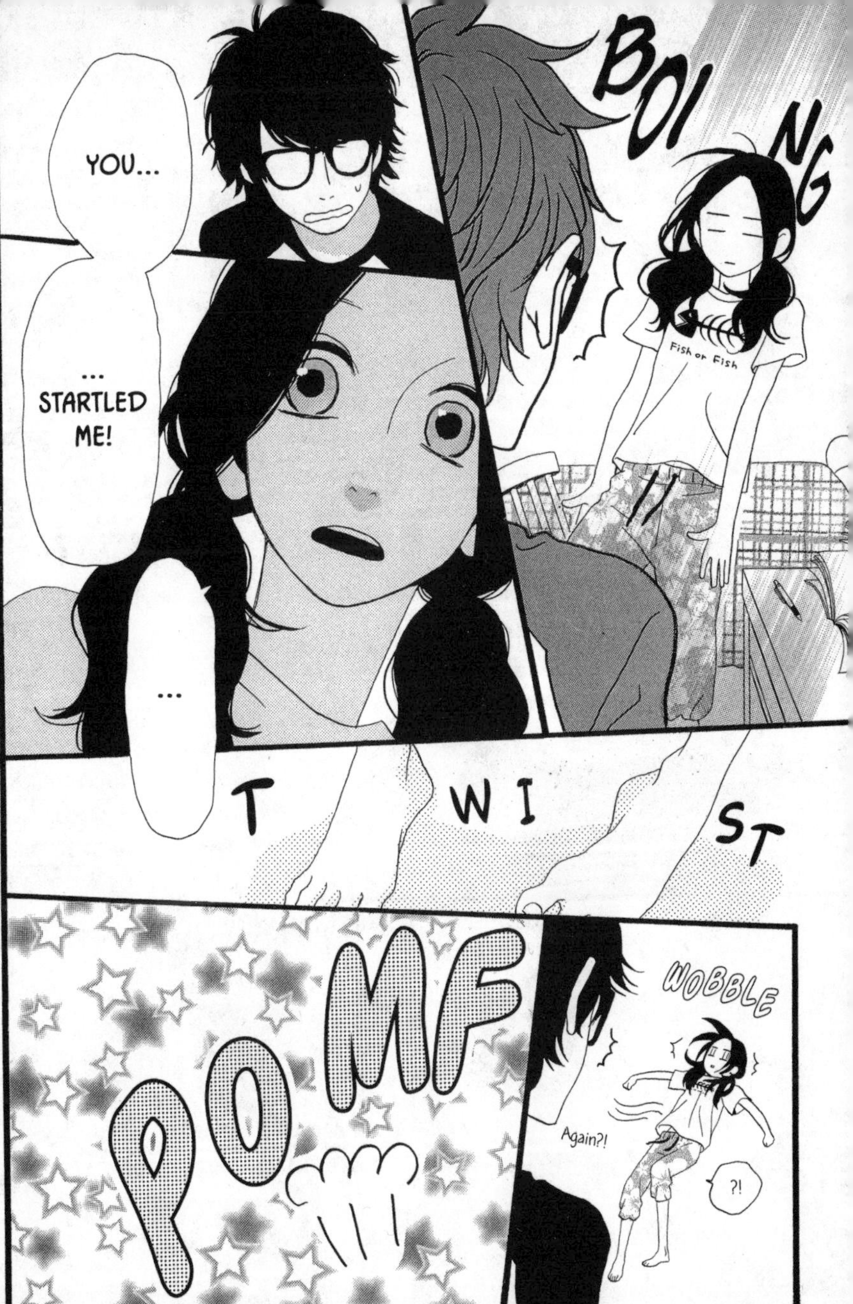

BOING
Fish or Fish
YOU...
... STARTLED ME!
...
TWIST
WOBBLE
Again?!
?!
POMF

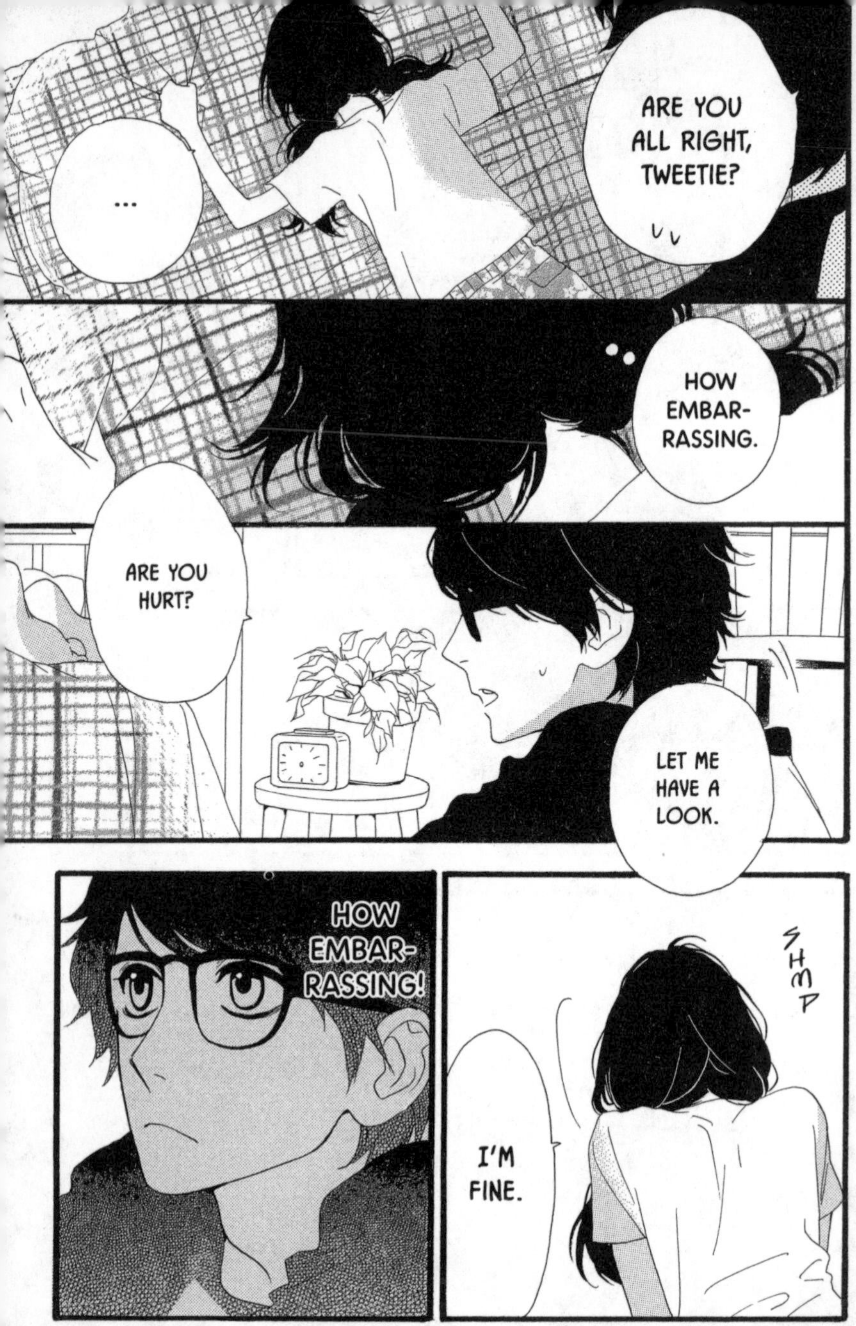
ARE YOU ALL RIGHT, TWEETIE?
...
HOW EMBAR-RASSING.
ARE YOU HURT?
LET ME HAVE A LOOK.
SHMP
I'M FINE.
HOW EMBAR-RASSING!

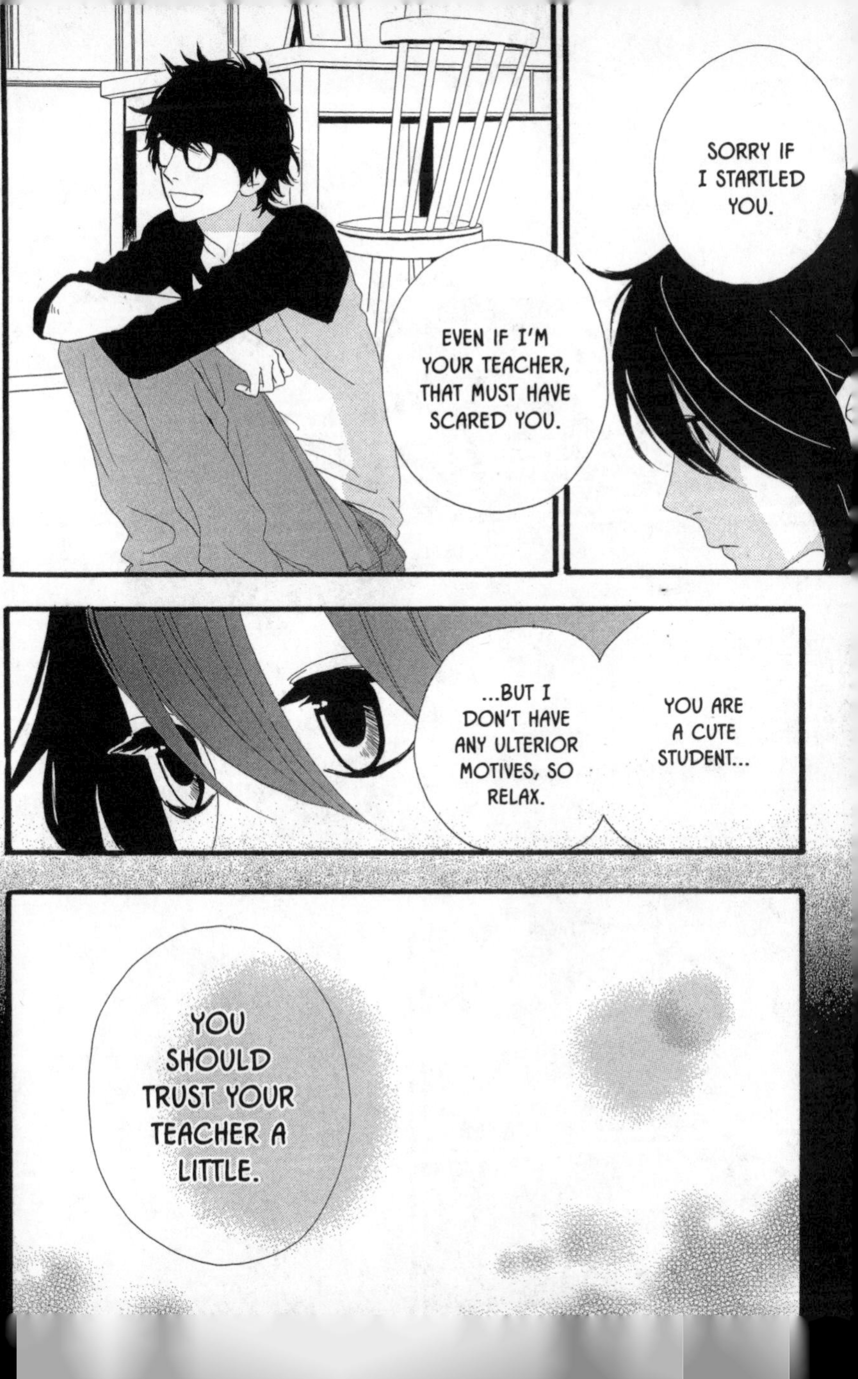
SORRY IF I STARTLED YOU.
EVEN IF I'M YOUR TEACHER, THAT MUST HAVE SCARED YOU.
YOU ARE A CUTE STUDENT...
...BUT I DON'T HAVE ANY ULTERIOR MOTIVES, SO RELAX.
YOU SHOULD TRUST YOUR TEACHER A LITTLE.

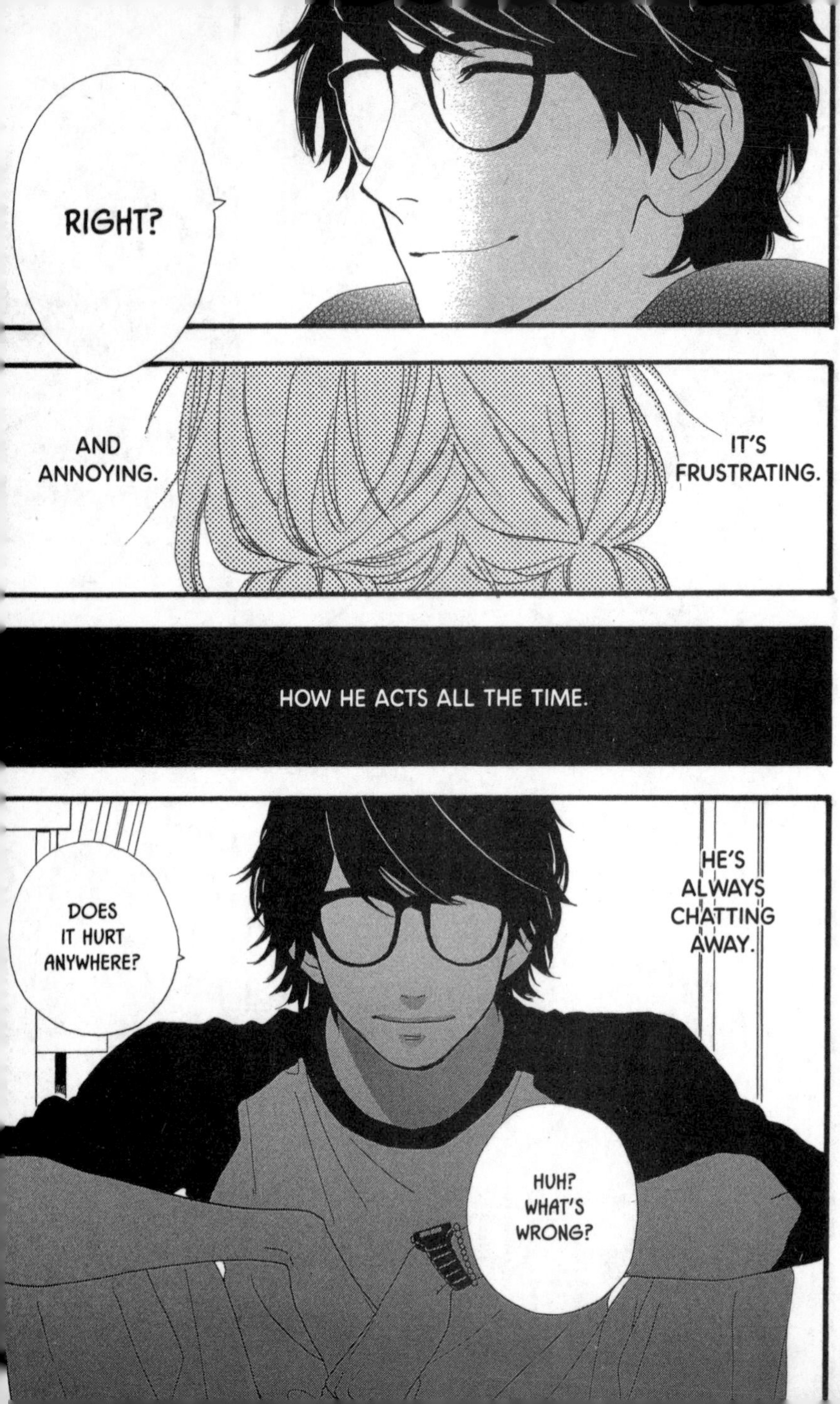
RIGHT?
IT'S FRUSTRATING.
AND ANNOYING.
HOW HE ACTS ALL THE TIME.
HE'S ALWAYS CHATTING AWAY.
DOES IT HURT ANYWHERE?
HUH? WHAT'S WRONG?

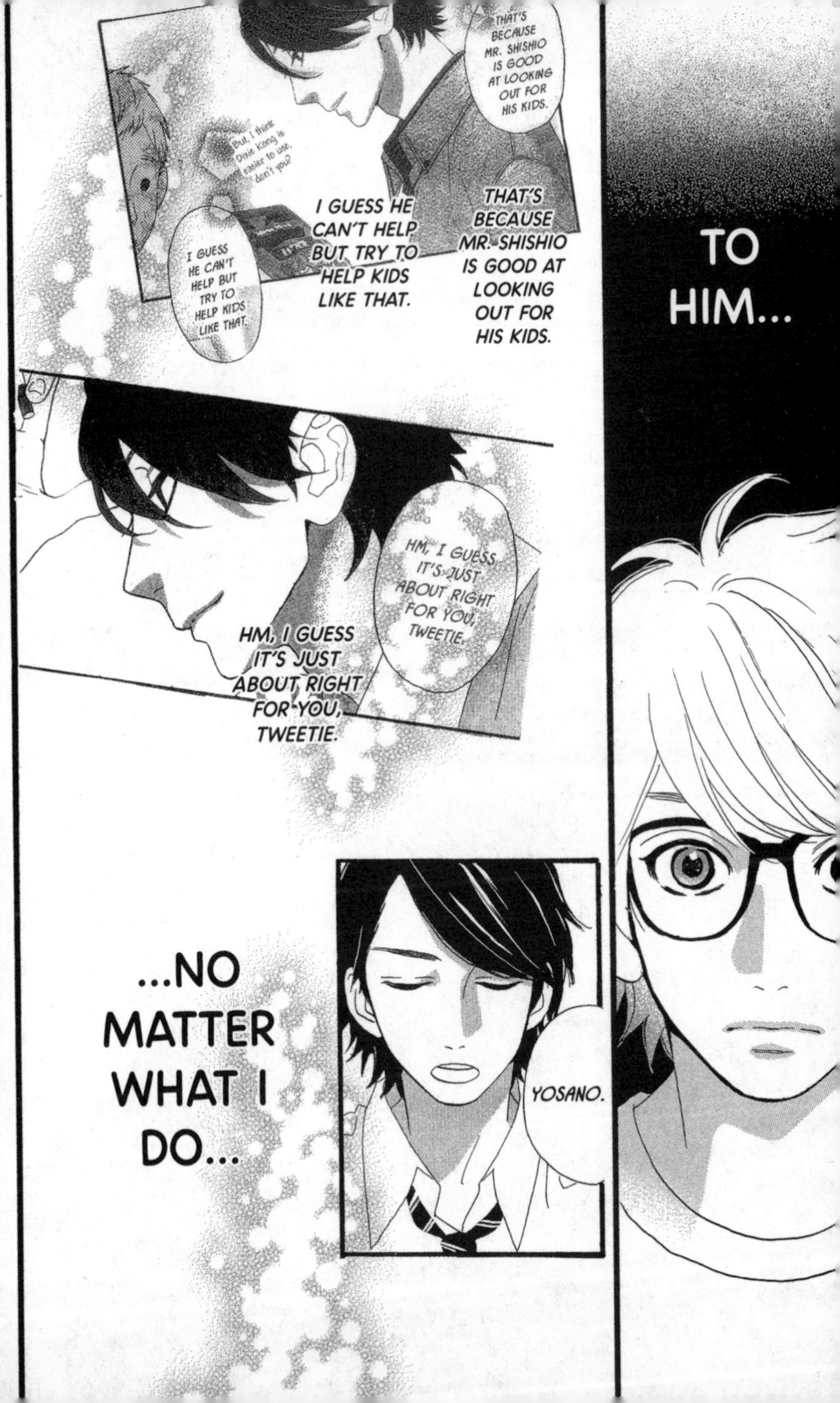
TO HIM...
THAT'S BECAUSE MR. SHISHIO IS GOOD AT LOOKING OUT FOR HIS KIDS.
But, I think Dixie Kong is easier to use, don't you?
THAT'S BECAUSE MR. SHISHIO IS GOOD AT LOOKING OUT FOR HIS KIDS.
I GUESS HE CAN'T HELP BUT TRY TO HELP KIDS LIKE THAT.
I GUESS HE CAN'T HELP BUT TRY TO HELP KIDS LIKE THAT.
HM, I GUESS IT'S JUST ABOUT RIGHT FOR YOU, TWEETIE.
HM, I GUESS IT'S JUST ABOUT RIGHT FOR YOU, TWEETIE.
YOSANO.
...NO MATTER WHAT I DO...

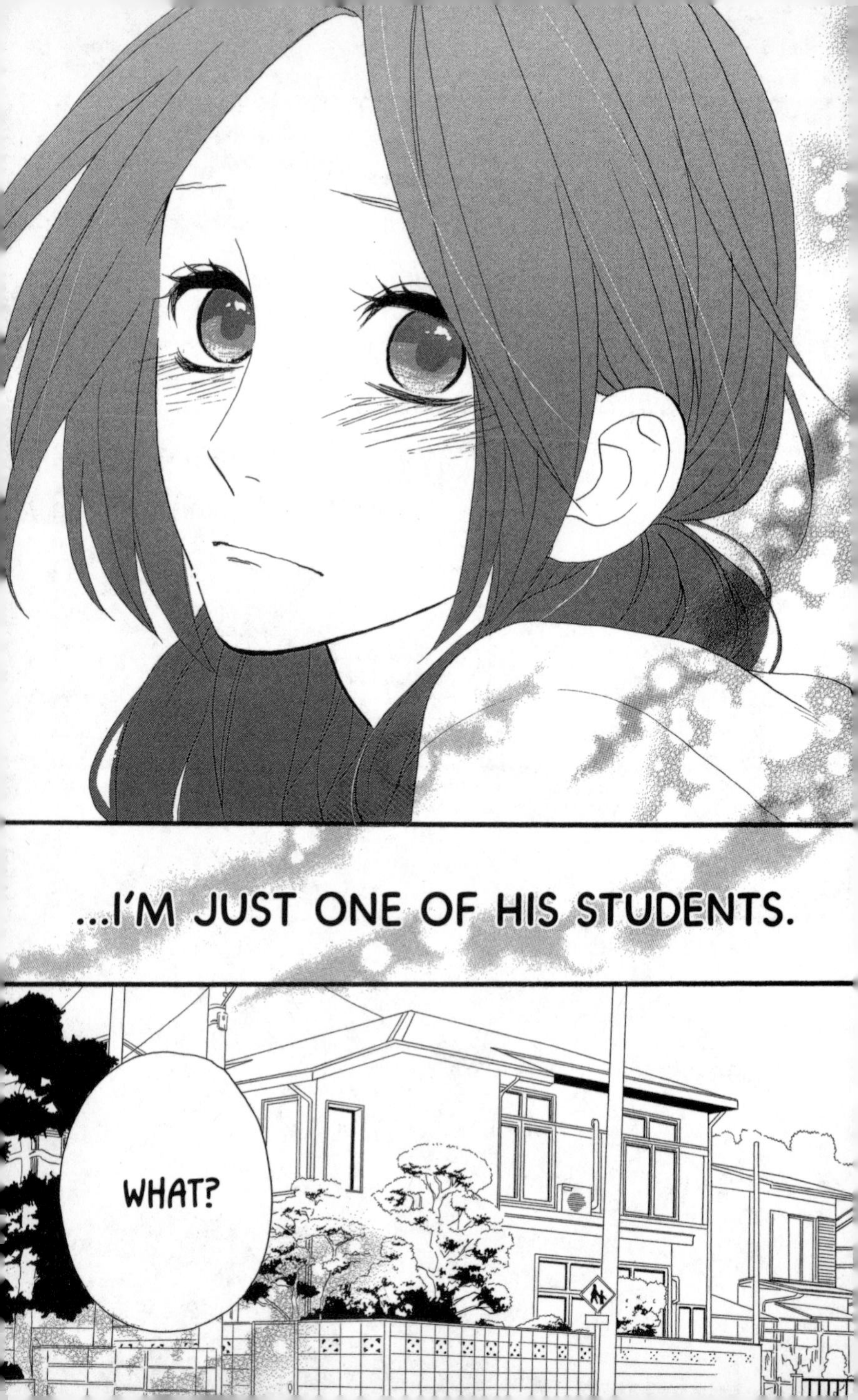
...I'M JUST ONE OF HIS STUDENTS.
WHAT?

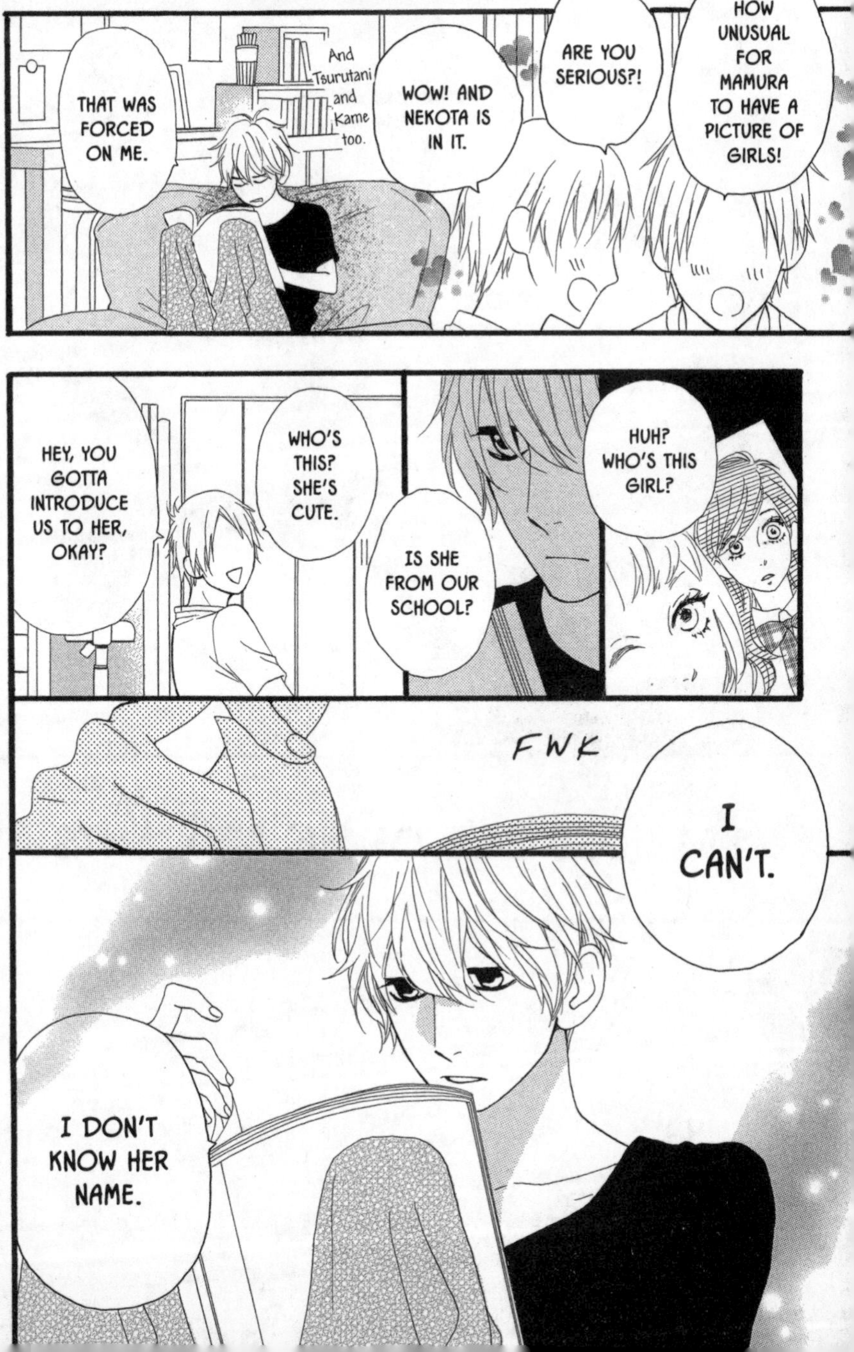
HOW UNUSUAL FOR MAMURA TO HAVE A PICTURE OF GIRLS!
ARE YOU SERIOUS?!
WOW! AND NEKOTA IS IN IT.
And Tsurutani and Kame too.
THAT WAS FORCED ON ME.
HUH? WHO'S THIS GIRL?
IS SHE FROM OUR SCHOOL?
WHO'S THIS? SHE'S CUTE.
HEY, YOU GOTTA INTRODUCE US TO HER, OKAY?
FWK
I CAN'T.
I DON'T KNOW HER NAME.

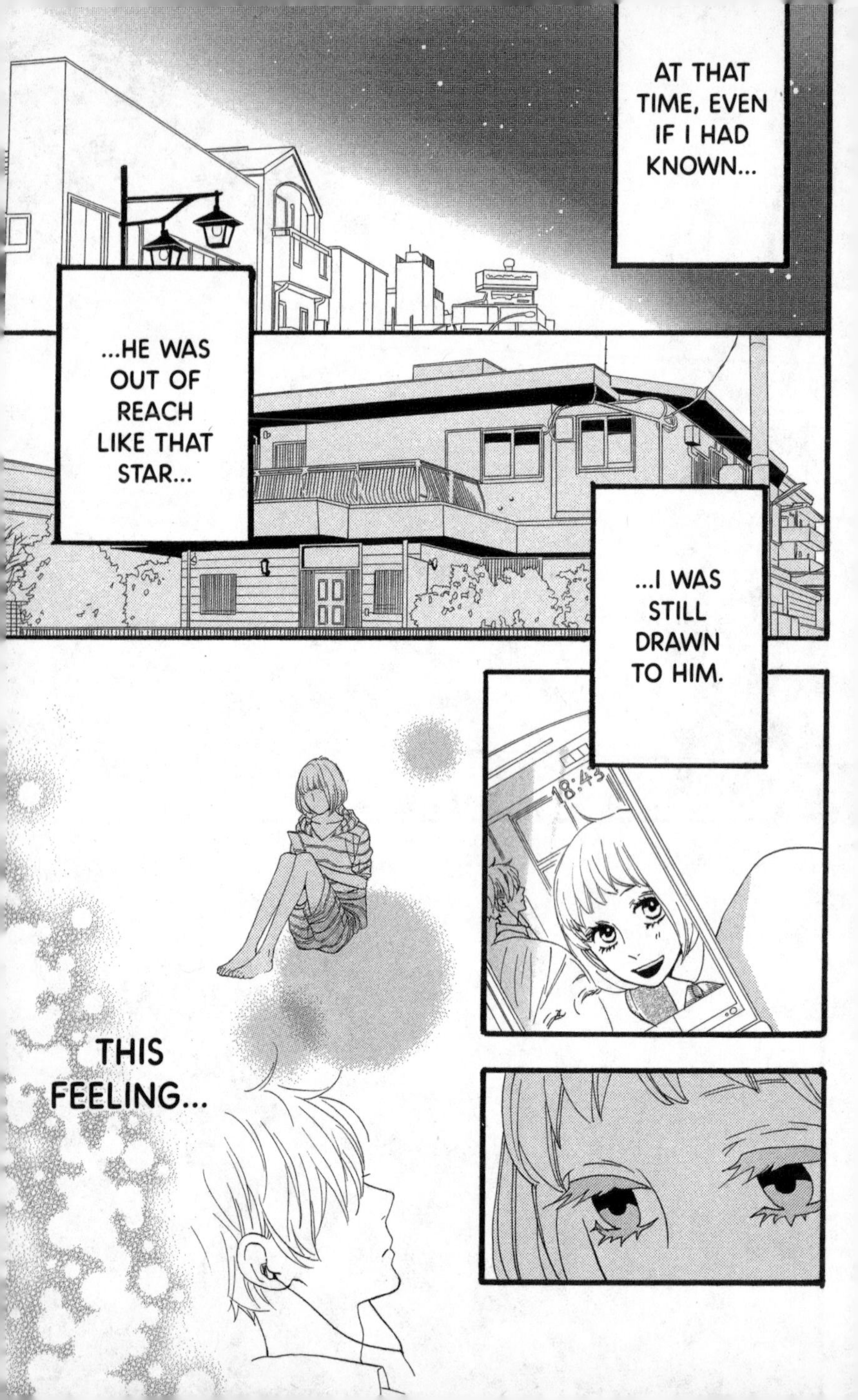
AT THAT TIME, EVEN IF I HAD KNOWN...
...HE WAS OUT OF REACH LIKE THAT STAR...
...I WAS STILL DRAWN TO HIM.
18:43
THIS FEELING...

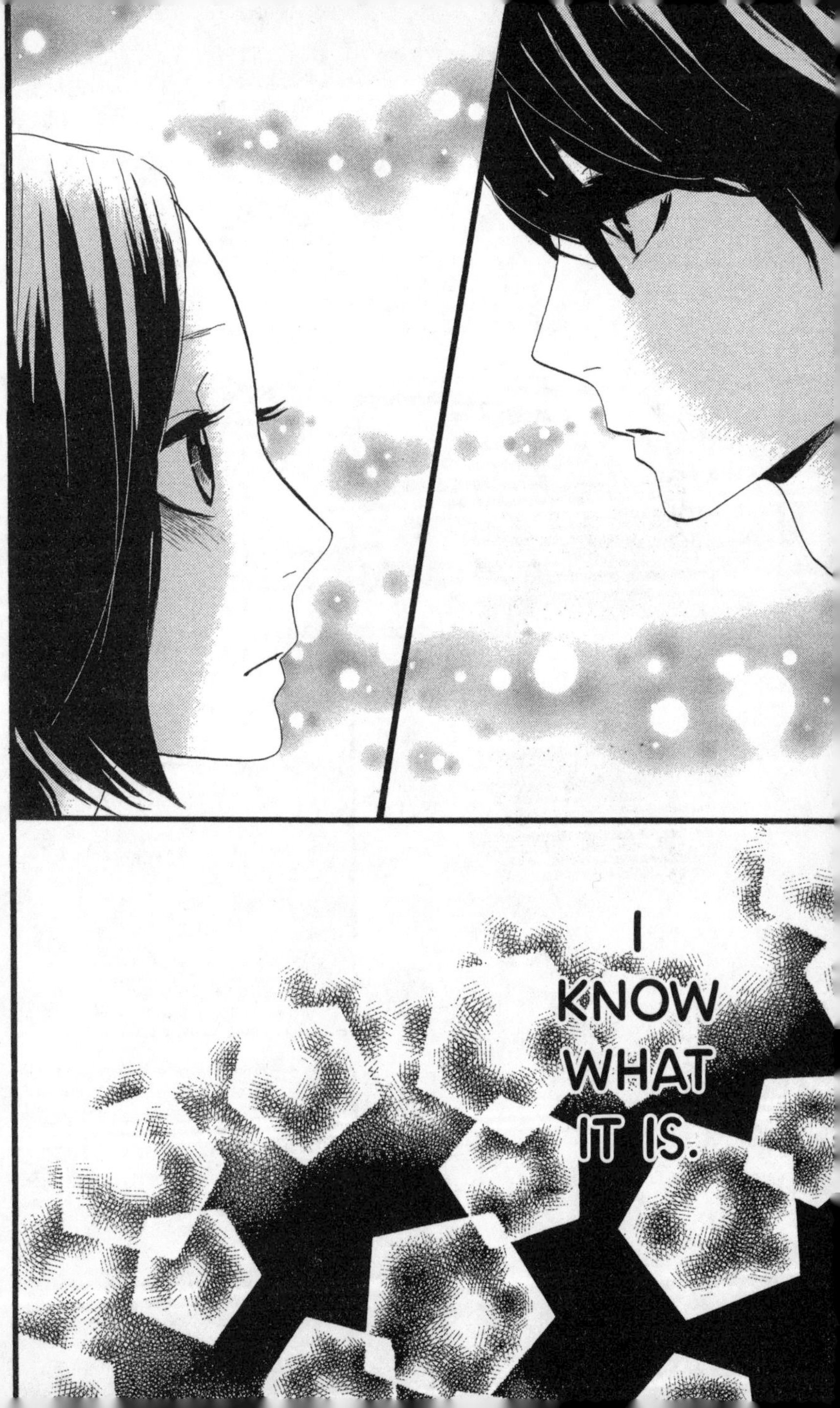
I KNOW WHAT IT IS.

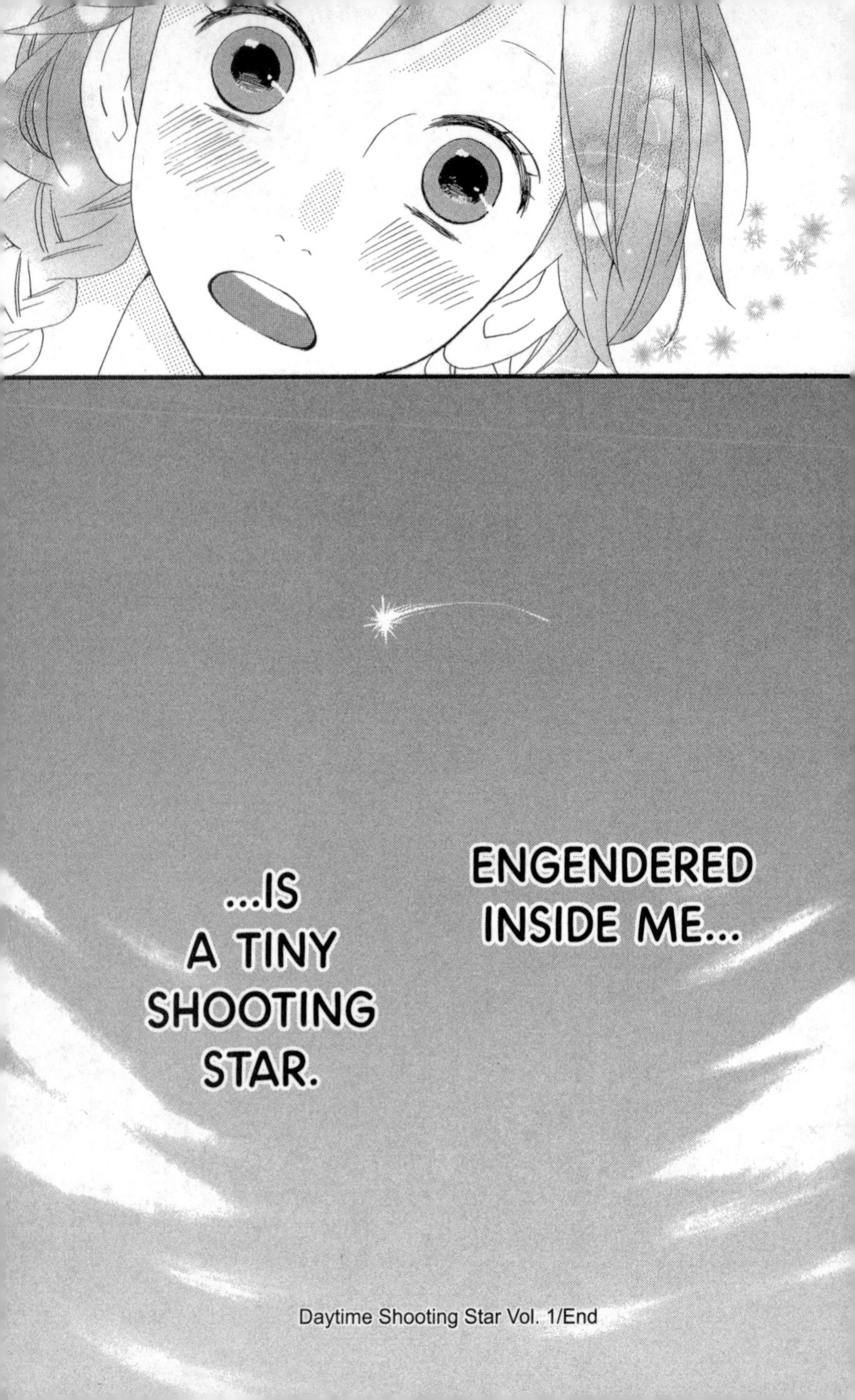
ENGENDERED INSIDE ME...
...IS A TINY SHOOTING STAR.
Daytime Shooting Star Vol. 1/End

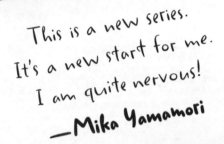

This is a new series.
It's a new start for me.
I am quite nervous!
—Mika Yamamori

Mika Yamamori is from Ishikawa Prefecture in Japan. She began her professional manga career in 2006 with "Kimi no Kuchibiru kara Mahou" (The Magic from Your Lips) in *The Margaret* magazine. Her other works include *Sugars* and *Tsubaki Cho Lonely Planet*.

★DAYTIME★SHOOTING★STAR★ *1*

SHOJO BEAT EDITION

Story & Art by
Mika Yamamori

Translation ★ **JN Productions**
Touch-Up Art & Lettering ★ **Inori Fukuda Trant**
Design ★ **Alice Lewis**
Editor ★ **Nancy Thistlethwaite**

HIRUNAKA NO RYUSEI © 2011 by Mika Yamamori
All rights reserved.
First published in Japan in 2011 by SHUEISHA Inc., Tokyo.
English translation rights arranged by SHUEISHA Inc.

The stories, characters and incidents mentioned in this
publication are entirely fictional.

Printed in the U.S.A.

Published by VIZ Media, LLC
P.O. Box 77010
San Francisco, CA 94107

10 9 8 7 6 5 4 3 2
First printing, July 2019
Second printing, May 2021

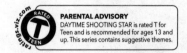

PARENTAL ADVISORY
DAYTIME SHOOTING STAR is rated T for
Teen and is recommended for ages 13 and
up. This series contains suggestive themes.

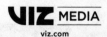

viz.com   shojobeat.com

STOP!

You may be reading the wrong way!

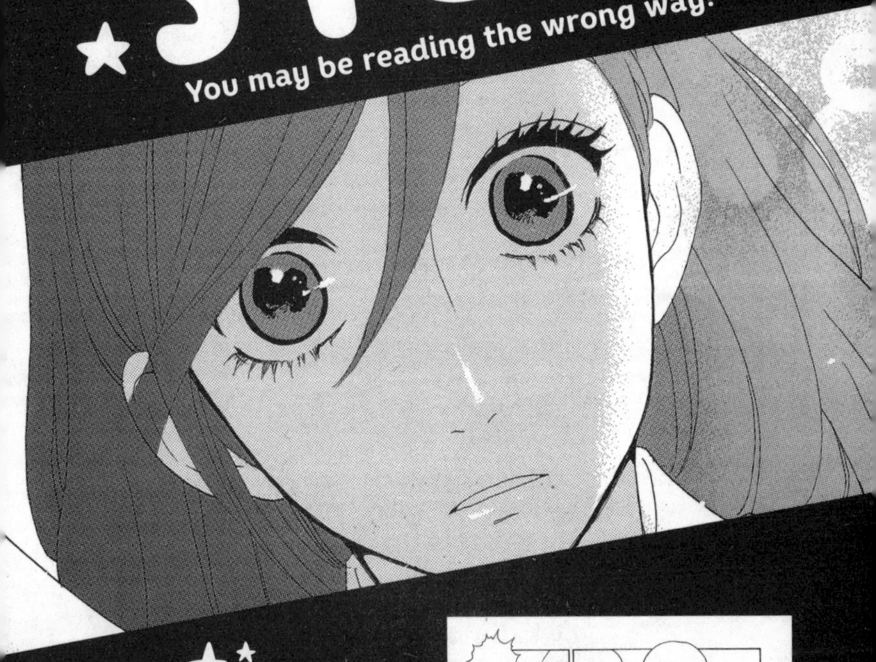

In keeping with the original Japanese comic format, this book reads from right to left—so action, sound effects and word balloons are completely reversed to preserve the orientation of the original artwork.

Check out the diagram shown here to get the hang of things, and then turn to the other side of the book to get started!

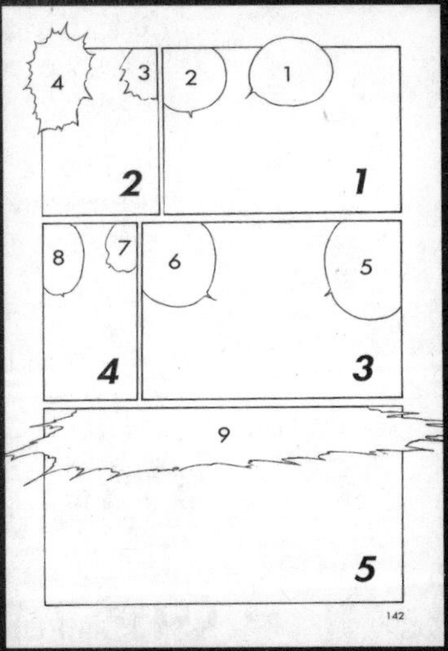
1
2
3
4
1
2
5
6
7
8
3
4
9
5
142